THREE DAYS DEAD

BOOKS IN THE
DONALD YOUNGBLOOD MYSTERY SERIES

Three Deuces Down (2008)
Three Days Dead (2009)

A DONALD YOUNGBLOOD MYSTERY

THREE DAYS DEAD

KEITH DONNELLY

HUMMINGBIRD BOOKS
Gatlinburg, Tennessee

Hummingbird Books

A division of Harrison Mountain Press

P.O. Box 1386

Gatlinburg, TN 37738

Designed by Todd Lape / Lape Designs

Library of Congress Cataloging-in-Publication Data

Donnelly, Keith.

Three days dead : a Donald Youngblood mystery /

by Keith Donnelly.

p. cm.

ISBN-13: 978-0-89587-372-9 (alk. paper)

ISBN-10: 0-89587-372-9 (alk. paper)

1. Private investigators--Tennessee—Fiction. 2. Male friend-

ship—Fiction. 3. Cherokee Indians—Fiction. I. Title.

PS3604.O56325T475 2009

813'.6--dc22   2009005293

Printed in the United States of America

by the Maple-Vail Book Manufacturing Group

York, Pennsylvania

*To Robert Lynn Donnelly, Mary Agnes Wiggins
and Geraldine Campbell Donnelly,
gone but not forgotten*

*And to Tessa,
without you, nothing matters.*

Prologue

The autumn of my senior year in college was a glorious explosion of colors on the University of Connecticut's Storrs campus. The leaves of early October were a powerful testimony of a force far greater than mortal man. I smiled at the thought as I walked across campus: *Donald Youngblood, philosopher.*

I was headed for the grill to meet Billy Two-Feathers, a full-blooded Cherokee Indian and my best friend, when I was distracted by a confrontation between an upperclassman I vaguely knew and did not like and a first-semester freshman. This was Rat Week, when all incoming freshmen were expected to wear rat hats and, within reason, to do the bidding of upperclassmen.

Daryl Osgood IV was an arrogant, self-important rich kid who acted like he owned the campus and could do as he pleased. Though he was about my height, Daryl was slight of frame. He had the pale-skinned, dark-haired look of the pampered rich. In my junior year, he had been in one of my upper-level economics classes, and I took pleasure stomping on some of his outrageous theories. As I approached, I heard foul language and witnessed a shove. That was enough: *Youngblood to the rescue.* I closed the gap between us.

"What's going on, Daryl?" I said pleasantly.

"This rat doesn't know the fight song," Daryl snarled, as only the snooty upper class can.

"Is that right, rat?" I asked.

"Yes, sir," the freshman answered.

He was a little guy about five-foot-eight and could not have weighed more than 130 pounds soaking wet. His rat hat sat atop his light brown hair like a beacon beckoning cruel upperclassmen. His brown eyes peered through John Lennon–style wire-rim glasses. I sensed that he was a couple of harsh words from a total breakdown. *Total geek*, I thought.

"Shame on you, Daryl," I said, still keeping my pleasant demeanor. "That's no way to treat an incoming freshman." I turned to the rat. "What's your name, rat?"

"Timothy Brentwood, sir," he said enthusiastically, sensing he may have found an ally.

"Well, Mr. Timothy Brentwood, you will meet me here tomorrow at this very spot at noon and sing the University of Connecticut fight song for me."

"Yes, sir."

"Butt out, Youngblood. This is none of your affair," Daryl hissed.

I moved closer to Daryl and said with a low, threatening whisper in his left ear, "Oh, but it is, Daryl. In case you haven't heard, University of Connecticut upperclassmen do not mistreat incoming freshmen. If you don't leave now, I will not only kick your ass, I'll report you to the dean of students."

Daryl went slightly paler than he already was. I thought he might actually cry—from fear or rage, I was not quite sure.

"You will regret this, Youngblood," he whispered back, and turned to walk away.

I grabbed his arm for one parting shot. "If you cause this freshman any more grief, Daryl, you will be the one with regrets."

Daryl broke free of my grip and left as if his pants were on fire.

I turned to Timothy Brentwood. "Are you called Timothy or Tim?" I asked.

"Tim, sir."

"Well, Tim, you have made an upperclassman friend, and for an incoming freshman, that's a good thing to have. Any enemy of Daryl

Osgood the fourth is a friend of mine. My name is Don Youngblood, and if you need anything, look for me in the college grill or the Economics Department. If I'm not asleep, I'll probably be at one of those two places. I do suggest that you steer clear of Daryl, and I do suggest you learn the fight song. Either that or take that stupid hat off and pretend you're a sophomore. Forget tomorrow at noon. I have better things to do than listen to a rat sing the fight song."

Tim smiled. "Thank you, sir. I have to go. I'm late for class."

I watched as Tim Brentwood walked away hatless in the opposite direction from Daryl Osgood. Fast learner. *Welcome to UConn*, I thought.

◆　　◆　　◆　　◆

Billy was waiting for me in the grill. At six-foot-six, he was hard to miss. Billy was sure to be a staple of the upcoming edition of the UConn basketball team, ranked number one in the preseason polls. Jim Clauson, Connecticut's coach, was famous for going to the far corners of the world to find basketball recruits. No one was surprised when he took the best that the Cherokee Nation had to offer, although Billy was anything but a typical Cherokee Indian.

Billy had grown up in Wilton, Connecticut, adopted by a wealthy, childless white family. I had met his parents for the first time during a short break our freshman year when Billy asked me to go home with him. His parents were loving and caring and downplayed their obvious wealth. I was impressed with the number of books, pictures, and artifacts in their home that dealt with everything Cherokee. Billy later told me that his parents took great pride in teaching him about his heritage.

"You're late," Billy said. It was not an accusation as much as a statement of curiosity. I was almost always on time.

"Had to rescue a rat," I said.

"A what?"

"An incoming freshman. A rat."

"The two-legged variety."

"Exactly."

"What happened?" Billy asked.

I told him about my encounter with Daryl Osgood IV and Timothy Brentwood.

"I never did like that guy. I may have to have a little talk with Daryl," Billy said.

"A little talk" meant Billy would probably scare Daryl into wetting his pants. Billy was a mother hen. He felt he had to protect me. At nearly six-foot-two and rather solidly built, if I did say so myself, I did not feel I needed protecting.

"Stay out of it," I said. "I can handle Daryl Osgood."

"The fourth," Billy smiled.

◆   ◆   ◆   ◆

A few days after the incident with Daryl Osgood IV and the freshman rat, I was in the college grill a few minutes past six in the morning. I was alone in a far corner with a *USA Today* and a cup of coffee loaded with half-and-half and sugar. Autumn meant college football, and being a native Tennessean, I was very interested in the latest edition of the Volunteers football team, undefeated and ranked number five in the country. *Not bad*, I thought.

The shadow that fell across my newspaper would compare to a total eclipse of the sun. I looked up. I was staring into the biggest University of Connecticut varsity football jacket I had ever seen—Mount Everest in blue and white leather. Farther up this mountain, resting on a pair of massive shoulders, sat a head adorned with a blond flattop. Pale blue eyes stared out of this head and down at me.

"You're Youngblood," the mountain said.

"And you are Bruiser Bracken," I said, remaining seated. I knew Bruiser by sight, but I did not know him personally. He was an offensive lineman on the football team, which meant he was probably mean and slow. Bruiser was approximately six-foot-four and weighed somewhere in the vicinity of a compact car.

"I hear you were picking on one of my brothers," he said casually.

I was encouraged that there did not seem to be menace in his voice. "I didn't know you had a brother," I said.

"Fraternity brother," Bruiser said.

"And who might that be?" I asked, although I had a pretty good idea.

"Daryl Osgood," he said.

"You mean Daryl Osgood the fourth, don't you?" I cracked.

A small smile curled at the corner of Bruiser's mouth. "Yeah, that's who I mean."

I smiled back at Bruiser, hoping he was here only to deliver a message.

"I'm here to scare you and mess you up a little for picking on a fraternity brother," he said, emphasizing *fraternity*.

I stood. If I had to defend myself against this Incredible Hulk, I would need to rely on my quickness.

Bruiser smiled again. "You scared?"

"Shitless," I said, and I halfway meant it.

"Then consider yourself properly reprimanded," Bruiser said. "Mind if I get a cup of coffee and join you?"

"Be my guest."

Bruiser returned with coffee and three small containers of half-and-half. He added raw sugar from the holder on the table, mixed in the half-and-half, and stirred. I liked my coffee the same way. He took a sip and made an approving sound.

"Nothing like that first sip of the day," he said.

"Couldn't agree more," I said.

Bruiser took a more aggressive drink. "Tell me why darling Daryl wanted me to mess you up."

I told him the story I now referred to as "the rat and the rich kid."

When I finished, Bruiser smiled. "I always hated that pasty-faced prick," he said. "Don't worry, Daryl won't be picking on any more freshmen."

"If you had no intention of messing me up, why are you here?"

"Long story. Normally, our fraternity wouldn't give a guy like me a second look. I come from a blue-collar family, and most of the brothers are rich kids, but I was on a football scholarship and had decent grades, and I think they brought me in to be the fraternity enforcer. We have quite a few geeks who from time to time do need some protecting. I don't just go out and beat people up. I try to get both sides of the story and act accordingly. If a brother is out of line, I'll go back and have a little talk with him. If the offending party is out of line, I issue a warning." Bruiser paused and smiled. "A warning is usually all it takes."

"I'll bet."

"In your case, I guessed that Daryl was being a prick. Besides, if I messed with you, I would get a visit from Billy, and that could get ugly."

"I don't let Billy fight my fights," I said, a little annoyed.

"Probably not," he said. "You look like you can take care of yourself. But do you think you could stop Billy from paying me a visit if he wanted to?"

I thought about that for a few seconds. "Probably not," I said.

"Well, there you go."

Bruiser and I spent the next half-hour getting to know each other. He had grown up in a coal-mining town in Pennsylvania and watched his father slowly commit suicide working day after day and year after year in the mines. He vowed not to end up like that. So, while other coal miners' kids were out raising hell, Bruiser played football, lifted weights, and hit the books. Bruiser was just a notch below what it took to play for a major college football power so when Connecticut offered him a scholarship, he jumped at it.

Bruiser looked at his watch. "Got to get to class," he said. "Nice talking to you."

"You, too," I said.

Bruiser pushed away from the table, stood, and smiled. "You have my permission to kick the shit out of Daryl Osgood the fourth anytime the need arises."

"Thanks," I grinned. "I'll keep that in mind."

The need to kick the shit out of Daryl never did materialize. Daryl Osgood IV stayed clear of me the rest of my senior year. I met Bruiser from time to time in the grill, where we had coffee and explored the meaning of life. The following year, Bruiser was taken in the third round of the NFL draft. He had a decent but short career as an offensive lineman for the Washington Redskins. After that, I lost track of him.

THREE DAYS DEAD

1

I was in the office early on a Monday, an unusually cold day for April. Billy had not yet made an appearance. Jake, my black standard Poodle, was curled up on his bed in the corner of my office, the inner office. The sign on the outer office door read,

CHEROKEE INVESTIGATIONS
Donald Youngblood and Bill T. Feathers
Private Investigators

Billy and I didn't start out as licensed private investigators. We were basically just hanging out. Then we got our licenses, and in the years that followed a lot of people began to take us seriously. A few even ended up dead. I didn't need the money, but I did want to help people. Becoming a private investigator seemed the perfect occupation to help people while creating a little excitement in my once-dreary life. In the previous six months, I had found plenty of excitement, but that's another story.

I heard the outer office door open. Jake raised his head and growled his less-threatening growl.

"Hello?" A female voice. *Young*, I thought.

"In here," I called out.

Seconds later, a young girl, fourteen or fifteen maybe, stood in my doorway. She was wearing blue jeans, beat-up tennis shoes, a navy peacoat that was too big for her, and a wool cap. She looked rather unkempt. Pulling off the cap to reveal thick blond hair cut short, she stared at me with piercing blue eyes. Those eyes looked old beyond her years.

"Can I help you?" I asked.

"I need you to find someone," she said.

"Who?" I asked.

"My mom."

"Sit down," I said, motioning to a chair. "How long has you mother been missing?"

"A week."

"A week? Who's been taking care of you?"

"I can take care of myself," she said with attitude.

I didn't doubt it. Something about this young lady suggested experience. Her mother was gone for a week, and yet I saw no panic. There was a matter-of-fact calmness behind those eyes that made me assume she had seen more and coped with a lot more than was normal for her age. I let the comment pass and stared at her in silence.

"How old are you?"

"I'll be fourteen my next birthday," she said with the same brashness.

"How did you hear about me?" I asked.

"I didn't. You're the only private investigator in the phone book. I did hear that you might have been the one who shot that bad guy at the police station."

Well, so much for my sterling reputation.

"Just a rumor," I said. "He was actually killed with a knife."

"I heard that, too," she said.

Rumors traveled fast in a small town. The news of a dead body in the local police station had spread like wildfire through a drought-ridden forest.

"Will you do it?" she asked. "I'll pay you whatever it costs, even if it takes me ten years." She handed me a roll of bills. "Down payment."

I unrolled the wad and quickly counted over one hundred dollars.

"What's your name?"

"Lacy," she said. "With a *y*. Lacy Malone. Born Lauren Lacy Malone. Has a nice ring to it, doesn't it?"

"It does," I said. "This is a lot of money, Lacy. Where did you get it?"

"Saved it from odd jobs. Cleaning houses mostly, some gardening work. I'm good with flowers and plants. Took me a year to save that."

I handed it back to her. "Keep it for now. You may need it. Now, sit down, relax, and tell me your story. Tell me everything you can think of. I have plenty of time."

She took a deep breath and started her story. I sat back and listened. Lacy Malone was born in East Tennessee to an unwed seventeen-year-old named Tracy Malone. Lacy had no idea who her father was, and the birth certificate she carried with her confirmed that the father of Lauren Lacy Malone was indeed *unknown*. A few odd comments over the years had led Lacy to believe that her mother knew who her father was but did not want to tell her. Lacy and her mother had lived with her grandmother in the grandmother's house during Lacy's preschool years. The house was a few miles outside Mountain Center. Her grandmother had died two years ago of a heart attack. Lacy's mother worked as a waitress in Newport. They got by okay, as her mother had inherited the grandmother's house free and clear of any debt, as well as some other money. The status quo held until about six months ago, when her mother was persuaded by a friend to take a job as a dancer at a topless bar outside Knoxville. The Bloody Bare, it was called. The money was so good it was hard to pass up, but problems ensued. Her mother—quite a looker, according to Lacy—started spiraling out of control. Booze, drugs, and staying out all night had turned her mother into someone she did not know. Finally, last week, her mother had packed up, left a note, and vanished while Lacy was at school. Lacy handed me the one-line note. It said, "You are old enough to take care of yourself."

"Why do you want to find her?" I asked.

"She used to be a good person, and she is probably hooked on drugs now and needs help. I have heard about rehab programs. I want to get her into one of those so I can have my mom back." Her cool demeanor was starting to crack as her eyes glistened.

Damn. I did not deal well with *adult* female tears. Adolescent female tears were even worse. I felt the urge to hold her and tell her everything was going to be all right, but I didn't. I had no idea if everything *was* going to be all right.

"Any idea where she went?"

"None."

"Give me ten dollars," I said.

Lacy peeled a ten-dollar bill off her roll and handed it to me without question. She had a puzzled look on her face.

"You have just retained my services," I said. "How can I get in touch with you?"

She smiled and handed me a slip of folded notebook paper with her name, address, and cell phone number. Everybody had a cell phone these days, even middle-schoolers.

"I have to get to school," she said.

"Want a ride?"

"Sure."

We left Jake in dreamland, chasing rabbits.

2

I dropped Lacy off at Mountain Center Middle School and pondered my present dilemma while driving back to the office. Lacy was in the eighth grade, a point in her life when youth would collide with adolescence and create all kinds of interesting side effects, emotional and physical. It was not a time to be living alone and unsupervised, no matter how mature she was for her age. It was plain to see she was going to be a very attractive teenager, drawing young males like a magnet. In one sense, it was none of my business. In another sense, I had encountered a youth in distress, and I felt bound to do something about it. I knew I couldn't leave this alone. If I contacted the so-called authorities, Lacy would end up with foster parents, and that was a crapshoot I was willing to gamble on only as a last resort.

I picked up my cell phone and called one of my two best friends in the world.

"Mountain Center Police Department."

"Hi, Susie," I said. "Let me speak to Big Bob."

"Hey, Donnie," said Susie. "How you doin'?"

"Very well, thank you," I replied. "And yourself?"

"Great. Hang on."

Susie was Big Bob's sister.

"What's up?" the big baritone voice boomed. Big Bob Wilson, high-school best friend and basketball star, was now the main defender of law and order in Mountain Center. Having a well-connected law officer as one of your best friends was not at all a bad thing, especially if you were a private investigator. Big Bob knew almost everyone and everything going on in Mountain Center.

"Meet me at the diner for breakfast," I said. "I'm buying."

"When?"

"Ten minutes, or whenever you get there," I said.

"I'll be there," the big man said, and hung up.

◆　◆　◆　◆

I drove back to my office building and parked in my usual space in the back. The Mountain Center Diner was two blocks from my office, and the walk took only a few minutes. I had my own table in the back, and Doris Black, the owner, made sure that no one sat there until after I left or nine o'clock, whichever came first. Doris always waited on me personally ever since I started giving her tips on various stocks that were outperforming the market. Having spent five years on Wall Street before returning to the safety of my hometown, I felt as qualified as anyone to hand out sage advice on the fickle market. Although she never told me how much she invested from my tips, I knew it was considerable, and I knew she had made a nice return. From time to time, I gave Doris tidbits, and she always followed up with a purchase.

"Good morning, Mr. Youngblood," smiled Doris.

Doris considered me a celebrity because I had worked on Wall Street, and I could not get her to call me Don. I gave up trying years ago and just enjoyed the status.

"Good morning, Doris."

"What'll it be?"

"I'm waiting for Big Bob, so I'll just take coffee for now," I answered.

"You got it," she said as she wrote on her pad and scurried off.

Doris reminded me of Shirley Booth on the old *Hazel* TV show. Doris was in her mid-fifties, slightly overweight, and attractive in a matronly sort of way. Her husband had died many years ago, and she had two grown sons who had moved away and another who was a senior in high school headed for the University of Tennessee on a golf scholarship. The diner was her life, and she loved seeing all her regulars. Doris had a great sense of humor and was always cheerful. I felt honored to call her a friend.

She scurried back with a pre-owned *USA Today*, laid it on my table, and hurried off again.

I located the sports page. Baseball season had just started. Once upon a time, I had been an avid fan of baseball in general and the Cincinnati Reds in particular, but free agency, strikes, and outrageous salaries had soured my outlook on our national pastime. After the last strike, I had vowed never to watch another game on TV, and so far I had fulfilled that vow. I had always enjoyed reading the sports page over breakfast, and I still looked at the major league box scores, although I did not recognize many of the players. The Reds were predicted to battle the Pirates for the cellar of the National League Central, which further dampened any spark of enthusiasm I might muster.

The diner got suddenly quiet. I looked up to see the chief of police walking toward my table. Big Bob Wilson had arrived for breakfast.

"Hey, Blood," he said. As he sat, the diner buzz resumed.

"How's it going?"

"Same ole, same ole," Big Bob said. "What's on your mind?"

"Let's order first."

I nodded at Doris, who rushed over. I ordered my favorite, a feta cheese omelet, sausage patties, home fries, and rye toast. Big Bob ordered pancakes, bacon, and a side of home fries. Mountain Center Diner home fries were legendary. I filled the void with local sports chatter while waiting on breakfast and getting to the point of my meeting with the big man.

"I need to talk to you off the record," I said. "You cannot hear this as the chief of police."

He glared. "I am the chief of police."

I stared back in silence.

"Okay," he said finally. "You going to tell me about Ronnie Fairchild?"

"No," I said. "Something else."

"When am I going to hear about Ronnie?" Big Bob asked as breakfast arrived.

"Another time," I said as I took my first bite of omelet. "I've got to put some distance between me and the Fairchild case before I'm ready to talk about it."

"Okay. Let me hear what's on your mind," Big Bob said, attacking the pancakes.

Between bites, I told him what I knew so far about Lacy. He listened as he ate. There was no expression on his face that let me know what he was thinking. He gave an occasional nod. I think he blinked a couple of times.

"What do you think?" I asked as he finished his breakfast, leaving a goodly quantity of home fries.

"Well, I don't think she should be living alone," he said. "For one thing, it isn't safe. You have to find her a place to stay with an adult or I'll blow the whistle to social services."

"So much for off the record," I said.

"Don't give me that shit, Donald," Big Bob said. "You knew I couldn't let this slide."

We called each other Donald and Robert only when we were pissed or wanted to get the other's undivided attention. Big Bob was slightly pissed.

Big Bob's beeper vibrated on his belt, and he snapped it off and took a look. He then picked up his coffee cup and drained it. "Got to go," he said. "You've got three days to work this out, and then I'm going to have to make it official."

I nodded.

"And thanks for breakfast," he said.

The big man turned and walked through the diner and out the front door. A couple of dozen sets of eyes followed his exit. I finished the last of my breakfast and went back to the office.

3

Less than a year ago, I was a confirmed bachelor drifting from relationship to relationship with some very fine women. Those women all had one thing in common. They were husband hunting. I was the dashing ex–Wall Street whiz kid turned private eye with one particular mission in life: *not* to get married. Sandy Smith had been the latest in the string of these nice ladies to issue an ultimatum. When I swallowed hard and went suddenly mute, she packed up and ran off to Atlanta to pursue her career and continue husband hunting. From time to time, we exchanged emails. She now had another guy on the hook.

My resolve to stay unattached began to waver when I was hired as a bodyguard for a Knoxville police officer wounded in action and still being stalked by a very bad guy. Billy and I had livened things up a bit by capturing her stalker and delivering him to the Mountain Center Police Station. I ended up helping dispose of the bad guy and falling in love with the good girl.

Luckily, she felt the same way about me, so much so that she agreed to give up the excitement of the Knoxville police force for the boredom of the

Mountain Center police force. Mary Sanders was now a fixture in my life, and I couldn't have been happier. I was still wondering what happened.

I called Mary on her cell.

"Hello, sweetie," she answered. She rarely called me sweetie, so she must have been in a good mood.

"Hello yourself, sweetheart," I said, feigning the tough private eye. "How about dinner tonight at the club?"

"Sounds good. What's the occasion?"

"I have a new case I want to discuss with you. It's pretty unusual. I need your female insight."

"Now I'm curious. What's this about?"

"Tonight," I said. "Call me at the office when you're ready, and I'll pick you up at our place."

"Okay, sweetie," Mary teased. "See you later."

• • • •

The very private Mountain Center Country Club was not in the city of Mountain Center. The club was situated on an unknown number of acres in a vastly underdeveloped area northeast of the city. MCCC offered golf, tennis, platform tennis, croquet, swimming, skeet shooting, archery, racquetball, and a fitness center with a full-time masseuse. You could soothe aching muscles with a variety of saunas, whirlpools, and steam baths. A first-class restaurant with a chef who had graduated from Johnson & Wales University in Providence, Rhode Island, sat atop the third floor of the main building.

The club was for the rich. It did not discriminate against color, only gender. It had no female members. Wives of members had full privileges with the exception of golf and the men's grill. The women had their own grill—off-limits to men—and their own pro shop. They could play only on ladies' day or with a male member on other days. Men could not play golf on ladies' day. Well, there you had it. Not Augusta National, but close.

I joined the club for a very dumb reason: to play racquetball during the winter. It would probably have been cheaper to build my own court. I played racquetball a couple of times a week, sometimes with Mary and sometimes with Billy. Mary was a really good racquetball player and almost impossible for me to beat. Billy and I were about even. Occasionally, Billy, Mary, and I would play cutthroat: every person for themselves. Mary always won, even if we tried to gang up on her. Sometimes, Big Bob would join us. Big Bob had a membership, compliments of his father, one of the richest men in town.

Club rules stated that in any activity you could only bring a guest twice a month. Since the courts were not in high demand the rule was not enforced for racquetball. Over the years, I had taken advantage of almost all the club had to offer with the exception of golf, which I considered a stupid frustrating game.

Mary and I sat in the MCCC restaurant at a corner table for four next to the front window, which overlooked Clubhouse Road and, beyond that, the first tee. The lights in distant Mountain Center were beginning to establish themselves as the sun set behind the hills. On the table in front of us was a bottle of Chateau Ste. Michelle Sauvignon Blanc for Mary and a bottle of King Estates Pinot Noir for me. I would probably drink half of my bottle, while Mary might very well finish hers and then help me with mine without showing the slightest effect. We clinked glasses.

"So what's the big mystery?" she asked.

"I have a new case," I said.

"So you told me."

"Missing person."

"Again? You said no more missing person cases after last time."

"This one is a little different," I said. "My client is a thirteen-year-old girl, and the missing person is her mother."

"What about the police?"

"She doesn't want the police. Drugs may be involved. The mother left a goodbye note and vanished to parts unknown."

"Jesus Christ," Mary said with disgust.

"Really," I agreed.

I told Mary everything I knew, including my conversation with Big Bob. In the meantime, the waiter arrived with our food—sea bass for Mary and salmon for me.

"What are you going to do?" Mary asked.

"First, I'm going to check out the girl and see if her story rings true. I think it will, but you never know. Then I'll need to find her a place to stay. After that, I'll go look for the mom."

"What about our trip to Singer Island with Scott?" Mary asked.

In early April, Mary had asked for and been granted two weeks of vacation from the Mountain Center police force. We had made plans to meet Scott Glass and his new trainee flame, Melinda, at Singer Island, Florida. We were supposed to leave the day after tomorrow.

"Damn," I said. I had completely forgotten about the trip.

"It's okay," Mary said. "We can postpone it. Sean is out sick, and I'm sure Big Bob will be relieved to hear I can stay and work."

"Sorry," I said. "I'll call Scott tomorrow."

"Never apologize for helping someone," Mary said.

4

I was late coming into the office the next morning. That happens when I drink a whole bottle of red wine and then have to fight off a frisky blond goddess. I didn't put up much of a fight, but it lasted until about two in the morning. Although I wasn't hung over, I wasn't in top form either.

Billy was working on his latest painting when I arrived. Since he rarely got to the office before I did, he gave me a curious look and a wry smile.

"I made a carafe of your brew," he said. "You look like you need it."

"My hero," I said, heading for the white carafe.

Most of the time, Billy drank his own hideous brew, which best resembled heated black cough syrup. He mixed a combination of French roast and espresso. Sometimes he added sugar and other times cream. Sometimes he added both. When I quizzed him about it, he would say he liked variety.

He had done me a favor by making my brew, a special order from Gevalia. I poured this elixir into my favorite cup, added half-and-half and raw sugar, stirred, took that first magical sip, and returned to the land of the living.

I had just sat at my desk and booted up my computer when the phone rang. I picked it up before Billy could get to it.

"Cherokee Investigations," I said in my radio announcer voice.

"Hey, Blood, what's happening?" Scott Glass asked.

Scott Glass was an FBI agent working out of headquarters in Quantico, Virginia. I had met Scott at UConn the day before I met Billy. Scott, Billy, and I were on the basketball team together before I was told that my walk-on status had been changed to walk-off. Scott was six-foot-five and looked like anything but a basketball player. He had a geeky, lanky, awkward, studious look that was more in line with an FBI agent than a basketball talent. But Scott was one of the finest shooting guards ever to wear the UConn blue and white. He had dark, curly hair and always wore glasses. He was quickly nicknamed "Professor."

"Unfortunately, I just picked up another case," I said. "I don't think we can make that trip to Singer just yet."

"That's good because I can't make it either. We've got a sniping serial killer on the loose in Maryland, and I've been assigned to the team."

"Yeah, I read about that. Good luck."

"Hang on, Blood." I was on hold momentarily. "Got to go," Scott said hurriedly as he came back on the line. "I'll catch up with you later."

"Okay, Scottie. Be careful out there," I said, hoping he heard me before he hung up.

I logged on to AOL to check out the stock market and review the portfolios of a few of the people for whom I still handled investments.

Unfortunately, the list was growing instead of dwindling. The market was hovering around twelve thousand, and yesterday had been a flat day with no news worth paying attention to. I sent a few emails and logged off as the phone rang. I got it before the second ring.

"Cherokee Investigations."

"You're all set for that appointment," Big Bob said. "Ten o'clock."

"Thanks."

"Keep me informed."

"You can count on it," I said, and hung up.

Big Bob and I were always competing for the last word.

◆　　◆　　◆　　◆

I sat in the principal's office. I hadn't been in a principal's office since the sixth grade, when I had gotten my backside paddled for fighting. I could not remember what the fight was about, or who it was with, but I remembered the size of the paddle and the man who wielded it. Boomer Jones was famous for busting butts and laughing about it later. We all loved Boomer, and you were nobody in grammar school unless your bottom had felt the sting of Old Thunderbolt, his legendary paddle. When Boomer retired to Florida, his paddle actually went on display in the school trophy case. Legend had it that there was a notch on the paddle for every fanny Boomer had blasted—pure myth, of course. Looking around the office as I sat and waited for the current principal, I did not see any sign of a paddle. What had happened to the good ole days?

Big Bob had arranged my meeting with the Mountain Center Middle School principal, Dick Traber. Dick was not a local boy, so I didn't know him personally. He had been in the job almost as long as I had been back in town, ten years.

Dick Traber came through a back door to his office and offered a hand in greeting as I stood. Dark, slender, and bespectacled, he had the look of composure and intelligence that would inspire trust if I were a parent of a child in his school.

"Mr. Youngblood, nice to meet you," he said. "I have never met a real-life private investigator."

"The jury is still out as to whether or not I actually am one," I said.

"Oh, from what I've heard, I don't think there is any doubt. Sit down, please, and tell me how I can help you."

"Thank you," I said, taking a seat in the chair directly in front of his desk. "May I ask you to keep this conversation confidential?"

"Certainly," he said.

"I need some background information on one of your students. She has asked me to look into a situation for her, but before I can do that I feel I need to know her a little better. Her name is Lacy Malone."

"Lacy Malone." He nodded. "Yes, I know who she is, but I don't know anything about her. Is she in trouble?"

"No, definitely not. I wonder if I might talk to her homeroom teacher."

Dick Traber immediately started tapping the keyboard on his desk and staring at the monitor to his right. "Lacy's homeroom teacher is Miss Phelps. She has a free period in a few minutes. I'll get word to her to come to my office. Excuse me for a moment."

Dick Traber went out to the office reception area and returned less than a minute later. He seemed a little nervous.

"I wouldn't be doing this unless the request had come from the chief of police. Can you tell me what this is about?"

"I cannot betray that confidence," I said. "But I can tell you that it has nothing to do with your school or anyone associated with it, and I promise to give you the full story once my services are no longer required."

"I understand," he said. I detected relief in his voice.

◆ ◆ ◆ ◆

Lori Phelps was a young, blond, good-looking eighth-grade English teacher. If she had been my teacher in the eighth grade, I would have either been the best student in school or I would have never gotten anything done, I'm not sure which. One thing was for sure: I would have definitely been in love.

I had been moved to a conference room, and Miss Phelps sat across the table from me with pad and pencil, confident and relaxed.

"I have never met a private detective before," she said.

Lot of that going around, I thought.

"How can I help you, Mr. Youngblood?"

"I need some information on one of your students," I said. "Just background. I am helping her with a problem, but I need to get a feel for who she is."

"Which student?"

I detected a little resistance.

"Lacy Malone," I said.

"Oh, Lacy. I'm not surprised," Miss Phelps said slowly. "I knew something was going on there."

I heard disappointment in her voice.

"How so?" I asked.

"Lacy is an excellent student, but lately her grades have been slipping and her homework has been late or incomplete or not done at all. Her mind wanders in class, and she looks less kept than usual. I tried to contact her mother, but no luck so far."

I nodded. *The mother starts to go downhill, and so does the daughter,* I thought.

"Does she have many friends?" I asked. "Is she popular?"

"Lacy keeps to herself a lot. She has no close friends, so far as I can tell. She seems much more mature than the other eighth-graders. Her attitude is one that seems to say, 'I can't be bothered.' "

I nodded again.

"Can you tell me what is going on?"

"Not yet," I said. "But Lacy does have some problems at home that I am going to help her work out. She may not be staying at home for a while. Do you have an email address?"

"Yes," Miss Phelps said as she started writing on her pad. She tore off a sheet of paper, folded it, and handed it to me across the conference-room table.

"Thanks," I said. "I'll be in touch. I am going to try to get Lacy back on track. I may need your help as far as her studies go. You let me know what she needs to do to get caught up, and I'll see that it gets done."

I stood and handed her my card. Lori Phelps rose and took it from me and gave it a quick read.

"I appreciate your getting involved. Lacy is a good girl with lots of potential."

"In what area?" I asked.

"Math and computers," she said as we walked into the hall.

A thought stirred in the back of my mind. A plan was forming.

The old, familiar sound of a school bell ringing interrupted my train of thought.

"It was a pleasure meeting you, Mr. Youngblood," Miss Phelps said, extending her hand. "Let me know if I can be of further help. I've got a class in five minutes."

I watched in appreciation as Lori Phelps turned and walked down the hall while students wandered out of classrooms in all directions. I stood there for a moment frozen in time with a sad smile on my face, taking in the sights and sounds of middle school, transported back almost thirty years to memories of happy times: good friends, loving parents, schoolrooms, teachers, sports, and very little responsibility. Times that it took years of fading memories to fully appreciate.

I walked out the front door of Mountain Center Middle School with an odd sense of jealousy. *Oh, to be an eighth-grader again, if only for a little while.*

5

I was in my office that afternoon playing chess on my computer and deciding how to approach finding the missing Tracy Malone. Jake was asleep in his usual place, probably concerned only about his next meal. My immediate concern was Lacy. Mary and I had discussed plans, both short term and long term.

I dialed Lacy's cell.

"Hello, Mr. Youngblood."

Damn caller ID.

"Hello, Lacy. We need to talk. Can I pick you up at school?"

There was a pause. "No, I'll take the bus and meet you in your office. I'll see you in about an hour."

"Fine," I said. "See you then."

◆　◆　◆　◆

She sat in front of my desk with a can of Diet Coke, staring intently, waiting for me to say something.

"How was school?" *A riveting conversationalist, me.*

I thought I saw a slight smile flicker, but she smothered it.

"Fine," Lacy said. "What else do you want to say to me, or to tell me or ask me?"

I hesitated as I tried to figure out a place to start.

"Let me guess," she said. "You are going to tell me I cannot stay by myself."

Smart kid.

"Well, there's that," I said.

"I pretty much knew that when I came in here to hire you," she said. "So you obviously have a plan. Why don't you tell me, and then we'll both know."

"Fair enough," I said. "We can do this officially, which means telling child services, or we can do this unofficially, which means you quietly move in somewhere under adult supervision."

"You prefer the latter, I take it," Lacy said. "And you have someone in mind, no doubt."

Too smart.

"I do." I couldn't help smiling. This kid could be a future partner. "But there would be all the usual rules—homework, chores, bedtime."

"Whom would I be staying with?"

Whom?

"For a while, with me," I said.

"You and the blond Wonder Woman? I can live with that," Lacy said. I detected a hint of enthusiasm.

"Blond Wonder Woman?"

"Yeah, that's what the boys at school call her. They all think she's hot. She directs traffic after school sometimes. One of the boys nicknamed her Wonder Woman. You know, after the TV character, because she's tall and good looking and all. Then another boy pointed out that Wonder Woman had black hair, so they started calling her 'the blond Wonder Woman.' "

"I see."

"Anyway, that would be cool, staying with you two, and I'll abide by whatever rules you make," she said excitedly.

"There is a question of back homework and sliding grades."

"You've been snooping."

"I'm a detective," I said. "We snoop."

"I did the crime, so I'll do the time," she said.

"Meaning?"

"Meaning I'll do the back homework and I'll study to pull up my grades."

"So we have a deal?"

"We have a deal," Lacy said.

◆　　◆　　◆　　◆

After I closed down the office, Lacy, Jake, and I went to Lacy's house to gather some of her things. Jake stayed in the car while we went inside. I was expecting a mess. Instead, I found the house neat and clean and everything in its apparent place. Lacy's room was a little less orderly, especially her desk. Books, notebooks, stacks of papers, catalogs, and unidentifiable items covered the work surface.

I watched as Lacy stuffed clothes in a duffel bag and crammed books, notebooks, and papers into a backpack until neither would hold any more.

"I would like to take my computer," Lacy said.

One look told me that Lacy's computer was probably an underpowered hand-me-down, but I did not want to insult her by suggesting it belonged in the trash.

"What operating program are you running?" I asked.

"Windows 98."

I nodded. "Are you online?"

"Not anymore," she said. "Mom didn't pay the AOL bill last month, and they cut me off."

"Which AOL were you running?"

"Eight-point-oh," she said.

I nodded again. "The bedroom that is going to be your room has a new desktop computer set up in it with a work station twice as big as your desk," I said as her eyes widened. "That computer is running Windows XP and AOL 9.0 Optimized. It has a hundred and sixty gigs of memory on the hard drive and two gigs of ram. You are welcome to use it. You can download anything you need off your hard drive and bring it with you."

She smiled and opened her top desk drawer, pulled out a floppy disk, and held it up for me to see. "I always back up every night before bed."

"That makes you a lot more diligent that I am," I said. "You ready?"

"Yes."

As I closed and locked the front door, I stopped and turned to Lacy. "Got another house key?"

"There's one hidden around back," she said.

"Get it."

She disappeared around the right side of the house and returned a few seconds later with another key.

"Give me both keys," I said, holding out my hand.

She smiled a small smile and handed me the keys. "Don't trust me, huh?"

"Trust has to be earned," I said. "Besides, I remember what I was like when I was your age."

"You shouldn't judge me based on what you were like," she lectured politely.

"True," I said as we walked back to my Pathfinder. "But until I build a database on you, I'll play it safe."

♦   ♦   ♦   ♦

When Lacy met Mary, it was instant hero worship. Lacy was in awe of the beautiful blond lady cop, and the warmth and friendship between them was instant and genuine. I was now outnumbered and outgunned in my own abode. Jake, the other male on the premises, would be of no help. He would cave in to the soft hands and gentle voices of the adoring females. Well, the same could probably be said of me. I was told politely to get lost while Mary helped Lacy move into the guest bedroom. I sat at the bar in the kitchen with my laptop, nursing a Michelob Amber Bock and listening to faint conspiratorial voices and muffled laughter from one level above. Mary had not lost the mothering instinct, and I was sure she would have an impact on Lacy.

I was halfway finished with my beer when Mary returned.

"Where is our guest?" I asked.

"Shower," Mary said. "There were some hygiene issues that I had to address."

"How'd she take that?" I asked.

"Like she was craving discipline," Mary said. "She really is a sweet girl."

"Remember, this is temporary," I said.

"I know."

"I'm going to find her mother."

"I know."

Mary started dinner, and I took one last look at the stock market. I didn't particularly like what I saw. My consternation was gratefully interrupted as Lacy came bouncing down the stairs and into the kitchen. Her blond hair was still damp from an apparent towel drying, and she had changed into fresh jeans and a T-shirt. She looked like a smaller version of Mary.

"That was fast," Mary said.

"That computer rocks," Lacy said. "It's so awesome that homework will even be fun."

"Speaking of homework," I said, "how much do you have?"

"About an hour's worth. Mary said I could do it after dinner."

I looked at Mary and smiled. "A step ahead of me, huh?"

"Or two," she grinned.

"Anything else I should know about?"

"If there is, we'll let you know, won't we, Lacy?" Mary teased.

"Sure thing," Lacy said.

There was silence as Mary poured herself a glass of wine and I sipped my beer.

"Want something to drink?" Mary asked Lacy. "Soda, tea, lemonade?"

"Do you have bottled water?" Lacy asked. "I don't drink anything with sugar in it."

"Good for you," Mary said. "Bottled water it is."

More silence.

Lacy looked around, apparently comfortable with the silence. She absent-mindedly patted Jake, who knew a good mark when he saw one. "I could get used to this," she said. "But I know it's only temporary, until you find my mom."

"You are wise beyond your years, Lacy," Mary observed. "How come?"

Lacy shrugged. "I don't know. Because of my grandmother, I guess. I spent a lot of time with her before she died, and she never talked to me like a kid, always like an adult. She taught me a lot of things. She was my real mother, if you know what I mean. I love my mom and all, but my grandmother really raised me. She said my mom was too much like one of her sisters. That neither one of them had a lick of sense."

I sat and finished my beer, listening and watching the exchange between these two special females and feeling a bit like a fifth wheel.

Mary had fixed spaghetti sauce earlier and was heating it on the stove. The water for the noodles was boiling, and at the appropriate time I would be expected to make my infamous Caesar salad.

"Want some help?" Lacy asked.

"Not this time," Mary responded. "I know you're dying to check out that computer in your room. Why don't you do that, and I'll call you when dinner is ready."

"Cool," Lacy said, and bounced off the barstool, out of the kitchen, and up the stairs in a flash.

Mary smiled at me. "Do kids still say 'cool'?"

"This one does," I said.

6

We sat on T. Elbert's front porch in the cool dawn of an April morning drinking coffee from Dunkin' Donuts and munching on various bagels with cream cheese. My mentor, friend, and ex-TBI agent, T. Elbert Brown, was now confined to a wheelchair, thanks to a drug dealer's bullet five years ago. T. Elbert lived in an old turn-of-the-twentieth-century two-story on Olivia Drive. The house was immaculately kept both inside and out.

Joining us on T. Elbert's front porch was Roy Husky. I had met Roy, a hard man ten years my senior, on the Fairchild case, and we had become unlikely friends. Roy was an ex-con turned jack-of-all-trades for powerful Mountain Center businessman Joseph Fleet. Even though our backgrounds were at opposite ends of the spectrum, Roy and I had found common ground in honesty, humor, and a single goal that had led to a growing friendship.

I talked about my new case.

"Thought you were through with missing persons cases," Roy said.

"I was hoodwinked," I said.

"You have a hard time saying no where women are concerned," Roy teased.

"Don't we all," chimed in T. Elbert.

I let it pass. I noticed T. Elbert was not using his motorized wheelchair.

"Is your motorized chair on the fritz?" I asked.

"Nope," T. Elbert said, slapping the arms of his wheelchair. "I like to use old faithful here when I'm rolling around the house. Helps keep my upper body fit. Feel this muscle."

Just to play along, I reached over and felt a very formidable bicep through his heavy cotton shirt.

"Impressive," I said.

"Helps the grip, too," T. Elbert said. "Want to shake hands?"

"I think I'll pass on that one, T. Elbert," I said.

"Roy?" T. Elbert said.

"Not me," Roy laughed.

We were quiet for a while, enjoying the sounds of a new day dawning. A light breeze moved newborn leaves in a nearby maple tree as rays of sunlight danced through.

"Want to take a ride later this week?" I asked Roy. "I want to visit the strip club where Lacy's mother worked. Be good to have a tough guy like you along."

"Why not?" Roy growled. "Someone has to protect you from yourself."

◆   ◆   ◆   ◆

Later that day, I sat in the office of the Mountain Center chief of police drinking steaming Earl Grey tea from a black mug with *MCPD* printed on it. I was giving Big Bob the complete update on Lacy Malone.

"Well, that's the story," I finished.

"Humph," Big Bob snorted.

"What's that mean?"

"Not quite legal, but I guess it's okay for now, while you look for her mother."

"How long are you giving me?" I asked.

"As long as you need. The less I know, the better. Lacy couldn't have better people looking after her than you and Mary. Besides, a good dose of teenager will do you good."

7

The Smoky Bare was advertised as a tasteful adult nightclub. It was located on the outskirts of Knoxville on the Alcoa Highway. We sat in a back booth in an area that served food. I sat next to Roy, who was on the inside, and I faced Mary, who was next to Billy. Mary had insisted on coming to keep an eye on me. She knew The Smoky Bare from her days on the Knoxville police force. She looked gorgeous in tight jeans, a white T-shirt, and a black leather jacket to match her black boots. *Be still, my heart.* We had ordered burgers on the advice of our server, who rivaled any Hooters waitress I had ever seen.

The Smoky Bare was not what I expected it to be. A long, wide, low, flat building from the outside transformed inside into what I could only describe as a classy strip joint. Not that I had been in many, but I had never seen one cleaner or more tastefully decorated than The Smoky Bare. It had a long bar, a large area that contained half a dozen pool tables, a dance floor, four dancer's cages, and a small stage on the far back right. One topless dancer swayed to soft, slow music in a cage on the other side of the dance floor, which was about as far away from our booth as it could be and still be in the building. I tried to take covert looks at the dancer, strictly for professional reasons, but Mary was having none of that.

"Keep you eyes on yours truly or sleep on the couch," she said firmly.

I think she was teasing, but I wasn't quite sure.

"I thought it was my room," I said.

She arched an eyebrow. I smiled.

"Want me to swap with him?" Billy asked.

"No," said Mary. "He has to be trained."

I heard Roy chuckle softly beside me.

"Something you want to say?" I snapped.

"Nope," Roy said quickly.

The food arrived. During that distraction, I took another quick look at the dancer. Whoever did the hiring had a good eye. If all the girls looked like this one, I could see why The Smoky Bare was a popular place. I scanned the bar. It was semi-full with an after-work crowd; about half wore suits. *Nothing promotes male bonding better than a good-looking topless dancer,* I thought.

I took a bite of my cheeseburger. *Not bad.*

"Tell me about this girl in Cherokee," Mary said casually to Billy.

I glanced at Roy. He glanced back. We kept our heads down and concentrated on our food.

"Somebody's got a big mouth," Billy said.

"Come on, Billy, what's the big secret?" Mary asked. "When are we going to meet her?"

"Soon," Billy said.

"Okay, so tell me about her."

Billy ate in silence while Mary stared at him and waited.

"She's a schoolteacher," Billy said.

"And?" Mary prodded.

"And she is attractive," Billy offered.

My mother would have described this scenario as "pulling hen's teeth." Billy would eventually give Mary the information she sought, but she would have to earn it. Mary, on the other hand, was an experienced and relentless extractor of information, and she would find out all she wanted to know.

"What's her name?" Mary continued.

Roy and I ate in silence. I tried hard not to laugh.

"Maggie," Billy said. "Maggie Morning-Song."

"Beautiful name," Mary said.

A shadow loomed over our table. I looked up to see a very large man around fifty years of age in a gold polo shirt and khaki slacks. The shirt was embroidered with *The Smoky Bare* in black and underneath that the word *Manager*. He was probably an inch or two taller than I was and beefy—not fat but thick, probably worked out. His dark hair was combed straight back.

"Is everything okay here?" Manager asked. He was looking at Mary.

"Fine," I said.

He was still looking at Mary. She was smiling back at him.

"Would you be interested in a job here, miss?" Manager asked. "You're certainly equipped for it, and the money is terrific."

I could feel my face get red. Mary laughed.

"Get lost," I said.

Manager smiled at Mary. Roy put his hand on my arm as if to say, *Calm down.*

Manager never took his eyes off Mary. "No doubt, the boyfriend," he said, cocking his head toward me.

Roy had a firm grip on my arm.

Mary stood and removed her leather jacket, which did nothing toward calming my mood. "I just might be interested in a job here," she said. "Why don't you show me around, and we'll talk about it."

I got the message. Roy relaxed his grip.

The waitress showed up.

"Beers are on me, Cindy," Manager said.

We drank free beer and finished our food. I watched another dancer fill another cage. She was as good looking as the first one. The place was slowly filling up. I was surprised at the number of young couples. Time passed, and I was becoming uneasy with Mary's absence. I knew she was a cop and could take care of herself, but my male ego was having a hard time sitting by and doing nothing.

Half an hour later, she returned, alone.

"Take the job?" I snarled.

"Will you grow up?" Roy countered.

"I'm teasing," I said defensively.

"Find out everything you wanted to know?" Roy asked.

"And then some," Mary said. "Come with me," she ordered, looking at me.

"Yes, dear," I teased.

I followed Mary around the right side of the bar and through a door at the rear. I found myself in a hall. Stairs on the left went down. A small

Dressing Room sign had an arrow angled down the stairs. Stairs going up on the right had a similar Offices sign. I followed Mary up the stairs and down the hall to a corner office. We walked in. Manager was sitting behind a desk tapping on a computer keyboard. The screen was angled away from me, so I could not see what he was working on. He looked up and smiled at Mary.

"Steve Wade, this is Don Youngblood," Mary said.

Steve stood and offered a hand. Confused, I accepted it, and we shook hands—a testosterone shake, pretty much a draw. I didn't want to hurt the guy.

"I'll leave you two alone," Mary said. "Steve will answer any questions you have regarding Tracy Malone."

"Sit," Steve said, motioning to a chair in front of his desk. "Sorry about the job offer thing, but Mary and I know each other from the Knoxville PD. I retired a few years ago, and I thought she might be on the job, so I had to get her alone to see what was up."

"Well, you sure had me fooled," I said.

"Yeah, you looked like you were going to come out of that booth and pound my ass," he laughed. "Mary filled me in on the last few months. I knew she had been shot. I followed it in the newspapers. I even talked to Chief McSwain, but he was very tight-lipped. Then I read about what happened with Teddy Wayne Elroy. I'm glad everything worked out for Mary. She is good people, and she seems happy. You're a lucky man."

"I am," I said, wanting to move on. "Tell me anything you can about Tracy Malone."

"First, let me tell you about The Smoky Bare, so you will understand things better. This place used to be called Bottoms Up, a lowlife hangout for perverts, boozers, drug users, and any other scum you can imagine. The girls were skanks and drug addicts and went topless and bottomless and would do about anything for twenty dollars. We used to bust this place about once a month and shut it down. They would pay a fine and somehow open back up, and the same scenario would repeat itself.

"About a month after I retired, the owner was shot and killed, and his daughter, who wanted nothing to do with the place, closed it up and put it up for sale. She went on the Internet, compiled a list, and contacted every adult entertainment business in the country that she could identify, to see if any were interested in buying the place. A few months later, she got a nibble.

"A very legitimate corporation, Adults Only, Inc., which owns gambling houses and high-class adult clubs around the world, contacted her and opened negotiations. A few months later, the sale was complete."

He was on a roll, and I just let him go without interruption. His thoughts were well organized and well presented, with emphasis in all the right places. *I'll bet DAs love this guy*, I thought. He would be great on the witness stand.

"The next week, I got a call to come in for an interview. I was surprised, since I already had a security job and wasn't looking. I found out later that they have a lot of ex-cops working as managers at their clubs. It makes sense. We're tough, we've dealt with all kinds of people, and we can enforce the rules. And believe me, there are rules. We run within the law, and any employee who does not follow the rules is out.

"Anyway, the money was so good I couldn't turn it down, and it is a hell of a lot more interesting than security work. Am I boring you?"

"Not at all," I said. "I'm all ears."

"We take particular care in hiring our girls. Background checks, drug tests, and complete physicals are required. We pay well and even offer medical after a three-month probation period. Seeing the girls topless is the last thing we do, and there are always a couple of my senior girls in the room when that occurs. We are proud of what we hire."

"From what I've seen, I can see why," I said. "Now, about Tracy Malone?"

"Tracy, yes." He pecked the keyboard of his computer and turned his attention to the screen. "Hired about four months ago and fired three weeks ago. Failed a drug test, a shame, really. She was a sweet girl. She was very good-looking and kind of shy and became a good dancer. Everyone really liked her."

"What happened?" I asked.

"Fell in with the wrong guy," he said. "Bad guy. And I know a bad guy when I see one. He had some kind of snake tattoo running down his right arm. Not bad looking, and a real charmer, according to some of the girls. I guess Tracy fell for his line."

"Got a name?" I asked.

"I don't know it, but one of the girls might," Steve said.

"Could I talk to one of the girls who might have been close to Tracy?"

"Sure." He punched an intercom on his desk. "Sally, you down there?"

We waited in silence for a few seconds.

"Yeah, Steve. What's up?" a female voice said.

"Could you get decent and come up to my office for a few minutes? There is someone I would like for you to meet."

"Sure thing, Steve. Be up in five."

◆   ◆   ◆   ◆

I sat facing Sally, a tall redhead with all the right qualifications for her job. She wore high heels, cutoff jeans, and a T-shirt. The T-shirt did nothing to diminish her fitness for work.

"Can you tell me about this guy Tracy Malone got mixed up with?" I asked.

"Victor," she said. "I don't know his last name. About your height, slender but muscular, if you know what I mean. Dark, like he had a perpetual tan, dark hair and eyes. He was scary and charming at the same time. He had some kind of snake tattooed on his right forearm. It was creepy. The head of the snake was on his hand with the mouth open, and the two fangs were on the first digits of the middle two fingers. And it was a really good tat. It scared the hell out of me. That snake looked real enough to bite you."

"You think she might be with him now?" I asked.

"Probably," she answered. "Tracy told me that Victor was going to take her to Vegas and she was going to be a showgirl. My ass. He'll keep her hooked on drugs until he's tired of her, and then he'll dump her. I've seen the type."

"Anything else you can tell me?"

"Not really. Tracy was a sweet kid until she met Victor, and then she slowly went out of control. I can tell you that Victor seemed to have plenty of money, and he spent some of it on Tracy. Clothes and jewelry, stuff like that."

"Did Tracy ever say what brought Victor to East Tennessee?"

"Business, that's what she said," Sally snarled. "I'd bet a week's pay whatever business he was into was illegal."

I handed Sally my card.

She looked at it. "Private investigator. Why are you asking questions about Tracy, if you don't mind my being nosy?"

"Her daughter asked me to find her," I said.

"Daughter?" she said, startled. "Tracy never told me she had a daughter."

"Thirteen years old," I said. "Tracy just left her a note and took off."

"That fucking Victor," she said softly.

"If you think of anything else, or if you see Tracy or Victor again, please give me a call."

"You got a steady girl, Don?" she asked invitingly.

"I do," I said. "But thanks for asking."

"It figures," she said coolly as she rose to leave. "Nice meeting you."

I watched her go. It was not an unpleasant sight.

8

Two nights later, Mary and I sat at the kitchen bar, drinks in hand, while Lacy did homework in her room. Mary could sense that I didn't feel very motivated about finding Tracy Malone, and Lacy had not mentioned the subject since she moved in.

"What are we going to do about Lacy?" Mary asked.

"I don't know," I said. "I'll think of something."

"In a way, I'd like to keep her," Mary said.

"I know."

"But I know we can't," she continued.

"I know."

"You and I need time to get to know each other better. Unfortunately, Lacy would just complicate things."

"True," I said.

"And Lacy knows that," Mary said.

"She's a smart girl," I said.

We sat in silence with our drinks, lost in our thoughts, neither of us demanding conversation from the other. I could hear the wind whistling past the kitchen window. It was cool for April, and a storm was moving in. Tomorrow's forecast promised cold temperatures and a steady rain.

"Are you going to look for Tracy Malone?" Mary asked.

"I don't know," I said. "I'll have to talk to Lacy."

No sooner than the words had left my lips, Lacy came bouncing down the stairs. She looked fresh and alert, a recovering flower that had received water after a long dry spell.

"Talk to me about what?" Lacy asked.

Elephant ears, my mother would have said. I changed the subject.

"Finished with all that homework?" I asked.

"Yes. Talk to me about what?" she persisted.

"About whether or not you want me to look for your mother," I said.

Lacy screwed her mouth up and stared into space, as if searching for an answer that was not immediately forthcoming.

"I think you should," she finally answered. "I might be better off without her, but she needs help."

Out of the mouths of babes.

9

The next day, heavy cloud cover and a misty rain hung over Mountain Center, delaying daylight for almost an hour. At eight o'clock, it was still almost dark. Daylight would eventually win, but the clouds and rain would give ground grudgingly. I was alone in the office reviewing yesterday's action on Wall Street and making decisions for more than a handful of people whose accounts I still handled.

Billy was not in the office, nor did I know where he was. He often disappeared for days at a time, not letting me know when he was coming back or where he had been. His disappearances were happening more frequently lately, and I suspected it had something to do with his new female acquaintance in Cherokee. Mother hen that he was, if I were to pull that same disappearing act, he would worry the entire time I was gone and yell at me when I got back.

So I sat alone at my desk with coffee and a sausage and egg biscuit from the McDonald's across the street and pulled up the Orbitz website on my desktop computer. I had grown less fond of flying because of all the restrictions imposed on travelers, but Las Vegas was just too far to drive. The best choice was through Memphis on Northwest, so I printed a tentative schedule while I mulled over travel dates.

The phone rudely interrupted this quiet time. Had it not been for caller ID, I would have let Bell South's voice mail system take the call.

"Cherokee Investigations."

"Hi, Don. I thought I would catch you at this time of morning. I hope I'm not disturbing your morning ritual," my ex-girlfriend said.

"No problem, Sandy," I replied. "What's up?"

Sandy Smith sounded subdued, unlike the Sandy I was used to, a woman who redefined the word *up*.

"I need your advice. Can you talk now?"

"Sure," I said. "Go ahead."

"I don't really know how to start. It's a little embarrassing, really."

"As you know, I am not easily embarrassed, so just start at the beginning and tell all," I encouraged.

"Okay. Well, a couple of months ago, I met this guy."

The story unfolded. Sandy was still husband hunting. When she had finally convinced herself that I was not likely to be husband material in the near future, she left Mountain Center for greener pastures in the form of a new job in the Atlanta area. Sandy was a financial advisor for Wachovia. Soon after starting the job, she had met this guy, Roger Allen, in a Starbucks near the industrial center where she worked. Roger said he was a consultant, but Sandy was never sure exactly what that meant. Anyway, they continued to meet about twice a week for coffee, and then it escalated to dating. When he started demanding too much of her time, Sandy decided to back off, but Roger was having none of it. Now, he seemed to be stalking her, demanding another chance.

"Did you sleep with this guy, Sandy?"

"No, Don," she said emphatically. "I did not, and he was not pleased."

"Good thing," I teased, "or you never would get rid of him."

"Cute," she said. "I know you are trying to calm me down with that sly Southern wit of yours, but this is serious."

"Sorry," I said. "When is the last time you saw this guy?"

"I saw him last night through the peephole in the front door of my apartment. He was begging me to let him in, and when I told him I would call security if he didn't leave he got nasty. He said I would regret the way

I treated him. Then he said, 'I'm going to get you, bitch.' The way he said it scared the hell out of me. What do I do, Don?"

I thought for a minute. Sandy waited.

"You could call the cops," I said.

"I thought about that, but it would be my word against his."

"Roger needs to be discouraged," I said. "Email me your business address, and I'll drive down tomorrow."

"Thanks, Don," Sandy said. "You're a good friend."

Before we hung up, we spent a few minutes getting caught up on things that had happened since Sandy left Mountain Center. After we disconnected, I sat and stared out my second-floor window at the nearly empty street below. *Mary's going to love this*, I thought.

◆   ◆   ◆   ◆

I had waited until after dinner. Mary stood with her hands on her hips and glared at me. The glare was not a put-on. Had the temperature in our condo been colder, I might have actually seen steam rising. I was a little surprised at her reaction, although I had never professed to understand women.

"Look," I said. "She is just a friend, and she's in trouble. She needs my help."

"Just a friend? The same friend you were sleeping with for a year? The same friend who was in love with you and left because you weren't ready to get married?"

"That's the one," I smiled. *Big mistake.*

"You go to Atlanta and I'm gone," Mary said as she stormed up the stairs and down the hall to the bedroom and slammed the door.

I stood there perplexed by what had just happened. This was the first time I had ever seen Mary mad. I don't do well with ultimatums, but maybe this little tantrum meant she really cared. On the other hand, maybe she was just plain jealous. *Women.*

Lacy bounced down the stairs from her room.

"What was that all about?" she asked.

"I'm not sure," I said.

"That wasn't about me, was it?" Lacy asked.

"Not at all," I answered.

"You guys fight a lot?"

"Never," I said. "I'm not even sure that was a fight. It was more like a blitzkrieg."

"A what?"

"Forget it," I said. "Go do your homework, and stay out of the line of fire."

I went down the stairs and turned left into the laundry room, where I kept my gun safe. I dialed in the combination and opened the safe and removed my Beretta 9000S Type F, my firearm of choice if I was going to carry a concealed weapon. I clipped the Beretta, still in its holster, to the left front of my belt and went back up the stairs to the kitchen. I left a note for Mary, grabbed a lightweight jacket and a duffel bag from the front hall closet, and quietly slipped out the front door.

Once in the Pathfinder, I called Big Bob on my cell phone.

"Want to meet me at the range?" I asked when he answered the phone.

"We don't allow civilians on our range," Big Bob said.

I could envision the large grin on his face.

"I am a friend of the Mountain Center police force and a personal friend of the chief," I cracked.

"Well, in that case, I'll see you down there in about ten or fifteen minutes," his big voice rumbled. "Try not to shoot anybody."

He hung up before I could get in another smart remark.

10

The newly remodeled and expanded Mountain Center Police Station had a firing range in the basement. The range had a dozen lanes and was sparingly used by members of the force. Contrary to popular belief, most cops did not particularly like discharging their weapons, and it was rare that a small-town cop would even have to remove his firearm from its holster. The likelihood of pointing and shooting at someone was almost nil. Combine that with the fact that most cops were family men who wanted to spend time at home and who had to pay for some of their practice ammo and the result was an almost empty firing range. I kept Big Bob's locker stocked with ammo for both of us. It was my way of supporting local law enforcement. After all, you would like to think that your chief of police was a good shot.

I went through the front door of the station and found Big Bob's younger brother Sean at the desk.

"Hey, Don, what's happening?" Sean asked.

"I thought you were sick," I said. "When did you get back?"

"Today is my first day back," Sean said. "So, naturally, Big Bob put me on the second shift."

"Brotherly love," I said.

Sean laughed. "Must be it," he said.

"I just want to get in a little target practice, Sean. Is it okay to go on down?"

"Sure, but I don't think you need any practice. I've seen you shoot," he said.

"Practice makes perfect," I said. "See you later."

◆   ◆   ◆   ◆

By the time Big Bob arrived, I had the ammo out and the targets set. I had a full clip loaded in my Beretta and was ready to go. Big Bob tossed his jacket on a nearby bench and un-holstered his Glock 21 forty-five automatic, a hand cannon suitable for the big man. Big Bob quickly loaded twelve rounds in the thirteen-round clip, inserted it into the butt of the Glock, and slapped it in place. We put on range glasses and ear-muffs. We were ready to go, our ritual about to begin.

The big man lifted the Glock and squeezed off three quick rounds. As soon as he fired the last of his three, I did the same. We alternated until we were empty, the Glock and the Beretta having their own private conversation. Then we retrieved our targets.

We both had twelve kill shots, the difference being that my grouping was tighter that his. My grouping was always tighter than his.

He smiled when he looked at the targets. "Well, you haven't lost your touch. It's been awhile since we've done this. We ought to do it more often. Here," he said, handing me his Glock, "let's see how you do with my piece. Give me that sissy gun."

We loaded and repeated the same sequence as before, with pretty much the same result, the difference being that Big Bob's grouping was more spread out. Mine was also not quite as good as my Beretta grouping.

Big Bob shook his head. "Good shootin'. Damn Beretta is too light for me."

We practiced for an hour, playing different games and taking breaks in between. One game was headshots, another was elbows and kneecaps, and yet another was hands and feet. Big Bob performed well, but I won every game.

"Blood, you're the best damn shot I have ever seen. You should have been a cop."

"Not me," I said. "I don't look good in blue. How about a game of fingers?"

"Fuck you," he said. "I've been humiliated enough. I'm going home and have a cold one. I'll talk to you later."

He reloaded, holstered his piece, picked up his jacket, and headed to the stairs.

I was alone on the range. I reloaded the Beretta. *Well*, I thought, *if nobody wants to play fingers, I'll play by myself.* I sent my target back down the range. The target I used was a full-sized silhouette that I had specially printed by a local commercial printer. The arms were slightly spread from the body, and the fingers were spread wide on the hands. Most police forces used a head-and-chest target. My target had small bull's-eyes on the forehead, heart, elbow joints, kneecaps, hands, feet, and crotch—the latter bull's-eye being a personal favorite of Mary and the few other females on the force she had shown the target to. The smallest of the bull's-eyes were at the fingertips and almost impossible to hit outside of thirty feet. I put my glasses and muffs back on, emptied a clip from fifty feet, and retrieved the target.

I sensed a presence next to me. I turned and found myself staring into the ice-blue eyes of a gorgeous six-foot blonde. I removed my glasses and muffs.

"Come here often?" she said.

"Only when I am running for my life," I said.

"Safe place to be," she said, "with the cops and all."

"You would think," I said. "Want to go a round?"

"One clip," she said, "and then I'll buy you a beer."

I attached a clean target to the carrier and sent it down the firing line. She removed her new Glock 20 ten-millimeter from its holster, aimed, and fired ten shots in succession. I retrieved the target. Ten kill shots. The grouping was tight. Not as tight as mine, but the girl could shoot.

◆　◆　◆　◆

We sat in a back booth at Jared's Grill. I ordered a Black and Tan and Mary a Blue Moon.

"I'm sorry," she said. "I overreacted. I guess I am a little more possessive of you than I thought, and I hate that. I trust what we have, and I shouldn't be worried about you going to Atlanta."

"Marietta," I smiled.

Mary gave me the hard cop stare. "Wherever," she said, annoyed. "I hate it when you do that."

"Do what?"

"Be a wiseass when I am trying to be serious."

"Sorry," I said. "Defense mechanism. I have trouble with serious."

We worked on our drinks and stared at each other.

"Look," I said finally, "my going to Marietta is no big deal. I will always like Sandy and consider her a friend. I was never in love with her, and she knew it. That's why she left. I do, however, love you."

She stared at me as I watched a tiny smile form.

"Serious enough?" I smiled back.

She raised her glass, I raised mine, and we touched them together.

"You be a good boy," Mary teased. "Or I'll use you for target practice."

11

With my ever-dwindling love of flying came a favorable disposition toward driving. And so late the following morning, I decided to drive to Marietta. Spring had sprung in the Smoky Mountains, and I chose to take U.S. 441 South over the Smokies and into Cherokee, North Carolina. I had thoughts of running into Billy, who I had not seen in days, but that didn't happen. I did have a message from Billy saying he was fine and would see me in a few days. He had called at six o'clock in the morning, knowing I would be sound asleep and my cell phone would be in the Pathfinder, where I usually left it. He did not want to do any explaining, so he called at a time he could leave a message.

When I came out of the mountains and into the town of Cherokee, I dialed Billy's cell. I heard his voice say, "Leave a message."

"Hey, Chief," I said. "Long time, no talk. I am in Cherokee and headed to Marietta on a little business. Be back in a few days. Call me if you need to." I hung up. I could be just as cryptic as he could.

I left Cherokee and went through the Nantahala National Forest, following the river, where whitewater rafting was in full swing. I had rafted here when I was in high school, and it was great fun. I vowed to bring Mary over and do it again sometime. I crossed into Georgia a few miles south of Murphy, North Carolina, and snaked my way down to I-575. The traffic increased as I headed south toward I-75. The speed-limit signs read 70, but the real speed limit was closer to 80, as evidenced by all the cars whizzing by me. I bumped the cruise control to 75 and tried not to get run over. Just before four o'clock, I-575 South took me to I-75 South, a six-lane nightmare that gave me an idea of what it might be like to drive the short track at Bristol. Luckily, I did not have to stay on it for long. I took Exit 261, hung a left, drove down Belk Road to a nearby Marriott Courtyard, and checked into a suite on the back corner of the top floor.

I called Sandy Smith.

"Your bodyguard has arrived," I said when she answered.

"Where are you?" she asked.

"The Courtyard on Belk," I answered.

"That's about a mile from where my offices are," she said with some surprise.

"You can run, but you can't hide," I teased. "Tell me exactly where your offices are in this industrial park."

She did.

"Still driving the Volvo?"

"Yes," Sandy said.

"Seen our boy today?"

"No, thank God."

"Okay," I said. "Here's what I am going to do."

•   ◆   ◆   ◆

I parked my car under a tree in a far corner of Sandy's office parking lot. I backed in so that I had a good view of Sandy's Volvo, parked a good fifty yards away in front of her building. I was hoping Roger would show up to confront her and I could come to the rescue. I didn't consider myself a bully, but I could be when playing the role of knight in shining armor, especially when the object of my bullying was threatening a woman I cared about.

Sandy came out casually at the end of her business day, taking her time about getting to her car and opening the door. She looked damn good in a sharp little light gray suit and white high-collared blouse. I felt a little stir in the pit of my stomach. *That's over*, I told myself. *You passed, remember?*

I followed Sandy to her condo complex in the Buckhead area north of Atlanta, staying a discreet distance behind. I didn't notice a tail if there was one. She parked in her designated spot and disappeared into an elevator that would take her to the top floor. I waited until I thought she had enough time to get inside. I got antsy and was starting to open the Pathfinder's door when my phone rang.

"Yes?"

"I'm in," Sandy said. "No sign of him."

"Too bad," I said. "I am kind of anxious to meet Roger."

Sandy ignored the comment. "Want to come up for a drink?" she asked.

"Better not," I said.

"Don't trust yourself?" she asked.

"Not for a minute," I said.

"That's sweet, Don, but I realize we're just friends, and I certainly wouldn't try to take advantage of you while you were doing me a favor."

"I'm not worried about you," I said.

"Go take a cold shower and call me in the morning," she teased.

"I'll do that," I laughed. "What time do you leave for work?"

"About eight-thirty."

"I'll be at a discreet distance in the parking lot," I said. "If Roger shows up tonight, call me."

"I will," Sandy said. "Thanks, Don. I'll see you in the morning."

I returned to the Courtyard, sent Mary an email, and went straight to bed. Mary was working second shift, and I longed to hear her voice, but it would be unprofessional to call a cop on duty unless it was an emergency. Well, it damn near was an emergency, but I resisted calling her and eventually drifted into a fitful sleep full of weird dreams that I couldn't quite remember.

12

I followed Sandy to work the next day with no incident. The same could be said of the uneventful return trip. I even managed to take Sandy out to dinner that night and keep my hands to myself. She helped me accomplish that unlikely feat by not flirting with me. I did not go up to her condo. I waited until she was safely inside and returned to the Courtyard and called Mary.

"Are you being a good boy?" she answered. Caller ID left no surprises anymore.

"As good as can be expected," I said.

"I expect a lot."

"I know."

"Have you confronted the villain?" Mary asked.

"Haven't seen hide nor hair of him," I answered.

"How long will you be gone?"

"As long as it takes or a week, whichever comes first," I said.

We talked awhile longer, and as we said goodbye Mary left me with an image of how I was going to be welcomed home. Luckily, Lacy's bedroom was far away from ours.

◆　◆　◆　◆

Two days later, I sat in the Pathfinder waiting for Sandy to get off work. Once again, I had backed in to give myself a clear view of her car. The last two days had been completely uneventful, and I was beginning to wonder if Roger had given up.

Sandy appeared from her building and headed toward her Volvo. She was just about to open the door when a silver BMW came out of nowhere and blocked her in. A tall, attractive man, snappily attired in gray slacks and a blue blazer, bounded out of the driver's side and quickly made his way toward Sandy, who had dropped her car keys in the excitement. I snapped a few quick pictures with my digital camera on zoom, and then I was on the move in the Pathfinder. I roared down the parking lot as the man I assumed was Roger Allen grabbed Sandy by the arm and spun her around. He said something and she replied, but I couldn't make out what it was over the roar of my engine and the screech of my tires as I came to an abrupt stop near the scene.

I was out of the Pathfinder and in Roger's face in an instant.

"Back off!" I yelled.

Roger let go of Sandy and spun to face me.

"Get lost," he growled. "This is a private matter."

I had to admit he was doing a pretty good job of being intimidating, but I was high on adrenaline and didn't much care.

"Get away from my sister," I said menacingly.

Roger did a double take. For a moment, he didn't know what to say. Then he got it.

"Bullshit," he said, still trying for intimidation. "If you're her brother, let's see some identification."

I guess it was the way he said it. Or maybe it was the arrogant asshole attitude. Whatever it was, it evoked a response that surprised even me. I quickly hooked him hard to the solar plexus with my left. *Finally, I'm making good use of all that speed bag work in Moto's Gym*, I thought as he went down to one knee, gasping for air.

I leaned down. "That's all the identification you're going to get."

Roger let out a hard groan. I seized him beneath his right arm and lifted him upright. I thought the fight was out of him, and then I saw his right fist clench and a look on his face that told me he was ready for a fight. Something in his eyes gave me pause, and I was immediately reminded of the Fairchild case and another killer I had confronted. He was beginning to recover from my sucker punch, and the will to fight was there. And then it was gone.

"Another time," he said, and the way he said it gave me a chill. This guy was dangerous.

He opened the driver's side door to the BMW, which was still running, and got in. He wouldn't look at me. He put both hands on the steering wheel and gripped it tightly. I could see his knuckles go white.

With the door still open, I mustered all the macho I could, bent down, and said softly and slowly in his left ear, "Stay away from Sandy."

He didn't respond.

He gave me another bone-chilling stare and slammed the car door. Then he smoked his tires as he left the parking lot. At that moment, I wished I had Billy or Roy waiting in another car to tail him. He would spot me if I followed, but I sure would have liked to know where he lived. I made a mental note of the license tag number.

I walked to Sandy. "You okay?" I asked.

She looked at me with concern on her face. "You've changed," she said.

I didn't answer.

"I mean, I'm okay, and I appreciate what you did, but you scared me."

"I believe Roger is a very bad guy," I said.

Sandy ignored that statement.

"I have never seen that side of you," Sandy said. She seemed a little in shock.

I still didn't answer. I guess I didn't have an answer. I opened Sandy's car door, and she got in.

"I'll follow you home," I said as I closed the door of the Volvo.

I went back to the Pathfinder and wrote down Roger's tag number while it was still fresh in my mind.

◆   ◆   ◆   ◆

I stayed in Marietta a few more days, repeating the same routine of following Sandy to and from work. We had dinner together the night before I left, but Sandy was distant and the small talk was forced. I could tell that whatever designs she once had on me as a potential husband had died when I punched Roger Allen in the stomach. She seemed relieved when I told her I was leaving the next day.

"I really appreciate all that you did," Sandy said as I dropped her in front of her condo.

"That's what friends are for," I said. I handed her a business card. "I know you have my number, but I want this to remind you that you can call me anytime."

She put the card in her wallet and then laid her hand on mine. "And we will always be friends, Don. But I think you and the lady cop sound like a real good match. I wish you the best with that."

She got out of the car, and I rolled down the driver's side window. "Stay in touch, Sandy," I said. "And call me on the cell once you are inside and locked up."

"I will," she smiled, and gave me a little wave as she walked toward the elevator.

Thirty seconds later, I got the call. I drove back to my hotel trying to figure out what Sandy had seen in me that scared her so much.

13

We were in bed.

"Wow," I said.

"Wow?" Mary asked.

"Wow," I confirmed.

"Is 'Wow' good?" Mary asked.

I kissed her lightly on the mouth. " 'Wow' is very good," I said.

"You were just super horny," she said.

"That, too," I said.

Lacy had conveniently spent the night with a friend. Whether that was a coincidence or a conspiracy was a matter better left unexplored. Either way, I had reaped the benefits.

"Good thing Lacy wasn't here," I said.

"Yes, we did get rather loud, didn't we?"

"She probably would have called nine-one-one," I said.

Mary laughed. Then I laughed. Then we were both laughing uncontrollably. When we finally calmed down, we held each other quietly and enjoyed the moment. I was finally beginning to figure out this love thing. It went far beyond the physical into a realm of togetherness that was hard to explain unless you were there. There are moments in your life that you would just like to freeze in time and live in for a while until you explore every aspect. This was one of those moments, and while relishing it I drifted off into a deep, uncomplicated sleep. And although I cannot confirm it, I am sure I was smiling.

◆　　◆　　◆　　◆

Early the following morning, I was in my office staring at the Orbitz home page on my computer screen and trying to figure out how to avoid flying to Las Vegas. Since transporter technology worked only on *Star Trek*, I could not come up with any reasonable alternative. Las Vegas was just too far to drive. I booked a flight that would arrive in the early afternoon two days hence. Then I booked a rental car and a room for a week at the Renaissance Las Vegas Hotel on Paradise Road. Exactly what I was going to do once I reached Vegas I had no clue. I had to at least make the effort. Lacy was probably better off without Tracy, but I had promised that I would try to find her mother, and I was big on promises.

I heard the outer office door open. I looked at Jake, who raised one ear but did not stir from his apparent state of sleep. A moment later, Roy Husky walked in and placed a medium-sized cup of Dunkin' Donuts coffee on my desk. Roy did this a couple of times a week, and we would sit and talk for a while. Billy was absent, no doubt in Cherokee with Maggie.

"Thanks," I said.

Roy nodded and sat in a chair in front of my desk. "What are you up to?"

"Planning a trip," I said.

"Where?"

"Vegas," I said. "Ever been there?"

"Yep, you?"

"No," I said.

"Is this about the girl's mother?" Roy asked.

"Lacy," I said. "Yes."

"Need backup?"

"Not right away," I said. "If I do, can you get away?"

"As far as Joseph Fleet is concerned, I'm at your beck and call."

Joseph Fleet was an industrialist I had worked for on my first big case. I had helped him bring closure to a very painful time in his life, and he felt he owed me. At the same time, Roy Husky and I had begun a friendship that continued to grow. Roy was Fleet's right arm.

"Good to know," I said. "I'll keep it in mind."

"Vegas takes lots of money," Roy said as he raised his coffee and took a drink.

"Do tell," I said.

♦ ♦ ♦ ♦

That night, Billy came over and brought pizza from the best place in town. Lacy was in her room doing homework or playing on her computer, I wasn't sure which. After Billy arrived and the smell of pizza drifted through the condo, Lacy made an appearance in the kitchen. She bounded down the stairs and around the corner and ran smack into Billy. She looked up at him in surprise, her mouth open. Billy smiled at her.

"Lacy," I said, "meet Billy Two-Feathers. Billy, meet Lacy Malone."

"God, you're big," Lacy said, staring up at the six-foot-six Cherokee.

"Nice to meet you, too," Billy smiled.

We settled down at the kitchen bar with Caesar salad and pizza. Mary had a glass of wine, I had beer, and Billy and Lacy had Diet Cokes. Billy did not drink alcohol.

"Are you an American Indian?" Lacy asked Billy.

"Yes," Billy said. "Cherokee."

"And you're partners with Don, and that's where Cherokee Investigations came from," Lacy said, rather pleased with herself.

"That's right," Billy said.

"Did you grow up on the reservation?" Lacy asked.

Mary and I exchanged a glance. Billy was getting the third degree.

"No, I grew up in Connecticut," Billy said.

"How did a Cherokee Indian manage to grow up in Connecticut?" Lacy asked.

"I was adopted," Billy said.

We continued eating salad and pizza as Lacy grilled Billy. Mary and I smiled knowingly at each other. Billy had at last met someone who was not going to accept one- and two-word answers.

"By who?" Lacy pressed. "How did that happen?"

"By an upper-middle-class white couple in Wilton, Connecticut," Billy continued. "My mother grew up in Cherokee, North Carolina, and became pregnant when she was very young. She was embarrassed and ashamed. She stole some money and ran away. Somehow, she ended up in a cheap hotel room in Stamford, Connecticut, and gave birth to me. She bled to death in that hotel room," Billy said quietly, "and I became a ward of the state of Connecticut. I never found out who my father was. I'm not sure I even want to know. My story was in the Connecticut papers, and this white couple in Wilton offered to adopt me."

I knew Billy was adopted. I had met his parents when we were at UConn, but I had never heard the full story. In fact, Billy's oratory was the longest response to a question I had ever heard from him. In Billy-speak, it was the equivalent of a congressional filibuster. I was surprised that he had shared so intimate a story. We ate in silence.

Not surprisingly, Lacy broke that silence.

"I'm glad you found a good home," she said as she touched Billy's hand.

I looked at Mary. I thought I saw tears forming. I knew what she was thinking. I looked at Billy. He patted Lacy's hand.

"Me, too," he said.

Lacy took Billy by the hand. "Come with me," she said. "I want to show you my room."

Mary gave me a knowing smile.

Billy and Lacy were gone for a long time as Mary and I sat at the kitchen bar and enjoyed our drinks. We heard sounds of muffled conversation that were indecipherable. Every now and then, I heard Lacy laugh. Billy never ceased to amaze me.

14

The night before I went to Vegas, I met Roy at The Brewery, a local microbrewery. Mary was working second shift, and Billy was in Cherokee. Lacy was baby-sitting Jake, or was it the other way around? I felt like going out for a burger and a beer. Jake loved burgers and would drink beer if I let him, but he was a lousy conversationalist. Lacy said she had too much homework. I wanted to get to know Roy Husky better.

We were in a booth on the second floor in the far left corner. The crowd was sparse and quiet. We both ordered burgers with fries and pints of Black Bear Ale. When the ale arrived, we raised our glasses in a quiet salute and took that first glorious drink.

"Not bad," Roy said.

"Never had the Black Bear Ale?" I asked.

"Never been here before," Roy said. "I don't get out much."

"Date?" I asked.

Roy smiled. "Kind of."

Just before I asked, it dawned on me what Roy meant by *kind of*, and I let it go.

"Friends?"

"You, Billy, and T. Elbert," Roy said with resignation. "If it weren't for you, I wouldn't have any friends. Is this an interview? You doing an article for the *Mountain Center Press*?"

"Relax," I said. "I'm just honing my interrogation skills."

"And doing a damn fine job of it, too," Roy teased.

The burgers arrived, accompanied by small mountains of fries. We were silent for a while as we ate our food.

"Good?" I asked.

"Umm," Roy nodded.

When we finished and ordered two more Black Bear Ales, Roy asked, "Why did you quit Wall Street and become a private detective?"

"Burned out and lonely," I said. "I needed to get back home. Being a PI seemed like it might be interesting. It turned out to be more interesting than I thought."

Roy nodded. We drank some more ale.

"Mr. Fleet told me you're a rich man," Roy said. "Millions, he said."

"What about it?" I asked. "You need a loan?"

"No," Roy laughed. "I was just curious. You don't live like a rich man. I mean, you live like you have plenty of money, but not like you have millions."

"I have all I want," I said. "I'm comfortable. If I went overboard with the money, it would be a constant reminder of what I lost to get it."

"Your parents," Roy said.

I nodded.

"Sorry I brought it up," Roy said.

"Not a problem," I said.

"There is something else I don't quite get," Roy said.

"Which is?"

"You seem to be awfully damn good at this work. You're a college guy and a Wall Street guy, so I know you're smart," Roy said. "But there is something underneath the surface. It's a toughness that I wouldn't have expected. You aren't afraid of things when the going gets tough, you know a lot of things you shouldn't know, and you're cool under fire. Why is that?"

Roy stared at me, and I stared back. Roy Husky was no dummy. We drank the ale and were silent for a long time as Roy waited for his answer.

"Are you sure you aren't imagining something?" I asked.

"I'm sure."

Roy waited.

"For now," I said, "let's just say I don't want to talk about it. Someday, I might tell you the whole story."

"Does Mary know?"

"No," I said.

"Big Bob?"

"No," I said.

"Billy?"

"Yes," I said, "and we are done with Twenty Questions."

"Sorry," Roy said, smiling slightly. "Just honing my interrogation skills."

"And doing a damn fine job of it," I laughed.

15

I was in row four of first class, staring out the window of the Boeing 767 at thirty-seven thousand feet, looking at snow-capped mountains and wondering if I would ever take the time to ski again. The skiing detective—it didn't quite fit. It was years since I had flown over the Rockies, and the sight brought back memories of my youth and my dream to be a ski bum. I certainly had the money for it, but I had lacked the resolve to throw my life away on self-indulgence. Instead, I finished college and went to work. Maybe when I retired I could be a ski bum. Now, that was a thought.

Las Vegas was heating up, even if it was only early May. I could feel the heat as I exited the aircraft and walked through the jet-way into the cool air conditioning of the terminal. I was dressed casually in jeans and a white short-sleeve pullover collared shirt. I refused to use the term *golf shirt*, since I did not play golf. My backpack with my laptop, latest novel, files, and various accompaniments that I needed was slung over my left shoulder as I headed to baggage claim.

♦   ♦   ♦   ♦

The Renaissance Las Vegas Hotel was a mere two miles from the airport. I picked up a rental car from Hertz and in thirty minutes was being led to my VIP suite by a young bellhop whose nametag read, "Lance—Houston, Texas."

"Anything else I can do for you, sir?" Lance asked.

"Not at the moment," I said, handing him a twenty.

He grinned widely, obviously thinking he had latched onto a big tipper. I had my reasons for over-tipping.

"Anything you need, you ask for Lance," he said excitedly.

"I'll do that, Lance," I said as I shut the door behind him.

In Vegas, money was all.

◆   ◆   ◆   ◆

I was admiring the view of the city from my suite on the concierge floor. The city known for gambling, glamorous women, wedding chapels, five-star hotels, and big shows spread out before me. Early on, the town had been most famous for the Flamingo gambling resort, built and opened in 1946 by the notorious gangster Bugsy Siegel. Bugsy didn't live long enough to see how successful the Flamingo would be or how Las Vegas would turn into one of the fastest-growing cities in the United States. Someone, no doubt the mob, bumped off Bugsy in 1947. The mob supposedly controlled much of Vegas in the fifties and sixties, but law enforcement finally caught up. By the seventies, Vegas was being controlled by big corporate money. It was common knowledge that the mob still existed in the Vegas underbelly.

Once again, I realized what an amateur I was. My only plan so far was to stumble around blindly, like a mouse with his whiskers to the wall, and hope I ran into something. Something like a guy named Victor with a snake tattoo on his right arm. I could call New York mob boss Carlo Vincente and cash in that favor he said he owed me, but I had no desire to talk to Carlo. I had no doubt that he could discreetly get a line on Victor, but I wanted to come up with a plan of my own. I would use Carlo only as a last resort.

◆ ◆ ◆ ◆

At five o'clock, I was in the club-level lounge nursing a beer and formulating a plan to find Victor with the snake tattoo. I surmised that if I found him, I could find Tracy Malone. That was not necessarily true, but I bet that Victor would at least know where Tracy was. Since I did not want Victor to know I was looking for him, I would have to be careful about whom I talked to and what I said. I had picked up a Berlitz pocket guide to Las Vegas. I was reading the section on adult entertainment. There were two basic categories: topless and all nude. I was hoping Tracy would stick to topless. I didn't know if my heart could handle cruising all-nude bars. I had a picture of Tracy Malone with me for identification purposes, in case I stumbled across her. Even though the picture was one of her with her clothes on, I had confidence I would recognize her just the same.

I decided to start at the Riviera, a hotel and casino that had the reputation of big, brassy adult entertainment. The likelihood of bumping into Tracy Malone or a man with a snake tattoo running down his arm was remote, but it was a place to start. I went back to my room and called Mary. We talked about nothing for half an hour, although I do remember a veiled threat about showgirls and such. After we hung up, I went to the Envy Steakhouse and had a filet mignon, medium rare, with all the trimmings. It was my first filet of the year.

◆ ◆ ◆ ◆

The Riviera was about a mile from the Renaissance, so I decided to walk. The sun was setting and the evening was cooling as I walked up Paradise Road. Plenty of people were on the street, and I could feel the energy that Vegas generated. I turned left on Desert Inn Road. A Marriott Courtyard was on my right. I walked down past the Royal and turned right on the Strip. The Riviera was just up the street on the right.

I spent three hours in the Riviera. I was not prepared for the opulence of the interior. I caught a show, *Crazy Girls*, which was an eye-opener. I practiced my skills of observation by giving every participant the once-over, slowly. I did not see Tracy Malone. In fact, there were times when I forgot I was looking for Tracy Malone. After being completely overwhelmed by T&A, I went to the bar for a drink. I was approached by three different women in a half-hour period all of whom I politely informed that I was waiting on someone. I paid my bill and went to the casino and played blackjack at the fifteen-dollar table for an hour. Not caring whether I won or lost, naturally I won. I hit the wall about eleven o'clock Vegas time, cashed in my chips, and walked back to the Renaissance. The streets were still humming. I was just able to get back to my room, get my clothes off, brush my teeth, and fall exhausted into bed.

◆　◆　◆　◆

The next morning, I was on the phone with Scott Glass.

"Hey, Professor, what's happening?"

"Hey, Blood. What are you doing in Las Vegas?" Scott asked.

Caller ID tells all, I thought.

"You could at least say good morning before you start interrogating me, Professor," I countered. "I'm working on that case I told you about."

"Let me guess," Scott said. "You want a favor."

"A small, insignificant favor," I said.

"Yeah, I'll bet," Scott scoffed. "What is it?"

I told him.

"I'm not going to find any mob connections this time, am I?" Scott asked.

"You might," I said.

"Great," Scott said sarcastically. "I'll get back to you, Blood."

16

The next three days were more of the same. I visited a number of topless clubs on or near the Strip, with the same result—no Tracy Malone and no man with a snake tattoo. I understood why nightlife in Vegas lasted all evening. The days were too hot to go anywhere. Even in May, the heat was oppressive. I took in about two clubs a night. That was about all I could stand. My interest in naked women was waning. I was beginning to worry about myself.

"I think I'm getting turned off to breasts," I told Mary on the phone the evening of my fifth night.

"I think I can fix that when you get back," she said.

"I certainly hope so," I said.

"Billy wants to take Lacy to Cherokee for this weekend," Mary said. "Is that okay with you?"

"Sure," I said. "What's going on with those two?"

"I think Billy relates to Lacy's predicament," Mary said. "Lacy may very well end up being adopted."

"Well, I'm glad he's taken an interest," I said. "Lacy needs a lot of affirmation right now, and this search is probably going to keep me out here a few more days."

"Think maybe you should go to the cops and see if they might be willing to help?" Mary asked.

"Would you be willing to help a PI who walked into the station unannounced?" I asked.

"Maybe, maybe not," she said. "It would depend on how good looking he was."

I ignored the tease.

"It's the 'maybe not' that bothers me. If I ask the wrong person and he knows who this guy is and tips him off, then I could have a problem."

"I see your point. Why not hire a PI out there?"

A private investigator hiring a private investigator. Now, there was a thought.

"Same problem," I said. "Who to trust."

"Why don't you give Scott a call?"

"I already did. No luck. No credit card charges, no bank accounts. Pardon the pun, but no trace of Tracy Malone."

"Cute," Mary said. "Did you ask him to check his database for a man with a snake tattoo on his right arm?"

Damn! I was silent on the other end.

"You didn't, did you?" Mary teased.

"I was so focused on Tracy that it just didn't cross my mind. I'll give Scott a call tomorrow. Thanks," I said.

"You would have eventually thought of it," she said. "All those naked women are clouding your mind."

"Topless," I fired back. "Topless."

◆　　◆　　◆　　◆

Having been unsuccessful in convincing Mary that my Vegas nightlife was strictly business, I nevertheless decided to brave the pitfalls of glitz and glitter by visiting the recently opened Velvet Slipper Casino on the south end of the Strip.

The Velvet Slipper was tastefully decorated in desert earth tones and dark wood. The horseshoe bar allowed patrons plenty of room to relax, have a drink, and hook up with the opposite sex. The casino floor seemed to be the size of a football field, with plenty of room to move around to play blackjack, roulette, and the slots. Girls danced at various locations. They were gorgeous and topless. I looked just long enough to not see Tracy Malone. I smiled at my lack of interest and went to the bar for a beer.

A pretty blonde appeared from nowhere. She wore clothes.

"Hi, handsome," she said.

"Hi, yourself," I said.

"Why don't you buy me a drink?" she asked.

"Why don't you buy me one?" I countered. *Mr. Charming.*

She took a few seconds to process my response. "Not likely," she said as she turned and walked away.

I stayed and had a few beers and watched girls come and go and perform their routines. I was about to leave when I felt a hand on my shoulder. I turned on my barstool and stared into a grinning face and vaguely familiar blue eyes from somewhere out of my past.

"Is that you, Don?" said the grinning face.

My senior year in college came rushing back.

"Bruiser?"

Bruiser grinned. "I haven't been called Bruiser in years. It's Dennis now."

"Dennis. I'll have to adjust to that," I said. "You're a long way from the East Coast. What are you doing in Vegas?"

"Living and working. I'm head of security here at the Velvet Slipper. I saw you on our security cameras. I thought it was you, but I wasn't sure. You haven't changed much."

"You haven't either," I said. "The hair is longer, but you're still about the size of a pickup truck," I teased. "You look like you're staying in shape, though."

"Thanks," Bruiser said. "I do the machines about three times a week. You look pretty fit yourself. What are you doing in Vegas?"

"I'm looking for someone," I said.

I gave him a brief history of my career as a private investigator. He laughed.

"Still got Billy looking out for you?"

"Most of the time," I said. "Billy is still a mother hen."

"Not a bad thing to have," Bruiser laughed.

I agreed. I could have done a lot worse than have a friend as loyal as Billy Two-Feathers.

"You might be able to help me," I said.

I told him about Tracy Malone.

"Damn," Bruiser said. "She just up and left her daughter?"

"Looks like," I said. "I think she is with a guy she met while she was dancing back home. I don't know his name, but he is supposed to be from Vegas. All I know is that he has a snake tattoo running down his right arm and his first name is Victor."

Bruiser's face went cold. "A snake tattoo? That can be only one guy, and you don't want to mess with him. He's a snake, all right. His name is Victor Vargas—professional gambler, thug, procurer of women for the sleazier clubs, and general bad-ass. He is probably mob connected, although not officially. Victor is independent, dangerous, and very charming where the ladies are concerned. They call him 'Victor the Viper.' The tattoo on his arm is a viper. A deadly poisonous snake, just like Victor."

"You know him?"

"Not very well, but yeah, I know him," Bruiser said with a snarl. "He comes in here sometimes looking to get in a high-stakes game in one of our back rooms. I usually tell him the table is full. He is very friendly toward me and has never caused me any trouble, but word gets around. Be careful around this guy, and don't let him know why you're here," Bruiser cautioned.

"I need to pick up his trail so that I can follow him. He could lead me to Tracy. Any thoughts?"

Bruiser ordered a club soda with lime from the bartender and went silent for a few minutes.

"It's best that you don't go looking for him," he said. "I'll try to set up a game in a few days and get the word out. He'll probably call me wanting a chair. If he doesn't, I'll call him and tell him I have an opening. Since I usually turn him down, he is likely to jump at the chance to play here."

"That would be great, Dennis. I appreciate it."

"You can call me Bruiser," Dennis said. "Coming from you, Dennis just doesn't sound right."

"Bruiser it is," I said, raising my beer in toast style.

"You married?" Bruiser asked.

"Close," I said. "But no. How about you?"

"No," he said distantly. "Too many women out here. Too many choices make you indecisive. I'll have to get out of this town before I can settle down."

The bartender ambled over and said softly to Bruiser, "They need you upstairs, Mr. Bracken."

Bruiser nodded and turned to me. "Gotta go. Where are you staying?"

I told him.

"Using your own name?"

"Yes," I said.

"Got a cell phone?"

"Doesn't everyone?" I said.

"Give me the number."

As I recited my number, Bruiser programmed it into his cell phone. In return, he gave me his.

"I'll be in touch," he said as he walked away.

17

For the next two days, I did the same thing I had been doing, with the same result. No Tracy Malone. Then I got the call.

"I have a game set up for ten tomorrow night," Bruiser said. "Your guy will be here. The game ends promptly at two in the morning. House rules. I suggest you be here by midnight, in case he leaves early."

"I'll be there before ten o'clock," I said. "I want a look at this guy."

•   •   •   •

I sat in the bar at the Velvet Slipper nursing a beer and taking in some of the scenery, which I now found only mildly interesting. It was funny how that worked. Bruiser came over and sat down a little before ten o'clock.

"They will all be arriving soon," he said. "If you're not here at ten, you don't play."

"Strict," I said.

"Yes, but it gives us a good reputation."

"What are the other rules?" I asked.

"Somewhat different for every game, depending on how big the buy-in is," Bruiser said. "This game is a ten-thousand-dollar buy-in. Not huge, but not small either. Table stakes, no limit. No hand can be dealt after two in the morning."

"How many players?"

"Six, and we furnish the dealer."

A very good-looking brunette in tight jeans and a bright red V-neck top walked by. As I'm sure she intended, the top didn't do much to cover what she was trying to show off. She nodded at Bruiser and headed toward the back of the casino.

"One of the players," he said.

"She wore that outfit on purpose," I said.

"You bet," Bruiser said. "Probably won't do her any good. Once the game starts, these players will be totally focused on the cards."

A tall man with salt-and-pepper hair and a mustache to match walked by. He also nodded at Bruiser.

"Another player?" I asked.

"Yep," Bruiser replied.

The procession continued—an attractive older redhead, a short, fat man wearing a beret, and a small, thin, much older man dressed in a suit with a bowtie. Finally, Victor Vargas.

Vargas came toward us, confident and assured, his eyes focused on Bruiser. He had movie-star looks, and his smile was casual and friendly, but the eyes were cold. He looked to be very fit. He wore a white suit with a black T-shirt. The suit was expensive. He nodded at Bruiser, which

Bruiser acknowledged with a slight move of his head toward the back of the casino. I glanced at my watch; it read 9:58.

"Now, you wait," Bruiser said. "I'll give you a heads-up if he starts to leave early. I've got to get back upstairs."

"Thanks, Bruiser," I said. "I owe you one."

"I think I know how you can pay me back," he said. "We'll talk about it later."

◆　◆　◆　◆

I do not wait well. I never have. I sat at the bar and nursed another beer. Sometime later, I called up Bruiser's number in my cell phone's speed-dial list and punched *Send*.

"Yeah?" Bruiser answered.

"What is Vargas driving?" I asked.

"Hang on."

I waited for Bruiser to come back on the line.

"Black four-door Mercedes sedan. It has a silver-and-black plate of a viper on the front."

"Thanks. I'm leaving the bar while I can still walk," I said. "I won't go far. Let me know when Vargas is on the move."

"Okay," Bruiser said, and disconnected.

I went outside to find the desert heat retreating. The humidity was nonexistent. The pleasant night brought a lot of activity to the Strip. The energy level was high. As I looked around the parking lot, I noticed a few spots had opened up. I spotted the black Mercedes. Vargas had backed it into a space, and the viper plate glistened under the lights of the parking lot. I quickly moved my rental car to a spot that allowed me a better view of the overall lot and the black Mercedes. Having done that, I went for a walk. It was unlikely that Vargas would leave anytime soon. I checked the time and calculated how far I could safely go, then started walking north on the Strip. It was a lonely walk. I was aching to share the sights and sounds of the Strip with Mary. I found the neon energy of Vegas exciting, but I missed the hills of East Tennessee. My mind wandered. I tried to figure out what I was really doing here. Then I remembered Lacy. This was for her.

When I had sufficiently depressed myself, I turned around and walked back to my rental car.

◆　　◆　　◆　　◆

Ricky Nelson was singing "Lonesome Town" on an oldies station I had found. I smiled at the irony. It was one in the morning, and I was beginning to doze as I listened to music from the fifties, sixties, and seventies.

My cell phone rang. I looked at the digital clock glowing on the dashboard. It was two o'clock. Bob Seger was singing "Night Moves." I had tuned to a clairvoyant radio station.

"Vargas is on the move," Bruiser said.

"Good," I said. "Did he win or lose?"

"He won, but not much," Bruiser said. "Be careful. You're playing with fire."

"I will," I said. "I'll call you tomorrow."

"No, you'll call me tonight," Bruiser said.

"Okay, Mother," I said. "I'll call you later." I hung up before Bruiser could get off a parting volley.

I was glad Vargas had won. I was hoping his mind would still be on the game and that he would pay little attention to what was going on around him. Like being tailed, for instance.

I spotted Vargas heading toward his black Mercedes. I turned the radio off, slid down a little in my seat, and watched as Vargas remotely unlocked the Mercedes and got in. As he started the Mercedes, I started my rental but did not turn on my lights.

Vargas drove out of the parking lot and turned right. I turned on my lights and followed at a discreet distance. Traffic was moderate. I could let a car or two get between Vargas and me and still have no problem keeping tabs on him.

I followed Vargas into North Las Vegas and then to a section known as Sunrise Manor. He made a right off Lake Mead Boulevard and then another right into a gated community. I watched the gate slowly slide left to right as I drove past. Vargas had not stopped as he rolled toward the gate, meaning that he probably had a remote gate opener in his car. I drove down the street and turned around, then drove back past the gate and continued to my hotel. On the way, I called Bruiser and let him know I was in one piece. He did not seem impressed.

There was nothing more to do that night. I had probably found where Vargas was living, and I had a feeling Tracy Malone was with him. Tomorrow, I would do my first stakeout.

18

At eight o'clock the following morning, I sat parked on a side street in my nondescript gray rental car drinking coffee and staring at the gate Victor Vargas had driven through the night before. A very tasteful monument next to the gate proclaimed it to be Hidden Valley Estates. Not one car had exited since I arrived. Las Vegans probably slept late—all that nightlife. But I was not concerned with cars coming out. I was concerned with cars going in. Finally, a car entered. The driver stopped and punched numbers into a keypad.

I was very interested in seeing how fast the gate closed, and I was not surprised that it was exceedingly slow. An eighteen-wheeler could follow a car through and still have time to change a flat tire.

I stayed another hour, hoping I might spot Tracy Malone. No such luck. If Tracy was dancing somewhere, she most likely was still asleep. Other cars entered. Some drivers used the keypad, and other drove straight through as the gate opened. They obviously had remotes for the gate. A woman from a house on the other side of the street came out to her mailbox and gave me a long, curious look, which meant it was time for me to go. I did not want a local cop asking me what I was doing sitting in my car for two hours on a residential side street. The curious lady went inside, and I left.

◆   ◆   ◆   ◆

I drove back to my hotel and did some work on my laptop. The market was hovering in the mid–twelve thousands, and most of my investments and my clients' investments were doing well. Private investigating was cutting into my investment time. Luckily, I was in for the long haul. I did not swim the shark-infested waters of the day-trader.

Around noon, I was back in the rental car. I stopped at a nearby Subway and picked up lunch, a turkey and cheese sub with a bag of Doritos and a Diet Coke. I headed back to Hidden Valley Estates. This time, I parked a block up on the corner on the opposite side of the street at a house with a For Sale sign in the yard. It looked empty. I backed up the driveway almost to the garage, into the shade of a very leafy unknown variety of tree. I had a perfect view of the gate to Hidden Valley Estates. I got out of my car and walked around the house as if I were interested in the property. A peek inside revealed the absence of furniture, a perfect cover. If anyone asked, I was just a prospective buyer having a bite to eat while waiting on the real-estate agent to show up.

Back in my car, I sat eating my lunch with the air conditioning on full blast. Thanks to the shade of the unknown tree, the air conditioning was able to keep the inside of the car at a reasonable temperature. I did not see any curious neighbors. In fact, I did not see anyone who paid the slightest attention to me.

A few minutes after I finished my lunch down to the very last crumb, my cell phone rang. It was Roy Husky.

"The world's greatest private investigator speaking," I said in as animated a voice as I could possibly muster.

"Sorry," Roy said. "I've got the wrong number."

"Funny," I said. "You missed your calling."

"You, too," Roy said, not missing a beat. "How's it going, gumshoe?"

"So you missed me and just had to hear my voice, right?"

"Hell no," Roy snarled. "That damn mother hen Billy was too stubborn to call, so he put me up to it. You really should call him once in a while, you being partners and all."

"Yeah, I should," I said, seriously regretting that I had not touched base with Billy. "When did you see him last?"

"This morning," Roy said. "We had coffee. Rather, I had coffee. I don't know what that swill he drinks is."

Over the past year, Billy and Roy had developed a friendship that only ex-cons could understand. I was on the outside of it, but I was glad for their friendship. Billy needed someone in his life other than me who he could talk to, and Roy was perfect. He was tough, smart, perceptive, and a good listener.

"Having any luck out there?"

"I am making progress," I said.

I filled him in on my adventures so far and my present stakeout.

"You actually ran into a guy from college who knows this Vargas?" Roy asked incredulously.

"Yep."

"I guess it's better to be lucky than good," Roy said.

"Anytime," I said.

As I was talking to Roy, a sweet little baby-blue Thunderbird, a 2002 or 2003, drove by with a very good-looking blonde driving. The convertible canvas top was down, and I got a good look at the blonde. If it wasn't Tracy Malone, it was her twin sister.

"Damn," I said. "Tracy Malone just drove by. I'm gone. I'll call you later."

"You've got to be fucking kidding me," I heard Roy say as I closed my cell phone.

◆　◆　◆　◆

I moved the gearshift from park to drive and followed the baby-blue T-Bird. Tracy turned into a shopping center, parked, and went into a Starbucks. I waited. Ten minutes later, we were headed back to Hidden Valley Estates. I was about fifty yards back when she turned and went through the gate. My timing was perfect. I was halfway through the gate when it started to close and made it through with time to spare. The baby-blue T-Bird made a left at the first stop sign.

Hidden Valley Estates was an upscale semi-secure community with expensive homes built on decent-sized lots, all of which were immaculately kept—a very nice neighborhood. The baby-blue T-Bird went two blocks and then turned right. I kept my distance. By the time I made the turn, it was gone. I spotted the back of the T-Bird and the back of a black Mercedes in the next block about six houses down on the right, just before a garage door came down and concealed them from my prying eyes.

I drove to the corner, went around the traffic circle, and headed back toward the house, making note of the house number and the street, 24 Hidden Valley Lane. I had no doubt found Tracy Malone.

◆　◆　◆　◆

Later that afternoon, I was in my suite enjoying a couple of beers and a snack plate of peanuts, cheese, and crackers that I had put together in the concierge lounge. I was at my computer reading and writing email. I had an email from T. Elbert wanting a full report on my escapades, so I wrote him the short version to satisfy his curiosity. I had an email from Sandy saying so far, so good, as to the stalker problem I had helped her with. I shut down my email and opened my games file. I started a game of Scrabble and began considering my next move as far as Tracy Malone was concerned. I decided to call Billy. I dialed his cell phone intending to leave a message, since Billy rarely answered. I was surprised when he did this time.

"Hello."

"Hey, Chief. How's it going?" I asked.

"Who is this?" Billy asked.

"Okay," I said. "I'm sorry I haven't called."

"We are partners, you know," Billy said.

"I know."

"And you are on a case," Billy pressed.

"True."

"And so is it too much to expect to get daily updates?"

"Okay, Mother," I said sharply.

"Relax, Blood, I'm teasing," Billy said. "But you deserve it. Tell me what's going on."

I told him everything.

"So what are you going to do next?" Billy asked.

"I'm not sure," I answered. "But I'll think of something."

About an hour and one phone call later, I had a plan.

19

The gleaming Learjet looked brand-new in the early-morning light, but I knew it wasn't, since I had been on it before. The name Fleet Industries was emblazoned on the tail of the aircraft in maroon lettering. The edges of the wings were tipped up at almost a 90-degree angle. The aircraft sparkled in the bright sunlight as it taxied toward a private hangar at McCarran International Airport.

I had been directed to a spot on the tarmac where I could wait. The sleek little bird taxied in and stopped about thirty yards from where I was standing. The pilot, Jim Doak, gave me a wave and cut the engines. I had met Jim the year before when I was working the Fleet case. Fleet had offered me the use of the jet anytime I needed it, as long as it was available and I paid the fuel cost. I waited as the stairs unfolded and reached the tarmac. Lacy was the first person off the jet, followed by Billy and then Roy.

Lacy bounded down the stairs and came toward me, almost running. I could see by her grinning face that she was excited.

"That was so cool," she said. "I've never been on a plane before."

"Pretty nice, huh?" I said. "Bet you had to get up really early."

"It didn't matter," Lacy said. "I was so excited I couldn't sleep. Me on a private jet to Las Vegas! I'll be the talk of Mountain Center Middle School."

"Calm down," I smiled. "You are not here to see Vegas, and the less you say at school the better. You do not want to draw attention to yourself."

"You're right, I know," she frowned. "I'm here to get Mom. What's the plan?"

"We'll discuss it later," I said as Billy and Roy joined us.

"Discuss what?" Billy asked.

"The plan," Lacy said before I could open my mouth.

"Let's get some breakfast," I said to no one in particular.

◆　　◆　　◆　　◆

After breakfast, I sat in my rental car with Lacy in the parking lot of the shopping center where Tracy Malone had gone to Starbucks. I told her how I had found her mother.

"How did she look?" Lacy asked.

"She looked good, as far as I could tell," I said.

"I'll bet she's still on drugs," Lacy said. "She was hooked bad."

We were waiting for the phone to ring. Roy and Billy were parked at my favorite empty house waiting for some sign of Victor Vargas. I was hoping they would spot Vargas leaving. If so, Roy was to call us and then tail Vargas to make sure he was not returning to the house.

We waited.

"Boring," Lacy said. "How long do we have to wait?"

"I don't know," I said. "We wait for the call, and then we go in. That's the plan. What are you going to do if she's there?" I asked.

"I don't know exactly," Lacy said. "But I'll handle it."

We waited some more.

"Boring," Lacy said again after a while. "Do private detectives have to wait a lot?"

"I don't know," I said. "Sometimes, I guess. I don't have a lot of experience with waiting, and I do not wait well."

We sat in silence for a while, and then Lacy began playing a game on her cell phone.

A half-hour later, my cell phone rang.

"A black Mercedes with a viper tag on the front just went past me," Roy said before I even answered. "I'm on him."

"Good," I said. "Keep in touch."

"You got it," Roy said. "And by the way, the keypad number to the gate is 1324." He hung up before I could ask how he knew that.

I turned to Lacy. "Showtime," I said.

◆　　◆　　◆　　◆

We pulled in the driveway of 24 Hidden Valley Lane. I started to open the car door to get out, but Lacy stopped me.

"Wait here," she said. "It would go better if I went alone."

I nodded. "Take your cell phone and make sure it's on," I said. "If I call and say it's time to go, then get out of there fast."

I watched Lacy go purposefully up the walk to the front door and ring the doorbell. A few seconds later, the door opened, and there stood Tracy Malone with her mouth open and an incredible look of surprise on her face. I could lipread, "Oh, my God."

Lacy pointed into the house, and Tracy turned and followed her as she went inside. The front door closed. I started the car and let the motor run as I waited. I felt exposed sitting in Victor Vargas's driveway, but I knew Roy and Billy had my back.

After the longest fifteen minutes in my recent memory, the front door opened and Lacy came out carrying a small suitcase, followed by Tracy. I popped the trunk. Lacy stored the suitcase in the trunk and slammed it shut. She opened the back passenger's side door, and Tracy got in. Then Lacy came around the back of the car and opened the back driver's side door and got in, too.

"Mom, this is Don Youngblood," Lacy said as I turned in my seat to look at Tracy. "Don, this is my mom."

"Hi," Tracy said shyly.

"Hello," I said.

In the rearview mirror, I saw Lacy take Tracy's hand. "It will be okay," Lacy said softly.

I backed out of the driveway at 24 Hidden Valley Lane and headed for the airport. If we were lucky, it would be much later before Victor Vargas realized that his prize had flown the coop.

     ◆ ◆ ◆ ◆

"I got what I came for," I said.

I had called Bruiser on my cell phone to say goodbye and thanks.

"You're leaving," Bruiser said flatly.

"Yes," I said. "Vargas will not be happy when he finds out his main squeeze is missing."

"You're sure that she was his main squeeze?" Bruiser asked.

"We took her from his house," I said. "She wasn't just visiting."

"Jesus!" Bruiser exclaimed. "If he ever finds out it was you, he'll cut your dick off."

"Thanks, Bruiser," I said. "I really needed to hear that."

"I'm just saying, watch your back."

"I will," I said. "And thanks for everything. Come visit me in the mountains sometime."

"You can count on it," Bruiser said. "Be careful, and stay in touch."

"You can count on it," I echoed.

20

I had first met Sister Sarah Agnes Woods at a fundraiser for a drug and alcohol rehab center during my Wall Street days. The center was being built in the backwoods of Connecticut and was to cater to the very rich and the under-thirty addict. The plan was that the very rich would support the center so that the less fortunate could get treatment at a reasonable price. But first, the center had to be built. Funds had to be raised, and since I had funds, I was a potential target for a considerable donation. I went to the fundraiser because I liked the idea of supporting the center. I had seen drugs and alcohol derail more than one life while I was in college.

A tall, rather attractive woman at least ten years my senior with short, curly salt-and-pepper hair and intense hazel eyes staring out through John Lennon–type spectacles had approached me with cocktail in hand. The glasses brought back memories of Timothy Brentwood.

"You are Donald Youngblood, Wall Street whiz kid," she said rather pointedly.

"I am," I replied. "Although I'm not sure about the whiz part."

"Modesty from someone who works on Wall Street," she said. "How refreshing. I am Sister Sarah Agnes Woods. I am chatting you up for the sole purpose of extracting money from you."

"Honesty from a fundraiser," I said. "How refreshing."

She laughed, and I think at that moment we became instant friends. Sister Sarah Agnes walked away with a rather large donation from me that night. We stayed in touch through the years, having the occasional dinner and many telephone conversations. Her directness, honesty, and pragmatic approach were qualities I looked for when I considered committing to a friendship. No surprise, she got the rehab center built. She named it Silverthorn. I was there the day it opened.

I had called Sarah Agnes the night before Lacy arrived in Las Vegas. "Do you have room for a new patient?" I asked without preamble.

"Well, hello to you, too," she said.

"Hello back," I said. "Do you?"

"For you, of course. Who is it, and when will they be here?" she asked.

I told her.

"Does she want to get better?"

"I don't know," I said.

After a short pause, Sarah Agnes said, "Okay, bring her and we'll see if she does or not."

♦   ♦   ♦   ♦

Unless you knew exactly how to get there, Silverthorn was impossible to find. I had been there a few times, and even though I was very good about remembering places, I wrote down the directions I had stored on my laptop. The drive took an hour from Bradley International Airport north of Hartford. Fleet's private jet had dropped us off and winged its way home with Roy and Billy on board. Lacy and I would return by commercial airline, a trip I did not look forward to.

It was late in the day when we turned into the entrance of the rehab center. Silverthorn reminded me of a huge European-style hotel. The main building was five stories tall, with three-story wings on both sides. In the years following its completion, Silverthorn had become one of the "in" places to rehab for the rich and famous on the East Coast. Sarah Agnes tolerated those people by charging them outrageous amounts of money, part of which went directly to the general fund for operational expenses and the balance to investment accounts that I handled. I knew she had little sympathy for the older ones and the repeat offenders, but they were a necessary evil. Sister Sarah Agnes' real mission was the younger and less fortunate addict.

I dropped Lacy and her mother at the entrance. Lacy retrieved her mother's luggage from the trunk of the rental car. They had been talking in hushed tones since we left Vegas. Every now and again, I caught bits and pieces of their conversation. Lacy was trying to reassure her mother that she was doing the right thing and that everything would work out. Tracy did not look convinced.

"Wait here," I said. "I'll park the car and be right back."

By the time I returned, Sister Sarah Agnes had come outside to greet mother and daughter. She smiled widely when she spotted me walking up the drive. I received a hug and a quick kiss on the cheek when I got to her.

"You're looking fit," she said.

"Mary says she has him in the best shape of his life," Lacy chimed in before I could respond. I was surprised at her boldness.

"Mary?" Sarah Agnes questioned.

Lacy smiled.

"I'll explain later," I said.

"Indeed you will," Sarah Agnes said, arching an eyebrow. "But for now, let's go inside and get Ms. Malone checked in. I have some guest rooms ready so that you and Lacy can stay the night."

◆　◆　◆　◆

After dinner, Sister Sarah Agnes and I retired to the study. Even in late May, nights in the backwoods of Connecticut can get very cool. We sat by the fire drinking red wine and taking in the silence. Not a creature was stirring, neither addict nor staff. Lacy was in her room doing homework on my laptop. One of her assignments was to book us a flight home. Tracy was fast asleep, thanks to a little blue pill from Sarah Agnes.

"What do you think about Tracy?" I asked.

"Way too soon to tell," Sarah Agnes said. "Give it a few weeks. They all come in here talking the talk. We have to see if she can walk the walk, and that is infinitely harder."

"But you will help her," I said.

"Yes, and I'll take charge of her personally."

"Thank you," I said.

"No thanks required. It's what I do. Now, tell me about this Mary," Sarah Agnes ordered, showing a slight smile.

I told her. She listened intently.

"And how long have you been together?"

"About eight months," I said.

"And you think this is going to last?"

"Yes," I said. "I do."

"Why?"

I felt as if I were on a psychiatrist's couch. I let the question resonate in my mind. Time passed.

"I have never felt that any relationship I had with a woman was perfect until now," I said.

"That's a very good answer," she said. "But understand that no relationship is perfect. Sooner or later, she will disappoint you and you will disappoint her. How you handle those disappointments will be the key to your relationship."

"Perhaps *perfect* was a bad choice of words. Maybe *complete* is a better way to describe it."

"It was not a multiple-choice question. It is what you think it is. But *perfect* does not leave any room for growth."

"Okay," I said, a little annoyed. "Stop trying to shrink me."

Sarah Agnes smiled, and we were silent for a while. We drank wine and watched the flames dance.

"A female cop," Sarah Agnes said finally, shaking her head. "Sweet Jesus!"

21

L acy and I had breakfast at Silverthorn and were joined by Tracy, who commented on how well she had slept and how good she felt. I was not convinced. She didn't look like she had slept well or felt good. Lacy made no comment.

Mother and daughter said goodbye at the front door under the supervision of Sarah Agnes, who nodded at me with an arched eyebrow, her trademark.

We had been on the road for a good fifteen minutes before Lacy broke the silence.

"She didn't sleep well last night," Lacy said.

"I know," I said.

"In her own way, she is trying to be brave," Lacy said.

"She'll have to be," I said. "She has a tough road ahead."

"I'll help all I can."

"I know you will," I said, "but there is only so much you can do. She has to want it."

We were silent for a while, then Lacy again broke the silence.

"Is this Victor a mean guy?" she asked.

"I think so," I said.

"My grandmother once told me that my mother was attracted to bad men. Why do you think that is?"

"I don't know," I said. "Perhaps it has to do with wanting to be punished."

"For getting pregnant and having me?" Lacy asked.

"Probably not," I said. "Probably has to do with something that happened before you were born."

"You're pretty smart," she said.

"You, too," I said.

Lacy was silent awhile longer, and then she asked, "Do you miss Mary?"

"I do," I said.

"Me, too," Lacy said.

And for some reason, that touched me.

◆   ◆   ◆   ◆

The flights home were uneventful. We changed planes in Charlotte, North Carolina. Between flights, we had lunch at a TGI Friday's. For me, the whole trip was a drag, but for Lacy it was an adventure, and I took pleasure in that.

"I never flew before," she said. "And now, I've been on three airplanes in two days."

"You are turning into a world traveler," I teased.

Lacy punched me good-heartedly on the shoulder.

◆   ◆   ◆   ◆

Billy was waiting for us when we landed at Tri-Cities Airport. His large frame and dark good looks were hard to miss. Security was probably on high alert.

Lacy ran to meet him. They had established a bond in the little time they had known each other.

"Hi, Chief," I heard her say.

Chief? Billy let very few people call him Chief and get away with it.

"Hey, Little Princess," I heard Billy say.

Little Princess? What the hell was going on?

"Three planes in two days," she said to Billy.

"You're a veteran traveler now," Billy said.

He did not get punched.

"I'll see you two at baggage claim," Lacy said, and took off up the escalator.

"How did it go?" Billy asked as we followed Lacy.

"About as well as could be expected," I said. "Little Princess?"

Billy smiled. "Need-to-know basis only," he said. "And you don't need to know."

22

My world was returning to normal. I had slept in my own bed with the woman I loved. Mary had rekindled my excitement for the nude female body, especially hers. Now, I sat in the Mountain Center Diner with a *USA Today* and a cup of coffee, waiting on a feta cheese omelet with home fries and rye toast. All was as it should be.

I was engrossed in the sports page when Billy sat down. I had not expected him, but I was not surprised. Billy had a way of just turning up.

"So I never had a chance to ask about the details in Connecticut," Billy said.

"Yeah, the Little Princess was really monopolizing your time," I teased.

"She's a terrific kid," Billy said. "I really like her, and I think we have some things in common. I'd like to help her. Be her friend until she gets her mother back. *If* she gets her mother back."

"Getting her back is one thing," I said. "Whether she stays is something else."

"Yes," Billy said. "And I have a bad feeling about that. So tell me about Connecticut."

I told him.

"Addictions are hard," Billy said. "I hope she makes it."

Before I could comment further, Roy Husky sat down.

"Figured I would find you two here," he said.

"The more the merrier," I said.

Doris appeared to take their orders. While she was doing that, Big Bob showed up. He sat down hard and tossed his hat on a nearby chair.

"Who called this meeting?" Big Bob cracked.

"It's an open forum," I said.

Doris took Big Bob's order and scurried away. In no time, she was back with not only my breakfast but theirs as well. The table went silent as we devoured the food. The diner had not yet begun to fill up, and most of the booths, tables, and counter stools were vacant. It could have been argued that the four baddest men in Mountain Center on the right side of justice now sat eating breakfast together.

"Nothing beats a Mountain Center Diner breakfast," Big Bob said.

"Amen to that," I said.

Roy and Billy, mouths full, nodded agreement.

"So how was Vegas?" Big Bob asked.

"Hot," I said.

"The weather or the women?"

"Both," I said. "And I got tired of both."

"Not the Donald Youngblood I used to know," Big Bob grinned. "Mary's got you pussy-whipped, that's what it is."

Billy and Roy, mouths still full, nodded in agreement and said "Uh-huh" simultaneously.

"Damn it," I said. "Just shut up and eat."

He laughed. One of Big Bob's most endearing qualities—or most irritating flaws, depending on your point of view—was that he said exactly what he thought at all times. I had learned to accept it, but at certain times it was annoying. And yet he was impossible to insult and never took offense at anything I might say. And I could say plenty when he went too far.

"Well, did you accomplish what you wanted to?" he asked.

"I did."

"Good," he said.

He made no mention of Lacy, and neither did I.

The conversation turned to the local high-school football team, which had been undefeated until losing a close 28–22 road game on Friday night to a Middle Tennessee team it should have beaten. Big Bob and his brother Sean went to all the games under the umbrella of "security," and therefore always got in free and always got to park inside the stadium. Truth be told, they were a welcome sight at any game, home or away.

We continued eating our food.

"Got to run," Big Bob said.

He threw money on the table, grabbed his hat, and was gone as quickly as he had appeared.

"Damn," said Roy. "That guy can sure fill up a room."

"He does live large," I said.

"Umm," Billy nodded, still eating.

23

My phone rang at midday, breaking the silence of my lonely office. Billy was I knew not where, but I suspected he was in Cherokee with Maggie Morning-Song, whom I had yet to meet. I had left Jake at home. I didn't want him getting used to coming to the office every day, but today I wished I had brought him. The caller ID on the phone read, "Out of area." I hesitated but decided to answer, since I had nothing else to do.

"Cherokee Investigations," I said in my most professional voice.

"Donald Youngblood, please," a very businesslike, slightly nondescript voice requested. *Telemarketer?*

"Speaking," I said warily.

"Mr. Youngblood, my name is Jim Murphy. I am a detective on the Marietta, Georgia, police force."

I swallowed hard. "Sandy?"

"How did you know?" he asked.

"Sandy Smith is the only person I know in Marietta. What happened?" I asked, although I already suspected. Roger Allen.

"Miss Smith was mugged and beaten up in a parking garage at a shopping mall. She is in a coma at a local hospital."

"Which hospital?"

"Kennestone Hospital," he said. "It's on Church Street in Marietta."

"How did you find me?" I asked.

"I went through the lady's wallet looking for clues. Imagine my curiosity when I discovered the business card of a private detective from Tennessee," Murphy said. "You're either very good, for her to go out of state to hire a PI, or you know the lady."

"I'm good enough," I said, a little bit annoyed, "and I do know the lady."

"Got any idea who might want to beat her up?" Murphy asked.

"I thought you said she was mugged."

"Whoever did this wanted to make it look like a mugging. Muggers don't stay around to beat the hell out of their victims," Murphy said. "They grab, maybe knock the woman down, and run like hell with the purse. This guy—I am assuming guy—beat the hell out of her, then dumped out the contents of her purse and left the purse. I don't know if anything was taken, but the money wasn't."

"House key?" I asked.

"Jesus, you think like a cop," Murphy said. "Her keys were on the ground near her car. There was a key to her condo on her key ring. I know because I went to the condo. I found a framed picture of a guy face down in one of the drawers. Made me think maybe the guy was someone she had just broken off a relationship with. Could it be your picture?"

"Maybe," I said.

"Guy was pretty good looking," Murphy said.

"Has to be me," I quipped, fear masking itself in humor.

Murphy chuckled.

"Any witnesses?" I asked.

"Maybe. The lady who found her and called it in thinks she saw someone running between cars, but she's not sure. My guess is that Miss Smith's attacker heard the car coming and took off. That may be the only reason she's alive."

"I'm coming down there," I said.

"You know something I don't know," Murphy said. "It would help if I know now."

I told him the story and gave him the license plate number.

"I'll put an APB out on this Roger Allen. Know where he lives?"

That question stung. "I should," I said. "But I don't."

"Not your fault," Murphy said, cutting me some slack. "You couldn't have known. Department of Motor Vehicles should have it."

"I am relatively new at dealing with real bad guys," I said. "But I am learning fast that you should assume the worst. I should have had the guy tailed."

"Spilt milk," Murphy said. "I'll see you when you get here. I want to catch this SOB."

24

The nurse's nametag said she was Laura Crowder. She was young and pleasant with sandy hair and clear blue eyes that showed awareness behind her calm demeanor. Taking into consideration that it was midnight, I was impressed. Her station guarded the entrance to intensive care—ICU, in hospital jargon.

"Can I help you?" she asked.

"Yes," I said. "I am here to see Sandy Smith."

I was fully prepared with a story about how I was the closest thing Sandy had to a family, and that I should be awarded next-of-kin status.

"Are you Don?" Nurse Laura asked.

The question caught me off-guard. "Yes, I am."

"She has been asking for you," Nurse Laura said.

"I thought she was in a coma," I said.

"She is drifting in and out of semi-consciousness. She has suffered severe head trauma, among other things. She is delirious when she is awake, partly due to her condition and partly due to the drugs we have her on. She has called for Don, though."

"Can you be a little more specific about her condition?"

"She has a skull fracture, but it is not compressed, which means there are no skull fragments pressing on the brain. That is good news, but she does have a scalp laceration that required stitches, along with a severe concussion. That means there is some brain swelling. She also has bruising on the rib cage and her arms, like she was trying to ward off the blows from her attacker."

"Can I see her?" I asked.

"Sure, but she is out of it right now. You can sit by her bed if you like. Third alcove on the left."

I nodded and walked into ICU to the third alcove on the left. What I saw made me livid. Sandy's head was bandaged. Her face was a collage of skin tones, grays, blues, and purples. The head of her bed was elevated, and she had an IV running to her left hand. A monitor displayed what I guessed were heart rate, blood pressure, and EKG. I wanted to cry and kill someone at the same time. This was my fault.

◆　　◆　　◆　　◆

Having recovered from the initial shock of how Sandy looked, I stood by the side of her bed and took her right hand in mine. It felt normal, neither warm nor cold. I squeezed. No response. I stood there for an indeterminate amount of time staring at her surroundings before I settled into a bedside chair. It was less than comfortable. I managed.

I had left Mountain Center at sunset, after Mary went on second shift. She was very understanding. *I guess an unconscious ex-girlfriend doesn't pose much of a threat*, I mused, then shook my head at my warped sense of humor. I was mad at myself, trying hard not to break something. If I ever found that son of a bitch Roger Allen, I would kill him. My dark side was on the prowl.

I sensed a presence behind me. I turned and observed a man standing in the hall and looking into Sandy's alcove. He was a beefy man with light brown hair, slightly taller than me. He had a tired look on his face.

I stood. "Murphy?"

"That's me," he said. He extended his hand, and I took it.

"Don Youngblood," I said. "Nice to meet you. I think."

"I know what you mean," he said. "Pisses you off, don't it?"

"Royally," I said. "I'd like to hit someone. Especially Roger Allen. Any sign of him?"

"Nothing," Murphy said. "The guy is a ghost. The address on the plate you gave me was bogus."

"Any sign of the car?"

Murphy looked at me like I had two heads.

"Yeah," I said. "Stupid question. Probably ten thousand silver BMWs in the Atlanta area. It's late and I'm beat. Speaking of late, what are you doing here at this hour?"

"Hell if I know," Murphy sighed, suppressing a yawn. "I just left the office after cleaning up some overdue paperwork, and I have no home life, and I was in the neighborhood. I thought you might be here, so I came on up. Let's go have some coffee."

We took the elevator down to the first floor and went to the cafeteria, which was marginally open. I got coffee and a blueberry muffin, and Murphy followed suit. We were both tired and acted like it. I ate the muffin, drank the coffee, and felt a bit revived. Murphy, too, appeared to perk up.

"So tell me the whole Roger story again, and don't leave anything out," he said.

I told him everything I could remember. But I didn't mention the pictures. I wanted to look at them first. He sat silently, finished his coffee, and went for another cup.

"So she said she didn't sleep with him," Murphy said as he sat back down at our table.

"That's what she said."

"And you believe her?" Murphy asked.

"I am easily lied to by women," I quipped.

"Welcome to the club," Murphy said.

"She was a little too quick to say no," I said, thinking back. "But I'd rather not bring it up again. Maybe you can get someone to check the bedroom for a stray hair or something."

"That might be a little tricky without a good reason, and Ms. Smith saying she didn't sleep with the guy is not a good reason," Murphy said.

"I get the point," I said. "I'll try to find out."

Murphy nodded and drank more coffee.

"Was there a security camera anywhere in the parking garage that might have picked up his car?" I asked.

Murphy grimaced. "Hasn't been working lately, which means the bastards are too cheap to fix it."

"Any listing anywhere of a Roger Allen?" I asked. "Phone book, DMV, rap sheet?"

"About twenty-five Roger Allens so far. None of them appears to be our guy. But we are still checking," Murphy said as he finished the last of his second cup of coffee. "I gotta go home and catch some Zs. Here's my cell phone number." He handed me a business card. "Call me if you come up with anything. I hope the lady is going to be okay."

"Thanks for calling me," I said.

"I checked you out with the local cops up there," Murphy said as he got up to leave. "They say you're hot shit. So I expect you to come up with something we can sink our teeth into."

"Hot shit," I said. "I'll have to remember to put that on my résumé."

Murphy smirked. "See you around," he said as he turned and walked away.

◆   ◆   ◆   ◆

I returned to Sandy's room and the less-than-comfortable chair and drifted into a restless sleep filled with a collage of sounds and colors. At some undetermined point, I heard a faraway voice. It was a faint voice, almost a whisper. I felt myself surface from the depths of sleep, and as I popped above the surface I heard, "Don."

I opened my eyes. The clock on the wall showed 6:05. I had slept about five hours.

"Don," Sandy said again. Her voice was weak. She reached out a hand.

I rose from the chair, took three steps to her bedside, and slipped her hand in mine.

"How are you feeling?" I asked.

"My head hurts," she said. "He tried to kill me."

"Who?" I asked.

"The guy in the black ski mask. He was after my purse."

"Did he say anything?" I asked.

" 'Bitch,' " Sandy said, struggling with the word. "He kept growling 'Bitch' over and over as he hit me. Then I fell and hit my head, and I heard someone running and tires screeching, and I guess I passed out."

"Do you think it could have been Roger?"

"Roger?" Sandy looked confused. "You think it could have been Roger? I don't know. I guess he was about the right size. Why do you think it could have been Roger?"

"Because the guy who did this did not take your purse, and muggers usually don't stay around beating up their victims," I said.

"Oh, God," Sandy moaned. A tear trickled down her left cheek. The realization that Roger Allen might have tried to kill her was sinking in.

"The police have tried to find Roger," I continued. "He seems to have disappeared."

Sandy was quiet, as if she were trying to remember something. "It could have been him," she said weakly. "It could have been his voice."

I felt a presence behind me.

"Good, you're awake," Nurse Laura said. From the other side of the bed, she checked Sandy's pupils. "Good," she said.

"I'm surprised you're still here," I said.

"I work eleven to seven," Nurse Laura said, then returned her attention to Sandy. "How do you feel?"

"My head hurts," Sandy said.

"I'll bring you something for that," Nurse Laura said.

Nurse Laura eyed the monitors, seemed to nod approval, and left the room.

"Sandy," I said, staring at her intently. "I need to ask you something about you and Roger, and I need an honest answer."

She looked away. Another tear escaped, then another. She knew the question.

"We tried," she said. "He couldn't perform. It was awful. He would get an erection and then lose it before he could get inside of me. He was so embarrassed and angry. He acted like it was my fault. He got dressed in a hurry and stormed out. That was the last time I let him in my apartment. The next day, he apologized and wanted to see me again, but I said no. Then he kept pursuing me, and two weeks later I called you."

I nodded and didn't comment.

Nurse Laura appeared with a couple of little pink pills. Sandy gulped them down, and Laura left.

"I'm tired, Don. I don't want to talk anymore," Sandy said as she turned away and closed her eyes.

I went back to the chair. Sometime later, when I was sure she was asleep, I left the hospital.

25

I drove to the same Marriott Courtyard where I had stayed the last time I was in Marietta. The time that I thought I had dispatched Roger Allen. The time I was wrong. Even if Sandy wasn't convinced he had tried to kill her, I was, and if I could I would see he paid the price. I checked in and got the same third-floor suite I had occupied before. Then I called Jim Murphy's cell phone.

"Murphy," came the terse response.

"Murphy, it's Youngblood," I said. "If you're free for lunch, I'm buying."

"I'm a cop. I'm always free for lunch when someone is buying," Murphy said. "Where are you?"

I told him.

"There's a Spaghetti Warehouse about a mile from you. Get directions at the front desk. I'll see you at noon."

He hung up before I could say anything. *Jim Murphy should meet Roy Husky*, I thought.

◆　◆　◆　◆

I arrived early and secured an out-of-the-way corner table with a view of the door. Murphy was right on time. He looked tired.

"How much sleep did you get last night?" I asked.

"About five hours, I guess," he said. "Goes with the territory."

The waiter arrived, and we ordered.

"Sandy woke up," I said. "It looks as if she is going to be all right."

"Good to hear," Murphy said. "But you're not buying me lunch to tell me that."

He waited.

"She kind of had sex with him," I said.

"Explain 'kind of,'" Murphy smirked.

I explained.

"Jesus Christ," Murphy said. "Some women can really pick 'em."

"Careful," I said. "She did pick me at one point."

"And let me guess. You're not the marrying kind, so she moved on, looking for a husband."

"Murphy," I said, "you are beginning to be annoying."

"Goes with the territory," he said.

I sipped my sweet tea and listened as Murphy talked about life "on the job." Ten minutes later, our food arrived. Murphy had veal parmigiana, while I had a grilled chicken Caesar salad. The portions were ample. We ate and drank in relative silence. Every now and then, I would ask a question and Murphy would respond with an answer as short as he could possibly make it. I couldn't believe how hungry I was, and then I remembered that I had missed breakfast. Murphy attacked his food like he hadn't eaten in days. Every now and then, he made sounds of approval.

When we finished, Murphy said, "Now, that was good."

I nodded.

"I guess the sort-of-sex thing could be enough for me to get one of the forensic guys to take a look," Murphy said. "I'll let you know. Give me your cell phone number."

I did.

"I'm outta here," Murphy said. "Thanks for lunch."

He was gone like a big wind, leaving me looking for the waiter with the check.

◆　　◆　　◆　　◆

I returned to my room at the Courtyard and went online and checked my email. Then I went to cbssportsline.com and read all the sports I could stand. Next, I checked a few stocks that I was tracking. Nothing much was happening. I unpacked. Having killed a couple of hours so the grilled chicken Caesar salad wouldn't feel like a brick in my stomach, I put on my gear and went for a long run.

Running helped me think. Finding Tracy Malone was one thing. I had a trail to follow. Finding Roger Allen was another thing. There was no trail. If I was going to find Roger, I needed some help and some luck.

An hour later, I was in the shower washing away the sweat and tiredness from the last twenty-four hours.

I called Mary at the condo. She was on second shift all week, and I knew she would be getting ready for work soon. She answered on the second ring.

"Mountain Center Brothel," Mary said in her sexiest voice.

"Sometimes, I hate caller ID," I said. "You can't surprise anyone."

"I knew it was you anyway," she said.

"You did, huh?"

"Sure. Telemarketers never call in the afternoon, and no one else ever calls here."

"Well, how are things in sleepy little Mountain Center?" I asked.

"Sleepy," she said. "Not much happening. We may be helping Sheriff Durham take down a suspected meth lab in the very near future."

Jimmy Durham was a local county sheriff and a longtime friend.

"He is waiting on confirmation so he can get a warrant," Mary continued. "Other than that, it's pretty quiet. How is Sandy?"

"Not good right now, but they think she'll be okay. She is lucky to be alive. I'm sure he meant to kill her."

"How is the local cop you're dealing with?" Mary asked.

"A piece of work," I said. "But I think he's pretty good."

"You're pretty good, too," Mary said.

"Yeah? At what?"

"Detecting," she said. "And other things, if you get my meaning."

I got it.

"Speaking of which, when will you be back?" she asked.

"A couple of days at the most," I said. "I want to be sure Sandy is out of the woods recovery-wise, and then I'm out of here. I am kind of missing other things."

"I've got to get ready for my shift," Mary said. "Get home as soon as you can."

"I'll do that," I said. "See you soon."

I hung up.

Get home as soon as you can, I thought. *Home.*

Interesting.

I felt a twinge. Maybe it was the chicken Caesar.

26

The next few days, I spent most of my time at the hospital with Sandy, who was awake now more than she slept. When she was moved out of intensive care, I made sure she had a private room. Friends from work visited, including her boss, an older gentleman named Ed, who seemed genuinely concerned and who I liked. Everyone made certain that I understood Sandy would be well taken care of.

Late in the evening of the third day, Sandy and I were alone. The last of her office friends had departed. Jim Murphy had been by a couple of times to ask what he said were follow-up questions. I wondered. I was thinking there might be more to it. Sandy was starting to look more like her old self, and her old self looked really good. Murphy did not mention forensics, and I did not ask. I was sure he would get to it.

"Murphy's nice," Sandy said.

"I think he likes you," I said.

"Are you kidding? I look terrible," Sandy said.

Typical woman.

"Terrible for you is still pretty good," I said.

Sandy laughed. "Haven't lost any of that charm, have you, Don? It just comes so naturally."

I smiled and let it pass. I didn't know whether that was a compliment or not, and I wasn't about to ask.

We were silent for a while.

"It's time for you to go back to your life," Sandy said. "I appreciate your coming down here, but I have friends who will help, and you have someone waiting."

It was the second time Sandy had referred to Mary. I didn't know how much she knew, but Mountain Center was not that big a town, and plenty of people were willing to get involved in other people's business. So-called friends would be more than willing to let her know what I was up to.

"I was planning on leaving in the morning," I said.

"Forget Roger Allen," she said. "Let the police handle it."

I was silent.

"This is not your fault, Don. It's my fault for getting involved with him."

I remained silent.

"I know you. And I have to be honest. I saw a side of you that scared me. You are not going to let this go, are you?"

"Not yet," I said. "And it's not all about you. Maybe he has done this before. And he more than likely will do it again. The guy needs to be locked up, or worse."

"It's the 'or worse' that bothers me," Sandy said.

"Relax," I said. "The chances of my finding Roger Allen are slim to none."

"Somehow, that doesn't make me feel any better," Sandy said.

◆　◆　◆　◆

The next morning, I packed up the Pathfinder and headed back to Mountain Center. I had said goodbye to Sandy the night before, and she promised to stay in touch and keep me posted on her progress. I wondered. I sensed that she was ready for me to leave.

I drove into North Georgia and back into the Nantahala National Forest, through the land of whitewater rafting. The traffic was slow, but I didn't care. The warm spring day held promise for all of those willing to slow down and enjoy it. I pulled off the highway and bought a Diet Coke with ice at a roadside stand. I sat on top of a picnic table drinking and watching various rafts finish their runs. I knew the fun they were having. I felt a little lonely. I missed Mary. I needed to get back.

I drove through Cherokee and into the Great Smoky Mountains National Park. The tourists were plentiful and in no hurry to get anywhere. On this particular day, I didn't mind. It took me an hour to reach Gatlinburg and almost another hour to get to Mountain Center.

I called Mary on my way into town.

"I'm back," I said when she answered at the condo.

"About damn time," she teased.

"How is Lacy?" I asked.

"She's fine," Mary said. "And she's at school." She drew out the *and*.

"Meaning?"

"Meaning get your butt home. I've got the day off. Put the pedal to the metal, big boy," Mary said in her most sexy voice.

"I might get stopped for speeding," I teased back.

"Not to worry," Mary said. "I know the chief of police."

I looked at the speedometer. I was doing fifty in a thirty-five-miles-per-hour zone. It was a good day to be alive, and it was about to get better.

27

My favorite time of day is the early morning when I am in my inner sanctum, the one private place I share only by invitation, my office. The quiet is like a warm blanket, that first cup of coffee a magical elixir. I was eating a poppy seed bagel with cream cheese and enjoying every scrumptious bite. I was playing my new game of choice, Spider Solitaire, and doing a damn fine job of it on the most difficult level. It took awhile, but with a lot of backpedaling and a second cup of coffee, I finally won. Fireworks went off on my computer screen. I closed down the game and picked up the phone. It was early to make a call, but I knew she would be awake.

"You're up early," Sarah Agnes said.

"I am always up early," I said, "in search of peace and quiet."

"Yes, I hear your life has been a little hectic lately. How was Marietta?"

"You seem to know a lot for someone living out in the woods," I said.

"Living out in the woods does have its advantages," Sarah Agnes said. "I hear things."

"Little voices in your head?" I teased.

"No, but patients do tend to share news."

"Okay, I get the picture. Lacy talks to Tracy, and Tracy talks to you."

"And they said you weren't a detective," she gloated.

"Who's they?"

"Never mind," she said, as if lecturing me. "Why did you call?"

"Maybe I need some counseling," I quipped.

"Maybe you do."

"I'm joking," I said.

"Maybe you aren't," she said.

Maybe I'm not, I thought. I was silent.

"You have had a lot of changes recently," Sarah Agnes said.

"Yes, I have."

"Since this Fleet case that you told me about, your world, as they say, has been rocked."

"Significantly," I said.

"You are basically a loner at heart, Don. Probably in part because you were an only child with doting parents, and in part because you lost them before you completely matured."

"I've completely matured?" I asked jokingly.

"We are never completely matured," Sister Sarah Agnes said seriously. "We are all just works in progress, but let's try to stay focused for a minute. You like order and routine. Then you get this case that changes everything. You meet dangerous people and get involved in killing and murder. You strike up a friendship with this Roy person who you would seem to have nothing in common with, your girlfriend du jour leaves town, you fall in love with a very challenging woman who is more than just a plaything, and now you are trying to make a difference in the life of a thirteen-year-old girl. On top of that, you have discovered your dark side. Have I missed anything?"

"I don't think so."

"That's a lot for someone like you to handle."

"I know," I said. "My head is spinning just listening to you talk about it."

"It's called life, Don. Want my advice?"

"Maybe," I said cautiously. "Let's hear it."

"Embrace it. Live it. Love it," she said with emphasis. "But be careful not to become an avenging angel. You cannot right all wrongs. Leave some of that to the authorities who are paid to do it, or to the higher power."

I let that sink in for a minute. My life had changed drastically in the last year, and I was certainly discovering different aspects of myself. Some I liked, while others scared me. Most of the changes were good, but I did feel myself pushing closer to the dangerous edge.

"Are you still there?" Sarah Agnes queried.

"Yes. Enough shrinkage," I said, feeling a little uncomfortable. "How is Tracy?"

"Did you hear anything I said?"

"I heard," I said with faked annoyance. "And since you have all those degrees, I'll take it under advisement. Now, let's move on."

"You are a control freak," Sarah Agnes said, exasperated.

"Pot calling the kettle black," I said.

"Touché," she laughed. "Okay, about Tracy. She seems to be doing fine, but something is there I have not yet uncovered. Something way back in her past that caused her to be the way she is today. I do not think she is really a drug addict. She has kicked it too easily, or so it seems. I'll keep you posted."

"How often does she talk to Lacy?" I asked.

"Every day. And she delights in that. She is very grateful that you and Mary are taking care of Lacy. She genuinely cares about Lacy but senses that she cannot give her the mothering she needs."

"Lacy is a good kid," I said. "How can she be so solid with all the chaos around her?"

"Happens all the time," Sarah Agnes said. "Role reversal. Although she may not be as solid as she appears. What is the long-range plan for Lacy?"

"I don't know," I said. "I'm working on it."

"Want my advice?" she asked.

"No," I said emphatically.

Sarah Agnes laughed, and then I heard muffled conversation in the background.

"Sorry, Don. I have to go now. Minor emergency."

"Okay," I said. "I'll call you soon. And Sarah Agnes . . ."

"Yes?"

"Thanks," I said.

"You're welcome," she said.

◆   ◆   ◆   ◆

Late that afternoon, my phone rang again, and I immediately recognized the number.

"Youngblood," I answered tersely.

"Do you always sound so tough?" Murphy joked.

"Only when I know it's the police," I said.

"I hate that fucking caller ID," Murphy said.

"Cops would," I cracked. "Who wants to answer the phone when the law is calling? Speaking of which, I assume this is not a social call."

"I got a CSI to go over to Sandy's place," Murphy said. "He cleaned the bedroom pretty good and found a few hairs, numerous female—Sandy's—and a few from an unknown male. We assume the male is our buddy Roger Allen. I ran the DNA through our computer and came up with zilch. I am pretty much at a dead end."

"Is Sandy home from the hospital yet?" I asked Murphy.

"Yeah, she's home. Going back to work next week. Looks pretty good. Still having a few headaches."

"You're doing a fine job staying on top of this one, Murphy," I teased.

"Fuck you, Youngblood."

"Easy, Murphy," I said seriously. "If you two like each other, that's fine with me. Listen, I may have an idea. Can you send me the DNA report?"

He paused.

"I'll send it, but it didn't come from me," he said.

"I understand."

"Give me your email address. I'll attach it."

"A cop who knows computers," I said. "I'm impressed."

"Comes in handy," Murphy said. "Got to keep up with the crooks. I'll send it tonight."

"Okay, Murphy. Thanks."

"One more thing," Murphy said.

"Go ahead."

"Sorry I bit your head off."

"No problem," I said. "I meant what I said. You two do not need my approval anyway."

"Thanks, Youngblood. Let me know if you come up with anything."

"I will, Murphy. Take care of yourself."

28

F riday night, I met Mary and Lacy at the lake house. About an hour's drive from Mountain Center, the house belonged to my parents before they were killed. Still immaculate, it sat on a ten-acre parcel of land, a lot of it lakefront.

Mary and Lacy had picked up pizza from our favorite local place, a large half pepperoni and half chicken and pesto. I had the makings of a Caesar salad laid out on the kitchen island. A bottle of 2004 Luna Sangiovese was breathing on a nearby countertop.

Mary and Lacy were on barstools on the other side of the island. They seemed to be watching me a little too closely, and they kept looking at each other and smiling. Lacy was drinking a Diet Coke.

"I love your Caesar salad," Lacy said.

"Me, too," Mary said.

I had the distinct impression that I was being messed with again. Two against one—bad odds, especially when the two were female and the one was male.

"You love it more because you don't have to make it," I smiled.

"That, too," Mary said.

"Uh-huh," echoed Lacy.

"Officer," I said. "Make yourself useful and pour the wine."

"Yes, sir," Mary saluted.

Soon, two lead crystal balloon goblets were half full of the dark red elixir. We touched glasses and sampled the full-bodied red from California.

"This is really good," Mary said.

It was indeed.

I continued with my masterpiece. I washed, dried, tore, grated, mixed, crumbled, and tossed until I was satisfied. Then I divided the salad into three equal portions. We took our drinks, the salad, and the pizza out the back door and down to the lower deck, which overlooked the lake. The night was pleasant—no wind, no humidity, and no bugs. Daylight saving time promised us one more hour of light. We ate, drank, and engaged in small talk.

"How is school?" I asked, a typical adult question to try to engage a thirteen-year-old in conversation.

"Almost over," Lacy said. "And before you ask, my grades are all As and Bs."

"Good to know," I said.

I caught Mary's eye. She smiled and kept quiet.

"I want to get a job for the summer," Lacy said. "Earn my own money."

"Sounds like a good idea," I said.

"Got any suggestions?" Lacy asked.

"I might," I said. "Let me think about it."

I actually did have a couple of ideas.

"I was thinking about taking the houseboat out tomorrow and going fishing," I said. "Anyone interested in joining me?"

"Me," Lacy said quickly with excitement.

"Me, too," Mary added.

"Okay," I said in my best Long John Silver imitation. "Captain Don will be responsible for the fishing gear and bait. Mates Mary and Lacy will be responsible for the food." I left off the *Arrgh*.

"Yes, sir," Mary saluted.

"Yes, sir," Lacy mimicked.

I was definitely being messed with.

29

The following morning, after I took the houseboat out of the boathouse and docked it, I went into the woods with a large Styrofoam cup and a garden spade. It did not take me long to find a moist spot beneath a cover of leaves and turn over the black soil, revealing a community of worms and night crawlers. I filled the cup and returned to the dock, where I had laid out fishing rods, tackle boxes, folding chairs, and life preservers. Mary and Lacy came down to join me. Mary carried a large cooler effortlessly, while Lacy carried a picnic basket that I knew was packed with sandwiches, chips, and probably a few surprises.

"First mates reporting for duty, sir," Mary teased.

"You can't have two first mates," I shot back.

"You can on this trip," Mary said. "And two first mates trump a captain."

"Permission to come aboard?" Lacy asked.

"Granted," I said. "Load up."

A few minutes later, we puttered away from the dock. The houseboat was really a glorified barge that my dad had built while I was growing up. Basically a wooden deck that sat on pontoons, it was approximately twenty feet long and ten feet wide, with twin engines on the rear. We never used both engines at once. When I questioned my father why we had two engines, all he would say was "Backup." Half the barge was covered to offer shade on hot days. The uncovered part we called "the sun deck." It made the barge sound like more than it was. The deck was painted light gray. It had three-foot railings all around with heavy-duty coated wire mesh, except for two door-sized openings on either side.

I stayed close to the shoreline to avoid the wakes of the weekend crazies who buzzed around the lake trying to impress their girlfriends with how fast their boats were. A half-hour later, we anchored in a shady cove where I knew bluegill had once hung out. I hoped they were still there.

"Have you ever fished?" I asked Lacy.

"No," she said.

"One of my best childhood memories is fishing with my parents," I said to no one in particular as I retrieved our live bait from a bucket at a rear corner of the barge. "Watch and learn," I said to Lacy as I chose a worm from our stash.

I impaled it on a small hook, leaving some wiggle room for the worm. I expected a "Yuck" or something similar from Lacy, but all I got was an intense stare at what I was doing. I added a small lead weight above the hook and attached a float about four feet above the weight. I hung the rod over the side of the barge and performed a delicate sidearm cast toward the bank. I let out some slack in the line.

"Watch the float," I said. "If it goes under, give a little jerk backward on the rod and start reeling it in."

I gave her a demonstration and then cast again.

"Got it," she said as she took the rod from me.

I turned my attention to another rod.

"You going to try it?" I asked Mary.

"Not right now," she said from a folding chair. "I would rather just relax and watch." She removed a thermos from the picnic basket and poured herself a cup of black coffee. A chill was still in the air.

I chose a rod with a medium-sized hook already attached, added a heavier weight, and removed a large night crawler from the Styrofoam cup. It squirmed in my hand as if it knew its doom was at hand. Escape proved to be futile as I swiftly baited the hook. I brought the tip of the rod up and slightly back over my right shoulder and skillfully flicked the bait about fifty feet out toward open water. I smiled inwardly at my success. *It's all in the wrist*, I thought. I started reeling my bait in, slowly dragging it across the bottom, hoping to entice an unsuspecting and hungry bass.

"My float jumped," Lacy said excitedly.

"That's good," I said. "It means fish are present. They're nibbling. Wait for the float to go under. Then do as I showed you."

I finished reeling in my bait, with no success, and then repeated the process.

I had just reeled in for the third time when I heard Lacy squeal.

"I got one!" she exclaimed as she started reeling in.

She did indeed. A good-sized bluegill had taken the bait and was putting up a pretty good fight.

"Nice and easy," I said. "He won't get away. Maneuver him to the opening, and I'll get him in the net."

I netted the bluegill and brought it on board.

"Congratulations," I said. "Your first fish."

Lacy beamed.

"Hold it up," Mary said.

Before we knew it, we had our picture taken, the memory preserved. I had a strange sensation. I could almost feel the presence of my parents.

◆   ◆   ◆   ◆

Lacy caught four more bluegill before noon, and I hooked one very nice-sized bass. The fish were imprisoned in a wire mesh cage hung over the side of the barge. At day's end, we would release them. A barge rule had always been, "Do not catch the same fish twice in the same day."

We took a break around noon and had lunch. Mary had made turkey and Swiss cheese sandwiches with romaine lettuce, honey mustard, and mayonnaise on jumbo deli rye bread. I put a sandwich on a paper plate, added potato salad and an ample portion of Doritos, and topped it off with a chocolate chip cookie from the Mountain Center Diner. Fishing is hard work. I needed to keep my strength up. I took a beer from the cooler and poured it into a Styrofoam cup.

I had just finished eating when I noticed a boat coming our way. As it approached, I recognized the driver.

Jimmy Durham was an old friend of mine from my high-school years who had played basketball for a rival school. In those days, we met twice a year when our teams played for county bragging rights. Jimmy was a great athlete whose career ended when he blew out a knee playing quarterback on a bad football team his senior year. These days, he was county sheriff. We still occasionally played pickup basketball together.

The boat slowed and pulled alongside. Jimmy was in uniform, and there was a sheriff's star on the side of the boat. Jimmy, ever the kidder, looked at Lacy.

"You got a fishin' license, little lady?" he drawled. Jimmy always acted like he wished he had been born in Texas.

Lacy looked at me in a panic. I couldn't let this go too far.

"Doesn't need one," I said. "She's thirteen years old and fishing with live bait."

"That so, little lady?" Jimmy asked, perpetuating the charade.

"Yes, sir," Lacy said. She was starting to relax. I wasn't sure about Mary.

"Okay, then," Jimmy said. "Got any beer on board?"

"Beer is not allowed on the lake," I said. "I might get in trouble with the law."

"Probably not for the next hour or so," Jimmy smiled.

I looked at Mary and Lacy. They had that look women get when they realize they've been duped. I opened the cooler and tossed Jimmy a Sam Adams Light.

"Damn," Jimmy said. "The good stuff. Thanks, Don. We had 'em goin' for a minute there, didn't we?"

"We sure did, Jimmy," I said.

I did the introductions as Jimmy drank down half the bottle of Sam.

"Nice to meet y'all," he said. Then he turned his attention to me. "I haven't seen you since that Fairchild thing. Rumor has it that you closed that out. I would like to hear that story someday."

"Someday," I said.

Jimmy took another long pull on the beer.

"What brings you out on the lake?" I asked.

"Stolen boat. Probably kids out for a joyride," Jimmy said. "Used to be cars, now it's boats. I'll probably find it abandoned in a little cove somewhere, but whoever took it will be long gone."

Jimmy finished the beer and tossed me the bottle.

"Want another one?"

"Naw, I gotta stay under the legal limit. Y'all have a good day," Jimmy said as he swung his boat around and moved slowly away. "See ya later, Don!" he hollered over his shoulder.

"So that's Jimmy Durham," Mary said, moving close to me as I watched Jimmy's boat fade into the horizon. "Quite a character."

"He is that," I said.

"We're still waiting to hear from him about the meth lab thing," Mary said.

◆　◆　◆　◆

After lunch, I moved the barge into the sun and Mary stripped off her clothes to reveal a very sexy bikini.

"I want to get some sun," Mary said.

Lacy followed Mary's lead, and although her bikini was not quite as revealing it left no doubt that Lacy was going to mature into a knockout woman.

"You two are liable to draw every boat on the lake," I teased.

"Shut up and hand me the suntan lotion," Mary said.

By four o'clock that afternoon, Lacy had caught another five bluegill and I had reeled in two more bass. Lacy was really into it. She was baiting her own hook and casting like an old pro. Exhausted, we packed up, released the fish, and puttered back to the lake house, enjoying the late-day breeze and the beauty of the lake.

As we approached the dock, I slowed, maneuvered the barge alongside, and jumped out with the front towrope to tie off. Lacy was right alongside, watching my every move.

"Tie it off like this," I said, demonstrating.

"Got it," she said.

"Okay, then you can tie off the rear."

"Yes, captain," she teased.

Mary threw her the rope, and she tied it off like she had been doing it for years.

We unloaded all of our gear.

"Stow this in the boathouse," I said to Lacy, pointing to the tackle and the life jackets.

"You bet," she said enthusiastically.

I picked up the cooler, and Mary grabbed the picnic basket. Lacy stowed the gear and was back in a flash.

"Don," Lacy said.

"Yes."

"I think today is the most fun I ever had," she said reverently.

Her words touched my very soul. In that one sentence, I understood that the thing Lacy was missing most was her childhood.

I glanced at Mary. She was behind Lacy and brushing away a tear. She turned away.

"I'm glad," I said.

"Can we do that again sometime?"

"How about tomorrow?" I asked.

"That would be awesome!" she exclaimed.

She gave me a hug before I knew what was happening.

"I feel yucky," Lacy said a minute later. "I'm going to take a shower. I'll see you-all in a little while."

She turned and ran up the walk, up the stairs that led to the lower desk, up the stairs to the upper deck, and through the back door with the energy only an excited thirteen-year-old could muster.

Mary was beaming at me. "That is one happy girl," she said. She moved close and kissed me gently on the lips. "And you are just an ole softie."

I was that.

30

I returned to work to get some rest. Lacy was a great kid, but all that thirteen-year-old vitality and enthusiasm were like a black hole draining my energy. We had spent Sunday on the lake much like we spent Saturday. We caught fish, soaked up sunrays, ate, drank, and generally enjoyed the day. We did not, however, see Jimmy Durham. I guess he found the missing boat.

We came back to the condo late Sunday night, and I made an early-morning escape to my inner sanctum before the womenfolk stirred. I had made a list of things to do for the day. First on the list was to check the stock market.

On the Street, the Dow Jones Industrial Average was vacillating around twelve thousand, over one day, under the next. I doubted any significant gains in the next year, so I had to be cautious in my investing. The price of gas was worrisome. I was predicting that the market would correct itself and fall under twelve thousand, maybe even below eleven. If gas went beyond four dollars a gallon, the market might very well go under ten.

One area I liked for long-term growth was stem cell research. I had recently purchased significant shares of stock in four different companies specializing in the field. I had little doubt that someday one or two of them would pay off handsomely. The trick was to be patient. As I scanned the listings for those companies I noted minor gains and losses, but so far they were all still in business, a good sign.

The next task on my list was to call Scott Glass. I dialed his direct number at Quantico.

"Smith," said the voice on the other end of the line.

"I was trying to reach Scott Glass," I said.

"Agent Glass no longer works at this location," the voice I knew only as Smith said.

"Can you give me a number where I can reach him?" I asked.

"Sorry, no can do," Smith said. "I was just transferred myself, and I don't know where Agent Glass was relocated."

"No problem," I said. "I'll try his cell phone."

I hung up and dialed Scott's cell phone.

"Hey, Blood, what's happening?" he answered.

"You tell me," I said. "You are not where you're supposed to be."

"I got promoted to special agent in charge of one of our field offices. Want to guess which one? You're going to be jealous."

Scott loved to play these guessing games when he had something special to tell me. I had no idea where all the FBI field offices were, but I would guess in most major cities.

"Sand or snow?" I asked.

"I guess I could say both."

"Denver?"

"Nope."

"Salt Lake City?"

"Bingo!" Scott exclaimed. "Remember that ski trip we took out here when we were in college?"

I was constantly surprised that the FBI had not dulled Scott's enthusiasm.

"Yeah, I remember," I said. "I also remember that you just about got thrown off the basketball team when the coach found out you went skiing. You ran laps forever."

"It was worth it," Scott laughed.

"The skiing or the California girl?"

"The California girl," Scott said. "Damn, I can't even remember her name."

"Karen," I said.

"Karen," Scott sighed. "Right. You never forget anything do you, Don? You have a memory like a portable hard drive."

"A blessing and a curse," I said.

"Well, enough of this," Scott said. "I would have called you in a few days, but you beat me to it. Is this more than a social call?"

I told him the whole Sandy Smith mugging story, complete with my initial participation and Jim Murphy's involvement.

"Can you take a look at the DNA report and see if anything in the FBI computer files matches?"

There was silence on the line. I was waiting for the inevitable argument.

"Sure," Scott said.

"You're not even going to put up a fight?"

"Why bother? In the end, you would just guilt me into doing it," Scott groaned. "Besides, after last time, I consider you a credible source."

The Fairchild case was one I would just as soon forget but couldn't. I remembered every aspect of it. *The curse.*

"Thanks, Professor. I'll attach it to an email."

"No, send it UPS or regular mail," Scott said.

"What's wrong with email?" I asked. "Are you paranoid?"

"Of course I'm paranoid," Scott quipped. "I work for the FBI."

"Are you in Salt Lake City now?"

"Yes," Scott said. "I arrived yesterday."

"Okay, give me the address."

He gave it to me as East 200 South Street.

"I have to go, Don," Scott said. "I am swamped."

"Later, Professor," I said. "And congratulations."

"Thanks, Blood," Scott said. "I'll be in touch."

◆   ◆   ◆   ◆

I left the office and walked to the Mountain Center Diner. It was late morning, and I had not eaten. *Man cannot live on coffee alone,* I thought, *especially with the diner a block or so away.* I wanted a late breakfast, and the diner served breakfast all day—my kind of place. The table where I normally sat still had the Reserved sign on it. I sat. Doris scurried over.

"You're late today, Mr. Youngblood," she smiled.

"I was actually working, and the time just got away from me," I said, picking up the Reserved sign. "I thought you held this table for me only until nine o'clock."

Doris shrugged. "Unless we're busy or someone specifically requests it, I usually don't remove the sign. What'll you have, the usual?"

"The usual sounds fine," I said.

Within minutes, I was devouring a feta cheese omelet with all my usual sides while reading the sports section of the *Knoxville News Sentinel*. The Cincinnati Reds were in first place in the National League's Central Division, a phenomena I knew would never last. Other than that, nothing very interesting was going on.

Doris came back with more coffee.

"Got a minute, Doris?" I asked.

"Sure, Mr. Youngblood. What do you need?"

"Sit down a second."

She sat, and I told her about how Lacy had come into my life.

"I was hoping she could work here part-time, maybe during the lunch hour," I said. "What do you think?"

"Well, sure," Doris said. "We'll give it a try. I can't afford to pay much. How about seven dollars an hour, and she can keep all her tips?"

"Cash," I said. "No records."

I was sure thirteen-year-olds were not supposed to have real jobs, even if it was part-time and even if we were in the hills of East Tennessee. However, I did know the chief of police personally, and the government agencies that might be interested had more important things to do than investigate thirteen-year-olds with part-time jobs. Besides, Lacy would soon be fourteen; she looked sixteen, and most of the time she acted like an adult.

"Sure," Doris winked. "I understand. Nobody is going to say anything anyway."

"I'm sure Lacy will be fine with seven dollars an hour and tips," I said. "Can you afford that?"

"Sure," Doris said. "We should be able to turn tables faster and make a little more money at lunch. Not that I need more money, you understand."

"I understand, Doris," I said. "You run this diner because it's your life, but having a little extra help wouldn't be a bad idea, would it?"

"Now that you mention it, I think it's a good idea," Doris beamed. "Have Lacy come by just before closing one day this week, and I'll show her the ropes. She can start as soon as school is out."

"Thanks, Doris," I said. "You're the best."

"Oh, Mr. Youngblood," Doris said, blushing as she rose to get back to work. "You do go on."

She bustled away with coffeepot in hand in search of an empty cup.

31

Stanley Johns lived just south of the heart of downtown Mountain Center in a quiet older section known as "the Tree District." Think of a common tree, and you would probably find its name on a street sign in the Tree District. Stanley lived at 418 West Locust Street in the modest two-story house his grandparents had built and where he had grown up. He was an odd little man I had befriended in high school. Short and round with dark, curly hair and a raspy, high-pitched voice, Stanley may have been the original geek. He was shy and sensitive, with an innocence found only in small children. In high school, Stanley was a flop in English, health, geography, psychology, and social studies, recording Cs and Ds and driving his teachers up the proverbial wall. Stanley, however, was a whiz in the sciences and math, and I was not surprised that he turned out to be a computer genius.

With the advent of the Internet, Stanley had a whole new world to explore. Had he wanted to, he could have been a world-class hacker. Instead, he turned his considerable talents toward writing anti-virus programs and became part owner of a software company. Stanley was one of the kings in the realm of virus protection.

I pulled in behind Stanley's ancient blue Chevy Malibu. My attempts to persuade him to purchase a new vehicle had been futile, so I had long since promised myself not to mention it. I got out of the Pathfinder and proceeded down the walkway on the left side of the house to the basement entrance that led to Stanley's computer domain. Going to the front door was a waste of time and energy. Stanley rarely was upstairs to answer the front door. I pushed the buzzer on the back door. While I waited, I stared at the small, yet tasteful, Software Unlimited sign. Eventually, Stanley would open the door. I had called him earlier that morning to let him know I was coming.

A minute later, the back door opened.

"Don," Stanley said with the exuberance of a child, "come in, come in."

"It's good to see you again, Stanley," I said. "It's been awhile."

I entered an outer room much like the reception area in a doctor's office. It was nicely decorated and had a desk for a receptionist yet to be hired. *Not unlike Cherokee Investigations*, I thought.

Directly opposite the back door was the entrance to Stanley's computer domain. I walked past a sign on the door that read "Oz," a gift from me. When it came to computers, Stanley Johns was the Wizard. Everywhere I looked, monitors, hard drives, and printers blinked, hummed, and whirred on various worktables in Stanley's twenty-by-twenty-five-foot world. Scanners, a few table lamps, Stanley's desk, a few chairs, bookshelves, and a huge mainframe computer occupied the rest of the space. The lighting was subdued and peaceful, and soft jazz played through multiple speakers spread around the room.

"It's good to see you, too, Don," Stanley said. "I haven't seen you since that awful business with Sarah Ann Fleet. You resolved that, I take it."

"I did," I said. "And before you ask, it's better that you don't know how."

"Right," Stanley said. "So what can I do for you this time?"

I told Stanley about Lacy.

"Her mother just ran off and left her?" Stanley exclaimed. "That's terrible."

"Well, we found Lacy's mother, and now we're getting her some help, so things might work out," I said.

"What can I do?" Stanley asked.

"Let Lacy work with you a couple of hours a day," I said. "She seems to have an aptitude for computers, and I think she is very smart. It would be for just the summer."

I could see the wheels turning in Stanley's head. On the one hand, he was a loner with limited social skills. People generally frightened Stanley. Lacy would be good for him in that respect. On the other hand, Stanley did not want to disappoint me by saying no, and so he was trying to work out how he could use a thirteen-year-old for two hours a day.

"Okay," Stanley said. "We'll try it for a couple of weeks to see if it works. If she does okay, she can stay the rest of the summer. I'll start her off at ten dollars an hour and raise her to twelve if she works out. I'll have to pay her cash. It will be kind of an unofficial job, since she's not fourteen."

"You know the law?" I asked.

"Sure," Stanley said. "The minimum age for a child working in Tennessee is fourteen. She can work forty hours a week during the summer and eighteen while going to school."

Stanley the businessman. I was very impressed.

"Thanks, Stanley," I said as I rose and headed for the door. "I'll bring Lacy around next week and introduce you."

I could tell Stanley was anxious for me to leave. He liked short visits.

I guess he thought some of those nasty computer viruses might escape and destroy the world while his back was turned.

"Bye, Don," I heard him say as he shut and locked the door behind me.

◆   ◆   ◆   ◆

That evening, we were sitting at the kitchen island eating takeout Chinese. I was having a beer and Lacy a diet soda. Mary was working second shift.

"Two jobs?" Lacy asked as she downed a wonton.

I couldn't tell whether she was excited or annoyed.

"They're both part-time," I said, putting my best spin on the two-job parlay while snaring a sesame shrimp. "Each is a few hours a day. One job, you get to work on your people skills. The other, you get to work on your computer skills."

"I guess that makes sense," Lacy said as she chop-sticked some fried rice into her mouth. She was warming up to the idea. "What do I get paid?" she asked.

I told her as I forked another shrimp and some broccoli. I never could get the hang of chopsticks—too much work.

"That's pretty good," she said as another wonton bit the dust. "I'll be the richest kid in my class."

"Best to downplay the rich kid thing, since you won't be fourteen until August," I said.

The food was disappearing fast.

"How did you know my birthday was in August?"

I gave her my best stare and knowing smile as I took a long drink of my Sam Adams Light.

"Right," she said. "You saw my birth certificate, and you remembered."

Lacy was a quick study.

"So what do you think?" I asked.

"I like it," she said, saluting me with her Diet Coke.

32

S oon after I arrived at the office the next day, the phone rang, inter-rupting the early-morning quiet and my first cup of coffee. *This better be important*, I thought. Caller ID was blocked.

"Cherokee Investigations," I answered.

"Stay put," Big Bob said. "I'll be there in a few minutes."

I opened my mouth to say something, but the line was long dead.

Five minutes later, the big man walked into the outer office, poured himself a cup of coffee, and came into my inner sanctum. He plopped his large frame down in one of the oversized chairs facing my desk. When you have friends as large as Big Bob and Billy, you better have oversized chairs in your office.

"Nice of you to make coffee," he said, taking a sip.

"You're lucky," I said. "Most days, I pick up."

"I really like this chair," Big Bob said. "I think I could get used to coming over here every morning for a cup of coffee."

"You didn't come for the coffee," I said. "What's up?"

"Mountain Center PD and the county sheriff's department are going to take down a meth lab out in the county in a couple of days," he said. "Could be dangerous. Naturally, I thought you would like to come along. Jimmy will temporarily deputize you for the occasion."

"Mary part of this?" I asked.

"She wants to be," Big Bob said. "And frankly, she is one of the best shots on the force, with one of the coolest heads. I'd be stupid not to take her."

"Then I'm in," I said.

"Hell, you'd be in anyway," he grinned.

He was right, of course.

"Still have one of those tranquilizer pistols from last year's excursion?"

"I do," I said.

"Got the darts for it?"

"I do," I said, "but I don't know if the sedative has lost any of its punch or not. We best not gamble on that. I can get fresh darts."

"Good," Big Bob said. "We can use the pistol, and fresh darts would be a good idea."

"Tell me about that," I said.

Big Bob laid out the plan. A lab out in the woods on private property in the far reaches of the county was producing large amounts of methamphetamine. It was well protected and well organized. Jimmy Durham had gotten a tip about it, and he and a deputy had scouted it out from a well-hidden spot in the woods. They had taken a lot of pictures with Jimmy's digital camera in order to convince a judge to sign a search warrant. The judge was told that the pictures came from a private citizen. Whether he believed that little white lie or not didn't matter. He signed the warrant.

A trail through the woods led to the lab, and an armed guard with a walkie-talkie at the mouth of the trail would alert the lab if anyone came snooping. The lab was set up in a big log cabin. Eight to ten people were probably inside at any one time, and the operation seemed to be 24/7. Most of the occupants carried guns. There very well could be a firefight.

"We need the element of surprise," Big Bob said. "Who would you pick to get close enough to the guard to take him out with that pistol?"

"Billy," I said. Billy moved as effortlessly and quietly as a big cat.

"My thinking exactly," Big Bob said. "Will you talk to him?"

"No problem," I said. "If I'm going, then he will want to go to look out for me. Besides, he hates illegal drugs and anything connected to them. He would take the place out by himself if you'd let him."

"Don't tempt me," the big man said.

"I'll talk to Billy," I said. "When do we go?"

"We'll go in two or three days, so get those new darts here as fast as you can," Big Bob said.

◆   ◆   ◆   ◆

A few minutes after Big Bob left, I was on the phone.

"You want what?" Raul said after our usual greeting.

"You heard me," I said.

Raul Rivera was a longtime friend from my college days who I had stayed in touch with over the years. Raul was good looking, rich, and single. Last year, he had helped me close the Fairchild case. Raul was on that short list of friends who I knew would do anything for me. I had hopes that Roy Husky was going to make that list.

"What are you into now?" Raul asked.

I told him.

"Sounds dangerous," he said.

"Billy will be watching my back," I said.

"And exciting," he added.

"Maybe," I said.

"And a very noble venture," he continued.

Raul also hated drugs. He was from Colombia, South America. People always took for granted that a rich Colombian was involved in drugs.

"Will you do it?"

"Of course, Donnie," Raul said. "I'll get them out today, and you will have them tomorrow. Send the old ones back to me, please."

"Will do, Raul," I said. "And thanks."

33

E arly in the morning three days later, we parked in and around a deserted barn on land owned by someone Jimmy Durham knew who was angry that a meth lab was on property bordering his. I didn't count heads, but we must have had fifteen to twenty law-enforcement officers on the scene. Only two were women, one being Mary. We were dressed like a SWAT team—all black, with protective vests. Billy and I had on our headsets that we had used during last year's Fairchild adventure. I gave the third headset to Big Bob. The headsets would allow us to communicate up to a range of five miles. I had my all-black gear from last year, so all I needed from the MCPD was a vest.

The day was dark and overcast. Rain had been promised, but so far none had fallen. We had at least a two-mile hike, maybe more. We met in the barn for final instructions. Jimmy and Big Bob stood above the rest of us in the bed of an ancient pickup truck that had not seen the light of day in who knew how long. A murmur permeated the barn.

"Let me have your attention," Jimmy Durham said in his country-boy drawl.

The barn went quiet.

"This is a joint operation between the sheriff's department and the Mountain Center PD. I appreciate the help of Chief Wilson and his staff and a couple of qualified civilian temporary deputies. I think most of you know who Don Youngblood and Billy Two-Feathers are, and we thank them for participating."

There was some nodding, some murmuring, and a few gentle back-slaps in approval of our help. Purposely, Mary stood with a female deputy on the other side of the group from Billy and me. She did not look my way.

"I am now going to turn this gathering over to Chief Wilson," Jimmy Durham drawled. "Chief."

"Thanks, Jimmy," Big Bob said. "We're here to take down a meth lab. From what Jimmy tells me, it's a big one. East Tennessee has a reputation of being a major methamphetamine factory. We're going to put a dent in that today when we take down this operation, which is housed in a large cabin deep in the woods a few miles from here. You might even know a few of the occupants, but remember that whoever is in there is on the wrong side of the law. Some are just dumb hillbillies looking for a fast buck, others are illegals working for peanuts, and last but not least are a few pros managing the whole thing. It's the pros I am most worried about. They will shoot first and ask questions later, so watch your butts. One more thing, do not get trigger-happy. Do not fire unless they come out firing. They might fire a few rounds at us from inside the cabin, just to see how serious we are and how many men we have. Let's keep them guessing."

Another murmur came from the group. A few rechecked their weapons. I caught Mary's eye from across the room. She gave me a slight smile and a wink. I knew she was feeling the rush. I was feeling it myself.

"We have some hiking to do," Big Bob said.

There was a collective groan.

"Billy will go ahead of us and take out the guard. Sheriff Durham observed through his surveillance that the guard gets a call every half-hour. Billy will wait until we reach our staging area. After we reach the staging area, Billy will take him out as soon as he gets his next call. After the guard is out, we will have to hustle to get to the cabin and get in position before the next call. When they call and don't get an answer, they will know something is up. Any questions?"

There were none. I looked at Billy and nodded. We turned our headsets on. Big Bob was not yet wearing his. Billy turned and walked out of the barn. I noticed four knives strapped to the back of his protective vest. He still refused to carry a gun.

The group left the barn ten minutes later. We made the trek through the woods single file to a stopping point out of view of the guard and waited to hear from Billy. He came over my headset a few minutes later.

"The deer has been spotted," he said. "Waiting for a good shot."

"Good luck," I said.

On the odd chance that anyone could pick up our channel, we were just two hunters out to bag a deer. Better safe than sorry. I wondered if it *was* deer season. Not being a hunter, I had no idea.

Fifteen minutes later, Billy was back in my headset.

"The deer is down and dressed," he said.

"Good work," I said. "Coming to your location."

Big Bob still did not have his headset on, and I saw no sign he even had it with him. Why did I bother giving it to him? I nodded to him, and he led us out. Jimmy Durham followed. I went next. Mary was somewhere near the middle of the pack. We double-timed it through the woods toward the cabin.

◆   ◆   ◆   ◆

The cabin was in a sort of bowl that had been cleared out in the middle of the woods, surrounded by thickly wooded slopes on all sides. I was sure the location was picked because it was hard to see unless you were practically on top of it. But it also gave us a distinct advantage if a firefight broke out.

As planned, we went in quickly and quietly and surrounded the cabin. Everyone had good cover.

Jimmy Durham turned on his bullhorn.

"You, inside the cabin," the bullhorn blared. "Throw out your weapons and come out with your hands up. You are surrounded."

The log shutters on the windows on either side of the front door flew open, and bursts of automatic weapons fire sprayed the forest. As we had been instructed, we held our fire, every last man and woman. I was a bit surprised. It showed a lot of discipline. Of course, I would have hated to be the man or woman who failed to follow Big Bob Wilson's instructions.

The firing from inside the cabin stopped.

"I repeat," Jimmy Durham said through the bullhorn, "throw out your weapons and come out with your hands up."

More weapons fire sprayed the forest. I hoped everyone was keeping his or her head down.

Big Bob in frustration grabbed the bullhorn from Jimmy Durham.

"This is Chief Wilson from Mountain Center," he said in anger. "You got one minute to throw out your weapons and get your butts out here, or I'm going to blow that drug-infested crap hole to kingdom come."

A few seconds later, a voice cried out, "We got children in here!"

"Collateral damage," Big Bob said into the bullhorn. "Forty-five seconds."

Another voice cried, "We got a pregnant women in here!"

"Just one more of you little dope dealers who doesn't get born," Big Bob blurted over the bullhorn. "Thirty seconds."

Then, so everyone could hear, he said, "Sean, get me that grenade launcher up here."

Ten seconds later, an AK-47 assault rifle came flying out the window, follow by an Uzi, then a shower of various handguns.

"Don't shoot!" a voice from inside the cabin said. "We're coming out."

A procession of nine men and two women walked through the door. Neither of the women appeared pregnant. No children were among the occupants.

"Get down on the ground with your hands behind your backs," Big Bob said over the bullhorn. "If I find anyone left inside that cabin," he continued, "I am going to shoot them on the spot."

"Don't shoot!" a lone voice from inside the cabin shouted in heavily accented English. "I'm coming out."

Another Uzi sailed out the window on the right-hand side of the cabin, and a final occupant emerged with his hands over his head.

A few seconds later, I heard Billy's voice in my headset. "Blood, I'm in the cabin," he said. "It's clear."

I relayed the message to Big Bob.

"Listen, everyone," he said, still using the bullhorn. "The cabin is clear. Billy is inside. Repeat, the cabin is clear. Secure the prisoners."

"Officer down!" I heard someone yell.

Off to my right, two Mountain Center police officers were bent over a prone figure. The blond hair was unmistakable. My heart went to my throat and back down again as I saw the officers help Mary to a sitting position.

"She's okay!" one yelled.

I covered the distance between us in seconds and yelled, "Out of my way!" as I knelt beside her.

She had a pained look on her face. "Ribs," she groaned, as if the words were painful to get out. "Must have been a ricochet. Get me on my feet."

I helped her up, but I could tell it was painful.

"Thank God for this vest," she said.

Big Bob, Jimmy Durham, and Billy walked toward us. Big Bob was barking orders. He had a walkie-talkie in his hand.

"Joe, you and Sam bring one of the vans and my SUV to the trail-head," Big Bob said into the walkie-talkie. "Leave the SUV with the keys in it and go back and get the other van. You copy?"

"Yeah, we copy, chief," came the reply.

"Sean, you drive Don and Mary to the medical center," the big man ordered. "I want Mary checked out."

Sean Wilson nodded.

"Billy, start taking pictures," Big Bob said. "You're on the clock now."

Billy nodded and walked off toward the cabin, removing his camera from a fanny pack.

"Jimmy, keep everybody outside until Billy is finished," Big Bob said. "Then have your guys inventory the place."

"Will do," Jimmy said, not the least bit concerned that Big Bob had apparently taken over his operation.

Mary waited patiently, but I could tell she was in pain.

"Get her out of here," Big Bob ordered with the wave of a hand.

* ◆ ◆ ◆

Sean drove, and I rode shotgun. The walk from the cabin to the SUV was obviously excruciating for Mary, but she made it in silence. Mary was spread out in the backseat trying to get as comfortable as possible. The road out could have been navigated only by an SUV. Sean took it as easy as he could, but there was no way to make the ride smooth.

"Fuck," Mary said as the SUV took a particularly hard bounce.

"Is that cop talk?" I said, trying to lighten the moment.

"Sorry," she said, then added, "God damn it, Sean, take it easy."

"Sorry, Mary," Sean said. "I'm doing the best I can. We're just about to the main road."

I saw a tear escape, but she refused to cry. Mary Sanders was as tough as any man. She endured in silence.

Once we reached the main road, the ride was smoother and faster. Sean hit the switch for the siren and the lights and drove like he'd had lessons from his older brother, Big Bob.

34

The Mountain Center Medical Center was new. It had replaced the old hospital less that a year ago. Sean called ahead to alert the staff that he was bringing an injured officer in, and Mary received the VIP treatment from the time we arrived. Sean left me sitting outside one of the examining rooms and went back to the meth cabin. Mary was in with the doctor on call. His nametag said he was Dr. Evan Smith.

A few minutes later, she was sent to x-ray in a wheelchair.

"Wait here," she said. "I'll be back in a few minutes." She sounded a little groggy.

I called Lacy at school and caught her just before she got on the bus. I explained what had happened.

"Is she going to be okay?" Lacy asked with concern.

"She is going to be fine," I said. "I don't think they'll keep her overnight. We should be home for dinner. Do your homework when you get in. That way, you can help me with Mary later."

"I will," she said. "Wow, a shootout."

Mary was coming back down the hall as I hung up with Lacy. The young Dr. Smith was giving her a lot of personal attention. He stopped her chair in front of me and locked the wheels.

"We'll wait for the x-ray, and then she can go," he said. "I do not think the rib is broken. It might have a hairline fracture, though. There is a lot of bruising, and she is going to be extremely sore for a few days. I have given her a shot for the pain."

He handed me a slip of paper.

"Pain meds. You can take this to the pharmacy and get it filled while we wait for the x-ray," he said. "We should have it by the time you get back. Go to the end of this hall, take a left, and then go all the way down, and it's on the right. You can't miss it."

I nodded. Dr. Smith turned and walked back toward X-Ray. I looked at Mary. She had a dreamy look on her face.

"You okay?" I asked.

"Tired," she said. "Whatever they gave me is making me sleepy, but I don't hurt as much. I didn't get much sleep last night, you know. I was revved up for the takedown."

"Wait here," I said. "I'll be right back."

As I was coming back with the pain meds—four days' worth of Percocet—Dr. Smith was coming out of X-Ray. He saw me and stopped and waited. He had the x-ray.

"No broken ribs," he said, holding it up to the light. "Looks like a hairline fracture on this rib here."

He removed a ballpoint pen from his pocket and pointed to a spot on the x-ray. I couldn't tell much, but I did see the tiny white line showing through all the variations of gray.

"It should heal fine in a few weeks," he said. "You can take her home now. Be sure she gets plenty of rest and takes it easy."

"I'll do that," I said.

He reached into the pocket of his white coat and removed a plastic baggie and held it up for me to see. Inside was a bullet in pristine condition.

"I removed this from the vest with forceps," he said. "I thought you might want it."

I nodded and took it from him. We shook hands.

"Thanks, doctor," I said.

An orderly wheeled Mary to the front door amid protests that she could walk by herself.

♦   ♦   ♦   ♦

Lacy took charge when we got back to the condo. She led Mary up the stairs and down the hall to our room and helped her get out of her uniform. I was told to get lost, so I waited in the kitchen. I booted up my laptop and went online.

Fifteen minutes later, Lacy was back.

"She's asleep," Lacy said. "Whatever they gave her knocked her out good. Want me to fix dinner?"

"Let's order takeout," I said. "No sense messing up the kitchen."

"Pizza sounds good," Lacy said. "We haven't had pizza in a while."

So we ordered pizza.

♦   ♦   ♦   ♦

Later that night, I sat at the kitchen counter cleaning the Beretta. I had not fired it, and it did not need to be cleaned, but I needed something to do. For the second time in less than a year, I had almost lost Mary. I was a little shook up thinking about it. Lacy was in her room finishing her homework. A few minutes later, she came quietly down the stairs and into the kitchen. She stared wide-eyed at the Beretta. Mary and I had already given Lacy the gun lecture, and Mary had promised to take Lacy to the firing range someday to let her shoot. We could not ignore the fact that we each had guns, knew how to fire them, and used them in our jobs.

"Did you shoot anybody today?" she asked cautiously.

"No, I didn't," I said, finishing my work. "I'm happy to say that I didn't fire my weapon."

"Good," she said.

"Shooting people is no fun," I said.

She was quiet.

"Taking a human life is about the worst thing you can do," I said.

She looked at the floor. I should learn to keep my thoughts to myself, I knew. I didn't need to be talking about such things to Lacy. She had enough to worry about.

"I guess so," she said, "but sometimes it has to be done, right?"

"Right," I said with a sigh. "It's been a long day. Time for bed."

Lacy turned and started for the stairs.

"Good night, Don," she said.

"Good night," I said.

When I heard her door close, I slapped a full clip into the butt of the Beretta and took it down to the laundry room and locked it in the gun safe. A few minutes later, I slipped into bed beside Mary. She was sleeping peacefully, but I knew the next few days would be rough.

◆　　◆　　◆　　◆

The next morning, I walked into the Mountain Center Police Station with bagels and Dunkin' Donuts coffee. It was early, but the big man was in his office. I entered and set the bag on his desk and sat down in front of him. He looked at me and then opened the bag.

"This is a rarity," Big Bob said, removing the bounty from the bag. "What's the occasion?"

"A reward for a job well done," I said, removing the lid from my cup of coffee.

"Remind me to bust more meth labs," Big Bob said, taking a bite of bagel loaded with cream cheese. "How's Mary?"

"She'll be okay," I said. "She was still asleep when I left. Lacy is staying home with her today."

"How is that working out?"

"So far, so good," I said.

"Umm," the big man uttered as he ate more bagel.

"How long were you out there?" I asked.

"My crew left around five o'clock. Jimmy's crew stayed and wrapped things up."

I drank some coffee and had a large bite of my own bagel. I tossed the baggie with the bullet inside on Big Bob's desk.

"From Mary's vest," I said.

He picked it up and stared at it.

"Clean," he said. "We should be able to get some good ballistics from this. If the weapon that fired this has fingerprints on it, I'll make sure attempted murder is added to the charges of the son of a bitch who fired it."

"Probably won't stick," I said, "but no harm in trying."

35

A couple of weeks went by and nothing happened, and I mean nothing. The phone didn't ring, and no one came through my office door looking for a crack private investigator. I picked the phone up a few times to see if it was working. It was.

Mary recovered nicely and was back to work. We spent some time at the lake house to avoid her going crazy cooped up in the condo. It was a good decision. Lacy spent a few nights with her friend Hannah.

I took advantage of the lull to thin out old files and generally straighten up my office. I even cleaned. Not very manly, but what's a bored PI to do? Billy came and went but did not stay at the office. He spent some time in his little art studio and a lot of time in Cherokee. *I might have to investigate Billy*, I thought.

I reviewed every file for every client for whom I handled investments. Many were pro bono. The others had been with me since the early days and had given me the opportunity to make lots of money. I felt a loyalty to them. A few dozen had basically said I could handle their accounts from Timbuktu, for all they cared. Wall Street or Tennessee, it didn't make any difference to them. I made a few purchases and a few sales. I generated and mailed reports. I sent and received emails.

Late in the afternoon on the fourth day, when I was so bored I could hardly stand it, the phone rang. I didn't bother to check caller ID. I would have been glad to talk to even a telemarketer.

"Cherokee Investigations," I answered in my very best radio voice.

"Damn," Scott Glass said. "For a minute there, I thought I was listening to a TV news anchor."

"Thanks," I said. "I've been working hard on that voice."

"Impressive," Scott teased.

"I'll bet you didn't call just to harass me," I said. "I hope you finally have some news."

"Sorry, we've been backed up," Scott said. "I have news, and I want to know your secret."

"What secret?"

"How have you managed for the second time in a little over a year to stumble upon a guy we're looking for?" Scott asked.

"You're looking for Roger Allen?" I asked incredulously.

"Not exactly," Scott said. "We are looking for a serial killer who has the exact same DNA as your alias Roger Allen."

"A serial killer?" I asked. "You're putting me on, right?"

"I wish I were," Scott said. "Got time for the whole story?"

"I do," I said.

Scott spun his tale. He took great joy in it, using dramatic voice inflections and pregnant pauses in the right places to build the suspense. I could not believe what I was hearing. About fifteen years ago in San Diego, a single woman in her twenties had been murdered late at night in the parking lot of her condominium complex. She was severely beaten. Cause of death was a broken neck. There were no witnesses. The only suspect was a boyfriend who the woman's friends had heard of but never seen. He was possessive, they said, and she wanted to break it off but was afraid of him. They could not remember his name—Randy, maybe. The boyfriend was never found, and no one knew what he looked like. Unidentifiable hairs at the scene were bagged.

Three years later in Los Angeles, also late at night, a similar murder had occurred in the garage of an apartment complex. A single woman in her late twenties with a mysterious, possessive boyfriend was badly beaten. Cause of death was a severely fractured skull. Skin samples underneath her fingernails were saved. Her closest friend thought the boyfriend's name was Rick or Richard.

Three more years passed, and another murder with a similar MO occurred in San Francisco in the garage of a shopping mall. Again the victim was a single woman, this time in her early thirties. She was beaten and strangled. No forensic evidence or reference to the boyfriend was found at the scene, but the victim was new to San Francisco. A sharp, computer-wise detective first grade made the connection to the San Diego and Los Angeles murders and called a friend at the FBI. Subsequent DNA analysis revealed a match between the hairs of the San Diego killing and the skin samples from the Los Angeles killing. The suspect went into the FBI files as an unknown serial killer and was soon forgotten as other matters took precedence.

"We found similar killings in Phoenix and Denver in the last six years," Scott said. "The Denver killing was two years ago."

"Think it was the same guy?" I asked.

"The first two, I would say definitely," Scott said. "The same DNA at both scenes is pretty overwhelming evidence. The others are hard to tell without DNA evidence. The San Francisco, Phoenix, and Denver cases had no mention of a boyfriend, and they all appeared to be muggings. We will look into those further."

My head was spinning. *A serial killer*, I thought. *Billions of people on the planet, and I sucker-punched a serial killer.* I had seen it in his eyes but did not realize at the time that what I was observing was a cold-blooded killer. I felt a chill that had nothing to do with the air conditioning.

"You still with me?" Scott asked.

"Yeah, I'm here," I said meekly.

"I'm reopening this case," Scott said. "I need you to get out here and work with my artist on a facial."

"Damn," I said.

"What?"

"I took pictures," I said. "I forgot all about them. I was going to give them to Jim Murphy. They're on my digital camera."

"How many?"

"Two or three," I said. "I never even looked at them."

"I need them ASAP," Scott said excitedly. "It would be real nice if I could crack this thing right after being promoted. I would owe you big time."

"The camera is at the condo," I said. "I'll bring it in early tomorrow morning and download the images to my desktop and email them to you. Unless of course you're so paranoid you want me to mail the camera to you."

"Email is fine," Scott said. "But use my personal email address."

"FBI geek at AOL dot com?" I asked.

"No, wiseass," Scott chuckled. "My Yahoo address. You have that, right?"

"I've got it," I said.

"Call me before you email," Scott said. "I'll be in early."

Totally paranoid, I thought.

"Okay, J. Edgar," I said. "I'll call you in the morning."

36

I was in the office early the next morning with my digital camera. I downloaded the photos of Roger Allen to my picture file on my office PC. In my opinion, they were not very good. I had taken them from a distance, and even though I had used maximum zoom the face of Roger Allen was still relatively small. I had three pictures, and none was full face. I knew the FBI had very sophisticated software, but I was skeptical about how close it could come to the actual face of Roger Allen. Well, at least the FBI had a couple of eyewitnesses who had seen Roger up close and personal.

I transferred the pictures to a ZIP file and booted AOL, then attached the file to an email and called Scott.

"Good morning, Blood," Scott said.

"Good morning, Professor," I said. "Don't you just hate caller ID sometimes?"

"I know what you mean," he said. "But officially, we at the FBI love caller ID."

"No big surprise," I said. "I'm ready to email you the pictures. I have three of them. You ready?"

"Ready," Scott said.

"Sending," I said.

"Got 'em," Scott said seconds later. "Hang on."

I took a drink of coffee that was about ten minutes old but still warm enough to be enjoyable. I could hear Scott mumbling to himself.

"Not too bad," he said. "I think we can work with these. When we're finished, I'll email you a head shot and see what you think."

"Any ideas on how you're going to proceed with this?" I asked.

"Well, since he left witnesses who can now identify him, I'm thinking he will try to leave the country," Scott said. "He might figure out that we have matched his DNA to some of the old murders. Serial killers are inherently smart. That's why they get away with so many killings before they're caught, if they're caught."

"He is probably long gone," I said.

"No doubt," Scott said. "But we can review tapes from Homeland Security at major airports and ports of call and hope we get lucky."

"That's a lot of tape," I said. "It will take forever."

Scott laughed. "It's faster than you think, it's all done by computer. You program the face with the tapes, and the computer will bring up a likeness, date, and location."

"Live and learn," I said.

"Gotta go, Blood. I'll be in touch."

"Later, Professor." I hung up.

If Roger Allen—an alias, I was certain—had left the country, he probably fled to a place where extradition laws were loose or nonexistent. So how would the FBI get him back? And if they couldn't get him back, how would good ole Roger get the justice he deserved?

Forget it, Youngblood, I thought. *You've been there and done that.*

◆　◆　◆　◆

The call from Scott came later in the day. It was without preamble.

"I am sending you an email attachment now," Scott said.

He sounded serious, so I kept a lid on the smart remarks and tried to remain professional.

"Online and standing by," I said.

"You've got mail," Madonna said, *AOL celebrity voice.*

"Who was that?" Scott said.

"Madonna," I said. "New office assistant."

"Bullshit," Scott said. "Look at the picture."

I did. I clicked "Download Now" and "Open File" and was staring into the face of the man I knew as Roger Allen.

"Bingo!" I said.

"What?"

"You guys nailed it. That's the guy. At least the way I remember him."

"Good," Scott said. "We're going to find this guy, Blood. When we do, I'll let you know. You stay out of it, okay?"

"Sure, Professor," I said. "Besides, I would have no idea where to start looking for him."

"Where have I heard that before?" Scott said.

◆　　◆　　◆　　◆

As the day slipped away, I managed to stay busy. I called T. Elbert at five o'clock and invited myself over for cocktail hour. We sat on his front porch on a warm, muggy day with two cold beers and watched an occasional car go by on his quiet street. Summer was fast approaching. The wind had taken the day off—not even a hint of a breeze. I was constantly longing for winter. I had never enjoyed summer. I just survived it.

"What's on your mind?" T. Elbert asked.

"What makes you think something is on my mind?" I replied.

"You usually come visiting in the morning. You coming over for a beer means something is going on."

We were quiet for a while. T. Elbert would throw things out there and then wait for a reaction. He was a patient, thoughtful man.

"Ever track a serial killer?" I asked.

"Serial killer?" T. Elbert exclaimed, straightening up in his wheelchair and leaning toward me with undivided attention. "Tell me about it."

I told him. He listened without interruption.

"So what is it you really need for me to hear?" T. Elbert asked with an unblinking stare.

I paused and took a breath.

"I should have had the son of a bitch," I said. "If I had tailed him, the cops might have nabbed him before he left town. Now he's out there, and he'll probably kill again."

"Not your fault," T. Elbert said. "If that's what you want to hear. And it's the truth. You couldn't have known. You handled it exactly how I would have handled it."

We were silent for a while.

"Thanks," I said.

"Let the FBI handle it. They have the resources, and from what you tell me your friend Scott seems motivated."

"Okay," I said reluctantly.

"I hear a *but*," T. Elbert said.

"But what if they find him in a place where they can't touch him?"

"Then," T. Elbert smiled, "it will be time for Youngblood and Company."

37

Midmorning a few weeks later, I was in my office with my feet up on my desk, leaning back in my chair and staring out my office window at the street below. Nothing much had happened except that the days had gotten longer, hotter, and muggier. I had done my usual investing things, kept in touch with Billy, Roy, T. Elbert, and Big Bob, frequented the Mountain Center Diner, and even managed to rendezvous with Mary a few times. Finding time alone with Mary was getting harder and harder. I was considering putting a bed in the office.

Mary had been through some excitement at work. A good ole boy robber wearing a Bill Clinton mask had successfully hit three area convenience stores over a seven-day period, until his beat-up pickup truck had a flat tire as he was making his escape from convenience store number four. Mary and Sean Wilson made the arrest three blocks from the store as the perpetrator attempted to change the flat. He wasn't too hard to identify. He still had the mask on. He was also on crack and higher than a kite.

Lacy had started her two jobs. Doris raved about her every time I came in for breakfast. At dinner, Lacy told funny tales about her Mountain Center Diner experiences. But it was Stanley Johns and his Land of Oz that really fascinated Lacy. She and Stanley had obviously bonded.

But I was still surprised when Stanley called. Stanley phoned me at the office about as often as Halley's comet passed earth. The ringing phone snapped me back to the present.

"Don," Stanley said without introduction. "Lacy is really working out. Her probationary period is over. She can work for me for the remainder of the summer."

Stanley the consummate employer.

"That's good to hear, Stanley," I said.

"She is very smart," Stanley said excitedly. "I think she should pursue a career in the computer field."

"She's thirteen, Stanley," I said. "I think it's a little early for her to be making career choices, but I appreciate your insight."

"You're right, of course," Stanley said, sounding embarrassed. "I'm getting way ahead of myself. Anyway, I just wanted you to know. She is very bright."

"Thanks for letting me know, Stanley."

"Right," Stanley said. "Anyway, how is her mother doing?"

"Okay, I guess," I said. "I haven't checked on her lately. All I know is what Lacy tells me."

"Well, then. Okay," Stanley said, struggling with the social aspects of conversation. "I have to go now. Bye, Don."

"Goodbye, Stanley," I said.

I stared at the fish swimming on my computer screen. The screen-saver program made them look as real as if they were in an aquarium. I thought about Stanley's call for a minute, then picked up the phone and called Sister Sarah Agnes.

"Hello," she said in that tightly controlled voice she always used at work.

"Hello yourself," I said.

"Well, hello, Don. How are things in your world?"

"Quiet," I said. "With a few surprises."

"Tell me."

I did. I started with Lacy and her part-time jobs, told her about Mary and her collar, and finished with Roger Allen.

"Jesus, Joseph, and Mary," Sarah Agnes said. "A real-live serial killer. Don, I think you're in the wrong line of work."

"It sort of looks that way, doesn't it?"

"You're going to let the FBI handle Roger Allen, aren't you?" Sarah Agnes asked sternly.

"As long as Roger gets the justice he deserves," I said.

Then I abruptly changed the subject before she could give me a lecture.

"How is your patient?" I asked.

"She is doing very well, thank you. She seemed in no hurry to leave, so I gave her a job working in the office. I am way behind in my record keeping, and Tracy is putting our old paper records on CDs and doing other odd jobs that I require. She is a fast study. If she stays awhile longer, my records will be the envy of my peers."

"Do you think she will ever be able to resume motherhood?" I asked.

"Maybe," Sarah Agnes said. "But it is going to take awhile. We have a session every day, but progress is slow. Something is buried deep that I cannot get to. She herself might not even know what it is."

"Anything you can share?" I asked.

"I am walking a very tight line here, Don. I cannot say too much."

"Okay, let me phrase it another way," I said. "Is there anything I can do to help?"

There was silence on the other end. I knew Sister Sarah Agnes was thinking, weighing the confidentiality aspects versus the good of the patient.

"Did you know she lived in West Virginia until she was about fifteen or so?"

"No, I didn't," I said.

"It popped out in casual conversation. You might look into that," Sarah Agnes said reluctantly. "Now she doesn't want to talk about West Virginia. She says she doesn't remember much of it. How much do you remember about the first fifteen years of your life?"

"Quite a bit," I said.

"Exactly!" Sarah Agnes said. "Something happened there. If you could find out what it was, it might help me get to the root of the problem."

"West Virginia is a big state," I said. "Do you know the town?"

"No," Sarah Agnes said. "And I am not going to find out anytime soon. You're a detective, so detect."

♦　♦　♦　♦

The day was shaping up. Sarah Agnes had given me something to do, and I could feel the boredom slipping away. I wasn't much into text messaging, but I needed an answer, so I sent a text message to Lacy asking for her mother's middle name. I got a quick response: "I'll call you."

The phone rang a few minutes later.

"What's going on?" Lacy asked.

"I am trying to track down a birth certificate for your mother," I said. "Did you ever see one?"

"No," Lacy said. "I don't think so. Why do you need it?"

"Do you know where your mother grew up?" I asked, ignoring her question, one I did not want to answer.

"Sure," Lacy said. "Bristol, Tennessee."

I had just stepped onto a very slippery slope. Obviously, Tracy had shared the West Virginia story with Sister Sarah Agnes understanding it would be held in confidence, and Lacy did not know about West Virginia. I certainly could not step into the middle of doctor-patient confidentiality.

"What is her middle name?"

"Lynn," Lacy said. "Her middle name is Lynn."

I braced for the next question, but I got a reprieve. I heard a cash register ring in the background.

"Gotta go, Don. It's time to get back to work. I'll talk to you later."

♦ ♦ ♦ ♦

I had a number of means to track down Tracy's hometown, but I decided to take the easy way out. Since I was now in Scott's good graces, I picked up the phone and called him. He answered on the second ring.

"Glass," he said.

I had blocked caller ID.

"Why not SAC Glass?" I asked.

"Half the people who call wouldn't know what it meant," Scott said. "What's up, Blood?"

"I need you to have someone track down a birth certificate for Tracy Lynn Malone. I think she was born in West Virginia within a year or two of nineteen seventy-nine or eighty."

"Hang on," Scott said. "Tracy Lynn Malone. Okay, got it. I'll get back to you."

"Got anything yet on Roger Allen?"

"Not yet, but I have put out a lot of feelers."

"I've been doing some thinking about it," I said. "Concentrate on the R. A. aspect, such as anyone who has closed a bank account who had the initials R. A. or a credit-card account that has gone inactive. Travelers leaving the country, things like that."

"We are thinking alike, Blood," Scott said. "You picked up on that, too. The fact that some of the witnesses mentioned names beginning with R."

"Great minds," I said. "Good hunting."

"I'll be in touch on this birth certificate thing," Scott said. "Say hello to Billy for me."

•   •   •   •

An hour later, I said hello to Billy. He came in and sat in front of my desk.

"Scott says hello," I said.

"Why are you talking to Scott?" Billy asked.

"Can't say," I said. "Something Sister Sarah Agnes asked me to do in confidence to help Lacy's mom."

I didn't dare mention the serial killer, or Billy would have had a fit. He nodded. Billy didn't know Sister Sarah Agnes Woods, but he did know who she was.

"We have to talk about something," Billy said.

I knew this was serious. In all the time I had known him, Billy had never used the words, "We have to talk."

"Okay," I said. "Sounds serious."

"I am thinking about moving to Cherokee," he said.

Translated, that meant Billy was going to move to Cherokee. He just said he was thinking about moving to soften the blow. Because he was a possessive mother hen who would have a fit if I told him I was moving somewhere, he would never understand that I didn't care where he lived. Our friendship was not about proximity.

"Why?" I asked, although I thought I knew why.

"Well, I have been seeing this woman, and we have become close, and she wants me to move in with her."

"Maggie," I said.

"Yes, Maggie," Billy said. He almost smiled. "Maggie really likes my art and photography and thinks I could sell much more of it if I was in Cherokee."

"So this is a business move?" I asked, and tried to keep a straight face.

This time, Billy did smile. "Not quite," he said.

"You're in love," I said.

"Yes," Billy said tamely.

"It's okay," I said. "It happens to the best of us."

"Like you?"

"Yes," I said. "Like me."

"I'll have to leave Cherokee Investigations," he said.

"No," I said firmly. "You will always be part of Cherokee Investigations. You are one of the founders. You'll be kept on retainer for special assignments, and believe me, there will be some."

"I was hoping you'd say that," he said.

"When am I going to meet Maggie?"

"Soon," Billy said. "Soon."

38

A few days later, early in the morning on a bright, clear day, I was in T. Elbert's Hummer H2, nicknamed "the Black Beauty," riding up I-81 toward Virginia. T. Elbert was driving. Every now and then, I asked him to help me do something just to get him out of the house. The last time, he had gotten Roy, Billy, and me out of a jam and made me look like a genius for having him along. I had not yet told him what I was up to, only that I was doing some detecting. He had jumped at the chance to come and said that I could tell him all about it later. We had been on the road for about an hour.

"So," T. Elbert said, "where are we going?"

"A little town called Saddle Boot in the southeastern tip of West Virginia," I said. *Thank you, Scott Glass.*

"What are we going to do in Saddle Boot?"

"I am looking for information on Lacy's mother," I said. "And before you ask, I cannot tell you why."

"No need for me to know," T. Elbert said. "I'm just happy to be here. But I am curious as to why you asked me to come along."

I knew the question was coming, and I was prepared.

"Well, for one thing, it's a long, boring trip," I said. "I could use the company. Most importantly, we are going to talk to the local county sheriff, and he is about your age. I figure the age thing and the fact that you are a semi-retired law-enforcement officer might cause him to open up a little more about what I'm after."

"And maybe the fact that I'm in a wheelchair after being shot in the line of duty won't hurt either," T. Elbert cracked.

"That, too," I said.

"That's pretty smart on your part, Donald," T. Elbert said. "Taking advantage of all your assets is the mark of a good agent."

"I'm not an agent," I said.

"No, but you think like one. Why is that?"

"All those cop shows I watched on TV when I was growing up," I said.

"That must be it," T. Elbert laughed.

"Want another cup of coffee?" I asked. I had gone out and filled a large thermos with Dunkin' Donuts coffee before T. Elbert picked me up.

"Sure," he said.

I poured T. Elbert a cup of black coffee, then poured a cup for myself and mixed in half-and-half and raw sugar from my small thermal soft pack. We were quiet for a while. Then I inserted the first disk of the latest John Sandford novel into the CD player. The unmistakable voice of Richard Ferrone began to unfold the latest Lucas Davenport tale. We listened without comment as we crossed into Virginia and headed toward Roanoke.

The first CD ended, and I ejected it.

"That's pretty good," T. Elbert said.

"Want me to put in disk two?"

"Sure," T. Elbert said enthusiastically.

Disk two got us through Roanoke, and we finished disk three a few minutes before we reached Saddle Boot. I gave T. Elbert directions to the county sheriff's office. We parked, and T. Elbert led the way toward the front door in his motorized wheelchair.

"You be the lead dog on this," I said. "I'll jump in when I think it's the right time."

"Sure thing," T. Elbert shot back.

T. Elbert was in full TBI mode and loving it. He maneuvered the wheelchair through the electronic front door, and I followed obediently, playing the role of underling. An attractive dark-haired female deputy at a desk near the door raised her head from her computer. Her nametag said she was Deputy Claire Thacker.

"Claire," T. Elbert said in a voice of authority, "I am here to see Sheriff Phillips."

Claire looked at T. Elbert and then at me and back at T. Elbert.

"Whom may I say is calling?" Claire asked professionally.

"T. Elbert Brown," T. Elbert said. "I am with the Special Projects Division of the Tennessee Bureau of Investigation."

"ID?"

T. Elbert showed his ID. I had only last year found out he still had an ID and was on the TBI payroll.

"Who is he?" Claire asked, looking at me.

I smiled at Claire. It had no effect.

"Bodyguard," T. Elbert said.

Claire ignored me, smiled at T. Elbert, and punched the Send button on her office intercom. "Sheriff, a T. Elbert Brown from the Tennessee Bureau of Investigation is here to see you."

After a pause, a voice said, "Send him in."

"Go straight, then take a right and go all the way down the hall. It's the last office on the left," Claire said, dismissing us and going back to whatever she was doing on her computer.

I followed T. Elbert.

"Bodyguard?" I asked softly.

"That was cop code for 'None of your business,' " T. Elbert said. "She got the message."

We took the right as instructed, and I saw a tall, lean man standing in the doorway of the last office on the left. As we approached, I read his nametag: Sheriff Dave Phillips.

"Come in, gentlemen," Sheriff Phillips said.

We shook hands and exchanged names. Sheriff Phillips had a firm grip, though it was no match for T. Elbert's.

"What can I do for the Tennessee Bureau of Investigation?" Sheriff Phillips asked.

"We are doing a background check on a juvenile in Tennessee whose mother supposedly grew up in these parts," T. Elbert said. "The family name is Malone. The mother in question is Tracy Lynn Malone. Born here thirty years ago."

"Sure, I remember the Malones," Sheriff Phillips said. "Tracy must have been about fifteen when they left."

"When they left, did they say where they were going?" T. Elbert asked.

"Told everyone around here they were goin' to California," Sheriff Phillips said.

"You've got quite a memory," T. Elbert said.

"Well, Betty Malone was memorable," the sheriff said.

"I see," T. Elbert said. "What can you tell me about the family?"

"Well, Tracy's father, Joe Malone, died in a truck accident when Tracy was a baby. She wouldn't remember him," the sheriff said. "Mrs. Malone—as I said, her name was Betty—must have got quite a bit of insurance or a regular check from the trucking company or somethin', because she didn't work, other than sell eggs. She was a good-lookin' woman, and a lot of guys went callin', but she wouldn't go out with any of 'em. Years later, she hooked up with some no-good drifter who would come and go. His name was John something. I can't remember the last name. He was kind of wild sometimes. He'd get drunk every now and then, and I would have to lock him up overnight. He liked to chase women, but other than that he didn't cause me much trouble."

"What happened to him?" I asked.

Sheriff Phillips looked at T. Elbert, and T. Elbert nodded.

"He left town a few months before Mrs. Malone sold her farm," Sheriff Phillips said. "I asked her about it once, and all she said was, 'He's gone, and good riddance.' Is Tracy okay? She sure was a sweet girl—nice lookin', too. All the young bucks around here were after her."

"She is fine," I said, looking at T. Elbert and then back to Sheriff Phillips. "Just going through a bit of a hard time right now. Got mixed up with some bad people, but we think she'll be okay. I really can't say more than that."

"I understand," Sheriff Phillips said sympathetically.

"Any other family around here?" I asked.

"There's Will Malone," the sheriff said. "Will was Joe Malone's older brother. When Joe married Betty, they split up their parents' property. Will still lives on his piece, about seventy-five acres, I'd say."

"Can you give us directions?" I asked.

"Be easier just to take you out there," Sheriff Phillips said. "No trouble. I have to go out that way anyhow."

I stood, and Sheriff Phillips did likewise. We followed T. Elbert out of the building to the parking lot and watched as he loaded himself into the Hummer.

"Nice wheels," the sheriff said. "The TBI's doin' okay."

"This is my personal vehicle," T. Elbert said. "Confiscated from a drug dealer. I bought it at auction."

T. Elbert slammed the driver's door, and the sheriff went to his cruiser as I got in the passenger seat beside T. Elbert. I wondered if the drug dealer story was true or if T. Elbert was just jerking the sheriff around. He liked to do that to people sometimes, even me.

We followed the sheriff out of town on the main road back the way we had come and took a right a few miles later. The road twisted and turned for a few more miles before the sheriff stopped at the mailbox of W. R. Malone. The driveway leading into the farm looked like a creek bed. The sheriff got out of his cruiser and walked back to the driver's side of the Hummer. T. Elbert lowered his window.

"It's been awhile since I've been out here," the sheriff said. "Looks like Will needs to get a road grader out here. Lucky you got that four-wheel drive. The house is about a mile and a half in. If Will won't talk to you, tell him to call me. It's okay to mention my name. I've known Will for a long time."

"You didn't give him a heads-up, did you?" T. Elbert asked.

Sheriff Phillips smiled. "No," he said. "I've been on the job for thirty years. I know the drill. You'll want to see his reaction to your questions, and you don't want to give him any time to prepare."

T. Elbert mellowed a bit. "Sorry I asked," he said. "No offense."

"None taken," the sheriff said. "We're all on the same side."

"Thanks for your time and the information," T. Elbert said, extending his hand out the window. "If you ever need anything from the TBI, come straight to me and I'll cut through the red tape."

"I'll do that," Sheriff Phillips said.

They shook hands, and T. Elbert gave Sheriff Dave Phillips his business card. Another surprise—I didn't even know T. Elbert had a business card. The sheriff nodded a goodbye at me through the window, and I nodded back. He turned, went back to his cruiser, got in, and drove away.

39

We bounced over ruts and rocks in the so-called driveway for about a quarter of a mile, then it improved right after we passed through a gate that I had to open and close. We went up and down a few times and finally reached a relatively flat piece of land and Will Malone's house. A rustic two-story with wraparound porches on both floors, it seemed well taken care of. A well-built barn stood about fifty yards back and to the right of the house. A few head of cattle grazed in an open field to the right of the barn, and to the left was a pigpen where some rather large hogs were asleep in the shade of an old oak tree.

A heavyset man in bib overalls came out of the house and down the stairs and walked toward the Hummer. He had a pleasant face that carried a look of curiosity. I guessed him to be in his early to mid-sixties. I opened my door and got out.

"Wait here," I said to T. Elbert as I shut the door and walked toward the man.

We met about fifty feet from his front porch.

"Will Malone?" I asked, as I got closer.

"That's me," he said warily.

"My name is Donald Youngblood," I said, extending my hand.

"Pleased to meet you, Mr. Youngblood," Will Malone said as we shook hands. He had a firm grip, presumably from years of working on a farm.

"Sheriff Phillips told me where I could find you," I continued. "I have a few questions about Betty and Tracy Malone."

"Betty and Tracy?" There was surprise and maybe something else in his voice, apprehension or fear, but he recovered quickly. "What about them?" he said. "I haven't heard from Betty and Tracy since they left. Betty promised to stay in touch but never did. Are they okay?"

A woman came out on the porch and stared at me.

"Will, is everything okay?" she yelled.

"Everything is fine, Thelma," Will answered.

Thelma nodded and went back into the house.

"Betty passed away awhile back," I said, watching for a reaction.

"I am sorry to hear that," Will Malone said. His regret seemed genuine.

"Tracy is fine," I said, "though she is having a bit of a rough time right now."

"What kind of a rough time?" Will Malone asked.

I opted for the truth—mostly, anyway.

"Tracy is in a rehab center right now," I said. "She has some issues she has to work out. I am a private investigator from Mountain Center, Tennessee. Her therapist hired me to look into her background to see if I could find anything that might help. Is there anything you can tell me?"

Will Malone proceeded to provide an expanded version of the story I had already heard from Sheriff Dave Phillips. Joe Malone met Betty in San Diego, California, while he was stationed there in the navy. They fell in love and got married. After Joe's tour was over, they moved to West Virginia. Betty never seemed too happy there, but she didn't complain. She got pregnant a few year later. Then Joe was killed, and Betty withdrew into motherhood. She left before Tracy's senior year in high school, saying she was tired of West Virginia and wanted to go back to California. She did not stay in touch.

"That's about it," Will Malone said.

I noticed that he hadn't mentioned John what's-his-name.

"Did Betty have any boyfriends?" I asked.

"Not that I know of," Will Malone said. His eyes looked away from me when he said it.

"Okay," I said. "Thanks for your time."

We shook hands again, and I turned to leave.

"Mr. Youngblood," Will Malone called. "Wait a minute, please."

I waited while Will Malone went back up the steps into the house. He emerged a few seconds later and came back down the stairs with a piece of paper in his hand, which he extended to me.

"Here is my phone number," he said. "Let me know how this thing comes out with Tracy."

"I'll do that," I said, handing him my card. "And if you think of anything else, give me a call."

Will Malone nodded, turned, and walked back toward the house. I got in the Hummer, and T. Elbert and I bounced and bucked our way in silence back to the main road.

◆   ◆   ◆   ◆

We drove for a while before T. Elbert broke the silence. I had been replaying my conversation with Will Malone over and over in my head.

"Learn anything interesting?" T. Elbert asked.

"Maybe," I said.

I recounted the entire conversation almost word for word as T. Elbert listened intently.

"Your conclusions?" T. Elbert asked.

"He knows more than he told me," I said. "He was nervous about something, and he didn't ask where Tracy was. Most kin like Will Malone would have said something like, 'Tell Tracy we send our love' or 'Tell Tracy she's in our prayers.' Something is not right."

"So what do you do now?" T. Elbert asked.

"Right now," I said, "I am going to make a phone call."

I dialed Sister Sarah Agnes.

"Hello?"

"This is your friendly gumshoe, reporting as ordered," I said.

"That was quick," she said. "You know something?"

"I do," I said.

I spent the next ten minutes revisiting in fine detail my conversations with Sheriff Dave Phillips and Uncle Will Malone. Sister Sarah Agnes never interrupted. When I finished, I thought maybe the line had gone dead.

"Sarah Agnes?"

"I'm here," she said. "You know, of course, there is something he is not telling you. It is probably very crucial to Tracy's mental health."

"I know," I said. "Want me to go back and break one of his legs?"

"Maybe later," she chuckled. "Let me work with what we have and see where it leads. And Don?"

"Yes?"

"Good work."

40

The following Friday night, we sat at the kitchen bar being mesmerized by Maggie Morning-Song. Billy had finally made good on his promise and delivered Maggie for dinner. Lacy and her best friend Hannah were upstairs in her room playing a video game. I didn't know what the video game was, but it had been "Mary approved."

Maggie was beautiful. She was tall and slender, and her dark skin, long, silky, raven hair, well-defined lips, dark eyes, and sharp nose combined for an incredible look. It was apparent that something in the mix was not Cherokee. Whatever it was had probably been the catalyst for this gorgeous woman. Maggie spoke softly and intelligently and seemed to deliberately select every word that came out of her mouth. She was obviously trying to make a good impression. She shouldn't have worried.

Billy looked at me and smiled, as if to say, *not bad, huh?*

"I'm moving tomorrow, Blood," Billy said. "Can you help?"

"Where are you moving to?" I asked, full well knowing.

"He is moving in with me," Maggie said with a little more spunk than she had shown so far.

"That's good," I said, smiling at Maggie. "Billy needs a keeper."

"You're the one who needs a keeper," Billy shot back.

"Well, he's got one," Mary chimed in.

"Good thing," Billy teased. "I was getting tired of the job."

"Enough," Maggie said. She seemed to be warming to the occasion.

"Tomorrow?" Billy asked. "I already rented a truck."

"Sure," I said. "Of course I'll help."

"No," Mary said, looking at a surprised Billy. "We will all help."

◆　　◆　　◆　　◆

Later that night, after some quietly passionate lovemaking, we lay in bed discussing the evening. Mary had prepared angel hair pasta alla Bolognese and fixed garlic toast, and I had tossed a Caesar salad. Maggie had warmed up to us as the evening progressed. She was charming and likable and obviously cared a great deal about Billy. I was happy for him and a bit melancholy for myself. Except for a couple of intervals, Billy and I had been watching each other's backs since our freshman year in college. As much as I teased him about being a mother hen, it was nice to know he was around. This move would be the first time we had not lived near each other since Billy got out of prison.

I was trying to analyze my feelings when I became vaguely aware Mary was talking to me.

"What?"

"I said that Billy is going to be all right," she said.

I hate it when women read my mind, I thought. I was willing to admit they were the superior species in many ways, but mind reading was truly unfair.

"I know," I said.

"So will you," she said.

Damn! There she goes again.

"I know," I said.

"You have me," Mary said.

"Thank God," I said.

We were quiet for a while.

"Think they'll get married?" Mary asked.

"Maybe," I said.

"I don't want to get married," Mary said awhile later.

"Okay," I said.

"Yet," she said as she kissed me. "Good night, my love." She rolled over and cut the light.

Yet?

She was messing with me again.

41

The next day, we helped Billy move—all of us, even Lacy's friend Hannah. The packing did not take long, as Billy didn't have much to move, mostly clothes and art and art supplies. He said he would get rid of the rest of his stuff before the lease was out. So we caravanned out of Mountain Center, down to Gatlinburg, over the Smokies, and down into Cherokee on a warm, hazy day, trying hard without much success to avoid the tourists who were out at that time of year. Billy drove the truck, with Maggie riding shotgun. I drove Billy's Grand Cherokee, and Mary drove with the girls in my Pathfinder. The plan was for me to drive the truck back and turn it in.

Maggie lived on the Bryson City side of Cherokee in a nice little ranch house about a mile off the main highway. She owned twenty-five acres of mostly wooded property with a creek running through it. I marveled at how quiet it was and knew Billy would like living there.

Behind the main house was a barn-style building attached to the house via a covered walkway. The two-story building looked new and had lots of large picture windows on the second floor and was to be Billy's new studio.

"Nice," I said to Billy. "Very nice."

Mary, Lacy, and Hannah had gone to the creek to scout the fish, and Billy and I were alone on the second floor of his new studio, having just brought up the last of his art and supplies. The room had plenty of light, but just enough trees were around to keep the building cool. I noticed an air-conditioning duct—never hurt to have backup.

"It's perfect," Billy said. "I helped design and build it. That's why I was gone so often."

"So your being gone didn't have anything to do with Maggie," I teased. I smelled the aroma of food coming from Maggie's kitchen.

Billy smiled. "Maggie had a lot to do with my being gone," he said.

"I like her," I said.

"I knew you would," Billy said.

"How did you meet her?" I asked.

"I was trying to track down my father," Billy said. "I was told to talk to Maggie. She knows a lot about local history."

"I thought you were going to leave that idea alone," I said.

"I want to know why my mother ran away," Billy said. "I want to know why whoever it was that got her pregnant didn't stand with her."

"And what if you don't like the answers you find?" I asked.

"Then I may have to avenge my mother's death," Billy said with a hard look on his face.

Maggie appeared out of the shadows at the top of the stairs. She silently glided over to Billy as he watched her come. She kissed him on the cheek, and I saw his face soften.

"Leave revenge to the Great Spirit," she said. "Dinner is ready. Come down to eat, please."

42

My life was returning to normal—or at least as normal as it could be, considering I was sharing it with two women. I had escaped the smell of soap and the sound of hair dryers and sought sanctuary at my office. The only other male in the house had seemed anxious to escape also. He lay asleep, content to be in a place of peace and quiet.

A man's retreat, however, can be turned upside down with one phone call. When I saw the caller ID, I knew it was not good news. Sister Sarah Agnes did not call in the early hours of the morning unless it was important.

"Good morning," I said. "I take it you have news, and it is probably not good."

"Right on both counts," she said without preamble. "Tracy is gone. I watched her leave from my room on the second floor."

"When?" I asked.

"A few minutes ago," Sarah Agnes said. "A man picked her up. I could swear he had the head of a snake tattooed on his right hand."

"You have very good eyesight," I said. "His name is Victor Vargas."

"What I have," Sarah Agnes said, "is a very fine pair of binoculars on my nightstand. They come in handy if I want to be nosy. The name Victor has come up in our sessions. I thought the man was probably him. Tracy never mentioned the tattoo."

"What happened to make Tracy leave?"

"I was getting too close to the truth," Sarah Agnes said. "She couldn't deal with it. Yesterday, I mentioned West Virginia, and you would have thought she saw a ghost. Then she clammed up and said she didn't want to talk anymore."

"So she called Vargas and told him where she was, and he dropped everything and came and got her," I said. "Maybe it's love."

"Or at least their perception of love," Sarah Agnes said. "I really can't say much, but their relationship is complicated."

"I'm sure this is not the first patient who bolted," I said. "Why did you call me so soon?"

"I don't know," she said.

I was not convinced. We were quiet for a long time, considering we were on the telephone.

"You're feeling guilty," I said.

I knew the feeling well, thanks to Roger Allen.

"I was so damn close to helping her, and I blew it," Sarah Agnes said.

"You had to mention West Virginia sometime," I said. "My guess is you would have gotten the same reaction whether it was yesterday or next month."

"We'll never know," Sarah Agnes said. "But you're probably right, and you're sweet to say so."

"I'll call you if I find out anything," I said.

"Let her go, Don," Sarah Agnes said. "I can't help her if she doesn't want to be helped, and I know this Victor guy is dangerous."

"I have to discuss that with my client," I said.

"Be very careful, Don," Sarah Agnes pleaded.

"I will," I promised. "Now, go take care of someone who does want your help."

◆   ◆   ◆   ◆

I had no intention of discussing anything with my client. I had every intention of returning to Vegas and finding out what was going on inside the head of Tracy Malone. I sat and pondered my next move. There was something I had to do, and it frightened me. I left the security of my desk and walked out of my office. I passed the elevators and proceeded around the corner and down to the end of the hall to an office door that read, "Roland G. Ogle, Attorney at Law." I went through the door.

"Well, hello, Don," Estelle Huff said as I entered.

"Hello, Estelle," I said. "Is Rollie busy? I need just a few minutes."

◆   ◆   ◆   ◆

Late that afternoon, Rollie Ogle sat in my office patiently waiting while I read the document he had prepared for me earlier that day. Rollie was ten years my senior, as Southern as grits, as smart as anyone I had ever met, and ruthless when it came to defending his clients. He was a general practice lawyer who did mostly divorce work with some petty criminal work tossed in for good measure. Rollie's knowledge of the law even outside his area of practice was impressive.

I finished reading.

"This is fine," I said. "Can you get it down to one page?"

"Sure," Rollie said in his sophisticated drawl. "I was just padding my fee."

"Would this hold up in court?" I asked.

"It might," Rollie said. "If you got the right judge. But from what you've told me, I doubt it will ever come to that."

"I need the final document by the end of today," I said.

"No problem, Don," Rollie said. "I'll have Estelle run it down later."

"Is there going to be a fee for that, too?" I teased.

"Why, naturally," Rollie smiled pleasantly.

43

I was listening to music on my laptop through headphones Wanda Jones had given me as a Christmas present. Wanda was the county medical examiner, my friend, and my confidante. We had known each other since high school. There had been a time when I might have considered a long-term relationship with Wanda, but she had still been trying to decide about her sexual preference. Instead, we became good friends. As the Eagles performed a song from their latest album, I watched from inside the Boeing 737 from thirty thousand feet as we flew over the snow-covered Rocky Mountains.

Two nights ago at dinner, Mary and I had told Lacy that her mother had left with Victor. We knew she would find out anyway. She did not seem surprised. Attempts by Lacy to reach her mother on her cell phone were unsuccessful. Against strong objections from the womenfolk, I had decided to return to Vegas and take one last run at Tracy. I wanted to hear for myself that she wanted to stay with Victor.

Call me stubborn. After all, I was a Taurus, the sign of the bull.

◆　◆　◆　◆

I was in the same room at the Renaissance Las Vegas Hotel looking out over the city on a bright, cloudless, scorching day. I had no intention of venturing out until the sun went down. I wanted to find Victor Vargas, but I wasn't too crazy about going back to his house. I hoped to find Tracy's place of employment. If I located Vargas, he might lead me there.

I flipped open my cell phone and called Bruiser Bracken.

"Youngblood!" he exclaimed. "What are you doing back in town?"

"Unfinished business," I said.

"I hope it doesn't involve Victor Vargas," Bruiser said.

"Unfortunately, it does," I said. "Where is the most likely place I can find him?"

"He is somehow connected to the Black Stallion," Bruiser said. "It's a topless and bottomless club over on Las Vegas Boulevard North."

Bruiser gave me directions from the Renaissance.

"I guess I would be wasting my breath to tell you to stay away from there," Bruiser said.

"You would," I said.

"Want some company?" Bruiser asked.

The offer was tempting, but I did not want to get Bruiser involved. He had to work and live in this town.

"No thanks," I said. "I'll try to keep a low profile."

◆　◆　◆　◆

The Black Stallion was a tastefully decorated establishment with a nice bar and plenty of unclad good-looking women. I was really kind of embarrassed. Topless was one thing, but all nude was something else. I didn't want to appear gay, and I did need to make sure none of the women was Tracy Malone. So I looked. No luck. I did not see Tracy Malone or Victor Vargas.

I did this for three nights running. I would stay a few hours, look for Tracy, look for Vargas, and then go back to my hotel room and call Mary and wish I were back in Mountain Center.

I finally gave up on the Black Stallion and on the fourth day returned to the house for sale outside the gate of Hidden Valley Estates. I sat for four hours and finally scored when I saw Tracy's baby-blue Thunderbird cruise by me and go through the gate. The convertible top had been stowed, and the hardtop was on. I was half asleep when the car passed and didn't get a look at the driver, but I assumed it was Tracy. I thought someone was in the passenger seat. I was too late to follow Tracy through the gate, so I had to wait for another opportunity. It came minutes later in the form of a black Jaguar. I followed it through at a discreet distance and headed for Vargas's house.

I made the turn on Hidden Valley Lane and as I approached the next block saw Tracy in her driveway talking to two very large men. I made a quick left at the intersection and doubled back to the main road. It appeared that Victor has supplied Tracy with bodyguards and that one of them accompanied Tracy wherever she went. Getting her alone was not going to be easy.

The next day, I sat in the parking lot of the shopping center at a safe distance from the Starbucks where I had tailed Tracy the first time I saw her in Vegas. I was parked under a tree in my nondescript rental car with the motor running.

About one-fifteen, the baby-blue Thunderbird pulled into an open space and Tracy got out. Seconds later, a big guy got out of the passenger's side and followed Tracy into Starbucks. He glanced around casually but didn't appear concerned about trouble. Fifteen minutes later, they came out, got in the car, and drove away, leaving me pondering my next move.

This was not going well. But I slowly developed a simple plan, one that would require two people. I thought about calling Billy, but I didn't want to drag him away from his newfound relationship with Maggie.

I called Roy instead.

"This is Roy," he answered.

"I need you in Vegas to back me up on something," I said. "Can you come?"

"What's this about?" he asked.

I told him.

"I'll call you back," he said, and promptly hung up.

If there were a contest for abruptness between Roy and Billy, I wasn't sure who would win.

I took my cell phone and my *USA Today*, locked the car, and made the hot walk across the parking lot to Starbucks. I ordered an iced mocha coffee and took it and my paper to an unoccupied table in a far corner away from the door. I muted my cell phone and settled down to read the money section. The market was struggling to stay above twelve thousand.

Fifteen minutes later, my cell phone vibrated.

"Youngblood," I said.

"I'll be there by sundown," Roy said.

"Private jet?"

"Yes."

"Fleet okay with this?"

"He is," Roy said.

"I'll get you a room at the Renaissance," I said. "Take the shuttle. I have a rental car. We'll have dinner after you get in."

"Okay," Roy said. "I'll see you tonight."

◆   ◆   ◆   ◆

I was in my room nursing a Sam Adams Light and munching dry-roasted peanuts from the concierge lounge. I was at my tinted picture window watching the sun sink low in the sky when my hotel phone rang. I pulled the curtains to cut down the glare, put my feet up on the desk, and answered.

"I'm here," Roy said. "Room 701. Nice room, gumshoe."

"When do you want to have dinner?" I asked.

"Give me a half-hour," Roy said.

I looked at my watch.

"I'll see you in the Envy Steakhouse at seven-thirty," I said. "It's in the hotel."

"Seven-thirty," Roy confirmed. "See you then."

◆   ◆   ◆   ◆

We sat at an out-of-the-way table in the Envy. On my recommendation, Roy had ordered filet mignon, and I had ordered a Caesar salad with grilled salmon. We had finished a beer each and shared a calamari appetizer when the food arrived. Roy looked at the steak and nodded approval. Then he looked at my Caesar salad.

"You eat like a girl," he said.

"And have a figure to match," I cracked.

"Yeah," Roy deadpanned. "I'm really going to have to back off on all this beef."

Roy Husky was the definition of lean. I had the feeling he worked out more than he told me.

"Is Jim Doak staying over?" I asked.

"Yeah," Roy said, swallowing his first bite of steak. "You're right. This is good. Jim is staying out by the airport. Wanted to be near the plane. That jet is his baby."

"Going back tomorrow?"

"Day after. Figured I might do a little gambling, as long as I'm here," Roy said. "Mr. Fleet said it was okay."

"Blackjack?"

"Only thing that makes sense," Roy said.

We ate in silence for a while.

"I'm curious as to why you didn't ask Billy to come out," Roy said.

"Billy is otherwise occupied with the opposite sex," I said.

I told him about Maggie Morning-Song.

"Well, I'll be damned," Roy said. "Good for Billy."

He was actually smiling.

"How do you want to play tomorrow?" Roy asked as he ate the last of his steak.

"Well, if they show up, straightforward," I said. "You keep the body-guard occupied, and I'll have a talk with Tracy. I'm hoping Starbucks is part of her daily routine."

I finished my meal, and Roy gulped down the last of his second beer.

"I'm going to check out the nightlife," Roy said. "Want to come along?"

"No," I said. "I've had enough of Vegas nightlife to last a lifetime."

"What time do you want me available tomorrow?"

"Meet me in the lobby at eleven-thirty," I said as Roy rose to leave.

He nodded and walked out of the restaurant and into the electric Las Vegas night.

I went back to my room and called Mary.

44

Sitting in my rental car under my favorite tree in the shopping center parking lot, we kept the motor running while we watched for any signs of a baby-blue Thunderbird. It was another scorching day in Vegas. Roy had not uttered one word since I met him in the lobby. He looked tired. He was drinking black coffee he had brought with him from the hotel. The aroma, one of my favorite smells, filled the car.

"Long night?" I finally asked.

"Uh-huh."

"Worth it?"

"Uh-huh."

"Blonde or brunette?" I asked.

Roy turned his head slightly and looked at me out of the corner of his left eye. A tight smile was on his face. "Redhead," he said, turning back and staring straight ahead.

I would have pressed to see how much Roy would give up about the redhead, but we were interrupted by the sight of a baby-blue T-Bird pulling into a parking space in front of Starbucks. Tracy was driving. As she got out of the car, the passenger's side door opened and the same big guy I had seen before emerged. He was about six-foot-two and bulky, with short dark brown hair. They walked casually into the coffee shop.

"Showtime," Roy said. "I'll go in first, order a coffee, and try to position myself behind the bodyguard. Give me a few minutes, then come in."

"Okay," I said.

I watched as Roy left the cool of the car for the hot Nevada sun, walked across the parking lot, and entered Starbucks. It was so hot that I was surprised he didn't leave footprints in the asphalt. I looked at my watch a few times as five minutes slowly ticked by. I could feel the adrenaline starting to flow.

I took the valise I had brought with me from the backseat and got out of the car. I felt the heat wave as my feet hit the pavement.

Thirty seconds later, I was enjoying the coolness of Starbucks as I ordered an iced cappuccino. The place was empty except for a couple of employees and the four of us. Tracy and the bodyguard were at a small table for two on the far left, and Roy sat at a table just behind them to the right, pretending to drink coffee and read his newspaper.

I paid for my drink and walked toward Tracy's table. The bodyguard gave me a curious look as I approached. I pulled a chair from a nearby table and sat down by Tracy.

"Hi, Tracy," I said. "Remember me?"

"Mr. Youngblood," she said, trying to act surprised. "What are you doing here?"

"I came to talk to you," I said.

The bodyguard stood. "You're leaving now," he said.

"I don't think so," Roy said from his nearby table.

In his lap in the folds of the newspaper, we could see the exit end of a silencer. I couldn't see the gun.

"You wouldn't shoot me in here," the bodyguard said.

"I would," Roy said convincingly. "Right in the kneecap, painful but noiseless. You'll probably walk with a limp for the rest of your life."

I thought I saw the bodyguard wince. The thought of a bullet in the kneecap made me cringe, and it wasn't even my knee Roy was talking about.

"Sit down, Ralph," Tracy said. "I don't want any trouble. I'll talk to Mr. Youngblood."

"Mr. Vargas won't like this," Ralph said.

"Then we won't tell Mr. Vargas," Tracy said with authority.

Ralph sat, and Tracy and I moved to a table up front.

"Why did you come?" Tracy asked. I could hear the annoyance in her voice.

"I wanted to make sure you weren't here against your will," I answered.

"I don't do anything I don't want to do," she said defiantly.

"Then you came here willingly," I said.

"Yes," she said firmly.

"What about Lacy?" I asked. "A girl needs a mother."

"I cannot be a mother to Lacy anymore," she said. "I just can't. I don't even know why."

I nodded. She seemed sincere. I looked back toward Ralph. He was watching me closely. I looked at Roy. His focus was solely on Ralph.

"Lacy is a smart girl," Tracy said intensely. "She'll be okay. I am not coming back."

I didn't think anything I said was going to change her mind.

"You should at least call her and explain," I said. "Let her know that it's not her fault."

"I will," she said, loosening up a little. "That's a good idea."

I removed from my valise the document that Rollie had prepared for me and handed it to Tracy.

"I would like for you to sign this," I said. "It appoints me as Lacy's temporary legal guardian until such time that you might want to resume parenting duties."

Tracy took the single-page document and read it without expression.

"Why would you want the responsibility?" she asked.

"I don't, really," I said. "But I don't want Lacy to become a ward of the state either."

"Does Lacy know about this?"

"No," I said.

"How about the lady cop?" Tracy asked.

"Mary," I said. "No, she doesn't know either. This is going to be our little secret. This is my ace in the hole in case someone shows up and tries to take Lacy."

"I see that we need to get this witnessed and notarized," Tracy said, looking at the document. "I do business with the bank a few doors down. They should be able to help us."

Tracy got up and walked over to Ralph. I followed.

"Mr. Youngblood and I are going to the bank," Tracy said. "Wait here. We will not be gone long."

Ralph started to say something, but Tracy cut him off.

"It's okay, Ralph," she said. "Victor will never know."

◆　　◆　　◆　　◆

We had the document witnessed and notarized in fifteen minutes and were walking back to Starbucks. I paused just outside the door.

"One other thing," I said. "What happened in West Virginia?"

For an instant, Tracy looked like she had seen a ghost. Then it passed.

"I don't know anything about West Virginia," she said in a low growl. "I wish people would stop asking me about West Virginia."

She went through the door and walked quickly over to Ralph.

"Let's go," she said tersely.

Ralph look at Roy.

Roy looked at me.

I nodded.

Roy nodded at Ralph, who got up and walked away with Tracy.

Tracy stopped and turned as she approached the door. Her face softened.

"Mr. Youngblood," she called.

I looked at her without responding.

"Thanks," she said.

I nodded.

She turned and walked out with Ralph following.

Roy got up, slipped the gun into his pocket, laid his newspaper on the table, and took one final drink of coffee. We left Starbucks and walked back to my rental car. I tossed my valise on the backseat, started the engine, cranked the air to max, and looked at Roy.

"Big gamble, bringing a gun along," I said.

Roy reached into his pocket.

"I didn't bring a gun," he said, holding up the shiny metal cylinder. "I only brought a silencer."

◆   ◆   ◆   ◆

We sat at the bar of the Velvet Slipper. We had decided to fly out later that night. I wanted to see Bruiser before we left. We were drinking drafts and taking in the scenery. It made me anxious to get back to Mountain Center.

"I'm going to play a little blackjack," Roy said, finishing his beer. "Come get me when you're ready to go."

"You ahead or behind?"

"Ahead," Roy said. "Couple of hundred."

I nodded, and Roy turned and walked toward the blackjack tables.

Fifteen minutes later, Bruiser sat down beside me and ordered a club soda with lime.

"What's happening?" he asked.

"I'm finished here," I said. "Just wanted to say goodbye. And thanks."

"Did it turn out the way you wanted?" Bruiser asked.

"No," I said. "But at least I feel like I have some closure."

"Closure is good," Bruiser said.

"You made things a lot easier for me," I said. "I owe you one."

"My pleasure," Bruiser said. "And you don't owe me anything. It was good to connect with you again. But I do have a favor to ask."

"Ask," I said.

"I would like for you to take over my investment portfolio," Bruiser said.

"Be glad to," I said.

"Thanks," Bruiser said.

"Fax me the details, and I'll take a look next week," I said.

"I'll do it tomorrow," Bruiser said.

"If you ever want to get away from all of this, come visit me in the mountains of East Tennessee," I said. "You have my number."

"And if you ever have a paying gig for some extra muscle, give me a call," Bruiser said. "I am always looking for some extra cash."

"You can count on that," I said.

The bartender came walking down the back of the bar and stopped in front of Bruiser. He picked up our drinks and wiped away the condensation and set our glasses back down on fresh coasters.

"As soon as you're free, Mr. Bracken," he said. He tilted his head and his eyes upward.

Bruiser nodded, finished his drink, and got off the barstool.

"The guy with you," he asked. "Friend or hired help?"

"Friend," I said. "And damn good backup."

"Yeah," Bruiser nodded. "He has that look. Well, take care of yourself, Youngblood. See you around."

"You, too, Bruiser," I said.

He nodded again and walked away. I thought he had a sad look on his face, and I wondered if Bruiser had any friends.

I finished the last of my beer and went to find Roy. I found him at a high-stakes blackjack table, and he seemed to be doing pretty well.

"Looks like you're on a roll," I said. "You want to stay awhile?"

"No," he said. "I'm about done."

"Okay," I said. "I'll get the car and meet you out front."

◆   ◆   ◆   ◆

I walked across the street and up the stairs to the second level of the parking garage. The lot beside the Velvet Slipper had been full. The rental car was parked at the far end. I had the keys in my left hand.

I was a third of the way to my car when I heard footfalls behind me. I caught a glimpse of a reflection in the side window of a parked SUV as I walked past. Two men were following me. They were closing fast. I could have run for it, but I decided to take a stand of my own choosing.

About halfway down, I stopped beside a pair of Cadillac Escalades, seemingly the car of choice in Vegas. One was black, the other white. The black Escalade was parked face in, the white one face out. I turned toward my pursuers—two thugs, I was sure, sent by Victor Vargas. I recognized one as they approached cautiously and spread out to the right and left. The Escalades guarded my back.

"Hello, Ralph," I said. "How's it going?"

"You know this guy?" the other thug asked.

"Not really," Ralph said.

"Had any good lattes lately?" I asked Ralph.

I didn't feel nearly as cool as I acted.

"Shut up, wiseass," Ralph said.

"Touchy," I said, waiting for someone to make a move.

"We have a message from Victor," Ralph grinned. "A sort of get-out-of-town message."

"How nice," I said. "But you're wasting your time. I'm leaving tonight."

"Too late," Ralph said. "The message has to be delivered. Orders."

He seemed to take a little too much pleasure in saying *Orders*.

"You can email it," I said. "I'll give you my business card."

"Funny guy for a man about to get the crap beat out of him, ain't he, Ralph?" the other thug said. He was slightly smaller than Ralph and had a scar over his left eye and shaggy blond hair.

I looked straight at Blondie. "Is that your real hair color, or is it Lady Clairol?"

To my left, I caught Ralph's movement out of the corner of my eye. I wanted him to think that I was being distracted by Blondie. He came in quickly, loaded for a roundhouse right. I was ready. I stepped in fast with a hard right jab and beat him to the punch. With a good shoulder turn and all my body weight going forward, I landed it squarely on Ralph's nose. His head snapped back, blood gushed, and he staggered backwards and went down hard on his rear end. I had no time to admire my work. Blondie came fast with a left. I ducked, then jabbed him in the stomach with the front end of the ignition key, which I held securely in my left fist between my middle and ring fingers.

"Fuck!" he screamed, and staggered backwards, holding his stomach.

I followed up fast with an overhand right, and Blondie went down.

I was about to say something cute when the back of my head exploded in a collage of pain, color, and bright lights, and down I went. Whatever I had been hit with glanced off my hard head and came down on my collarbone. The pain engulfed me. For good measure, on the way down, I hit my head on the front bumper of the white Escalade and then on the concrete floor of the parking garage. All of a sudden, my head was having a very bad day. I saw feet with tennis shoes, the third man. I hadn't been ready for a third man, and now I was about to pay a dear price for that mistake. Dazed, I rolled away and got kicked for my efforts. I felt some ribs cave in on my right side and the air rush from my lungs. I couldn't breathe. I was gasping for air when another kick landed on my hip. I knew I was in big trouble.

"Victor said not to kill him."

I think it was Blondie's voice, but my hearing was not exactly perfect at that precise moment.

"Fuck Victor," I heard another voice say.

Ralph, I thought. I guessed the nose hurt pretty bad. I rolled again and received another kick in the side just below the ribs. My head was killing me. I reached under the Escalade and grabbed for anything to hold onto. I found something, maybe a tie rod, and pulled myself partially under the SUV.

"Drag that piece of shit out from under that truck."

I was pretty sure it was Ralph's voice again.

Someone grabbed my leg and started to pull. I held on for dear life, literally. I tried to kick free. Then I heard a shout, and then the hands let go of my leg.

"Let's get the hell out of here," said a voice I did not recognize.

I heard running footfalls from both directions. My head was spinning, and I felt as if I were floating away. And like I wanted to throw up.

"Youngblood!" Roy said in a distant voice. "Let go. Let me get you out from under there."

I let go from underneath the SUV and felt myself sliding out.

"Goddamnit," Roy said. "They really fucked you up."

More footfalls rang out in the parking garage, coming toward us.

"Call nine-one-one!" Roy shouted. "We need an ambulance."

I heard the faint beep of a cell phone.

"This is Dennis Bracken," Bruiser said urgently. "A man is down and badly hurt on the second level of the parking garage across from the Velvet Slipper. I need an ambulance immediately."

I felt a hand on my shoulder.

"Hang on, Youngblood," Bruiser said.

Then I didn't feel the hand anymore, and Bruiser's voice was very far away. Then the darkness came.

45

My eyes fluttered open. Hearing the beep of a monitor, I turned my head slowly and looked up. The head turn was agonizing, almost blinding. Green lights broadcast my heart rate, blood pressure, and some things I was not quite sure of. I guessed that the squiggly line was my EKG, or maybe my brain waves, if I had any brains left. I was in a private room. It was not small. Someone had obviously found out I had money.

The room was dimly lit. I painfully turned my head in the other direction and spied a figure asleep in the chair next to my bed. Mary. I tried to lift my arm to touch her, but I couldn't. Moving my arm felt like I was lifting a lead weight.

"Mary," I croaked. I had very little voice.

"Mary," I said, slightly louder.

Mary stirred and looked at me sleepily. Then it registered, and she was wide-awake.

"Oh, God," she said, coming close and kissing me gently on the lips. "Oh, thank God." She smelled wonderful.

Mary grabbed the call button pinned to my bed and thumbed it. Seconds later, a nurse appeared. She was a stern-looking black woman, and I could tell at a glance she was all business.

"He's awake, Helen," Mary said.

First-name basis. Not a good sign. I must have been here awhile.

"About time, Miss Mary," Helen said. "Let's take a look."

Nurse Helen checked my pupils with a penlight. She made sounds that I thought to be approving. She nodded at Mary.

"Dr. Chang should be in by eight. Try to keep him awake. Talk to him. Get him to sit up."

"I will," Mary said. "Thanks, Helen."

Mary adjusted the back of the bed to a more upright position, then put her arms under me and scooted me upward. She was a strong woman.

My head screamed, but I kept silent. The throbbing was almost unbearable. I moved my head slowly to find a position that was less agonizing. The throbbing subsided.

"I saw my parents," I said, my words thick and labored.

"You were dreaming," Mary said.

"I don't think so," I said slowly. "It was too real."

"It's probably the drugs," Mary said.

I wanted to argue, but I didn't have the strength and could not locate the argument inside my screaming head. I took a deep breath, which killed me. My ribs were screaming along with my head, a terrifically painful duet.

"How long?" I winced.

"Over three days," she said. Tears were streaming down her cheeks. "We thought we had lost you."

"How long have you been here?" I asked in a voice so weak I did not recognize it as my own.

"Roy sent the plane for me hours after it happened. I was here the next morning. Billy is here, and Roy is still here, and Big Bob calls every couple of hours so he can report to T. Elbert and Doris."

I laughed, and my head hurt. "Yeah," I said. "Doris is better than Western Union."

Mary laughed through the tears and then turned serious. "Roy is really beating himself up for letting you go to the parking garage alone. If Dennis hadn't seen those guys on the security cam, you might be dead."

"You met Bruiser?"

"Bruiser?" Mary asked.

"Dennis," I said weakly. "College nickname."

"Bruiser," Mary said. "Yeah, it fits. Dennis has been wonderful. He's been by every day. So has a police detective named Rodriguez. He's hoping to talk to you. Can you identify who did this to you?"

"I don't know," I lied. I remembered it all vividly. "Things are still pretty fuzzy."

* ✦ ✦ ✦

I drifted into and out of sleep as Mary talked and tried to keep me awake. Around eight o'clock, Roy came in. I sent Mary to my hotel room to get some rest, convincing her that I was not going back into a coma. My head still hurt, and I felt like I was mired in quicksand.

"Nice to see you back," Roy said. "I thought for a while we had lost you."

"Nice to be back," I said with as much energy as I could muster.

"I should have been there," he said with a pained look on his face.

"Not your fault," I said. "I had it under control until the third guy got me from behind. I should have known better. Rookie mistake."

"We'll get those bastards," Roy said. "I swear."

"Let it go for now," I said weakly. "Your job is to get me out of here and take me home. I need time to heal."

"I can do that," Roy said.

Billy walked in and came to my bedside. He was silent as only Billy could be. The concern and anger on his face were evident. I had seen that look before.

"You should be more careful," he said.

"You're right," I said. "I was careless, and I paid the price."

We were all silent for a while, until a doctor entered my room. His nametag said he was Dr. Sam Chang. He smiled and nodded at my visitors.

"Everybody out," he said pleasantly.

"Sure," I said. "But I may need some help disconnecting all these tubes."

"Not you, funny man," Sam Chang smiled.

Roy and Billy headed for the door.

"Billy," I said. "Leave it alone for now."

Billy looked at Roy, and Roy nodded. Billy looked back at me and nodded, and they left.

"Want to know how I'm feeling?" I asked.

Sam Chang smiled again. "I know how you're feeling. Your head hurts like nothing you have ever felt before, you're having difficulty breathing, you cannot get comfortable, and you want the hell out of here. Did I miss anything?"

"I'd like to get rid of these tubes," I said. "Especially that one." I nodded toward my lower extremities.

"As long as you're doing okay, we'll jerk that one out by the end of today," he grinned.

"Ouch," I said. "I'll settle for gently removing."

Dr. Chang laughed. "I'll put my best nurse on it," he said. "And when I remove the IV, you'll have to drink plenty of liquids and try to eat something, so we can get all your plumbing going."

"When can I go home?"

"Normally, I would say a week, but I have already been told by your wife how stubborn you are, so I'm guessing three or four days."

Wife?

"What's the damage?" I asked.

"Hairline fracture of the cranium, severe concussion, fractured collarbone, two broken ribs, and some nasty bruises. The ribs are going to take the most time to heal. You'll need lots of rest, and you absolutely must take it easy. What I want is no running, no racquetball, and no going to the gym unless you promise to take it very, very easy."

He had obviously talked to Mary and learned about my exercise routine. Dr. Sam Chang was going to be a hard man to fool.

"What do you mean by very, very easy?"

"Very low weights, and watch the reps. You'll be able to tell what I'm talking about."

"How long for the ribs?"

"Six to eight weeks," Dr. Chang said. "But you can walk all you want. You are going to be sore for quite a while."

"Are you going to have them wrapped?" I asked.

"We don't do that anymore," he said. "It is generally considered to do more harm than good."

"What about the collarbone?"

"Before you leave, we'll put you in a clavicle strap. The strap will give the collarbone a little extra support while it heals."

"How long will I have to wear it?"

"It's obvious the head injury did not impede your ability to ask questions," Dr. Chang chuckled. "I would recommend wearing the strap six weeks."

"When will I start to feel like myself?" I asked. "I feel like I'm not all here."

"I've heard that from other patients who suffered severe head trauma," Dr. Chang said. "Everyone is different. Some take a week, some a month, and others longer."

"And some never recover," I said.

"Now you're putting words in my mouth," Sam Chang smiled. "I didn't say that. The body has a wonderful way of healing damage. I cannot think of a single patient with injuries consistent with yours who did not recover fully."

Sam Chang had a terrific bedside manner. He was friendly and authoritative at the same time. I liked him. He checked my pupils with a penlight and seemed to approve.

"I'll drop back by before I leave," Dr. Chang said as he walked toward the door. "And I'll send the nurse in with some pain meds after you've been awake awhile and continue to be responsive."

"Thanks," I said.

* ◆ ◆ ◆

Dr. Sam Chang was true to his word. I was unhooked from the IV later that day, and the catheter was removed, an experience I wished never to have again. The pain meds that night were first-rate—narcotics, no doubt.

The pain in my head was still there but had taken a seat in the back row. I felt as if I were floating above my bed. Roy and Billy took turns staying with me until Mary returned. I watched TV most of the next day as they sat in silence. For me, talking was too much effort. I occasionally dozed off. I drank ginger ale through a straw and nibbled on cheese and crackers. I tried to get out of bed to go to the bathroom, but I couldn't find the strength. With some effort, I was able to use a bedpan. It was a humiliating experience, and I felt a mixture of stupidity and rage when I thought about how I had arrived at this predicament.

At dinnertime, I had trouble getting the fork to my mouth, and Mary ended up feeding me. The sliced turkey and mashed potatoes with gravy tasted good. The peas and carrots didn't taste at all. There was anger in every bite. I ate about half the meal.

"How are you feeling?" Mary asked.

"Not much," I said. "I'm floating out there somewhere."

"You don't have to talk," she said. "I'm here if you need me."

"Question," I said.

"Go ahead."

"Did we get married while I was unconscious?"

"No," Mary laughed. "*Wife* sounded better than *live-in lover*, and it allowed me to be with you 24/7."

"Kind of sounds good," I said.

"You're being influenced by the drugs," Mary said. "Now, be quiet and get some rest."

46

On the morning of my third day of consciousness after getting my brains scrambled, I woke feeling that a haze had lifted. I was more alert, and my head hurt less. Breathing was still an adventure, but I seemed to have more energy. Dr. Chang came by and seemed to feel that I was progressing nicely. I was able to get out of bed and go to the bathroom on my own. Later that morning, I slowly walked the halls with Mary, rode the elevator down to the cafeteria, and enjoyed a cup of coffee and a bagel with cream cheese. By the time I got back to my room, I was exhausted but proud. At least I didn't feel like I had to take a nap. I took one anyway.

At lunch, Mary told me that Lacy was staying with Doris and that they seemed to be getting along, and that T. Elbert was driving her crazy with emails. Mary had brought her laptop and was keeping all my friends apprised of my condition. She had to email T. Elbert twice a day with details. And she called the MCPD once a day to give Big Bob the latest. He would settle for nothing less than a phone call.

Mary left early that afternoon to go back to the hotel for a while, leaving me alone with my thoughts. I pondered my situation. I was down but not out. I had taken a beating from some very bad guys and lived to tell about it. In some ways, it was a rite of passage. Maybe I could be a real, honest-to-God private investigator, with all the bumps and bruises that came with the job. Time would tell.

I could sympathize with Sandy Smith. I knew what it was like to be beaten half to death in a parking garage. *Even worse for a woman*, I thought. I found it ironic that we had suffered similar fates within a couple of months. I was angrier for Sandy than for myself. She was an innocent. I was not. I had brought this on myself by messing with bad people. It was a path I had chosen, and I would have to bear the consequences. I wanted very much to see Roger Allen again. I hoped I had the chance.

Revenge was really not part of my makeup, but I would not mind roughing Roger up a bit. Someday, I would also get the chance to settle my score with Victor Vargas. I was almost certain of it.

◆   ◆   ◆   ◆

Mary had brought my laptop from my hotel room, anticipating that when I was able I would want to get online. She was right, of course. That afternoon, alone in my room, I spent an hour online. It was good therapy. Just as I was shutting down, my cell phone rang. The caller ID read, "Out of Area."

"Youngblood," I answered.

"I knew that hard head would come in handy someday," Scott Glass said.

"Hey, Professor," I said, sounding a little more like myself. "Caught our bad guy yet?"

"Don't worry about that," Scott said. "We have cast a wide net. He'll turn up sooner or later. How much damage did those guys do to you?"

"Enough," I said.

I gave him the full medical report as Dr. Chang had given it to me.

"Six weeks?" Scott exclaimed. "You'll be climbing the walls."

"I hope," I said. "I can barely climb into bed right now."

A shadow fell across the foot of my bed, cast by a rather large Hispanic fellow in a cheap suit. He was carrying a briefcase. I knew immediately that the man had to be Detective Rodriguez.

"Gotta go, Professor," I said. "Someone here wants to talk to me."

"Take it easy, Blood," Scott said. "I'll be in touch."

I flipped the cell phone shut.

"I'm Detective Rodriguez from Las Vegas PD," the man said. "I'm investigating the incident that occurred in the parking garage across from the Velvet Slipper." Rodriguez pulled out a notebook and sat in the chair beside my bed. "Tell me what happened, Mr. Youngblood."

"They said they wanted my wallet," I said. "I didn't feel like giving it up."

"I see," Rodriguez said, sounding skeptical. "Three guys, and they wanted just your wallet. Would you recognize any of them?"

"I don't know," I said. "Things are still pretty fuzzy. I saw only two of them, and I cannot get a fix on their faces. I can tell you that the third man wore tennis shoes. Nikes. I got an up-close-and-personal look at the Swoosh."

The minute I said this, I regretted it. I had wanted to keep this information to myself, but the drugs must have been clouding my head. I still was not thinking clearly.

Rodriguez smirked and wrote in his notebook.

"Then what happened?" Rodriguez asked.

I described the fight pretty much the way it happened. Rodriguez made a few notes.

"Did they get your wallet?"

I assumed he already knew they hadn't. He was looking for a reaction from me.

"No," I said.

"Why not?" he asked. "You were down and out."

"The cavalry showed up," I said. "They ran."

"The cavalry being one Roy Husky and one Dennis Bracken," he said, looking at his notes.

"Yes," I said. "That would be the cavalry."

"Lucky for you," Rodriguez said.

"Yes," I said. "Real lucky."

"What were you doing in Vegas?"

"Gambling," I said.

"I see," Rodriguez said, again sounding skeptical. "What do you do for a living, Mr. Youngblood?"

"I'm retired," I said. "I used to be on Wall Street."

Rodriguez nodded and wrote in his notebook. We were playing a game. I knew that he didn't believe I had been mugged, and he probably knew that I knew that he didn't believe it.

"Do you know a Victor Vargas?" Rodriguez said.

He was good. He just tossed it out nonchalantly, but I had guessed that Victor's name would come up, and I was ready. I played dumb.

"Vargas?" I questioned. "Isn't he an artist?"

"No," Rodriguez smiled. "Not this Vargas." He reached into his briefcase and pulled out a sheet of photos encased in plastic. "We call this a photo array," he said, handing it to me. "Do you recognize anyone?"

I recognized Ralph immediately. I stared at the photos for an appropriate amount of time and then said, "I don't think so."

"Anyone vaguely familiar?"

"Not really," I said, laying the photo array beside me on the bed. "Like I said, things are still pretty fuzzy."

"Are you a licensed private investigator in the state of Tennessee?" Rodriguez asked.

He had done his homework. I was not surprised.

"I am," I said.

"I thought you were retired."

"I am," I said. "The private investigator thing is just sort of a hobby."

"I see." Rodriguez nodded and closed his notebook, then picked up the photo array. "See this guy right here?" he asked, pointing to Ralph. "His name is Ralph Marquette. They call him Ralphie East because he comes from the East Coast. He works for Victor Vargas. Word on the street is that he got in a fight last week and someone broke his nose."

"So?" I said.

"So, off the record, here is what I think," Rodriguez said. "You came to Vegas working a case that somehow involves Victor Vargas. You obviously pissed Victor off, and he sent some of his boys to rough you up, and it got out of hand. He must think highly of you to send three of them. For whatever reason, you choose not to tell me the real story. I'm okay with that. I'll file my report, and we'll chalk this up to an unsuccessful mugging, but I do not believe a word of it. Anything you want to add?"

I was silent for a while as Rodriguez sat patiently, waiting for an answer. My first impression was to like this guy. He was street smart and straightforward, like most cops I had met.

"Someday when my head clears, I'll probably remember more, and I'll give you a call and fill in some of the blanks," I said. "Right now, I am telling you as much as I can tell you. Tomorrow or the next day or the day after that, I am going back to Tennessee, and I do not ever expect to come back to Las Vegas."

Rodriguez stood and put the photo array and notebook into his briefcase and walked toward the door. He stopped in the doorway and turned and looked at me and smiled.

"For what it's worth, anyone who breaks Ralph Marquette's nose is a friend of mine," he said. "If you ever get back this way and need any help, let me know."

"Thanks," I said.

"Take care of yourself, Mr. Youngblood," Rodriquez said as he turned and left.

◆　◆　◆　◆

Late that night, I drifted into and out of sleep. I was becoming more alert each day, and the nighttime hospital noises woke me from time to time. I heard the faint sound of a siren growing louder as it approached the hospital then abruptly go silent. I became aware of a presence in the room.

"Who's there?" I asked.

A large figure stepped out of the shadows and sat in the chair beside my bed.

"Relax, it's me, Bruiser," Dennis Bracken said.

"You're out late," I said, slowly waking up. I located my bed control and raised the back so I was nearly in a sitting position.

"I just got off work," Bruiser said. "I've been by every night, but you've been asleep."

"Thanks for stopping by," I said.

"That night," Bruiser said, "I tried to call your cell phone to warn you, but my phone was dead. I saw those guys on the security cameras."

"Could you tell who they were?" I asked.

"Not specifically," Bruiser said. "Doesn't take a genius to know they were sent by Victor Vargas. What are you going to do?"

"For now," I said, feeling the pain in my ribs as I tried to get comfortable, "I am going home and try to heal."

"You know that Billy is not going to let this drop," Bruiser said. "And I don't think that guy Roy will either. They are both pretty pissed."

"Billy will do what I tell him," I said, sounding tired. "And so will Roy."

"If you say so," Bruiser said. "But if anything goes down, I want in on it."

"If anything goes down," I said, "it'll be good to have you on our side."

"Thanks," Bruiser said. "Now go back to sleep. I'm going to sit here for a while."

I didn't argue. I lowered the back of my bed and drifted off.

When I awoke, it was light outside. A folded piece of paper lay on my bedside table. With some effort, I retrieved and opened it.

The note read, "Keep in touch. Bruiser."

47

Two days later, I left the hospital. The nurse on duty wheeled me to the front door. Hospital rules. It was just as well. I still found walking difficult. My head was not hurting much, but my ribs were sore as hell.

Dr. Chang was on hand to give me a lecture about taking it easy. I had a feeling he knew he was wasting his time. He took one parting shot.

"Now listen, champ," he said with his hand on my shoulder. "Do not forget what I said, and call me if you have any problems."

Billy and Roy had left two days earlier, at my insistence. Their hovering had reached the annoying stage, and I was worried that they might go off half-cocked in search of Ralph Marquette. That meant Joseph Fleet's jet was not waiting to take me home. Mary and I had to settle for first-class commercial. Mary thought first-class commercial was great. She had not been corrupted by Fleet's private jet. We took a very early flight to Atlanta, then connected to Tri-Cities, arriving in the late afternoon.

Billy and Lacy were at the airport. Lacy raced to meet us as we came past security. She slowed and stopped in front of me.

"Can I give you a hug?" she asked, looking on the verge of tears.

"Sure," I smiled. "I like hugs. Just take it easy on the ribs. They're still pretty sore."

I opened my arms, and she stepped into my embrace. She gently wrapped her arms around me and laid her head on my shoulder. Then she started to sob. I looked at Mary. She made a gesture to Billy, and they walked away toward baggage claim, leaving us alone. I gave Lacy a squeeze that sent pain through my rib cage.

"Hey," I said softly. "What's wrong?"

"I almost got you killed," she blurted. "It's all my fault."

I pushed her away and held her by her shoulders at arm's-length.

"Look at me," I ordered.

Lacy raised her head to meet my gaze.

"This was not your fault," I said sternly.

"But if I hadn't asked you to find my mother, none of this would have happened," she sniffed.

"Finding people is what I do," I said, ignoring the fact that I had vowed to stop. "Sometimes, that can be dangerous. You never know. I got hurt because I was careless. That had nothing to do with you."

"Are you sure that you're not just trying to make me feel better?"

"I'm sure," I said. "Now, let's get my luggage and go find something to eat."

Lacy smiled and wiped away her tears.

"Okay," she said as if nothing had happened. "Let's go."

"Slowly," I said. "I'm not moving at full speed just yet."

Lacy took my hand and we made our way at a leisurely pace toward Mary and Billy, who were waiting at baggage claim with our luggage.

"What about my mom?" Lacy asked as we made the walk.

"I'll tell you all about that after dinner," I said, a task I was not looking forward to.

◆　　◆　　◆　　◆

The four of us had dinner at the Mountain Center Country Club. I liked eating there because it was never crowded, the food was good, and it was quiet. Lacy had never been to the club and was in awe at the idea of being there. She was quiet and wide-eyed, and had I not known better I would have thought we were in a church sanctuary.

"Wow, the country club," Lacy said quietly as we walked toward the dining room. "I never thought I would get to come here."

We were seated at a table by the window that overlooked the eighteenth hole of the championship course. Darkness was still hours away, and golfers were sprinkled throughout the course as far as the eye could see.

Lacy watched a group putt out on the green below us.

"Bummer," she said. "He missed a short one."

We turned our attention to our menus. After ordering, we engaged in small talk, except for Lacy, who was intent on watching foursomes approach and putt out on eighteen. When we tried to draw her into the conversation, we got one-word answers.

The food arrived. I struggled to remain focused. I felt like lying down in a corner somewhere and going to sleep.

"Good shot," Lacy said as a player hit an approach shot close to the hole.

I ignored that comment and asked, "How are things at the diner?"

In my present condition, conversation was work, but I was determined to get Lacy involved.

"Good," Lacy said. "I like it there, and Doris is great to work for."

"How about Stanley?" I asked. "How is he to work for?"

"Stanley's fine," Lacy said. "He doesn't really like to talk, and he gets annoyed if I talk too much, but I'm learning a lot. Doris talks all the time, and she is real funny."

As we ate, Lacy took center stage and told some new funny Doris stories. Every now and then, I would laugh or make a wrong turn in my chair, and my ribs would remind me of the beating I took in Vegas, a hard lesson learned.

Mary noticed and put her hand on my knee under the table and squeezed.

"How are you doing?" she asked quietly.

"Fine," I lied.

She saw right through that. She patted my knee and gave me a sad smile that said, *I am worried about you.*

When we finished dinner, Mary asked Billy to show her the tennis courts. Mary knew where the courts were, and Billy knew that she knew, but he played along, and they left Lacy and me alone to have the talk I did not want to have. None of this was lost on Lacy. As soon as they were out of earshot, she pinned me down with those blue eyes and a very serious expression.

"So tell me about my mom," she said. "Did you see her?"

"I did," I said. "And she looked fine, and she is not staying in Las Vegas against her will."

"Is she coming back?"

I didn't know how to sugarcoat my answer, so I just gave it to her straight the way I saw it.

"Not right away," I said.

Lacy sat in silence. I could tell she was on the verge of tears, and I felt lousy for her.

"She said she would call," I said. As soon as the words were out of my mouth, I thought maybe they were a mistake. I was drowning. I had no idea how to handle this situation.

"I'll bet," Lacy said sarcastically.

"Whatever happens," I said, "I'm in your life for as long as you want me in it."

"You and Mary and so many others have been great," Lacy said. And then the tears came.

I scooted my chair next to hers, and she laid her head on my shoulder and sobbed.

A couple of minutes later, she stopped abruptly and wiped away the tears and regained control.

"Why would she do that?" she asked angrily.

"I don't know," I said. "But it has nothing to do with you."

"What, then?"

"I don't know," I said.

In truth, I had a good idea. Something had happened in West Virginia. Whatever it was had surfaced, and Tracy had decided for whatever reason that Lacy was better off without her, or that she was better off without Lacy. I had a theory that I would check out with Sister Sarah Agnes later.

"What do I do now?"

"You do the best you can and get on with your life," I said.

"I can't stay with you and Mary forever," she said.

"No," I said. "Not forever. But for now, let's just concentrate on tomor-row and next month and the rest of this year."

"So I can start school just like always?"

"I don't see why not," I said. "Same rules apply."

"I can live with the rules," Lacy said seriously. "I'm just glad I can stay. Thank you so much."

She kissed my cheek and left me speechless.

"Let's go get Billy and Mary," I said, finding my tongue.

We walked slowly from the restaurant to the front doors and out toward the parking lot. In the distance, I saw Mary and Billy waiting by the car, engaged in casual conversation. It seemed like it took us forever to reach the car.

"Think I could learn how to play golf?" Lacy asked.

"I don't see why not," I said. "Do you want to?"

"I think I do," she said.

48

July morphed into August with little recognition from me. Hot was hot, and it was hot and muggy in East Tennessee. I slept a lot and was depressed. My head felt okay, but I was not quite all there. It was as if a part of me were missing. My battery was low, and I could not get it charged. I had short periods of thinking I was back, and then I was gone again. The more I slept, the more tired and the more depressed I got. I could barely force myself to get out of bed. When I did manage that feat, I would shower and shave, put on fresh pajamas, and return to bed to work. I would work an hour or two on my laptop and then turn out the lights and go back to sleep. I was sleeping sixteen hours a day. I did not want visitors. I unplugged the phone and turned my cell phone off. Mary refused to serve me in bed after a few days and went back to work. Lacy was gone most of the time, working her two jobs, so I was alone with my two new friends, self-pity and depression. If I wanted to eat, I had to go to the kitchen. I went once a day when no one was around.

I was still wearing the clavicle strap. My collarbone was okay, but my ribs didn't seem to be getting better. I turned on my cell and called my local doctor to complain. He told me that ribs take a long time to heal and show little progress early on. I asked how long and was told six to eight weeks. Wasn't that what Dr. Chang had said? I couldn't remember. I was in my fourth week. At this rate, I would go crazy before I healed. I turned off my cell and hurled it across the room. It hit a lampshade and fell harmlessly to the floor, still intact.

As the days passed, Mary and even Lacy got more and more annoyed with me. I knew everything they said was right, but I didn't care. Billy came over to visit and gave me a lecture about mind over matter, and I told him to get lost. Roy stopped by once to tell me to let him know if I needed anything or wanted some company. Otherwise, he would stay away and let me work things out. T. Elbert wrote more than one email telling me to "get your ass in gear." I wrote back and told him to mind his own damn business. I was beginning to hate myself because I knew I was not myself.

One day at dinnertime around the five-week mark, I heard the condo door open and shut a number of times in a very short period. I wondered what was going on. Part of me said, *Screw it. I don't care.* But my curiosity got the better of me, and I silently made my way to the hall that overlooked the living room, staying out of sight. I could peek around the corner and see into the kitchen–dining room area. I felt like a little kid, but I couldn't help myself. I saw Mary, Billy, and Roy and the back wheels of T. Elbert's wheelchair. I heard Big Bob's voice, a meeting about me, no doubt. I felt ashamed. I had alienated the people who cared most about me. I had been stubborn and willful and drawn a line in the sand.

The stubborn, willful part of me quietly took the whole of me back to bed, vowing that whatever they were planning was not going to work.

Man, oh, man, was I in for a big surprise.

49

The lights came on, and the shades went up. It was daylight.

"What the hell?" I mumbled. I peeked at the clock, which glowed a red 6:00.

"Get up and get in the shower," Mary said. She sounded none to happy.

That little kid emerged again, and I pulled the covers over my head and hunkered down. All of a sudden, the quilt and top sheet were ripped off the bed and thrown on the floor. Mary grabbed the front of my shirt and pulled me to a sitting position.

"Ow! That hurt," I said with some gusto, mixed with a whole lot of surprise.

"You're going to hurt even more if you don't do what I say," Mary growled with animal intensity. "Now get in the goddamn shower."

Mary rarely cursed or lost her temper, especially at me. Now I had seen and heard both in a matter of seconds. I had hit the daily double. Her "cop-ness" had surfaced.

"Okay," I whined. "I'm going."

Best not to mess with a six-foot blonde on a rampage.

"When you're finished, get dressed and come downstairs," she ordered. She didn't wait for an answer.

I must admit the shower felt good. My ribs were still sore, but I thought I detected a slight improvement. Maybe my detecting skills were coming back. While I was in the shower, I shaved. A shave in the shower is the best and closest a man can get. The whole process took some time, but I finally made it out of my bedroom and down the stairs. Mary was in the kitchen. I smelled bacon and coffee. It smelled good. I came into the kitchen and stood as if waiting for more orders. Mary smiled slightly.

"You certainly look better," she said. "Now, sit."

I pulled myself up on my usual barstool while Mary scrambled eggs. The willful part of me considered being a stubborn jerk and refusing to eat, but the sensible part did not want to start World War III.

We ate in silence.

"It's good," I said finally, even though I hadn't felt hungry.

"Thank you," Mary said formally.

I noticed suitcases by the front door. My heart skipped a beat. Was she leaving me?

"You going somewhere?" I asked meekly.

"We are going for a little ride," Mary said.

The *we* was such a relief that I didn't bother to argue.

Mary cleaned up the kitchen while I had a second cup of coffee. I didn't know what it was, but I felt a missing piece of my old self fall into place.

"Let's go," she said as she motioned me to the front door.

"Do I need to pack?"

"I have everything we need," Mary said, pulling up the handles on the two suitcases. "I think you can handle one of these, since they have wheels."

We wheeled the suitcases out of 5300 to the elevator and took it down to the parking lot. Mary loaded the luggage while I slowly maneuvered my way into the passenger seat. The clock on the dash read 7:44.

◆　◆　◆　◆

We sat on the balcony of my penthouse condo at the Seascape on Singer Island, Florida, with our wine and watched darkness creep across the Atlantic toward us. We had made the marathon drive in less than twelve hours, stopping only for restroom breaks. After much convincing, Mary had actually let me drive for an hour, confining me to no more than five miles per hour over the speed limit. She, of course, drove much faster. *Cops.*

I had not drunk any alcohol since the parking garage incident. I wasn't sure why. Sitting next to Mary with a warm breeze and a glass of robust red seemed just what the doctor ordered. I thought Dr. Chang would approve. Another piece of me dropped into place.

"Thanks," I said.

It was only one word, but it contained volumes, and Mary knew it.

"You're welcome," Mary said.

That was the sum total of our conversation.

50

The next morning, we went to breakfast at the Sailfish Marina. Breakfast has always been my favorite meal of the day, and the Sailfish Marina was one of my all-time favorite places to have breakfast. It ranked right up there with the Mountain Center Diner, the Mountain Lodge in Gatlinburg, Tennessee and the Silver Fork Lodge in Brighton, Utah.

"I love it here," I said to Mary as I looked out through the glass at the many small yachts and fishing boats tucked neatly into their slips.

"I know you do," she smiled.

I felt the real me starting to emerge. I think Mary felt it, too.

We had a table by the windows. The windows ran floor to ceiling and opened by pushing outward from seams in the center. They went around most of the restaurant, allowing views of the dock, the boats, and the girls in their bikinis that were feeding the fish. Our window was slightly opened to allow a little warmth to intrude on the air conditioning and to let us feel and smell the warm sea air.

"What day is it?" I asked. I had completely lost track and hadn't cared.

"Sunday," Mary said.

"August?"

She laughed. "Yes, August."

Breakfast arrived, and I realized I was hungry. I ate with gusto for the first time since the beating.

"Today, we get to rest," Mary said. "Tomorrow, we start to work."

"Yes, master," I smiled.

"Where have I heard that before?" Mary teased.

She knew damn well where she had heard it—from herself, less than a year ago.

♦   ♦   ♦   ♦

For the next week, we worked. Oh, how we worked. The Donald Young-blood Rehabilitation Program was being thrown back in my face. We walked early, worked out in the pool, went to the local gym to do some very light weightlifting, and then spent the late afternoons at the beach. I could feel my depression going out with the tide. I looked forward to each day under Mary's relentless encouragement, but I was still missing a piece of my old self.

The following Saturday afternoon, I was in the calm Atlantic running in knee-deep water. I wasn't covering much distance, and despite its being very low-impact exercise my ribs still felt the slightest jolt. Mary was walking beside me in ankle-deep water. She looked gorgeous, and I felt something stir. We hadn't had sex since the parking garage incident, and I was puzzled why I didn't feel the need. We had not even discussed sex, and I knew that Mary had to be concerned, given our history. We might miss a day or even two, but this was ridiculous, and I was surprised that it had taken so long to occur to me.

"I think you've got the better end of this deal," I said, panting like a dog that had been out in the sun too long.

"What goes around comes around," Mary said.

"Meaning?"

"Meaning, do you remember last year when we were down here?"

"How could I forget?" I said.

I had driven her unmercifully as I helped her recover from the results of a bank robbery shootout. During that time, we had fallen in love, and we'd been together ever since.

"Well, payback is a bitch," Mary said.

I laughed. "You got that right," I said. "Payback is definitely a female."

Mary kicked water at me. "Good to see that Youngblood sense of humor returning," she said.

◆　◆　◆　◆

I awoke the following morning, sat straight up in bed, and immediately knew something was different. The last missing piece of me had somehow found its way home in the middle of the night. I didn't know how, but I knew it as surely as I knew my heart was beating. I smiled to myself. I was back.

As usual, Mary was up before me. Her routine was to fix coffee and take it to the balcony to watch the sunrise. I knew that was where I would find her.

I quickly went to the bathroom and brushed my teeth. Then I gargled. Then I shaved and took a quick, wonderful shower. Everything was just a click different, that one tiny adjustment that separated good from perfect. I was myself for the first time since my brain had gone tap dancing inside my head.

I toweled off, pulled on a pair of shorts and a T-shirt, and went out through the bedroom door and into the living room. Through the sliding glass door, I saw Mary cuddling her coffee cup in both hands and staring at the ocean. I quietly slid the door open and stepped onto the balcony. The view was spectacular. Far out on the ocean, the sun was peeking from the cover of darkness through scattered clouds and promising another typically hot August day on Singer Island.

Mary felt my presence and turned and smiled.

"Good morning," she said.

I smiled and kept silent.

"What?" she asked.

I held out my hand, and she took it. I pulled her close and kissed her passionately. I led her back through the sliding glass door and into the living room. I took her top off on the way down the hall to the bedroom, and she returned the favor. As we reached the bed, Mary slid gracefully out of her shorts and helped me off with mine.

"Good thing I had a shower," she said.

"Wouldn't have mattered," I said as I pulled her down on the bed.

◆　　◆　　◆　　◆

An hour later, we lay locked together by arms and legs about as close as was physically possible for a man and woman. I was amazed at the perfect fit. I was floating outside myself, as if I were on drugs. Time had no meaning. I didn't want to move. I wanted this moment to last as long as possible.

Mary moved her head slightly and kissed my earlobe and whispered, "Welcome back."

"Good to be back," I said reverently.

"I was very worried about you," she said.

"I was worried about me, too," I said. "I was having a hard time finding myself. You have been very patient."

"My patience was about to run out," she said. "But then I started seeing signs that you were making your way back."

"I think Singer Island was the key," I said. "The pieces started falling into place here. It was a good idea to bring me here."

"Not my idea," Mary said.

"Whose?"

"Sister Sarah Agnes's."

"Sister Sarah Agnes? You talked with Sister Sarah Agnes?" I asked incredulously.

"I talked to everybody I could think of for advice," Mary said. "Most everyone said to give you space and you would come out of it. But you didn't seem to be coming out of it. Finally, Lacy said, 'Call Sister Sarah Agnes.' Smart girl, that Lacy. Anyway, Sister Sarah Agnes spent a lot of time with me on the phone asking about our relationship, our love life, how we met, and how we got along. I told her everything."

Mary disentangled from me and rolled and propped herself on one elbow, giving me an arousing view of her breasts. I tried to focus on our conversation.

"Everything?"

"Everything," Mary said. "Anyway, after a long pause, all she said was, 'Take him to Singer.' So I said, 'Singer?' And she said, 'Do for him what he did for you. I think he will associate and find his way back. What have you got to lose?' So here we are."

"Smart woman, that Sarah Agnes. I seem to be surrounded by smart women."

"Lucky for you," Mary smiled, kissing my ribs. I didn't notice any soreness.

"You were without sex for a long time," I said.

"I was," Mary said.

"Must have been difficult," I said.

"It was," Mary said. "I was considering an online search for vibrators."

"And?"

"And I decided to wait for the real thing," she teased.

"I'm glad you did," I said. "Sounds like we have a lot of catching up to do."

"We do," Mary said.

"Then let's get started," I said.

"Let's," Mary said.

51

The following week, I felt reborn. I rehabilitated with greater enthusiasm. The return of my sex drive, the blond goddess, the great weather, and the beautiful surroundings made for optimum healing. How much better could it get? The collarbone was mended and the clavicle strap removed. My bruises had faded. My head had long since stopped hurting, and the fog that had clouded my brain was finally gone. The soreness in my ribs remained but was fading each day. I could take deep breaths without effort. I could run at the ocean's edge with minimal discomfort. Physically, I was almost back.

That Tuesday night, we sat on the balcony sharing a bottle of chilled Chateau Ste. Michelle Sauvignon Blanc that, if it was lucky, had a life expectancy of maybe a half-hour. The half-full bottle was nestled in a Tervis wine bucket surrounded by slowly melting ice cubes. A soft breeze meandered in from the Atlantic. The sun was behind our building, and the shadows that fell across the beach told of its imminent departure over the western horizon. I could not remember feeling so content. I was alive, and all was right in my world.

"I need to see Raul," I said to Mary. "He would kill me if I came down here and we didn't get together."

"You should," Mary said.

"I think I'll ask him to meet me for lunch on Thursday. Want to come?"

"No," Mary said, pouring more wine for both of us. The bottle was now empty. "You two do the guy thing. I'll go shopping. I want to check out the Gardens Mall."

"Cops shop?" I teased.

"This cop does," Mary laughed.

◆　◆　◆　◆

"So, Donnie, where is the lovely Mary?" Raul asked in his cultured Spanish accent.

We were having lunch in a restaurant in Pompano Beach, roughly halfway between Singer Island and Miami.

"Shopping," I said.

"Shopping? She chose shopping over lunch with Raul Rivera?" Raul asked with mock disdain.

"Hard for you to believe, I know," I said. "But that ego of yours needs a reality check every once in a while."

"Yours, too, probably," Raul said.

"Mine recently had one," I said quietly.

"Tell me about it," Raul said, picking up on the seriousness in my voice.

I told him. The farther I went into my story, the redder his face got. He looked like he was going to explode.

"And why was I not told this before?" he demanded, a little too loudly.

A couple of heads turned.

"Calm down, Raul," I said softly, hoping he, too, would lower his voice. "I chose not to tell you because I didn't want you going off half-cocked, defending my honor."

"What is this half-cocked?" Raul asked. "I have not heard that expression before."

"It is American slang that means rushing to do something without completely thinking it through," I said.

"You mean like a half-cocked pistol?"

"Like that," I said.

"I might have rushed into something, Donnie, but I would have been fully cocked," Raul said, smiling.

"Uh-huh," I grunted.

"So when *do* we defend your honor?"

"*We* are not going to do anything," I said. "I put myself in harm's way. Vargas was just being Vargas."

"But he tried to kill you."

"No, he didn't. He sent his men to rough me up, and it got out of hand when I fought back," I said. "If I have a beef, it's with a guy named Ralph."

"So let's go after this person, Ralph," Raul said.

"No," I said. "Ralph was also just being Ralph. He was doing what his boss ordered. I pissed him off when I broke his nose, and he wanted payback. He wasn't even the one who hit me from behind. The guy in the Nike tennis shoes did that. If I went after anyone, it would be him."

"So let's go after Mr. Tennis Shoes," Raul said, not content to let it slide.

"No," I said. "Other people could get hurt. It's not worth it. If he had beaten up Mary, I would track him to the ends of the earth, but not for myself. I know it's hard for you to understand. It's just the way I feel."

"You are too nice to be messing with the people you have been messing with," Raul said. "I wish you would marry that good-looking woman of yours and go back to full-time investing."

I smiled at Raul.

"But you will not do that, will you, my friend?" Raul said. "You like solving the puzzles, and you like the possibility of danger."

I didn't know how to answer that, so I didn't.

52

On our last night at Singer, we went to Max & Eddie's Cucina, my favorite restaurant on the island. I had known David, the proprietor, for a number of years. The food was consistently good, the wine list extensive, and the service friendly.

We sat in a corner booth in the back. It afforded as much intimacy as the restaurant had to offer. The crowd was typically sparse for an August weeknight. The noise level and lighting were subdued. A candle flickered on our table, bathing Mary in a glow that made her even sexier than I could imagine, and I could imagine a lot.

The calamari appetizer arrived, enough for two and then some, the best I had eaten anywhere.

"This is really good," Mary said.

"Umm," I responded, my mouth full.

"I wish we didn't have to go back," Mary said. "But I promised Big Bob I would take only two weeks."

"Maybe I could bribe him with a big donation to the Mountain Center PD," I said.

"Bribing the chief of police could get you thrown in jail," Mary teased. "Besides, I need to go back to work so I can get some rest."

The main course arrived; grouper francese for me and shrimp parmigiana for Mary. We ate and smiled a lot and made little noises that let each other know how good our food was. We shared forkfuls across the table.

We had just finished eating when I smelled cigarette smoke. I located it a few booths down, toward the front. Florida has a no-smoking-in-restaurants law, and I couldn't imagine anyone not knowing about it. Our waitress arrived to inform the offender of the policy, and I heard a raised voice that seemed to be giving her a hard time. Mary turned to see what was going on as I rose from the booth to give my support to our waitress. Then Mary was on her feet, blocking my path.

"I'll handle this," she said, reaching into her purse.

She turned and headed toward the front of the restaurant with me in pursuit.

"Sir," Mary said in full cop mode, flashing her badge. "The state of Florida has passed a law forbidding smoking in all restaurants. Please put out your cigarette."

The waitress stepped away from the table, content to let Mary handle the situation. I looked around for David, but he was nowhere in sight. Just as well. I was enjoying watching Mary work.

I saw the surprise on the offender's face, brought on by the sight of a beautiful six-foot blonde with a badge. He recovered quickly and smiled.

"Why?"

Mary leaned in and said quietly, "Because if you don't, I'll call this in and have you hauled off to jail."

"Bernie," the woman with him said, "put out the damn cigarette."

Bernie dropped the cigarette in his water glass and looked at me for the first time.

"Who's he?" he asked.

"My partner," Mary said. "And he hates cigarette smoke more than I do."

I tried flexing my muscles, but I don't think Bernie noticed. I would have sucked in my stomach, but I didn't have one. The twenty pounds I had lost already made my pants too big.

Mary looked at the waitress.

"Has he paid his check?"

The waitress nodded.

Mary looked back at Bernie.

Bernie took the hint.

"Come on, Bernice," he said. "We're leaving this dump."

Bernie and Bernice? You've got to be kidding.

Bernie and Bernice left as indignantly as possible, pretending it was their idea. But I could hear Bernice giving Bernie an earful as they walked outside. They got in a red Corvette and drove away.

David came out of the kitchen.

"What just happened?" he asked.

The waitress told him how my beautiful blond date had come to the rescue.

"You missed all the fun," I said.

"Story of my life," David said.

He looked at Mary. "Your dinner is on me," he said.

"No," Mary said. "It was just too delicious not to pay for. Besides, my date here has lots of money."

"Okay, then," David smiled. "After-dinner drinks are on me for both of you."

Mary smiled. "We accept," she said.

53

The following Monday, Roy sat on the other side of my desk drinking coffee from Dunkin' Donuts that he had brought in a few minutes before. I let him stay because he also had coffee for me, as well as a poppy seed bagel with cream cheese.

"I was worried about you for a while," Roy said.

"Me, too," I said.

"Are you back?" Roy asked.

"Other than the ribs being a little sore, yeah, I'm back."

"Going back to Vegas?" Roy asked.

"No plans to," I said. "For now."

"You know Billy and I are not going to let this rest," Roy said matter-of-factly.

I digested that for a minute.

"Billy I can understand," I said. "But you?"

"You, Billy, and T. Elbert are the only friends I have in Mountain Center," Roy said. "Hell, you're the only friends I have anywhere. A guy has to look out for his friends. Besides, it happened on my watch, so to speak."

"I appreciate the thought," I said. "Let it lie for now. I want to see how things shake out."

Roy nodded as he got to his feet to leave. "For now," he said.

◆   ◆   ◆   ◆

News traveled fast in our small town. My office door opened and closed more in one day than it usually did in a week.

Midmorning, Big Bob showed up.

"About damn time you woke up and smelled the coffee," he said, hands on hips, not bothering to sit down. "Welcome back, Blood."

"Good to be back," I said.

He promptly left.

Just before lunch, Doris called.

"Welcome back," she said.

"Thanks, Doris."

"I'm sending over lunch," she said. "On the house. Don't argue. What time do you want it?"

"Anytime," I said.

Lunch turned out to be country-fried steak with gravy, mashed potatoes, green beans, and half a dozen homemade yeast rolls. I usually didn't have a big lunch, but I had twenty pounds to gain, and so I ate with guilt-free gusto.

That afternoon, I got the shock of my life. If the pope had paid me a visit, I wouldn't have been more surprised. Stanley Johns walked into my office.

"How are you, Don?" Stanley asked in that raspy voice of his. "I was worried about you."

"I'm fine, Stanley," I said. "Sit down and I'll make some coffee."

"No," Stanley said, looking anxious and moving toward the door. "I can't stay. I have some shopping to do and lots of work. You know, viruses. I just wanted to drop by and see how you're doing and tell you I'm glad you're better."

"Thanks, Stanley," I said as he opened the outer door. "Drop by anytime."

I don't think he heard the last part. I was beginning to get a complex. Nobody wanted to stick around and visit.

Around four o'clock that Monday afternoon, I had my final visitor of the day. The blond-haired, blue-eyed female looked a little more grown up than the last time I saw her, although it had been only two weeks. Lacy had spent the night with her friend Hannah on Sunday, and I had left the condo very early Monday morning.

She came in, sat down, and looked right at me.

"How are you doing?" she asked.

"Much better, Lacy," I said.

"I knew you would make it back," she said.

"Really?" I asked. "Everyone else was wondering."

"You're like me," Lacy said. "You're tougher than people think you are."

"Well, thanks for that," I said, smiling at her comparison. "But that's not why you came to see me in my office."

"And we are both real smart," she continued. "No, I came because I'm worried about something."

"Tell me."

"Well, school starts next week, and we have to tell them who to call in case of emergency and where we live and all of that, and I was worried that someone might show up and take me away," she rambled.

"First," I said, "stop worrying. Nobody is going to take you away. My guess is that so many kids actually need help that the authorities are not going to waste time looking at a kid who doesn't."

"You think?" Lacy said, straightening up in her chair.

"I think," I said, not mentioning the tenuous document I had stashed away in my safe-deposit box. "I will also look into legal guardianship if it ever becomes an issue. So relax. Looks like you're stuck with me."

"Why would you do that?" Lacy asked.

"I like you," I said. "And I know what it's like not to have any parents around, although I did have mine until I was in college."

"Thanks," she said, getting up to leave. "I'll see you at home."

"Want a ride?" I asked. "I can close up now."

"No need," Lacy said. "I'm meeting Hannah at the diner, and we're walking home together. Remember, she lives just up the street from us."

"You be careful," I said.

She grabbed her backpack and was out of the office faster than Bob Kesling could say, "Touchdown, Tennessee!"

◆　◆　◆　◆

I had begun the process of shutting down the office when the phone rang.

"Cherokee Investigations," I answered.

"Hey, Blood," Scott Glass said. "How are you feeling?"

"Not too bad, Professor."

"Well," Scott said, "I'm going to make you feel even better. Guess who Homeland Security caught trying to leave the country?"

"Britney Spears?" I cracked.

I knew damn well it had to be Roger Allen.

"Britney who?" Scott asked.

I hoped he was kidding.

"Forget it, Scott," I said. "You need to get out more. Are you going to tell me you have Roger Allen?"

"Or whatever his damn name is," Scott said. "But we have him."

"Where?"

"In a federal facility in Miami."

"When?"

"Two days ago," Scott said. "I just got the DNA match."

"How could you detain him long enough to do a DNA match?" I asked.

"Hell, Blood," Scott said. "We're working with Homeland Security. They can do whatever they damn well please."

"Well, I'm glad I'm on your side," I said.

"Want to go down and see ole Roger and gloat a bit?" Scott asked.

"How can I do that?"

"You're in the FBI computer now as a consultant," Scott said. "I can get you access."

"I appreciate the thought," I said. "But I'll pass. I do know a cop in Atlanta who might want to take you up on that offer."

"I might just let him do that," Scott said. "He would have to bring Sandy down to ID Roger. She wouldn't have to see him."

"Oh, she'll want to see him, all right," I said.

I gave Murphy's cell phone number to Scott before we hung up.

54

The days turned into weeks, and the college football season kicked off. The Tennessee Volunteers had lost a number of key players to the NFL, so the prognosticators were predicting a good but not great season. Not surprisingly to me, they lost their opener on the West Coast.

Mary's son, Jimmy, had been a first-round pick of the Tennessee Titans, which thrilled us both. I used up some favors and secured tickets to four games. Mary and I went to two early-season games and afterwards had dinner with Jimmy and his fiancée, Diane. Jimmy was the backup quarterback for now but always had to be ready to play. He was only one hard hit away from being the starter. Such was life in the NFL.

The leaves were starting to show some color, and the nights were longer and cooler. I was glad to see summer retreat. I loved winter and liked spring and autumn. Summer I tolerated. I was one of those people always on the lookout for the first snowflake of the season.

Physically, I was all the way back. My ribs were the last injury to heal, and they felt normal. Mentally, I still had a ways to go. I had flashbacks of the parking garage beating. I wondered if that memory might stay with me forever.

In late September, I got a surprise phone call.

"Hey, Youngblood, it's Murphy."

"Hey, Murphy," I replied, remembering the first time he had called. "Everything okay?"

"Yeah, everything's fine," Murphy said. "I wanted to thank you for the Roger Allen thing."

"How'd that go?" I asked.

I knew what Scott Glass had said, but I wanted to get Murphy's version.

"Beautiful," Murphy said. "Sandy identified him and then walked right in and slapped his face so hard I could hear the echo. I know it hurt like a bitch. Roger was so surprised he just sat there with this dumb look on his face. Then he recovered and started screaming, 'Get this bitch out of here!' It sure was good therapy for Sandy."

I had seen Sandy's temper a few times. She was spunky and really strong for her size. I almost felt sorry for Roger. Almost.

"Wish I had been there," I said. "Too bad you didn't video it."

"Surprised the hell out of me," Murphy said. "That woman has grit."

"She is quite a woman," I said.

"Speaking of which," Murphy said, "we're getting married."

I was stunned. Sandy was marrying a cop? Didn't make sense. Then it hit me.

"Congratulations," I said. "When are you leaving the force?"

"How'd you know?"

"I know Sandy," I said. "She couldn't deal with that lifestyle."

"I put my papers in last week," Murphy chuckled. "I'm leaving at the end of the month. I have accepted a job as head of security at a company in Atlanta that's doing stem cell research. They must be close to a breakthrough because they are paranoid about security. What they have now is laughable."

"Nice to be wanted," I said. "And take good care of them. I think I own some of their stock."

"What's nice is the paycheck," Murphy said.

"Money is the master motivator," I said.

"We want you and your lady to come to the wedding," Murphy said. "Sandy still considers you a good friend, and I'm fine with that. I hope you'll come."

"Murphy," I said, "you can count on it."

55

The weather gods were kind and granted a classic October Sunday for Sandy's wedding. To my surprise, it was held at the Jekyll Island Club Hotel on Jekyll Island. The guests numbered at least a hundred people, and a few were cops from Marietta.

The Jekyll Island Club dated back to the late 1800s. It started as a private getaway for the very rich. Over the years, its membership grew to include names like Goodyear, Macy, Pulitzer, Rockefeller, and Vanderbilt. The club started to decline during World War I and by the end off World War II was completely shut down. The state of Georgia stepped in and bought the entire island in 1947 and turned it into a state park. Certain portions of the island were leased to various investment groups. One such group began the restoration that transformed the original club into the luxury hotel it is today.

The wedding was a two-day marathon event. It started with a ladies' breakfast and a men's breakfast. After breakfast, the women went horseback riding and the men skeet shooting. Mary, of course, would rather have gone skeet shooting, but she was a good sport and went along with the other women.

The rehearsal was on Saturday, and I had to go because to my surprise I had been asked to do a reading for the wedding. Afterward, we attended the rehearsal dinner.

The Catholic priest kept things moving the next day, and the wedding went off on time and without any surprises.

"You headed back tomorrow?" Sandy asked.

We were outdoors at the dockside restaurant watching daylight disappear. The wedding was long over, and the reception was winding down. People were scattered around the dock area in small groups having quiet conversations, drinks in hand.

"Yeah, we're heading out early," I said. "Long drive."

Sandy took another drink of her beer, and I took a drink of mine. Sandy was one of the few women I knew who liked beer as much as she did wine. I caught Mary's eye, and she smiled and gave me an almost imperceptible nod. I had no idea what it meant. *You're next?*

"I'm glad you came," Sandy said.

"I'm glad you invited us," I said. "It's been fun."

We drank more beer, leaning on the railing and staring out over the water into the night.

"I hear you're one hell of a shot," Sandy said. "Jim said you were by far the best shot out there today."

"Luck," I said. "But Jim's being modest. He is pretty good himself."

"And Mary tells me you're good with handguns."

"Good enough," I said.

We drank a little more beer.

"I am so glad Jim is quitting," Sandy said. "He was married to the job, and now he is divorcing the job and marrying me. I am a lucky girl."

She wasn't drunk yet, but she was feeling pretty good. I was still nursing my second beer.

"You certainly are," I agreed.

"It could not have been you," Sandy said, looking me. "I know that now."

"No," I said. "It couldn't. I am a firm believer in 'What will be will be.' It was always supposed to be Murphy."

Sandy smiled. "Thanks," she said. "That's a nice thing to say. I think Jim and I make a good match."

"Hard for me to tell," I said. "But I like Murphy, and I know he's crazy about you."

"And I'll tell you something else," she said, slightly slurring the word *else*. "Mary is the woman for you."

"So I've been told," I said.

The wind was picking up and causing ripples on the water like endless corduroy.

"I hope you realize it," she said. *Realize* didn't come out quite right either.

"I am beginning to," I said, sipping my beer.

"Good," Sandy said, and paused. "I think I'm getting drunk."

"Relax," I said. "It's your wedding day."

◆　　◆　　◆　　◆

"It has been a really nice day," Mary said.

We were back in our suite. The digital clock glowed 12:05, way past my bedtime. Mary and I were usually in bed by ten o'clock at the latest, but we were running on wedding day adrenaline and needed some time to come down.

"It has," I said, sipping a glass of red wine I had carried back from the restaurant.

Mary was having a glass of white from a half-empty bottle we had brought from Mountain Center. We sat on the couch with our feet on the coffee table.

"I haven't been around this many people socially in years," she said. "I had such a good time."

"I'm glad," I said.

Casual conversation was not my forte, but I knew how to keep it going. Mary liked to talk. Most of the time, I was a good listener, which made us a perfect fit.

"I like Sandy."

"She likes you, too," I said. "She thinks you're the one."

"The one what?" Mary asked.

"The one for me," I said.

"I am," Mary said, kissing me lightly on the cheek. "Want me to prove it?"

"Please do," I said.

And she did, right there on the couch.

56

October faded into November, and the brilliant-colored leaves faded with it. The glorious fall colors in the mountains of East Tennessee grudgingly gave way to the early signs of coming winter. Like me, the leaves that were left showed their age as they clung in desperation. I tried to cling to the glory days when everything had been easier physically. I ran, went to the gym, and played racquetball with the same enthusiasm as always, but the price was higher. Muscles ached, little injuries popped up, and getting out of bed in the morning was an adventure. I was like an aging prizefighter hanging on for one last fight. I wondered if I could ever get back to the way I was before the parking garage encounter. Maybe age was just catching up. In the end, I knew, age would win, but I would not go quietly.

A cold front moved into East Tennessee, and the temperature dipped into the thirties, accompanied by a stiff breeze. From my second-floor vantage point, I watched the few people on Main Street bow their heads into the wind, their collars turned high. I gave thanks for the warmth of my office and the cup of coffee I cradled in both hands.

"Heard from Billy?" Roy asked.

Roy was sitting in his usual chair on the other side of my desk.

"Mary, Lacy, and I went to Cherokee for the weekend," I said, turning away from the window. "Billy's fine. He seems happier than I've ever seen him."

"Ain't love grand," Roy said.

"It is that," I said, ignoring the sarcasm.

"So, Youngblood," Roy said, "is it better to have loved and lost or to have never loved at all?"

"You tell me," I said.

"I don't know," he said. "I only know the *lost* part hurts like hell."

I knew Roy was hurting, and I knew why. Death sometimes had a way of leaving things unresolved and scarring your soul.

"Someday, when you're ready, you might want to share that with someone," I said.

Roy gave a slight nod and remained silent. He took another drink of coffee. He was about to respond when the phone rang.

"I gotta go," Roy said, rising quickly.

"See you later," I said as I pushed the *Talk* button on the portable phone, knowing who was on the other end of the line. "Cherokee Investigations," I answered as Roy disappeared into the outer office.

"Hello, Don."

"Hey, Sister Sarah Agnes. How are things?"

I heard the outer office door close.

"I have a concern," she said.

"Tell me," I said.

"Tracy Malone called me on Friday and asked if she could come back to Silverthorn," Sister Sarah Agnes said. "I said sure, and she said she would be here Sunday afternoon. She hasn't shown up. Furthermore, she gave me her cell phone number, and I have called a couple of times and have not gotten an answer. I'm worried."

"How did she sound on Friday?" I asked.

"Like someone who had made a decision," Sarah Agnes said.

"Explain," I said.

"I have heard it from patients before," she said. "You can hear it in their voices. They have come to terms with something and have decided to deal with it. She was ready, and she wanted my help."

For a minute, I was sorry I had answered the phone. My practical side did not want to get further involved with Victor Vargas and Tracy Malone. It might not end well, and I was tired of things not ending well. But then my stubborn side took over. I had considerable time invested in Tracy Malone. I needed to see that investment through to the end, if not for myself, then for Lacy.

"I'll go look for her," I heard myself say.

"Couldn't I just call the police?" Sarah Agnes asked.

"And tell them what?"

There was silence on the other end of the line. I hoped I had not been too abrupt.

"You're right," Sarah Agnes said with a sigh. "What would compel them to get involved?"

"I'll go," I said. "I'll call you tomorrow."

When I told Mary this bit of news, I was going to need backup.

◆　◆　◆　◆

After lunch, I called Billy's cell phone.

"Hey, Blood, what's going on?" he answered.

"I need you in the office later today," I said. "Pack for a trip. We are leaving tomorrow."

"Vegas?" Billy asked.

"Yes," I said.

"About time," Billy growled.

I then called Roy Husky.

"Hey, gumshoe. What's up?" Roy cracked.

"I need you at the office about five o'clock today," I said. "Can you make it?"

"Sure. What's this about?" Roy asked.

"Backup," I said. "This is about backup."

◆　◆　◆　◆

Later that afternoon, I made my last call of the day.

"Hi," Mary said. "I'm surprised to hear from you. Anything wrong?"

"No," I said. "Everything's fine. Come by the office after your shift."

"Why?" Mary asked. "What's going on?"

"Don't be so nosy," I said. "It's a surprise."

"Okay," Mary said. "I'll see you after work. I love surprises."

Oh, yeah, I thought, *you're going to love this one!*

◆　◆　◆　◆

Billy arrived first, and I filled him in. He listened without interruption.

"It's the right thing to do," he said. "I'm glad you didn't try to do it alone."

"If I did it alone, Mary would leave me," I said.

Roy walked in. He looked at Billy and nodded. Billy nodded back.

"Now, somebody tell me something," Roy said.

"We're going to Vegas," Billy said.

"About damn time," Roy said.

"My sentiments exactly," Billy said.

"When do we leave?" Roy asked.

"Tomorrow," I said.

"I'll see if one of the jets is available," Roy said.

I heard the outer office door open. Seconds later, Mary appeared in the doorway. She stopped, looked at Billy and then Roy, put her hands on her hips, and looked at me. Her face started to color.

"Some surprise, you coward," she said.

"Guilty as charged, officer," I said.

"You're going back to Vegas," she said angrily.

"Before you blow up," I said, "sit down and let me explain."

Mary sat in the one remaining chair, and I told her about the phone call from Sister Sarah Agnes. She shook her head from time to time but remained silent.

"I hate the thought of you going back there," Mary said, "but I don't see any way around it."

"Don't worry," Roy said. "We'll take good care of your man."

"Like last time," Mary said sharply.

Ouch!

Roy grimaced.

"I wasn't there last time," Billy said.

"Hey," I said. "Stop it. Last time was my fault and nobody else's. It's ancient history."

"If he doesn't come back," Mary said, looking from Billy to Roy, "you two better not either."

"We'll all be back," Billy said in his bass voice.

I wasn't sure about Mary, but it certainly made me feel better.

57

The weather in Las Vegas was a pleasant sixty-eight degrees, according to our pilot, Jim Doak. I rented a Lincoln Navigator. I was way beyond caring about blending in, although in Vegas the Navigator blended in just fine. We had flown out in a Fleet Industries jet. I had recently negotiated a partial interest in the older of the two Fleet jets. Joseph Fleet had not hard-bargained. He was doing me a favor, and we both knew it. I was basically paying for maintenance, fuel, and pilot time.

I felt a little strange being back. It was almost as if I expected another beating. Then there was that other side of me that hoped I had the chance to get even. Being surrounded by people I trusted and who would look out for me reinforced my bravado.

Billy was in the passenger's side of the Navigator, and Roy was in the back with Bruiser Bracken. I had promised Bruiser that if something went down, he would be in on it. I tried hard to keep my promises.

"What's the plan?" Bruiser asked.

"Go out to Vargas's place and see if Tracy is there," I said. "If she is being held against her will, we take her."

"If Vargas gets in the way, I'll kill him," Roy added coldly.

"I sure hope I get to meet that Ralph fellow," Billy growled.

I thought the car might explode from all the testosterone.

"You packing heat?" Bruiser asked.

"Yes," I said. "You?"

"Yes," Bruiser said. "Roy?" he asked.

"Yeah," Roy said.

"Billy?" Bruiser asked.

"Billy likes knives," I said.

"Got carry permits?" Bruiser asked.

"Not for the knives," I said.

Roy, even though an ex-con, had a carry permit, thanks to Joseph Fleet. Money talked.

"Tennessee carry permits probably won't do much good if something goes down in Vegas," Bruiser said.

"If something does," I said, "I know a cop who might cut us some slack."

"Dangerous and armed to the teeth," Bruiser said.

"That'd be us," I said.

◆　　◆　　◆　　◆

The drive to Victor's house took half an hour in pre-noon traffic. I stopped at the entrance to Hidden Valley Estates and punched in the gate code. I was hoping it hadn't changed. It hadn't.

"Impressive memory, gumshoe," Roy said.

"You never did tell me how you got the code," I said.

Roy smiled and remained silent.

I took a left at the first stop sign and went two blocks and took a right on Hidden Valley Lane. I cruised down to number 24 and turned into the driveway.

"Showtime," Roy said as all four doors on the Navigator opened almost simultaneously.

The black Mercedes was not in the driveway. I was a little disappointed. I went to the garage and peeked in through one of the small windows across the top of the door. No baby-blue T-Bird, and no black Mercedes. The garage was empty. Bruiser and Billy headed around back. I walked toward the front door. Roy was already there. He tried the doorknob and looked back at me.

"Locked," he said.

"Ring the doorbell," I said, stopping on the front walkway and looking around.

I heard the faint sound of the doorbell ringing inside the house. We waited. Roy rang it again, and we waited some more. Bruiser and Billy came from the back of the house as Roy rang the doorbell one more time.

"No sign of life around back," Bruiser said.

"Okay," I said. "Let's get out of here."

We drove to the Starbucks where I had confronted Tracy on my last trip to Vegas. We got coffee and found an out-of-the-way table.

"So what's the plan?" Billy asked.

"If it's okay with Bruiser, I'll go with him and we'll make the rounds of places where Vargas might be," I said.

Bruiser nodded. "I have a few ideas," he said.

"You and Roy sit on the house," I said to Billy. "I noticed that house that was for sale is still for sale. It has a good view of the gate."

Roy looked at Billy. "Are you ready for a little surveillance work?" he asked.

"Eagle Two is always ready," Billy said seriously.

Roy laughed.

Bruiser glanced at me with a questioning look.

"Inside joke," I said. "We did a little caper once, and we had code names. Billy was Eagle Two. He *wanted* to be Eagle One."

We finished our coffee and split up. Billy and Roy took the Navigator, and Bruiser and I took a taxi downtown to pick up Bruiser's car.

◆   ◆   ◆   ◆

Bruiser and I made the rounds of the well-known local hangouts. We drank a few beers and watched a few boobs while Bruiser discreetly asked questions about the whereabouts of Victor Vargas. His cover story was that a big card game was brewing that Victor might like to attend. But no one had seen him for at least a week.

Around four o'clock, Bruiser dropped me at the Renaissance and went to the Velvet Slipper. I checked in and upon request was given the same suite I had stayed in twice before. I also reserved rooms for Billy and Roy. I had a small carry-on with enough clothes to get me through a couple of days. If we stayed longer than that, I would have to use laundry service or buy more clothes.

I called Billy's cell.

"Eagle Two," he answered.

"You've been hanging around Roy too long," I said. "You're actually starting to develop a sense of humor."

"Did you call to insult me, or does this have a purpose?" Billy asked sharply, trying to sound annoyed.

"Any activity?" I asked.

"None," Billy said.

"Come on in," I said. "I reserved rooms for you two at the Renaissance. They're already paid for. Roy knows how to get here. Call me when you're settled in."

◆　　◆　　◆　　◆

"So what's the plan, gumshoe?" Roy said.

We were having dinner in the hotel restaurant. Darkness lay across the city like a mistress in dazzling attire beckoning the unsuspecting to come out and have some fun. For me, the darkness was only a reminder of the fatigue I felt from a long day. I ate slowly as I nursed my second beer.

"More of the same, I guess. Maybe Bruiser will turn up something," I said.

We finished dinner in silence. We were not a talkative group.

"I'm going to play a little blackjack," Roy said. "Want to come along?"

I shook my head.

"I don't gamble," Billy rumbled.

"Want to watch?" Roy smiled. "There will be plenty to look at."

"I could use some practice on my skills of observation," Billy said straight-faced.

"Go," I said. "I'll take care of the bill."

They left.

I went back to my room and called Mary to say good night. She was in a talkative mood. After she explained in great detail why it would be a good idea for me to hurry back to Mountain Center, the conversation turned more serious.

"Did you find Tracy?" Mary asked.

"No," I said. "No trace of her, pardon the pun."

"Vargas?"

"No trace of him either," I said. "The house was locked up tight, and no cars were in the driveway or the garage."

"What now?"

"We wait," I said, "and see if they turn up."

"What if they don't?"

"I don't know," I said. "I'll think of something. I owe Lacy some closure on this."

"Speaking of Lacy," Mary said, "did you know she was going out for basketball?"

"No, I didn't," I said, surprised. "Why do you think she's doing that?"

"Wake up, Don," Mary said. "The two men she loves most in the world are basketball jocks. I think she and Billy might have played some when Lacy went to Cherokee. She is being very secretive about the whole thing."

We wrapped it up and said good night, and I went to the bathroom to prepare for bed. I was out soon after my head hit the pillow. If I dreamed, I could not remember.

58

Early the next morning, I was in the concierge lounge having coffee when my cell phone rang.

"Did I wake you up?" Bruiser asked.

"No," I said. "I'm an early-to-bed, early-to-rise kind of guy."

"You're in the wrong city," Bruiser said.

"No doubt about it," I said. "What's up?"

"Victor Vargas is in Mexico," Bruiser said. "I heard from a reliable source that he has family there. My source said his younger brother is in some trouble and Victor went down to straighten things out."

"Any idea if he took a girl with him?" I asked.

"No girl," Bruiser said. "I checked with a friend of mine at the airport, and Vargas flew out last Thursday to Mexico City. He was alone."

I thought about that. Vargas flew to Mexico City on Thursday, and Tracy called Sarah Agnes on Friday and then seemingly left town. *So where is she?* I wondered.

"Thanks, Bruiser," I said. "You have been a big help."

"I'll keep asking around about the girl," Bruiser said. "But it looks like she split."

"I think you're right," I said. "Thanks for everything. I'll be in touch."

I was settled down with my second cup of coffee when Billy walked in. He filled a cup from the urn, picked up a newspaper, and came to my table and sat.

"Good morning," I said as he took his first sip.

"Umm," Billy nodded.

"Long night?" I asked.

"Kind of," Billy said. "We'll talk about it later."

He opened his paper and tried to ignore me. I understood about not being sociable before the first cup of coffee, so I shut up and went back to reading my paper. Tennessee football was having a historic season—in a bad way, unfortunately. The coach had been forced to resign, and one more loss would tie the all-time record in Tennessee's storied history. Fortunately for Vols fans, Tennessee basketball was alive and well. I was lost in that thought when Roy sat down with a cup of coffee and a newspaper.

"Good morning," I said.

"Vargas is in Mexico," Roy said as he exchanged glances with Billy.

"How do you know that?" I asked.

"Ralph told us," Billy snarled.

"As in Starbucks Ralph?" I asked, looking at Roy.

"One and the same," Roy said.

"I see," I said.

I did see. Even though I had said to leave it alone, they had gone looking for Ralph to get even for me. And while they were at it, they decided to extract some information. I understood it was as much for them as it was for me, so I let it slide.

"And Ralph just volunteered this information," I said.

"Not exactly," Roy smiled. "Some persuasion was involved."

I looked at Billy. He shrugged.

"How much persuasion?" I asked Roy.

"Well," Roy said, "let's just say that Ralph will be moving pretty slow the next few days. But he agrees we're even and that our little feud is over."

I would like to say I felt sorry for Ralph, but I didn't. If my beating was going to be avenged, I should have been the one to do the avenging, but I wasn't all that unhappy Billy and Roy had done it for me. I pushed on.

"Did he say if Tracy was with Victor?" I asked.

Of course, I already knew the answer, but I decided not to mention my conversation with Bruiser. I might as well let them think they had contributed to the hunt. And it never hurt to get confirmation.

"Ralph said she didn't go with Victor," Roy said. "He was supposed to be watching her, but she skipped in the middle of the night last Friday, and he's worried about what Vargas might do to him when he finds out."

"Ralph will probably blame it on you two," I said.

"Let him," Roy said. "Maybe Victor Vargas will come looking for us, and we'll get this settled."

"Did he tell you who the guy in the tennis shoes was?" I asked.

"No," Roy said. "He wouldn't give him up. He said the guy would kill him, so we let it go."

"Good work," I said.

They seemed pleased with themselves.

"What are we going to do now?" Billy asked.

"I have an idea," I said. "I need to make a phone call. You two take one more run out to Vargas's house. If you see any sign of Tracy, call me. If not, meet me in the lobby at noon."

◆   ◆   ◆   ◆

Back in my suite, I dialed Scott's number from my room phone.

"Don't you ever learn?" Scott answered.

"Meaning?"

"Meaning, didn't you get the crap beat out of you the last time you were in Vegas?"

"My memory is a little foggy on that," I said. "Besides, it won't happen again."

"Why not?" Scott asked.

"Well, for one thing, Victor Vargas is out of town and probably doesn't know I'm here," I said. "And this time, I brought Billy and Roy Husky. They have already extracted a measure of revenge on my behalf."

"Tell me everything," Scott said excitedly.

I did.

"Nice to have tough friends," Scott said. "What do you need from me?"

"Take this down," I said, and gave him Tracy's cell phone number. "I need a GPS track on that number."

"And if someone wants to know why, what do I tell them?" Scott asked.

I knew he could do it on his own authority. He just wanted to make me squirm a little.

"Possible kidnap victim," I said.

"Okay," he said. "It shouldn't take long. I'll call you back."

I plugged the cell phone in to charge, went to the bathroom, stripped, and took a long, hot shower.

◆　◆　◆　◆

An hour later, I was dressed and having breakfast in my room. I had just finished when my cell phone rang. I knew it was Scott.

"Special Agent Youngblood," I answered.

"You can get in trouble for impersonating an FBI agent," Scott said.

"Sorry," I teased. "I'm just in such awe of you guys."

"You should be," Scott teased back.

"You have news?"

"Tracy is in Green River, Utah," Scott said. "Or at least her cell phone is. She rented a unit from Green River Cottage Rentals. I know this because I ran her credit card."

"Good work, Scott," I said. "I take it all back. You guys are the greatest. I'm not looking at a map. How far is Green River from you?"

"It's a haul," Scott said. "It's off I-70. Looks like she was headed for Colorado."

"Was?"

"She paid for a week," Scott said. "She's been there three days. Unless she took off without checking out."

I didn't like the sound of that, but I kept it to myself.

"Thanks, Scott," I said. "I've got to go. I'll call you later."

I called Billy's cell.

"Hey, Blood. What's up?" he answered.

"You two get back here," I said. "We're leaving Las Vegas."

I hung up and called Hertz and arranged to drop the Navigator at the Denver airport. I planned to fly home from Denver. I was finished with Las Vegas.

An hour later, we were on I-15, North headed for Green River, Utah.

59

We arrived at Green River in the late afternoon with enough daylight to find the cottage Tracy Malone had rented, thanks to Scott's help and the navigation system on the Navigator. The cottages were scattered over a large, partially wooded tract a few miles outside Green River. We could see a dozen or so cottages, and most seemed to be unoccupied.

At the top of a small hill, surrounded by a few trees, was a cottage with a baby-blue Thunderbird parked in front. I drove up the narrow, paved, winding road and parked beside the T-Bird. We got out and walked to the door. I knocked. No answer. I knocked again. We waited. No answer.

"Tracy!" I shouted. "It's Don Youngblood. I need to talk to you."

No answer, and no sound from inside the cottage. I opened the screen door and tried the doorknob. It turned.

"Tracy!" I shouted as I pushed the door open.

The smell hit me like the heat of an August day at Singer Island when I left the comfort of the condo's air conditioning.

"Damn," I said, and turned my head away from the door, nearly gagging.

Billy pushed past me and went in, leaving the door open.

"Stay here," he said.

Roy started in and caught the smell.

"Jesus," he said as he turned away. "How can he go in there?"

"Billy is just different," I said. "Has to be genetic."

I heard windows opening. Billy was trying to air the place out. I thought I heard another door open. Maybe the cottage had a back entrance.

Billy was back out in less than two minutes.

"She's dead on the bed," Billy said. "Looks like an overdose. Stay here. I'm going to take some pictures."

Billy removed a small digital camera from the carrying case attached to his belt and went back inside. I looked at Roy. He shook his head.

I went back to the Navigator for my cell phone.

"Nine-one-one," a female voice answered. "State the nature of your emergency."

"I would like to report a dead body," I said. "Looks like a drug overdose."

"What is your name and location?" the voice asked.

I gave her the information and was promised someone would be there in approximately ten minutes. I then went to my suitcase, pulled out a white T-shirt, doused it in my favorite cologne, and walked back to the cottage. I stopped at the front door, covered my nose with the T-shirt, and went inside.

A living area with a kitchen was in the front. A door led to the bedroom. I went through it and to my left saw Tracy, face up and eyes open, spread-eagled on the king-sized bed. It was as if her pose said, *Here I am. Come and get me.* She was fully clothed. A syringe was on the nightstand, and an elastic strap was on the floor. The smell of death seeped through my T-shirt as I became aware of the clicking from Billy's camera. I had seen enough.

I returned to the front room and looked around. Tracy's cell phone was charging on the kitchen counter. I unplugged the charger from the wall and unhooked the phone from the charger. I walked outside and put them in the console of the Navigator.

In the distance, I saw a sheriff's cruiser coming unhurriedly up the road to the cottages. When it reached the top, it pulled in beside the Navigator and a man got out. He was perhaps in his mid-fifties and about six feet tall with a ruddy complexion that led me to believe he could be all or part Native American. He wore blue jeans and a white short-sleeve shirt with a button-down collar. On his belt were a sheriff's badge and what looked to be a Glock .45 in a black holster. His black cowboy boots were in bad need of a shine. He did not wear a hat, and his black hair showed flecks of gray.

"You Youngblood?" he asked in a voice that sounded strangely like Billy's, although not quite as bass.

"Yes," I said.

He extended his hand, and I took it.

"Tommy Joe Smith," he said. "Sheriff of Grand County. Pleased to meet you, although, I'm sorry about the circumstances. Body in there?"

"It is," I said.

He walked through the front door as Billy walked out. He seemed to take no notice of Billy or the smell.

He was back outside in a few minutes as a white SUV pulled up. The driver's side door read, "Grand County Medical Examiner."

A short, round, bald man emerged from the SUV smoking a cigar that looked way too big for him. He nodded to Tommy Joe. "Sheriff."

"She's inside, Leon," the sheriff said.

Leon picked up a medical bag from the back of the SUV and disappeared inside the cabin, cigar smoke trailing after him.

"Let's go sit in my cruiser for a minute," the sheriff said, looking at me. He paid no attention to Billy or Roy.

Inside the car, Sheriff Smith turned to face me, making himself comfortable against the driver's side door.

"So tell me how you came to find this young lady," he said.

"Tracy Malone," I said. "Her name is Tracy Malone."

He flipped open a little notebook and wrote down Tracy's name as I began her story from the time Lacy entered my office. I gave him the *Reader's Digest* version, omitting any reference to Victor Vargas. As far as he was concerned, I was strictly looking for a missing mother who had a drug problem. He listened without interruption, although his eyes were like lasers looking deep inside me, searching for any hint of a lie.

I finished, and he was silent. I remained calm and quiet.

"And who are those two?" he asked with a smile.

"They're my assistants," I said.

"Ex-cons, I think," the sheriff said. "I know the look."

Sheriff Tommy Joe Smith was a lot smarter than he wanted you to know.

"Friends," I said. "I hate to travel alone."

"Uh-huh," he mumbled. "Well, I have no reason to suspect foul play. And I think you are telling me the truth, although not the whole truth, but at least enough of it so you-all can go. I'll need to keep the body for an autopsy."

"Call me when you're finished with the body, and I'll make arrangements to have it sent back to Mountain Center," I said, handing him my business card. The card said that I was an investment consultant.

He took my card, looked at it, nodded, and slipped it in his shirt pocket.

"What tribe is you friend?" he asked.

"Cherokee," I said. "You?"

"Navajo," he said. "Mother's side."

I nodded, and he straightened up in his seat, signaling that the interview was over. We got out of the car as the medical examiner exited the cottage and walked back to the SUV.

He looked at the sheriff.

"I'd say she's about three days dead," he said.

◆   ◆   ◆   ◆

By the time we left the cottage, the sun was all but gone and the pleasant daytime temperature was turning considerably colder. Not wanting to drive any farther, we decided to spend the night at the Best Western River Terrace in Green River. It was a surprisingly good hotel, considering Green River was a town of fewer than one thousand residents. I was guessing that tourism was its number-one industry.

We ate dinner at the Tamarisk Restaurant next door. The food was good and the service friendly. The place was less than half full, and we had a back table overlooking the river that would have afforded quiet conversation, had we chosen it. We didn't. We ate in reverent silence, as if honoring the recent dead.

In my room, I took Billy's camera and downloaded the pictures of the death scene to my desktop and burned a CD. I was going to leave it at the front desk for Sheriff Smith as sort of a thank-you for not jamming us up. I went online and checked my email. I would have checked the market, but my heart wasn't in it.

Mary was working second shift, so I decided to wait and call her on our way to Denver. I really needed to hear her voice, but I denied myself that pleasure. Maybe in my subconscious mind, it was punishment for not finding Tracy Malone alive. I felt terrible about that. I knew I would have to tell Lacy. I felt terrible about that, too.

I was ready to undress for bed when I remembered Tracy's cell phone. I went down to the Navigator and brought the phone up to my room. I walked to the desk and sat with anticipation. I took a breath, flipped open her phone, and looked at the call log.

Under the missed calls were a name and number that gave me a chill. Victor Vargas had called Tracy on the day she died. She had not called him back.

I wrote down the number and put it in my computer backpack, then deleted the call from the missed-calls memory. I sat for a long time trying to decide what to do. I was no closer to a decision when I turned out the light and fell into a rather restless, fitful sleep.

60

The next morning, I was up early. I shaved, showered, packed the few belongings I had with me, and headed for the Navigator. I saw no signs of Billy and Roy.

As I exited a side door of the hotel, I noticed a sheriff's cruiser parked in the parking lot in front of the Tamarisk. Sheriff Tommy Joe Smith was leaning against the left front fender and drinking something from a Styrofoam cup. I nodded, went to the back of the Navigator, and put my overnight bag inside. By the time I closed the tailgate, the sheriff was standing next to me.

"Good morning," he said pleasantly.

Why didn't I believe this was a social call?

"Good morning," I said, equally cheerful. "You're up early."

"Well," he said slowly, "you've heard about the early bird?"

"I have," I smiled. "I just hope I'm not the worm."

He laughed. "Had breakfast?" he asked.

I shook my head.

"Then let's go have some," Sheriff Smith said.

The invitation was not a request, but more like a friendly order. Breakfast sounded good, so I nodded, and we walked across the parking lot to the Tamarisk Restaurant. Everyone inside seemed to know the sheriff and called him Tommy Joe. We were seated at the corner table by the window where I had sat the night before. The waitress came.

"Hey, Tommy Joe," she said. "The usual?"

"Sure, Allyson," Sheriff Smith said, to a pretty brunette with green eyes.

Allyson turned to me, and I gave her my order.

"I have something for you," I said, trying to get off to a positive start. I took the CD out of my coat pocket and handed it to him.

He looked at it curiously. "X-rated, I hope?" he smiled.

"For adults only," I said.

"Pictures from yesterday?"

I nodded.

"I noticed your Cherokee friend had a camera," he said.

The sheriff turned his attention from me and scanned the room. He found what he was looking for.

"Hey, Hubert," he called to a man across the room. "Let me borrow that laptop for a minute."

"Sure, sheriff," Hubert called back. "Let me get back to my desktop, and I'll bring it right over."

A few minutes later, the sheriff inserted the CD and began to run a slide show of the late Tracy Malone and the cottage where she died. Billy had been thorough, taking pictures inside and out from many angles.

"Your friend has done this before," Sheriff Smith said. "He's good."

"For some law-enforcement departments in our area," I said.

"Including Chief Wilson's," Sheriff Smith said.

"You checked out my story," I said.

"Had to," he said. "Part of the job."

"And it checked," I said.

"It did," he said.

Breakfast arrived. I had scrambled eggs with biscuits and chorizo gravy. Sheriff Smith had something far more daring, featuring mushrooms, peppers, and onions. I hoped he was riding alone. We dove right in.

"One thing I'm curious about," Sheriff Smith said.

"Uh-huh," I grunted with my mouth full.

"Her cell phone," he said. "I didn't see a cell phone. No woman goes anywhere today without one, especially on a trip."

I took Tracy's cell phone out of my jacket pocket and laid it on the table. He gave me a look that I could not interpret and went back to devouring his breakfast. When we finished, he picked the phone up and flipped it open. I knew he was scanning the call log.

"No calls the day she died," he said.

I did not respond.

"Unless somebody erased them," he said.

"Unless that," I said.

"And if someone did erase them," Sheriff Smith said, "they would probably have a very good reason."

"Without a doubt," I said.

Tommy Joe nodded and flipped the phone closed and handed it to me. I slipped it back inside my jacket pocket.

"And I probably wouldn't want to know anyway," he said.

"Probably not," I said.

"Chief Wilson said I could trust your judgment," Sheriff Smith said. "He said you're unusually smart and intuitive."

"That'll cost me," I smiled.

Allyson came with the check and refilled our coffee mugs. I started to reach for the check, but the sheriff beat me to it.

"This one is on the county," he said. "Don't get to do breakfast interviews very often. It'll look good on my expense report, me being up early and all."

"Thank you, and thank the county," I said.

We walked outside and across the parking lot to the sheriff's cruiser. He got in and rolled down the window and looked up at me.

"Any reason to believe that this wasn't an accidental overdose or a suicide?"

"None," I said. "But I sure hope the M.E. decides on accidental overdose."

"Anything you can add that might help me convince him?" Sheriff Smith asked.

I thought about that for a few seconds.

"She checked in and paid for a week," I said, leaning down and grabbing the bottom of his window with both hands. "Then she died the next day. Does that sound right?"

"Maybe she didn't want to be found for a while," the sheriff said.

"Maybe, but I found her cell phone attached to the charger," I said. "Not a detail you bother with if you're expecting to kill yourself."

"That sounds right," the sheriff said.

"And no suicide note," I said. "I think she would have left one."

"Okay, I'll talk to the M.E.," the sheriff said. "I'll give you a call in a few days when the autopsy is complete. Then you can make arrangements to get the body."

"I'll wait to hear from you," I said.

"If you're back this way again, Youngblood," he said, "drop in and say hello."

Before I could respond, his window was up and Sheriff Tommy Joe Smith was driving away.

61

Mary met me at Tri-Cities Airport late the next afternoon. Billy, Roy, and I had driven to Denver and rendezvoused with Jim Doak earlier that day. We had spent the three-hour ride to Denver in an uncomfortable silence, knowing bad news traveled with us.

Mary was waiting beside the Pathfinder when the Fleet Industries jet taxied into the private hangar. The sight of her standing there sent some unknown force through my body. She met us at the bottom of the jet's stairway, nodded to Billy and Roy, and hugged me. Billy and Roy went to retrieve our overnight bags from the cargo hold. I was carrying my laptop.

"Welcome back," Mary said softly.

"It's a bitter homecoming," I said.

She knew, of course, that Tracy Malone was dead. Lacy had not been told. We walked in silence to the Pathfinder and waited for Billy. He came with my overnight bag, raised the tailgate, and put it inside.

"I'll ride with Roy," he said. "You two need to be alone."

"Thanks, Billy," Mary said.

Billy looked at me with a sadness I had not seen in him. "You want me to tell Lacy, Blood?" he asked quietly.

"Thanks, Chief," I said. "This is something I have to do. But I would like for you to talk to her later."

He nodded. "Call me if you need me," he said, and walked toward the black limousine.

I got in the passenger's side of the Pathfinder. I usually liked to drive, but today I didn't have the energy. I was physically and mentally drained. Mary seemed to understand and drove without question.

We were silent for much of the ride, and then Mary broke the silence.

"I can tell her," she said.

"No," I said. "I have to do it."

"I understand," she said. "Want me to be there?"

"No," I said. "I have to do this alone."

I let out a long sigh. I wondered how long it would take to get the image of Tracy Malone spread-eagled on a king-sized bed in Green River, Utah, out of my mind. *A lifetime*, I thought. In the last two years, the hotshot detective had gotten a lot more than he bargained for.

"I'm tired of finding dead people," I said.

"I understand that, too," Mary said.

◆　◆　◆　◆

I have had to do a few hard things in my life, but telling a barely teenaged girl that her mother was dead ranked right at the top. I felt like a six-year-old going to the dentist knowing he was going to get his teeth drilled. My stomach was performing the kind of dance it used to do before a big game. I hated the feeling.

Lacy was in her room working on her computer when we got to the condo. She yelled, "Hello, welcome back!" and went right on working. I wondered if she knew what was about to unfold.

Mary and I went to the kitchen.

"Want a drink?" Mary asked.

"No," I said. "I have to do this now."

I went up the stairs to Lacy's room on legs that were not quite steady.

"How's it going?" I asked as I pulled up a chair and sat beside her.

"Good," she said. "I'm working on a report for geography class. We had to pick a country and write a report about it. We drew slips of paper out of a bowl. I got Colombia, South America."

"Really," I said, almost forgetting why I was in her room. "I was there last year."

"I know," she said. "Mary told me."

I watched her as she searched different links for Colombia. I had the feeling she knew what was coming and was avoiding the hearing of it.

Finally, she looked at me.

"She's dead, isn't she?"

"Yes," I said. "She is."

62

The next day, I was in my office with a list of phone calls to make and no motivation to make them. My mind kept wandering back to the previous evening. Lacy had shed some tears, but they were tears of resignation that had been stored up, waiting for the time when they would escape those sad blue eyes. Somehow, Lacy had known this day would come, and she seemed resigned to face it and get it over with. Afterward, Mary had joined me, and we stayed with Lacy in her room. She would cry a little, tell some stories about her mother in happier times before the drugs, and cry some more. The cycle repeated itself a few times until around midnight, when Lacy fell asleep with Mary sitting on the side of her bed stroking her hair and shedding silent tears of her own. I snuck silently away and went to bed. Much later, I felt Mary slip in beside me. I heard, "Good night, my love," whispered in my ear, and the next thing I knew it was morning.

Mary had taken the day off, and she and Lacy went to the lake house. Mary had decided it would be best if Lacy did not return to school until after the burial service. I made those arrangements with the local funeral home.

The portable phone on my desk rang, snatching me back to the here and now. Caller ID read, "Private caller."

"Cherokee Investigations," I answered.

"Hello, Don."

This was another conversation I did not want to have.

"Hello, Sister Sarah Agnes," I said rather vacantly.

"Oh, no," Sarah Agnes said, reading my voice. "She's dead, isn't she?"

Lacy's words exactly. Like Lacy, Sarah Agnes had expected it.

"Yes," I said, "she is. Overdose, probably accidental."

"Tell me about it," Sarah Agnes said.

I told her what I knew.

"I think you are probably right that it was accidental," Sarah Agnes said after I finished. "How is Lacy taking it?"

"I think she is doing pretty well," I said, "although it's really hard to tell. I may need you to talk with her at some point."

"I would be glad to," Sister Sarah Agnes said. "How are you doing?"

"I have spent the morning feeling sorry for myself and Lacy," I said. "I know what it is like not to have parents."

"Understandable," Sarah Agnes said. "And I will probably spend the rest of the day and the weeks that follow wondering what I could have done to keep Tracy alive."

"You did what you could," I said.

"And so did you," she said.

"Unfortunately," I said, "I was three days late."

◆　　◆　　◆　　◆

An hour later, the phone rang again. The caller ID read, "Grand County sheriff."

"Cherokee Investigations," I answered.

"Youngblood, it's Sheriff Smith."

"Hello, sheriff," I said. "Did you catch the worm this morning?"

Tommy Joe laughed. "In a matter of speaking," he said. "That first cup of coffee at the Tamarisk is just as good."

"So much for coffee talk," I said. "You have news for me."

"The autopsy is finished," he said. "Official cause of death is heart failure due to an accidental overdose of cocaine. No mention of suicide. The body can be released anytime."

"Someone will be in touch with you," I said. "Can I give them this number?"

"Sure thing," Sheriff Smith said. "Stop in sometime and tell me the rest of the story."

"I will," I promised.

"Take care of yourself, Youngblood," Sheriff Smith said.

◆　　◆　　◆　　◆

I hate loose ends; they drive me crazy. When I have questions, I want answers. Something was nagging me. What was Victor Vargas doing in East Tennessee when he met Tracy? Certainly, he wasn't recruiting the local talent. Then it hit me. Could it be that simple?

I called Big Bob.

"What's going on with the meth lab arrest?" I asked without preamble.

"The two ringleaders are still locked up," he said. "One of which we think fired the bullet that hit Mary. The guy won't give us his name, and he is not in the system. He didn't have any ID on him either."

"You got them?" I asked.

"No, Jimmy Durham has them in the county jail," Big Bob said. "What are you after?"

"Just a theory, right now," I said. "I'll let you know if it pans out."

I left the office and drove to the county jail, located about twenty miles from Mountain Center. On the way, I called Jimmy Durham.

"I want to take a run at the guy with no name who might have shot Mary," I said.

"He won't talk to anybody," Jimmy said.

"Give me a crack at him," I said. "What have you got to lose?"

"Okay," Jimmy said. "I'll have someone bring him over from the jail and put him in one of our interview rooms."

◆　　◆　　◆　　◆

He was sitting at a table when I walked in. He was a dark-skinned man who looked to be in his mid-thirties. I guessed him to be about five-foot-ten. He looked to be in decent shape.

I tried to act casual. I extended my hand and said in my best Spanish, "*Donald Youngblood. Nice to meet you.*"

I had caught him off-guard. Without thinking, most people will take your hand and reply in kind. The man with no name was not an exception. He stood and reached across the table and took my hand.

"*Oscar Morales,*" he said. "*Nice . . .*"

And then he realized what he had done.

"*Clever,*" he said. "*You tricked me.*"

"*If I am going to help you,*" I continued in Spanish, "*it is appropriate for me to know your name.*"

He stared at me, shaking his head. I wanted him as relaxed as possible. I thought he probably knew English and was trying to act like he didn't. He might use that secret to his advantage. I was hoping he thought I was his counsel. If he asked me directly, I would have to say no, and the charade would be over.

He didn't ask.

"*You are in a lot of trouble, Oscar,*" I continued. "*There are a lot of charges against you, even attempted murder.*"

Actually, that was not true. Oscar had not been officially charged with attempted murder. Not yet, anyway. But I needed all the leverage I could get.

"*Attempted murder?*" he asked, wide-eyed.

"*One of the bullets you sprayed into the woods hit a female police officer,*" I said. "*You could have killed her. You know how the police are when one of their own gets shot, especially a woman.*"

"*I was not trying to kill anybody,*" he pleaded. "*It was just a show of force, you know. That charge will never stick.*"

"*I think it will,*" I said. "*They will not care about your show of force. This is conservative East Tennessee, not liberal Miami.*"

"*How did you know—*" He stopped abruptly. "*You did it again. No one knew I am from Miami. You are very good. Easy to talk to. Your Spanish is very good, too. It is very aristocratic, and you have almost no accent.*"

"*I had a very good teacher,*" I said. Raul would have been proud. I wanted to keep Oscar talking. "*Do you have a family, Oscar?*"

"*A wife and three children,*" he said sheepishly.

"*It would be a shame if you never saw them again,*" I said sympathetically. "*You need to help yourself.*"

He nodded.

"*Where did the drugs go?*" I asked.

He was quiet for a while, and I waited patiently. Finally, he shrugged and nodded, as if he realized he was in a tough spot and needed all the help he could get.

"*The drugs went to four places,*" he said. "*New York, Atlanta, Miami, and Las Vegas.*"

"*Were they picked up here, or did you deliver them?*"

"*They were picked up here most of the time,*" Oscar said. "*Sometimes, we made connections in Knoxville.*"

"*How often did Vargas pick up?*" I asked. I slipped it in casually, as if I were asking about the weather.

"*Vargas picked up . . .*" Oscar Morales slammed his hand down on the table and pointed his finger at me. "*You are the devil,*" he said. "*I'm not talking anymore until we have some kind of a deal. If I keep talking to you, I will not have anything left to bargain with.*"

It didn't matter. I had what I came for.

"*I suggest you get a good lawyer and cut the best deal you can,*" I said, feeling a little sorry for Oscar Morales.

"*You are not a lawyer?*" he asked incredulously.

"*No, I am a private investigator,*" I said. "*I am after Victor Vargas.*"

"*Good luck with that one,*" he smirked.

I rose from the table and walked to the door and was just about to open it when Oscar called to me.

"*Mr. Youngblood.*"

I turned and looked at him without speaking.

"*Is the lady police officer okay?*" he asked sincerely.

"*She is fine,*" I said.

"*That is good.*" Oscar Morales sounded relieved. "*That is very good.*"

"*Have you ever been in jail before this, Oscar?*" I asked.

"*Not in the United States,*" he said.

"*Do you want some advice?*" I asked.

He nodded.

"*Do the time and then find another line of work.*"

"That is good advice," he said in passable English, "but this is all I know how to do."

"Find another line of work," I said slowly and firmly.

I closed the door after me. Jimmy Durham stood in the hallway behind the two-way mirror to the interview room. He flipped off the PA system.

"Damn if you aren't a snake charmer," he drawled. "Want a job as an interrogator?"

"Did you understand all of that?" I asked, ignoring his question.

"Yeah, I did," he said. "I spent some time in Texas while you were up north. I understand Spanish better than I speak it. You speak it a lot better than I do."

"Get him a lawyer and let him flip on his other connections," I said.

"He's just another pawn in this drug game. I'm going to call a friend of mine at the FBI. They might be interested in him, since the drugs are going across state lines."

"You missed your calling, Blood," Jimmy Durham said. "You should have been a cop."

"Not likely," I said. "You have to put up with too much political bullshit."

♦   ♦   ♦   ♦

That same afternoon, I was online checking the market and having a hard time concentrating. In the last few days, I had thought a lot about my parents. The plane crash that claimed their lives had robbed me of a priceless gift, much in the same way that Victor Vargas had robbed Lacy of the only parent she had ever known. I knew I would never completely recover from that loss, and I didn't think Lacy would either. I felt the anger smoldering inside me. Vargas was a drug dealer and a home wrecker. I wanted Victor Vargas to pay for his sins. *This is not over*, I thought.

I picked up the phone and dialed a number I had not planned on calling. I got an answer on the second ring.

"Bruiser," I said, "it's Youngblood."

"I've been hoping to hear from you," Bruiser said. "What happened?"

I told him the sad story, and when I finished we sat in silence hundreds of miles and two time zones apart, wondering what to say next.

"Son of a bitch," Bruiser finally said. "Not the ending you were looking for."

"I'm still looking for the ending," I said. "I need you to spread the word on what happened to Tracy. Casually mention that the funeral is on Friday. I need for it to get to Victor Vargas. A graveside service will be held on Friday in Mountain Center at the Center of Angels Cemetery. You can also brag that I had a hand in taking down a big meth lab near here. It was supplying Vargas. That should really piss him off."

"I can do that," Bruiser said, "but you are playing with fire."

"Yeah," I said. "But this time, I'll be playing with the home field advantage."

63

Friday was a cold, overcast day with a breeze that made it seem colder. I was under a tent near the casket that held the body of Tracy Malone. Since Lacy had no other relatives she knew of, she had asked Doris, Stanley, Billy, Mary, and me to sit with her in the front row as "family." I was really surprised that Stanley came, but he did.

I half-listened to the preacher as he talked about the sadness of a life ending suddenly with so much apparent living left to do. I remembered a funeral from a year ago and another life cut short. And I remembered my parents.

My eyes continuously scanned the area for signs of something or someone out of place. I knew Billy was doing the same. Roy stood at the back of the crowd outside the tent. He could have been a stone monument except for his eyes. They were moving constantly.

I was surprised at the crowd. I had expected a meager turnout. Instead, it seemed that the teachers, parents, and students of Lacy's entire class had turned out. The principal was also in attendance, along with many of the Mountain Center Diner locals Lacy had waited on through the summer. This girl had touched people, and they were here to pay her back.

Lacy was sobbing. Mary had her arm around Lacy and was crying silently and comforting Lacy at the same time. I felt Lacy's pain and fought hard to keep it bottled up. In the end, I lost. A tear escaped and rolled down my cheek. Then another. I sat silently and stared straight ahead, jaw clenched, as if I didn't notice. I was glad I had on sunglasses.

The minister finished, and we stood. The crowd filed by, offering condolences.

Billy leaned near me and whispered in my ear, "Over your left shoulder, up the hill in the trees. He's wearing a long black trench coat."

I moved slowly behind Billy so I would be blocked from the view of anyone on the hill, then looked over his shoulder into the trees. It took a minute, but I saw the partial silhouette of a man. I glanced toward Roy, but he was no longer there. The crowd was thinning.

I moved close to Mary. "Stay with Lacy," I said. "There is something I have to do."

"Okay," she said, not picking up on what was happening.

Just as well, I thought.

I turned back to Billy, but he, too, was gone. I slipped from the tent and started walking slowly across the cemetery. I crossed the cemetery road and started up the long incline that led to the trees. I could feel my black dress boots sinking slightly into the moisture-laden soil. My right hand was in my long, dark brown leather overcoat gripping my Beretta.

The figure emerged from the trees and started walking slowly down the slope. Even at a distance, I knew it was Victor Vargas and not one of his thugs. His right hand was down at his side and out of sight. I had no doubt that it held a gun. Mine was out and in the same position. He couldn't see my Beretta, but he must have known it was there.

This was a showdown spawned by hate. I knew Victor hated me for ruining his relationship with Tracy. I had no doubt that he blamed me for her death. I found it hard to hate anyone, but I hated Victor. He had come between a mother and a daughter, and I blamed him for Tracy's death and my beating.

We moved slowly toward each other. "Be careful what you want," my mother always said. "You might get it." I had wanted this showdown, and now that I was in it there was no turning back. Instead of fear, I was surprised to feel big-game excitement. In less than a minute, one of us was probably going to die. I just could not imagine it would be me. But

I was also sure Victor Vargas was imagining it could not be him. We would see.

When we were about thirty yards apart, Vargas stopped. Then I stopped.

"This is your fault!" he screamed. I could hear the anger and the wrath. "If you had stayed out of it, she would still be alive." He spit out the words like daggers.

"You got it wrong, Victor," I snarled. "If you and your drugs had stayed out of East Tennessee, none of this would have happened. It ends today, Vargas. No more Tracy Malones for you to corrupt."

Our talk was over. *He's a target on a firing range*, I told myself. *Stay focused.*

I saw his right hand move. Mine moved almost simultaneously, but he got off the first shot a millisecond before I squeezed off two. His round found the flesh of my left shoulder, and I felt the sting of it as I fired. His second round ricocheted wildly off a nearby headstone as he collapsed to his knees and fell face down into the soft turf of the hillside. I knew when I fired that my rounds had found their mark in the center of his chest.

I walked up to him. A Ruger SR9 lay near his shooting hand. I kept my gun pointed at him and kicked the Ruger away. Still keeping my Beretta aimed at the back of his head, I reached down, grabbed a handful of trench coat, and rolled him over.

His eyes stared at me and blinked. He coughed up blood and said the last thing I expected to hear.

"I loved her," he gurgled.

Why he felt the need to tell me that, I'll never know. Then his eyes rolled back, and his last breath rattled out of his lungs as he died.

I stood there wondering how a demon like Victor Vargas could love anyone. Then I noticed blood dripping beside my boot and realized my left arm was hanging limply by my side. I was beginning to feel woozy. The adrenaline high was wearing off. I sat on a nearby headstone and saw Mary running toward me. She looked panicked.

"My God, you've been shot," she said. Then she morphed into full
cop mode. Out came the cell phone. She punched in 911. "Susie, it's Mary.
Send an ambulance to the cemetery. Don's been shot," she said. "No, he is
not going to die. Hurry up, Susie." Mary flipped the phone closed and put
it away. "Get that coat off," she ordered. "I need to slow the bleeding. Sit
down and lean your back against this headstone."

With Mary's help, I did as I was told. *My leather overcoat is ruined*, I
thought. I smiled. I could be bleeding to death, yet I was thinking about
my overcoat; it's funny how the brain reacts in extreme situations.

I heard sirens in the distance as she put pressure on my wound. The
sirens were growing louder. Soon, instead of growing louder, they slowly
faded. After that, I didn't hear anything.

64

I awoke in a hospital bed. I assumed I was in the Mountain Center
Medical Center. Mary was asleep in a chair near my bed. I looked at
the digital clock on my nightstand. In glowing red numbers, it informed
me it was 6:33. A small red dot confirmed that it was morning. I looked
around. I was in a private room. The shades on my window were down,
and the slats were closed. Early-morning light was visible between the
slats. I was hooked to an IV and monitors. My arm throbbed, and I felt
groggy, probably from painkillers.

Beaten up and shot on the same case, and all I was trying to do was
find a missing mother. Tracy was dead, Victor Vargas was dead, and I was
back in the hospital. *I may have to rethink this private investigator thing*, I
thought.

I watched Mary sleep. She was beautiful and serene curled up in the chair; covered by a blanket. She had a contented look on her face that told me I was going to be all right. I felt a surge. Did I love this woman? I guessed that by my definition of love, I surely did. I certainly had never felt this way for any other woman.

Mary stirred and opened her eyes. Maybe she had felt my stare. Our eyes met, and she smiled sleepily. She threw off the blanket, got up, and closed the distance between us. She kissed me lightly on the lips.

"How do you feel?" she asked.

"Okay, I guess. How bad is the arm?"

"You won't be using it for a while," she said, "but the doctor expects a full recovery."

"I'm getting tired of rehabbing," I said.

"And I'm getting tired of sleeping in hospital chairs," Mary said. "I'll yell at you later, but what in the hell were you thinking? You scared me to death. By the time I realized what was happening, you were faced off with Vargas."

"I think you're starting to yell now," I said.

Mary glared at me.

"It was between Vargas and me," I said weakly. "I didn't want anyone else involved."

"You could have been killed," she said.

"But I wasn't."

She glared at me some more, and then her face softened into a smile.

"Pretty damn good shooting from that distance," Mary said. "Wanda said the two rounds were only about an inch apart."

"Practice makes perfect," I said.

Mary turned and pulled the chair close beside my bed and sat.

"The other two are in jail," she said.

"What other two?" I asked, the grogginess fading.

"Billy and Roy apprehended two men in the trees above Vargas," she said. "One had a rifle with a scope."

"Pays to have backup," I said.

"Pays to have Billy and Roy as backup," Mary said. "The one they called Ralph took a beating from Billy. Roy said he resisted being apprehended."

"I'll bet," I chuckled. I didn't mention the first beating from Billy that Ralph had taken. Ralph was obviously not the brightest bulb in the fixture. "Was the other one wearing Nike tennis shoes?"

"I don't think so," Mary said.

The door to my room opened, and Billy and Roy walked in. They ignored me and looked at Mary, who was rising from the chair to face them.

"How is Wyatt Earp doing?" Roy asked Mary.

"No smarter today than he was yesterday," Mary answered.

"I heard that," Billy said.

"Funny," I said. "I'm awake, if you'd like to talk to me."

"The doctor said you can leave later today," Mary said. "I'm going back to the condo and get Lacy out of bed. She was here until midnight. I'll be back later."

Mary gathered her things and left. Roy sat in the chair, and Billy stood at the end of my bed with a dark look on his face. I knew he wanted to give me a lecture, but he remained silent.

"Thanks for the backup," I said, looking from one to the other.

"Billy did all the heavy lifting," Roy smiled.

I looked at Billy.

"Ralph is sorry he came to East Tennessee," Billy said with no trace of humor.

"Real sorry," Roy chuckled.

"Ralph is a slow learner," I said.

"Real slow," Roy said.

Billy reached out and put his hand on my leg. It was as close to a hug as I would ever get from him.

"I have to go, Blood," he said. "You take care. I'll be in touch."

He turned to leave. I stopped him with a word.

"Chief."

Billy turned to face me.

"Tell Maggie hello," I said.

For the first time since he had been in my room, he smiled. I looked at Roy. He smiled. Billy closed the door behind him.

"That Indian is pussy-whipped," Roy said.

"Not a bad way to go," I said.

"True," Roy said.

We were quiet for a while.

"I hear one of the guys you collared had a rifle with a scope," I said. "I wonder why he didn't use it before I killed Vargas."

"Orders from Vargas," Roy said. "He told me he was to use the rifle only if you killed Vargas. Vargas wanted to kill you face to face."

"Huh," I said. "Thanks for showing up in time."

"My pleasure, gumshoe," Roy smiled.

"Was the guy with Ralph wearing tennis shoes?" I asked.

"No," Roy said. "And I looked to make sure."

65

Early the following Wednesday, we were on T. Elbert's front porch. The dull throb reminded me that my left arm was going to be in a sling for a while. I had assigned coffee and bagel pickup to Roy. I had learned quite by accident that Roy visited T. Elbert on a regular basis. I was glad for that. Both men were in need of friendship, however unlikely.

"Two in the chest about an inch apart, I hear," T. Elbert said proudly. "And from fifty yards, no less."

"Maybe sixty," Roy said with a sly smile, perpetuating the myth.

"More like thirty," I said, taking a sip from my Dunkin' Donuts coffee cup.

"Still," T. Elbert said, "one hell of a shot."

"Shots," Roy corrected.

"Right," T. Elbert said. "An inch apart."

"Enough," I said. "The guy is dead. Let's leave it at that."

Roy and T. Elbert exchanged a glance. I knew T. Elbert wanted to lecture me on not feeling guilty, but he kept quiet. It would have been a wasted lecture. I did not feel guilty. I had killed Victor Vargas in defense of my life, and maybe a few others. Whatever mean things Victor Vargas would have done in the coming years, he would not do now. Some would argue that I had forced the issue. Maybe I had, but I was convinced that Vargas was out to kill me one way or another. The only way to deal with that had been head on.

"Tennessee is not having a nice year," T. Elbert said, changing the subject. "Only three wins."

"Forget Tennessee football," I said. "Let's talk Tennessee basketball."

"I need a favor from you-all," Roy said, interrupting the sports talk.

"Let's hear it," T. Elbert said.

"Mr. Fleet wants to have a big Thanksgiving Day meal at the mansion," Roy said. "Problem is, he doesn't have any family left to do it with. He knows that I've become friendly with Youngblood and company, and he thought you could help me put something together."

"Count me in," T. Elbert said. "I've never been inside the Fleet mansion, and the food will be a hell of a lot better than what I would be eating."

Roy looked at me.

"Might be fun," I said. "How many people, do you figure?"

"I'd say no fewer than twelve and no more than twenty," Roy said.

"It will give me something to do," I said, rising to leave. "I'm going to the office."

I went down the porch steps.

"Did I ever tell you about the time . . . ," I heard T. Elbert say as I got in the Pathfinder.

◆ ◆ ◆ ◆

I had been ignoring my investment accounts of late, and I diligently tried to make up for it by spending the entire morning on my computer, buying and selling what the Street had to peddle. The market had taken a tumble, and bargains were to be had. By noon, I was mentally exhausted.

I went to the diner for lunch. Doris had not seen me since the shooting and was her usual flustered mother hen self, making sure I had everything I needed. When she saw my arm in a sling, I half-expected her to offer to feed me. I managed quite well with one arm. When I asked her about Thanksgiving at the Fleet mansion, I thought she would faint. I did manage to get a *Yes,* among all the *Oh mys.*

When I got back to the office, Big Bob was sitting in front of my desk waiting for me. I hung up my coat and sat.

"I could have sworn I locked that door," I said.

"I have a key, remember?"

"Even with a key, wouldn't that still count as a B and E?" I asked.

"Not if you're the chief of police," Big Bob said.

"Right," I said. "So what brings you to my inner sanctum?"

"I just thought I'd let you know that the county prosecutor is not pressing charges against you or Billy or Roy."

"Really?" I said, a little annoyed. "Was there ever any doubt?"

"No, not really," Big Bob said. He seemed uneasy. "Also, I need to know what to do with the body after the autopsy is finished."

"Call Las Vegas PD and ask for Detective Ed Rodriguez," I said.

"Yeah, I remember him," Big Bob said. "He called here after you were mugged. I told him you were a hot-shit private investigator."

"I heard," I said.

He had more he wanted to say. I could tell he was agitated. I had seen this mood before. He had a bone to pick, and I was the "pickee."

"That's not what you came here to tell me," I said. "So out with it."

"You set Vargas up," he said. "You played judge, jury, and executioner. What gave you that right?"

I was a little surprised by his attack, and then it hit me. He was pissed that I had not let him in on it.

"It was going to happen sometime," I said, starting to get a little hot myself. "I wanted it sooner rather than later. And I wanted it on my turf. Besides, it was a fair fight."

"Fair fight, my ass," Big Bob said. "I've seen you shoot, remember?"

"Targets at the firing range," I said, calmly trying to defuse the big man. "Not a live thug who shoots back. I was hit just before I got off my two shots remember? A foot to the right and a few inches lower and I'd be dead. Vargas wasn't such a bad shot himself."

As I watched him fume, I realized he was mad at me for risking my life. I hadn't thought of it that way, but there it was. I had risked my life.

"And another thing," I said. "What about those guys in the trees? One of them had a scope rifle."

I was quiet as Big Bob fumed some more. Then he leaned forward in his chair with a look that told me he would like to rip my head off.

"Anything like this goes down again," he snarled, "you'd better tell me."

"I promise," I said, and I saw him relax a bit.

"Hell, I could have shot the bastard myself," he said. "It would have looked good on my record." Then Big Bob sat back in his chair and smiled. "Two in the chest an inch apart," he said. "Damn good shooting, Blood."

◆   ◆   ◆   ◆

Later that afternoon, I was working on the Thanksgiving list. So far, it was comprised of Joseph Fleet, Roy, T. Elbert, Billy, Maggie, Lacy, Mary, and me. The list had grown to eight people. I needed at least four more. Lacy would probably want to bring a friend. That would make nine. Stanley would make ten. I would probably have to kidnap him, but I would not take no as an answer. Then I remembered that I'd asked Doris, and how excited she was about seeing the Fleet mansion. I needed at least one more person when the phone rang.

"I read in the paper that Victor Vargas met his match in the back-woods of East Tennessee," Bruiser Bracken said. "Very efficient, you killing him in a cemetery and all."

"I think that's called irony," I said.

"Whatever," Bruiser said. "I call it good work. Are you okay? The paper said you were wounded."

"I took a bullet in the left shoulder in exchange for two in his chest," I said. "I'll be fine in a few months."

"I guess this pretty much wraps up your case," Bruiser said.

"Unless somebody in Vegas comes looking to settle the score," I said.

"Won't happen," Bruiser said. "Vargas went off his turf looking for trouble and got himself killed, end of story. Besides, nobody really liked him much anyway. You did Vegas a favor."

"Thanks for the sentiment," I said.

"Gotta go," Bruiser said. "Stay in touch, Youngblood."

I started to hang up when a thought hit me.

"Say, Bruiser, do you have plans for Thanksgiving?"

◆　　◆　　◆　　◆

We were in the kitchen seated at the bar, having a pre-dinner glass of Malbec, a very nice red that our local wine shop owner had dubbed "the new Merlot." Mary was looking at the Thanksgiving list. Lacy was in her room doing homework. Tortellini was boiling on the stove, and an Alfredo sauce was simmering beside it. Freshly made Caesar salad was cooling in the fridge. All was right in my world.

"I hope you're okay with going," I said.

"You better believe I'm okay with going," Mary said, taking another drink of wine. "Going means I won't have to cook."

I breathed a sigh of relief.

"Why didn't you put Wanda on the list?" Mary asked.

"I didn't think about it," I said, a little white lie.

"Liar," Mary teased, seeing right through me. "You thought I might be jealous. You're wrong, big guy. She's your one true female friend. Ask Wanda."

"Yes, ma'am," I saluted.

66

Inside the Fleet mansion, the Thanksgiving feast was laid out on a table that spanned at least twenty-four feet. All the traditional fare was there, along with a few surprises.

"God bless this food and this time of fellowship," Joseph Fleet said before we started.

"Amen," we all said in unison.

We ate well and then scattered throughout the first floor of the mansion in small groups. Through the wide entrance to the dining room I could see Mary and Wanda in the hallway drinking wine and absorbed in quiet conversation. Doris and Maggie were at the far end of the table where Doris was doing most of the talking. Maggie listened and occasionally laughed as Doris recounted tales from the Mountain Center Diner. Joseph Fleet and Stanley Johns had wandered off somewhere to continue their discussion on computer security. T. Elbert was zipping from room to room in his motorized wheelchair, exploring. The last I had seen of him, he was headed toward the kitchen to give our compliments to the chef. Lacy and Hannah were still in the dining room seated on opposite sides, text messaging each other. I had no idea why. Billy, Roy, and Bruiser had wandered outside for a tour of the grounds before darkness set in.

I strolled toward Mary and Wanda. They looked at each other and smiled when they saw me coming. I was struck by how attractive and alive both women were.

"What's going on?" I asked, slightly paranoid.

"Nothing," Mary said.

"Nothing," Wanda said. "I'm just telling Mary everything I know about you."

God, not everything, I thought.

"It's pretty interesting," Mary said. "I'm probably going to have to interrogate you on certain subjects."

Wanda laughed. "Now, move on and let Mary and me get back to our girl talk," she coaxed.

Getting nowhere, I gave up and wandered alone into the study, drawn by the fireplace. I sat on the couch with a glass of very good Brunello and let myself be mesmerized by the fire. I completely lost track of time. It grew dark as I sat there and remembered the first time I had met Joseph Fleet. It had been in this room. So much had happened between then and now that it seemed a lifetime ago.

I was reflecting on the past two years when I felt a presence behind me. I turned as Joseph Fleet walked into the study and sat in the chair to the right of the couch. In his right hand was a brandy snifter.

"Thanks for helping Roy put this together," he said. "A nice and interesting group of people. I can't remember when I have had a better time."

"My pleasure," I said. "I had a good time myself."

"That Stanley Johns is quite a character," Fleet said. "He has agreed to take a look at my computer security and set up a special program for us."

"I'm surprised," I said, taking another sip of red wine. "Stanley is pretty much a hermit. You must be very persuasive."

"Well, I promised him the royal treatment," Fleet said. "Told him we would pick him up in a limo every day, dine him at the country club, and implement all of his recommendations. He seemed flattered."

"I'll bet," I chuckled.

"Roy is taking Stanley and Doris home now," Fleet said. "Bruiser and Billy and Maggie are going to stay the night. I have had guest rooms prepared."

I stood up, finishing the last of my wine.

"I think it's time to round up the girls and make tracks," I said.

Fleet finished his brandy and set the glass down. He took my glass and set it beside his.

"I hope we can do this again," he said.

"I don't see why not," I said as we walked into the hall.

Fleet stopped and turned toward me.

"One more thing," he said, concern on his face.

I felt a lecture coming. He paused and took a deep breath.

"You've had a tough year," he said. "I hope you find some time to relax and take care of yourself."

"I intend to do just that," I said.

◆   ◆   ◆   ◆

The next day, I drove Bruiser to the airport. I had sent him a plane ticket and told him I used frequent flyer points. He had graciously accepted, but I don't think he bought the frequent flyer story. Roy had insisted that Bruiser stay at the mansion.

Bruiser had arrived the day before Thanksgiving, and I gave him the tour of downtown Mountain Center, including the office of the town's only private investigator. If he was impressed, he had contained it well.

I dropped him at curbside check-in, and we shook hands.

"Thanks for the invite," he said. "I had a blast."

"It might turn into an annual event," I said.

"If it does, you can count me in," Bruiser said. "It was nice to get out of Vegas for a few days. I enjoyed my time with everyone. There is something about small-town life I find really appealing."

"I'm glad you came, Bruiser," I said. "Thanks for all your help in Vegas."

"My pleasure," he said. "Stay in touch, Youngblood."

Bruiser turned and walked inside the terminal and never looked back. I was sorry to see him go. Certain people are special but are infrequently in your life, and every time you see them you wonder if it is for the last time. Bruiser was like that. We might stay in touch, and we might not, but we were connected in a way that would always make us friends.

I drove from the airport feeling a small piece of me had left with Bruiser.

◆　◆　◆　◆

That same afternoon, I was in Moto's Gym working with light weights and feeling generally depressed. I wasn't sure why. The gym was empty. It had an early-morning crowd, a noonday crowd, and an evening crowd, but in between only a few stragglers. Billy and I had been part of the nighttime crowd, but Billy now spent most of his time in Cherokee. I was sure he was working out somewhere, but he never said. I wasn't very motivated to get back to the gym, but I knew I had to. I still had some muscle to gain back. I had been in pretty good shape after Florida and had stayed that way by running and playing racquetball, but the cemetery showdown had set me back.

I heard the yipping and growling of the dogs playing outside in Moto's dog run. Moto's beautiful Siberian Husky, Karate, and Jake loved to romp and get in mock fights. They would eventually wear themselves out and come inside to lie down.

"Why you here now?" Moto asked. "Wrong time for you."

Moto could speak perfect English, but he loved playing the typical movie version of the Oriental sage. He also thought it was good for business. Moto taught a variety of martial arts.

"I felt like coming now," I snapped. "Okay?"

"Sure, sure," Moto said dismissively. "How is shoulder?"

"Getting better," I said with less of an edge, "but still sore."

"Good," Moto grunted. "Where is that dumb Indian? I have not seen him in a long time."

For Moto, *dumb Indian* was really a term of affection for Billy, but that's a long story best saved for another time.

"Billy is spending a lot of time in Cherokee, North Carolina," I said. "He has a lady friend there."

"You tell him he needs to work out more," Moto said.

"I'll tell him," I said, pretending to focus on my weights.

Moto turned and walked back toward his office.

"Lady friend," I heard him grumble.

◆   ◆   ◆   ◆

Even later that afternoon, I was back at the office and shutting down for the night. Thanksgiving was history, and we were moving toward Christmas. The days were getting shorter and shorter and the nights colder and colder. The lights of Main Street cast a surreal glow in the semidarkness of the cold late-November day. I tried to imagine I saw snow flurries. I was waiting on that first ground covering of the season. Something was still bothering me, but I was having a hard time coming up with what it was.

The phone rang. "No data," caller ID said.

"Cherokee Investigations," I dutifully answered.

"How's the arm?" Scott Glass asked.

I had emailed him some sparse details of the cemetery shootout with "Showdown at Sunset" in the subject line.

"Stiff and still a little sore," I said.

"You're racking up points fast on the FBI computer," Scott teased. "We might have to make you an honorary agent."

"Does that mean I get the secret decoder ring?" I cracked back.

"Certainly not," Scott said. "Those are only for special agents in charge."

"Did you call for a reason, Professor, or is this just routine FBI harassment?"

"I wanted to hear every little detail of the cemetery showdown," Scott said.

I told him in painful detail. The retelling frightened me more than the event itself. We talked for about ten minutes, covering myriad subjects from sports to home buying. Scott was looking for a house in the Salt Lake City area.

"Did you make any use of the meth lab info I gave you?" I asked.

"Sure did," Scott said. "Turned it over to a local agent. He got some good leads from your guy Oscar Morales. I might have to put you on the payroll."

I ignored that statement and changed the subject to Tennessee basketball. Scott changed it to Connecticut basketball, and we argued about who was going to have the better team.

"You have to come out and go skiing this year," Scott said.

"You buy a house and I'll come," I said. "Lord knows you have enough money."

"Will do, Blood," Scott said. "Now, stay out of gunfights, will you?"

"You can count on it," I said.

◆　　◆　　◆　　◆

I bolted straight up from a deep sleep. Mary was sleeping peacefully on her side of the bed, the right side. She had tossed all her covers off and discarded her pajama bottoms. Luckily for her, she was wearing bikini panties. Watching her in the darkness of our bedroom at 2:33 A.M., I almost lost my train of thought. I got up and went downstairs to the kitchen and fixed myself a Diet Coke with lots of ice. I booted up my computer and sent an email to T. Elbert. The subject line read, "Want to take another trip?"

67

We were in the Black Beauty on I-81 North. We had just crossed the state line into Virginia when CD number one of a Harlan Coben novel featuring Myron Bolitar ended.

"I like this one, too," T. Elbert said.

"I thought you might," I said.

We rolled up I-81 as disk two played. I had heard this one on my recent trip to Florida with Mary, so my mind wandered to the task at hand. I knew more answers were to be found in Saddle Boot, West Virginia. I figured Tracy's death might shock Will Malone into telling me why Tracy and her mother really left.

By the time we reached Saddle Boot, we had finished listening to disk three. Myron Bolitar was knee-deep in trouble. I could relate. We found the entrance to Will Malone's farm. The road in looked somewhat improved. The Hummer took whatever it had to offer and rolled on. In a few minutes, we pulled up in front of the house. The yard and field were covered with a dusting of snow.

I had gotten out and headed for the front steps when I saw Will Malone coming out of the barn. I walked to meet him. He spoke first.

"Mr. Youngblood," he said guardedly. "What are you doing here?"

There is no good way to deliver bad news. I didn't dance around the issue. I gave it to him straight.

"Tracy is dead," I said.

His face sagged, and he shook his head slowly.

"Oh, God," he said. "I am really sorry to hear that. What happened?"

"Drug overdose," I said.

"On purpose?"

"It appears to have been accidental," I said.

"I hate that," he said, shaking his head again.

"I need to know why they left," I said.

When he didn't answer right away, I knew he had something more.

"I'll keep digging until I find out," I said. "Tell me now and I'll go away, and that will be the end of it."

He let out a long breath. Then he looked at me with a forlorn expression and nodded.

"I need to tell somebody," he said. "I've been keeping the secret way too long. Somebody needs to know, and I guess you're as good as any, being you knew Tracy and all. Come on in the house."

I followed him up the stairs, through the front door, through the living room, and into the kitchen. We sat at the table. I heard footsteps coming down from upstairs, and seconds later Thelma entered the kitchen.

"Why, Mr. Youngblood," she said. "What brings you back?"

"Tracy is dead," Will Malone said to his wife. "Accidental drug overdose."

Thelma Malone's hand went to her mouth to cover her gasp.

"That is so sad," she said as tears welled up.

She turned away briefly and dabbed her eyes with her apron. Then she turned back to us.

"I'm going to tell Mr. Youngblood about Betty and Tracy," Will said, looking at his wife. Whether or not he was seeking her approval, I couldn't tell.

Thelma was silent for a few seconds, as if trying to make a decision.

"It's time," she said, looking at her husband. "I'll make some coffee."

Thelma began the process as Will Malone turned toward me and started his story.

"Betty came knocking on my door one night around eleven o'clock," Will began. "We go to bed early, so I knew it couldn't be good news for Betty to come and get me out of bed. Thelma sleeps like the dead, so she didn't hear the knock. So I got out of bed and went down and opened the front door, and there stood Betty lookin' like she had seen a ghost or somethin.'"

I had the urge to tell Will Malone to cut to the chase, but I let him tell it in his own way and in his own time.

"She begged me to come with her," he said. "She said there had been an accident. So I got in her truck, and we were at her barn in a couple of minutes. An old road used to run from here over to her place, but it's grown over now."

My cell phone rang, interrupting Will Malone.

"Yes?" I said.

"Everything okay in there?" T. Elbert asked as Thelma set coffee in front of us.

"Everything is fine, T. Elbert," I said.

"Ask your friend if he would like some coffee," Thelma said before I could hang up. "I'd be glad to take it out to him."

"Mrs. Malone would like to know if you want some coffee," I said into my phone. "She'll bring it out."

"I would love some," T. Elbert said.

I nodded to Thelma, and Will Malone continued his story.

"So we went inside the barn, and there lay Johnny Cross dead as a doornail, and Tracy huddled in a corner white as a sheet, starin' off into space like she was in another world. Johnny was this drifter Betty took up with. God knows why good women take up with bad men."

I thought about Tracy taking up with Victor Vargas.

"Betty said she came home from a PTA meetin' and found Johnny rapin' Tracy," Will Malone continued. "So she stabbed the son of a bitch with a pitchfork. Those were her words, not mine."

I nodded. He was on a roll, and I wanted him to get it all out. Thelma had left the kitchen to take T. Elbert his coffee. I heard the front door open and close.

"I wanted to call the sheriff, but she begged me just to get rid of the body, and nobody would know the difference. I figured she was just ashamed and wanted to save Tracy the embarrassment of havin' to talk about gettin' raped, so I said okay. I told her to take care of Tracy, and I would take care of the body. So I used some old shower curtains and some duct tape, and I wrapped him up good so the smell wouldn't get out and carried him deep into the woods and found a nice little open area where the soil was soft. I dug a grave and buried him deep. I came back and told Betty it was done, and she said we would never speak of this again. About two months later, she came and told me she was leavin'. She said she would stay in touch, but I knew she wouldn't."

We sat in silence as I put the pieces together. Betty and Tracy had realized that Tracy was pregnant, and they left town. Betty was probably still afraid that the law might catch up with her, so she made up the California story. I would have to discuss this with Sister Sarah Agnes, but I was guessing that Tracy had gradually suppressed the memory of that night until something brought it all back. Maybe it was Victor Vargas. Maybe Vargas reminded her of Johnny Cross.

"Did you ever see Tracy after that night?" I asked.

"No," he said vacantly. "I never did."

We were quiet for a while, sitting and drinking coffee. I watched Will Malone as he stared into space.

"What else is bothering you, Will?" I asked.

"It's nothin'," he said.

I heard the front door open and close, and then I heard footfalls as Thelma climbed the stairs to the second floor.

"You don't think it was rape, do you?"

"I don't know," he said. "Betty had a bad temper, and Tracy was a little wild, and Betty really panicked when I mentioned callin' the sheriff. I believed her at the time, but over the years I have had my doubts. Maybe Betty caught 'em in the act. Maybe I helped cover up a murder."

I thought about that for a minute. There was a fifty-fifty chance he was right.

"What's done is done, Will," I finally said. "Let the dead stay buried."

68

I was in the office talking to Sister Sarah Agnes about the events of my long trip to West Virginia the day before. Jake lay eavesdropping on his bed. He pretended not to be interested.

"Are you going to tell Lacy?" Sister Sarah Agnes asked.

"No," I said. "Not now, maybe not ever. Some things you're just better off not knowing. Either she is the product of a rape, or her grandmother is a murderer. Either way, not a very pleasant family history."

There was silence on the other end.

"You disagree?"

"No," she said. "I very much agree."

"What is your best guess?" I asked. "Rape or murder?"

"You're the detective," Sarah Agnes said. "What's yours?"

"I think Betty Malone in a fit of anger killed Johnny Cross," I said. "I think it probably drove Tracy crazy for a while, until she found out she was carrying the child of the man she loved. Maybe that snapped her out of it. Tracy was probably feeling it was her fault that Johnny was dead, and that her only choice was to stay with her mother and raise Lacy. Betty obviously loved Lacy once she was born, but I'll bet Tracy and her mother were always at odds."

"What else?" Sarah Agnes prodded.

"I believe Victor Vargas reminded Tracy of Johnny Cross," I said, "a charming, good-looking bad boy. And then it started to unravel. In order to bury the past again, she had to get Lacy out of her life, so she ran away with Victor. We pretty much know the rest."

"How is Lacy doing?" Sister Sarah Agnes asked.

"She seems to be doing fine," I said. "She is turning into the typical teenager, but she hasn't caused us many problems, and she idolizes Mary, which helps."

"Be that as it may," Sister Sarah Agnes said, "you are walking a slippery slope. Tread lightly."

"I will," I said.

"And for God's sake, try not to get beaten up or shot again."

"That, too," I said.

◆　　◆　　◆　　◆

Back in my office after brunch at the diner, I went online to do some research on a new gas grill for the lake house. I had an ancient Ducane that was falling apart. I had settled on a new mid-priced Ducane when the outer office door opened. Jake's head lifted and immediately returned to snoozing position. Seconds later, Big Bob came into my office. He was carrying an unfinished pine box that was slightly smaller than a shoebox. It had a hinged lid and was secured by a metal latch. He set it down on one of my worktables.

"Got any coffee?" he asked.

"I just made some," I said. "It's in the carafe."

He returned to the outer office and seconds later was relaxing in one of my oversized chairs, coffee in hand. He took a drink.

"You've got to come to the station and teach Susie how to make a decent cup of coffee," he said in his rich baritone voice.

"It's not Susie," I said. "It's that cheap coffee you use."

"Maybe," he said, taking another drink.

"What's in the box?" I asked.

"Victor Vargas," he said, nonchalantly drinking more coffee.

"Vargas?"

"His ashes," Big Bob said, feigning annoyance. "Nobody wanted the damn body, so we cremated the son of a bitch. Since you killed him, you can decide what to do with the ashes."

"Any suggestions?" I asked as he stood to leave.

"If it was me," Big Bob said, "I'd flush 'em."

"That's cold," I said as Big Bob stopped in my doorway and turned and faced me.

"You know your problem, Blood?" he asked. It was a rhetorical question. "You're too damn nice to be getting mixed up with all these bad guys. It just might get you killed someday."

He turned and left me sitting there wondering how I could be friends with a guy who had such a good heart but no tact and no regard for anyone's feelings. The big man just said what he thought, and to hell with the consequences. Most of the time, I was okay with that. Today was not one of those times.

I looked at Jake. He had no comment. I looked at the pine box that held the ashes of Victor Vargas. Now, what in hell was I going to do with them?

I took my keys from the key rack and left Jake sleeping peacefully on his dog bed. With any luck, he would never know I had left.

◆　　◆　　◆　　◆

No one was at the receptionist's desk when I went through the front door, so I continued through the double doors to my left and down the hall that led to her office. I hoped she was not in the middle of cutting up someone. When I walked in, she was studying her computer screen. She looked up in surprise, smiled, stood, came over, and gave me a light kiss on the lips.

"Well," Wanda said. "This is a surprise. What brings you to the land of the dead?"

"That kiss," I flirted.

"Not likely," she said. "I know Mary, remember?"

"Did you work on Victor Vargas, or did your assistant?" I asked.

"I did," Wanda said. "What's up?"

"What can you tell me about the autopsy?"

"Well, he died from injuries consistent with gunshot wounds," she said. "One barely missed the heart, the other didn't. Damn fine shooting, Don."

I was getting tired of that compliment, so I ignored it.

"Anything else?" I asked.

"Why?" Wanda asked. "What does it matter?"

"It matters, Wanda. Was there anything else?" She was starting to annoy me.

"He had a brain tumor," she said. "It wasn't big, but it was in a bad spot. Might explain some of his bad behavior."

"Terminal?"

"Sooner or later," Wanda said. "Hard to say how long."

"Thanks," I said. "I'll see you later."

I was almost out the door when Wanda called after me.

"Donnie."

I turned.

"For whatever reason, Victor Vargas was a bad guy," she said. "Forget him."

I nodded and left.

◆　　◆　　◆　　◆

That night, at his request, I met Billy at The Brewery for dinner. I knew something was up. Billy rarely asked me to meet him for dinner. I usually had to ask him. We sat in a back booth with our drinks, waiting on our food. I was drinking Black Bear Ale, and Billy had sweet iced tea. Both of us had ordered pan-fried trout. A fried calamari appetizer sat on the table between us. It was slowly disappearing.

"I want to open a satellite office of Cherokee Investigations in Cherokee," Billy said.

"Sure," I said. "Think you can bring in any business?"

"I do," Billy said. "I'm an outsider, but I am Cherokee. Maggie thinks being an outsider might be to my advantage, since I don't have any pre-conceptions and won't want to mess in anyone's business."

"Sounds good to me," I said.

"I found a place downtown," Billy said. "Second floor, overlooking the street. I'll need some start-up money, and I'll want to hire a receptionist, since I'll still be spending a lot of time in my studio."

"Not a problem," I said as the food arrived. "I'll take the start-up money out of the business account. How are you personally fixed for money?"

"Fine," Billy said. "I don't need much money, and you know I have some."

"I know," I said.

We had this conversation about once a year. Billy knew that I felt guilty about having so much money. In truth, Billy was fine financially. Over the years, his bank account had grown to six figures. Still, that was a drop in the bucket compared to what I had. If I tried to force too much money on him, he got stubborn.

"And I know what's yours is mine and what's mine is yours," Billy said.

"Keep that in mind," I said.

"I will," Billy said. "Relax and enjoy your food."

We ate in silence. We were like that. We didn't talk just for the sake of talking. I knew there was more, but it would come in Billy's time. I was in no hurry. The food was good, and I was with my best friend.

"There is something else," Billy said.

"I figured," I said.

"Maggie and I are going to get married," Billy said.

I was not surprised by this announcement, but it had come sooner than I expected. I smiled. I almost laughed.

"Well, I'll be damned," I said. "Congratulations. Have you set a date?"

"Not yet," Billy said. "Probably in the spring."

Billy had a wide smile. It might have been the happiest smile I had ever seen on his face.

"I am in love, Blood," Billy said. "I never thought I would get married. I never thought I would find anyone I would want to spend the rest of my life with. Then, like magic, here is this smart, attractive, caring woman, and she loves me. We get along so well. It is hard for me to believe my luck."

"It's not luck," I said. "Some things are just meant to be."

"Whatever it is," Billy said, "I'll take it."

"I'm glad for you, Chief, I really am," I said. "I like Maggie, and she is certainly a smart and good-looking woman."

"So is Mary," Billy smiled again.

"We are two lucky guys," I said.

"We are," Billy said.

69

Late one afternoon a week before Christmas, I sat at my desk staring out the second-floor window of Cherokee Investigations, watching the first real snow of the season start to blanket Main Street. The wind was blowing and the temperature dropping. Across the street, the thermometer on the side of the Mountain National Bank building said it was twenty-nine degrees. The Weather Channel promised colder temperatures and six inches of snow by morning. Area schools had sent kids home early and had already announced they would be closed tomorrow, no doubt thrilling Lacy and hundreds of other kids.

The door to the outer office opened and closed. Jake moved one ear and continued his nap. He still thought he was a puppy and played like one, but like all of us who are getting older, he required more rest and more recuperation time. Jake would be ten years old next August.

A few seconds later, Lacy and Hannah walked into my inner sanctum, red-faced from the cold, blowing snow.

"Did you hear?" Lacy said excitedly. "No school tomorrow."

"I heard," I said with faked annoyance. "Hello, Hannah."

"Hello, Mr. Youngblood," Hannah said.

"Will you take us to the lake house tomorrow so we can go sledding?" Lacy asked. "That one big hill would be perfect."

Driving to the lake house on snow-covered roads was not my idea of fun. *But I do have four-wheel drive*, I thought, *and I haven't had a chance to test it out this year.*

"You don't have a sled," I said.

"I do," Hannah said. "A big one."

"We'll see," I said, feeling outnumbered.

"We'll see" is the male adult's way of evasively saying "No" or "Probably not." Kids take it to mean "Yes" or "Probably."

"Great," Lacy said. "Can Hannah spend the night?"

I was hoping you could spend the night with Hannah, I thought, but I kept that to myself. Instead, I fell back on another oldie but goodie.

"You'll have to ask Mary," I said.

"Okay," Lacy said. "Let's go, Hannah."

"Don't you want a ride?" I asked.

"No," Lacy said like I was crazy. "We want to walk in the snow."

They zipped their jackets, put on their caps and scarves, and walked toward the door.

"Bye, y'all," I said.

"Bye," they said in unison.

I heard the outer door open and close. In less than a minute, I watched them cross Main Street and head north toward our condo. They were laughing and kicking snow at each other, completely unaware of the cold.

Teenagers!

•   •   •   •

I was just about to rouse Jake from his nap when the phone rang. "Out of area," caller ID said.

"Cherokee Investigations," I answered, the tough, hard voice of a seasoned private investigator. Mike Hammer would have been proud.

"Donald Youngblood, please," a male voice said.

"Speaking," I said.

"Mr. Youngblood, this is Detective Rodriguez of Las Vegas PD. Do you remember me?"

"Sure do, detective. What can I do for you?"

"I heard about the Vargas shooting, and I have a piece of information to share that you might be interested in, if you would be so kind as to tell me why Vargas had you beaten up in the first place."

"Why not?" I said. "The case is pretty much closed."

I told Rodriguez the basics, leaving out some of the details he didn't need to know. He got the gist of it.

"Too bad about the mother," Rodriguez said when I finished. "Good riddance to Victor Vargas. Vegas will not miss Vargas."

"Catchy," I said. "What have you got for me?"

"A few nights ago, a lowlife known as Willie the Pipe was found in a dumpster in North Vegas, beaten unconscious," Rodriguez said. "Willie got the name because he never carries a gun. He carries a pipe or a piece of rebar or a tire iron. You get the picture. Anyway, I always thought that Willie might have been your third man in the parking garage. Now, I'm pretty sure."

"What makes you so sure?" I asked.

"I went to interview Willie when he woke up," Rodriguez said. "His story was that some monster of a guy in a ski mask beat him senseless, took his shoes, and tossed him in the dumpster. When I asked if the guy said anything, Willie said all the guy said was, 'Payback's a bitch.'"

"The shoes," I said. "Tennis shoes?"

"Nikes," Rodriguez said. "Almost new."

70

I left the lake house and took Jake to the office early on the morning of Christmas Eve to escape all the girl talk. Mary's daughter, Susan, had come in from Wake Forest to visit for the holidays, and Susan, Mary, and Lacy were having a grand time. Mary and Susan talked on the phone every day, so I was amazed they still found so much to discuss in person. Susan was a starter on the Wake Forest women's basketball team, and Lacy was suffering from a slight case of instant hero worship. I felt like the proverbial fifth wheel. My waving goodbye and slipping quietly away were barely acknowledged.

Roy had called the night before and said that he and Billy would bring coffee and bagels. They arrived in the limo fifteen minutes after me and parked across the street. Billy was carrying the goodies, and Roy had a shopping bag with what looked to be a wrapped present inside. Snow still lay in patches on Main Street, and the thermometer on the bank clock glowed thirty degrees. No warming trend was in sight. Hallelujah!

Less than a minute later, the office door opened and shut. I went to the outer office, where Billy and Roy were discarding coats and spreading out the coffee and bagels on the conference table. The shopping bag sat beneath the coatrack. I ignored it.

When all the lids were off the coffee cups, Billy raised his cup and said, "Merry Christmas, Blood."

"Merry Christmas, you two," I said.

"Dinner is at six tonight," Roy said.

"We'll be there," I said.

Joseph Fleet so enjoyed Thanksgiving that he had asked Roy to invite a few people over for Christmas Eve dinner. Billy, Maggie, Mary, Lacy, and I had graciously accepted. I felt sorry for Fleet and didn't have the heart to say no. And besides, I liked the man. Fleet and Roy would make their traditional trip to Amelia Island on Christmas day.

I took a bite of my poppy seed bagel with cream cheese.

"Think the Titans will make the playoffs?" Roy asked.

"I do," I said.

"Think Mary's son can get me a couple of tickets?"

"I gave you my tickets to two games already," I said, feigning exasperation.

Jimmy had played in one game when the Titans' starting quarterback had rested a sore shoulder. He had performed well in a winning effort, thus creating the dreaded quarterback controversy.

"I'll see what I can do," I said.

My curiosity finally got the best of me.

"What's in the shopping bag?" I asked.

"Don't know," Roy said. "It came UPS to the mansion, but it had your name on it. No return address."

"I hope it's not ticking," I said.

"Doesn't seem to be," Roy said.

Roy got up and retrieved the shopping bag from underneath the coat rack and placed it on the conference table. It took both hands to lift the wrapped box from the bag. I put it to my ear. No ticking. I methodically unwrapped the package to prolong the suspense. Beneath the paper was a box with "Payback's a bitch" written in big black capital letters on the top. I looked from Billy to Roy. They shrugged. I opened the lid to find a pair of almost-new Nike tennis shoes.

"Okay," I said. "Which one of you did this?"

"Not me," Billy said.

"Me either," Roy said.

I lifted the tennis shoes from the box and saw an envelope at the bottom with my name on it. I opened the envelope and pulled out a slip of paper folded once. I opened the handwritten note and read, "They probably won't fit, but it's the thought that counts. I had a great time at Thanksgiving. Thanks for the plane ticket. Bruiser."

71

Christmas Eve dinner at the Fleet mansion was a joyful success. On Christmas day, we slept late, fixed brunch, and exchanged gifts. Then we retreated to the lake house, not intending to come back to Mountain Center until it was time for Lacy to return to school.

The ashes of Victor Vargas loomed in my office as a constant reminder of the conflict between good and evil that rages inside us all. For most of us, most of the time, good wins. Inside Victor Vargas, good lost.

In the early morning on New Year's Eve, I left the lake house and drove to the office and made a phone call.

"Park headquarters," the voice said.

"I would like to speak with Ranger Roberts," I said.

"Hang on," the voice said.

Baine Roberts was a senior park ranger in the Great Smoky Mountains National Park who I saw a couple of times a year when I went hiking. He had once hired me to follow his wife because he suspected her of cheating. He had said they were not getting along and that all of a sudden she wanted a girls' night out with her friends. Baine, being a little paranoid, didn't believe her, so he came all the way to Mountain Center and hired me. I put Billy on the case. Despite his size, Billy was much better at being invisible that I was, and I didn't much care for following wives who might be cheating on their husbands. As it turned out, Baine's wife was going out with the girls and no one else. The girls drank and had a good time, but that was the extent of it. When I reported back to Baine, he had been so relieved that he said if I ever needed a favor, all I had to do was ask. I was about to ask.

"This is Roberts," he said.

"Baine," I said. "This is Don Youngblood."

"Mr. Youngblood," Baine said. "How are you?"

I had the same problem with Baine that I did with Doris. I could not get him to call me Don. I'd tell him, and he would say okay, and then he'd go right back to calling me Mr. Youngblood. After a few futile attempts, I had given up.

"I'm fine, Baine," I said. "How are you, and how is the wife?"

"We're both fine," he said. "I finally took your advice and got her to go with me for counseling. It helped a lot. We are getting along real well."

"Good to hear," I said. "Listen, Baine, I need a favor. How are the roads in the Smokies right now?"

"The roads are fine, Mr. Youngblood," Baine said. "What have you got in mind?"

"Is the road to Clingmans Dome open?"

"No, we keep that closed in the winter."

"Is it passable?"

"Sure," Baine said. "Why?"

◆   ◆   ◆   ◆

I drove through Gatlinburg and into the Great Smoky Mountains National Park, an 814-square-mile refuge for many kinds of wildlife and numerous tourists seeking escape from the real world. "God's country," my parents had called it. The park attracted millions of visitors annually. The free admission probably added to the total.

I took U.S. 441 South toward Cherokee. *Billy probably knows this road like the back of his hand*, I thought. I made Newfound Gap in twenty minutes. There was no traffic. The Clingmans Dome road was a right-hand turn just after the Newfound Gap parking lot. The gate was closed, and a park ranger's cruiser was parked in the left lane facing U.S. 441. Baine Roberts was behind the wheel. He was drinking what I guessed to be coffee. The exhaust from the back of his cruiser was a testament to the freezing temperature. I pulled the Pathfinder alongside the cruiser and lowered my window. The cold air rushed in. It felt good. Baine lowered his window.

"Colder than a witch's tit up here," Baine said without preamble.

The temperature gauge on the rearview mirror of the Pathfinder read twenty-nine degrees.

"Thanks for doing this," I said.

"No big deal," Baine said. "Just don't cut down any trees or nothin'."

"Not to worry," I said. "I left my chain saw at home."

Baine laughed. "Why in the world do you want to go up to Clingmans Dome on a day like today?" he asked.

"I'll tell you someday," I said. "Right now, it's personal. It's just something I need to do."

Baine nodded. "How long you figure to be?"

"I figure fifteen minutes up and fifteen back," I said. "Plus the hike up and back and a few minutes at the top. What do you think? An hour fifteen to an hour and a half?"

"Sounds about right," Baine said. "I'll be here waiting on you. You can reach me on your cell phone if you have a problem. We just put in a new tower at Newfound Gap."

He gave me his cell phone number and then got out of his cruiser, unlocked the gate, and swung it open. I drove through and watched in the rearview mirror as the gate swung shut.

◆　　◆　　◆　　◆

At 6,643 feet, Clingmans Dome was the highest point in the Great Smoky Mountains National Park and the third-highest peak east of the Mississippi River. Only Mount Craig and Mount Mitchell, both in western North Carolina, were higher, and only by a few feet.

I drove the curving seven-mile road with no sense of urgency. The day was cold and overcast, the wind brisk. I thought I saw an occasional snowflake. I watched the temperature gauge drop as the Pathfinder climbed. The views as I ascended to the parking lot at road's end were both barren and spectacular. I was totally alone and comfortable with the feeling.

By the time I parked, the temperature had dropped another nine degrees. I knew where I was going would be even colder, but I also knew I would be warm enough in my ski jacket, ski gloves, and toboggan. I loved cold weather and was prepared for it.

I removed the pine box from the back of the Pathfinder and began my half-mile hike up the steep paved trail in front of me. I moved steadily, being careful not to break a sweat. I heard the wind in the trees and watched the evergreens wave at me as I made my climb.

A short time later, I was standing at the base of the observation tower at Clingmans Dome. I stopped and looked up, then slowly climbed the walk that spiraled the final fifty feet to the observation deck. The wind had picked up, and my face was getting colder. When I reached the top, I set the pine box at my feet and took in the view. On a clear day, you were supposed to be able to see seven states from the top of the tower. Though today was not one of those days, the clouds were high and I could still see a great distance. Snowflakes danced on the wind. They were sporadic but excited me nonetheless.

I slowly made the 360-degree trip around the tower, taking in the spectacular view and wondering what it must have been like for the Cherokee when they occupied this land all by themselves. It was a shame how much damage could be done to a culture and the environment in the name of progress.

A gust of wind reminded me why I had made the trip as I came back around to the pine box. I unlatched the lid and opened the box. Inside, Victor Vargas's ashes were in a clear plastic bag fastened with a plastic tie.

Suddenly, I changed my mind. I was all set to do something noble for the man I had killed, even though he didn't deserve the sentiment. Then a tiny voice inside my head asked a question. Did I really want the ashes of this thug scattered over these beautifully preserved mountains? I did not. The answer I had been seeking was finally clear. Victor Vargas came from Vegas, and to Vegas he would return.

The wind was increasing, and I guessed the wind chill factor to be near zero. I closed the pine box, picked it up, and made a quick descent to the Pathfinder. In the warmth of my SUV, I made my way back to the main road. Baine saw me coming and opened the gate and waved me through. I stopped and lowered my window.

"Thanks," I said. "I owe you one."

"No way," he said. "I still owe you."

"Give me a shout if you're ever in Mountain Center," I said. "I know a great little diner."

"I'll do that," Baine said. "Call me when you come down this way again."

"Will do," I said, giving him a two-fingered salute as my window went back up.

I made a left and went down the mountain toward Gatlinburg.

72

On New Year's Day, I watched football. Unfortunately, I did not watch the Tennessee Volunteers. Tennessee had finished a disastrous football season without winning the mandatory six games required by the NCAA in order to participate in a postseason bowl game. At least Tennessee basketball was alive and well.

Two days later, Bruiser Bracken picked me up at the Las Vegas airport. I carried an old gym bag. Inside was the pine box that held the ashes of Victor Vargas. I opened the tailgate and placed the gym bag in the back of Bruiser's SUV.

"Where to?" Bruiser asked.

"Drive out into the desert and find the hottest place you can think of," I said.

"Great," Bruiser said, sounding delighted. "I've been dying to get this thing off-road."

"This thing" was a new white Range Rover. The new-car smell was still present.

"Nice wheels," I said. "When did you get it?"

"A Christmas present," Bruiser said. "From me to me."

"Speaking of Christmas presents," I said, "thanks for the tennis shoes. You shouldn't have."

"My pleasure," Bruiser laughed. "What did you end up doing with them?"

"I donated them to the Salvation Army."

"Appropriate," Bruiser said. "The original owner is not likely to find salvation where he's going."

Bruiser drove for half an hour on a state highway that seemingly led nowhere. He finally turned onto a dirt road and drove another ten minutes before we went off-road.

"The desert is not that hot this time of year," Bruiser said. "But come summer, the place I'm taking you will be hotter than hell."

We bounced and bucked until we came to a ravine. I got out of the Range Rover, opened the tailgate, and unzipped the gym bag. I removed the pine box, set it next to the gym bag, and opened the lid. I lifted the plastic bag from the box and carried it to the edge of the ravine.

I turned to Bruiser. "Any last words for the deceased?"

"Fuck him," Bruiser said.

"Well put," I said as I unceremoniously tossed the ash-filled plastic bag into the ravine. The bag seemed to fall in slow motion and finally exploded on the floor of the ravine with a dull thump. The ashes ballooned upward and outward and slowly settled. With a little help from me, Victor Vargas had found his final resting place. Not exactly Vegas, but close enough.

"Find a dumpster, and I'll toss the pine box and the gym bag," I said.

"I know where there's an incinerator," Bruiser said. "I'll burn them."

"Perfect," I said.

As Bruiser drove me back to the airport, I felt a sense of relief. I had put the final touches on the Tracy Malone case. The only thing that bothered me was that I didn't know whether Tracy had died accidentally or on purpose. Had Victor Vargas's phone call pushed her over the edge, or had she just wanted one final, glorious high before making her way back to Silverthorn? And why did she pay for a week? Those were mysteries that I would never solve.

73

We sat in the stands and watched as the Mountain Center girls' team ran away from the visitors from Nashville. The undefeated Lady Mountaineers were very good, and the half-full gym held an enthusiastic crowd. The Lady Mountaineers were coached by an ex–Lady Volunteer from the University of Tennessee. She had obviously been influenced by Pat Summit. She even had the Pat Summit stare, although nothing could match the original.

By halftime, the score was 44–20. Lacy had not played in a real game so far, but the coach had told Mary that tonight might be the night. She did not want to put Lacy into a close game.

"Her coach told me Lacy is improving fast," Mary said. "She said Lacy was going to be a player."

"And how did you happen to talk to the coach?" I asked. "Pull her over for speeding?"

"No, silly. She stopped and talked to me one day while I was directing school traffic."

"Using your badge to curry favor for Lacy?" I teased.

"Shut up and watch the game," Mary shot back, giving me an elbow to the ribs.

The score at the end of the third quarter was 60–26. Lacy and two other reserves started the fourth quarter. Lacy, at five-foot-seven and growing, was playing small forward—the "three," in basketball terminology. When the ball came to her on offense, she passed it. She didn't seem interested in scoring. On defense, she was tenacious, and I could tell the coach loved that. In the first four minutes of the quarter, she had three rebounds, two blocked shots, and two steals. Just under the four-minute mark, she grabbed an offensive rebound and put it back for a score and was fouled. She made the free throw like a seasoned veteran, showing off an excellent shooting stroke. At the two-minute mark, she took a pass and launched a shot from behind the three-point line. It found the bottom of the net without ever touching iron. Her first career three-pointer! With less than a minute left, she scored two more points on a beautiful pick-and-roll. The final score was 74–36. Lacy had seven points, four rebounds, two blocks, and two steals in one quarter—not a bad night's work for a freshman playing her first game. She *was* a player.

"You were great," I said after the game.

"Thanks," Lacy beamed.

"Were you nervous?"

"At first," she said. "And then I forgot about it and just started playing."

Billy appeared from nowhere. Lacy's smile was from ear to ear. If she had smiled any wider, she would have split her face.

"Good game, Little Princess," Billy said.

"Thanks, Chief," Lacy said. "I'm glad you came."

74

In mid-January, I took Mary and Lacy to Ober Gatlinburg and introduced them to skiing. They were immediately hooked. The next weekend, I had to drive them to Knoxville and buy them all new equipment. From the looks on their faces, it was worth every penny.

In February, during Lacy's winter vacation, I commandeered the older of the two Fleet jets, and we flew to Utah and met Scott Glass and his latest flame for a week of skiing. By the time we left, Lacy was skiing black-diamond trails. She was a natural athlete, maybe a really special one. She was also fearless, which sometimes can get you in trouble.

In March, we went to Nashville for a wedding, my second in less than a year, with another on the horizon. Mary's son, Jimmy, married his college sweetheart. There were hints that Mary might be a grandmother in the not-too-distant future, although Jimmy assured Mary that the bride was not pregnant yet.

The winter passed without my getting shot or beaten up. I had a few minor cases to work, but no heavy lifting. Billy opened the Cherokee office and immediately began to get business. I went back to my daily routine. The market was experiencing wild swings, but I watched closely, and my accounts all did as well as could be expected under the circumstances. I had not lost the touch. I was afraid the financial markets were close to making a major correction, so I moved toward insured money market accounts and mutual funds that I felt were secure.

Lacy was doing well in school and not causing us any major trouble. Big Bob warned me that would change, but he was a cynic whose own two kids were permanent teenagers. Lacy, on the other hand, had temporary teenager status. She stayed on her best behavior. Her worst offense was a sloppy room. When it got to the point that my neatnik self couldn't stand it, I would close her door and post a sticky note that said, "Caution: Toxic Waste." She usually got the message, and her room would be clean the next day. No one knocked on our door asking, "What's this kid doing here?" Lacy continued to work for Stanley two hours a day after school and for Doris four hours on Saturday at the diner.

Mary had a few exciting moments, but otherwise her work was routine. Although we were becoming more and more like a family, the M word had not surfaced again. We spent most weekends at the lake house. My life finally had some meaning and purpose.

I had not yet mentioned West Virginia.

75

The water cascaded over Cataract Falls into a small pool that exited into a shallow stream that would eventually reach the Little Pigeon River. On this beautiful, clear, calm day in late April in the Great Smoky Mountains National Park, we were gathered in front of the falls for the marriage of Maggie Morning-Song and Billy Two-Feathers. A local wedding-chapel minister, Dan something—I couldn't remember his last name—had obtained a permit from park headquarters and was presiding over the ceremony. The gathering was a mixture of Maggie's and Billy's friends, a blending of two different cultures coming together for a special event. T. Elbert had driven Mary, Lacy, and me in his Hummer. Roy had driven Wanda, Stanley, Doris, and Joseph Fleet in the limo.

Maggie and Billy had met with the Reverend Dan the week before and planned the wedding. They knew exactly what they wanted, a blend of modern civil and traditional Cherokee ceremonies.

Maggie wore a white dress with white buckskin moccasins, and Billy wore a roe-colored ribbon shirt, black pants, and elk-skin moccasins—traditional dress for a Cherokee wedding. A Cherokee holy man was in attendance to bless the union. The couple recited the vows they had written for the occasion.

"I give you my heart," Maggie said, staring into Billy's eyes. "I give you my promise to stay by your side and take care of you always. I pledge you my love until the end of time."

Billy was trancelike. He took a deep breath.

"I give you my heart," Billy said in his magnificent bass voice, staring back at Maggie. "Now, they beat as one. I give you my promise to protect you with my life and never leave you. I pledge you my love until the end of time."

In that moment, the world seemed to hold its collective breath, as if pausing to hear their declarations. All was silent except for the cascading water.

I stood beside Billy as his best man. I nodded to him and handed him his ring for Maggie, and he took it and slipped it on the third finger on her left hand.

"Forever," Billy said, looking at Maggie.

A friend of Maggie's, another schoolteacher in Cherokee, stood as her maid of honor. She gave Maggie her ring for Billy, and Maggie slipped it on Billy's third finger on his left hand.

"Forever," Maggie said, looking at Billy.

In the ancient tongue of the Cherokee, the holy man blessed the union and all of us present.

Then minister Dan stepped in front of the couple to make the ceremony official and legal.

"Do you, Maggie, take Billy to be your lawful wedded husband?" he asked Maggie.

Maggie, smiling at Billy, said she did.

"Do you, Billy, take Maggie to be your lawful wedded wife?" he asked Billy.

Billy, looking a lot more serious than Maggie, said he did.

"By the power invested in me by the state of Tennessee," minister Dan said, "I now pronounce you man and wife. You may kiss the bride."

Billy kissed Maggie. I looked at Mary in time to see a tear escape. She looked at me and smiled. That familiar feeling of electricity ran through me. *Your days are numbered*, a small voice whispered inside me. I smiled and congratulated the bride and groom.

Those gathered filed by to offer best wishes. I moved away to let others share the moment with the newlyweds. I felt disconnected. I was happy for Billy and a little sad for myself. Billy and I had been like brothers since our freshman year in college. We watched out for each other. He always had my back, was always there when I needed him. I hoped that wouldn't change.

I watched as the last of the guests congratulated the bride and groom, dispersed into small groups, and started casual conversations, in no hurry to leave.

Maggie caught my eye and moved toward me. She embraced me and kissed my cheek. She had a calmness about her that was hard to describe.

"You are not losing a friend," she said, reading my mind. "You are gaining one."

"That's good to hear," I said, my voice almost cracking, my eyes close to tearing.

"You and Billy have a bond that can never be broken," Maggie said. "Billy needs you as a friend as much as he needs me as a wife."

"You are very wise," I said.

"Thank you," she smiled demurely.

"I am curious about one thing," I said. "Why was someone as beautiful and smart as you still single?"

"That is quite simple," Maggie said cryptically. "I have always been waiting for Billy."

Epilogue

On a beautiful, warm day in early May, Lacy and I drove through the gates of the Mountain Center Country Club. I waved at James, our guard, and he waved back.

"I can't believe I'm doing this," Lacy said.

"It's what you want, right?"

"Yes, but I can't believe that I am actually going to do it."

I followed the road past the clubhouse and around to the practice tee. Tony Price, the club pro, was waiting for us. I had arranged golf lessons with Tony on Saturday afternoons for as long as Lacy was interested. I parked the Pathfinder, and we got out and walked over to Tony. A golf bag with new clubs I had purchased for Lacy stood beside him. I made the introductions. Lacy was wide-eyed with excitement.

"Have you ever hit a golf ball?" Tony asked.

"Never," Lacy said.

"Great," Tony said. "This should be fun."

"Call me on my cell when you're finished," I said to Lacy.

"Okay," she said.

"Thanks, Tony," I said.

"No problem," Tony said.

◆　　◆　　◆　　◆

I was on my way to the office when my cell phone rang. I did not recognize the number.

"Youngblood," I answered.

"Hey, Blood," Jimmy Durham said. "Are you busy right now?"

"No," I said. "What's going on, Bull?"

"Do you know the picnic area about a mile downriver from Campbell Bridge?"

"Sure," I said. "Campbell Bottoms. What about it?"

"Meet me there as soon as you can," Jimmy said, ignoring my question.

"On my way," I said. "What's this about?"

I didn't get a response. Jimmy had already disconnected. He hadn't sounded happy.

I took a right out of the club and drove the ten or so miles to Campbell Bridge and took another right on a secondary road just before the bridge. The picnic area was a few miles down on the left. The leaves on the trees in the thickly wooded area surrounding Campbell Bottoms had yet to reach full maturity. When they did, the sun would have a hard time penetrating the thick foliage. Sunlight danced off my windshield as I snaked my way down to the Bottoms.

I made a left-hand turn into the Campbell Bottoms parking lot. The Bottoms was a favorite weekend picnic area for Mountain Center residents. I had been here many times with friends when I was a teenager.

At least fifty picnic tables with outdoor grills were scattered throughout the area, with individual parking spots for vehicles. Cinder-block buildings at the north and south ends of the parking area housed restrooms. Through the trees, I saw two sheriff's cruisers parked at the far north end of the parking area. As I closed the distance, I saw Jimmy leaning with his arms folded against the front fender of his cruiser. I parked a couple of spots down and got out. I walked to meet him. He looked forlorn.

"You okay?" I asked.

His light blue eyes stared back at me with the resigned look of a county sheriff too long on the job.

"There is something I need you to see. . . ."

Acknowledgments

My thanks go to the following people for valuable medical information: Dr. Sarah Sheets Cook and Dr. Daniel P. Marshall.

Thanks also to: Meri Saffelder, the web-master of the donaldyoungbloodmysteries.com website and to Todd Lape for all his hard work on the text and jacket design.

A special thank you to Jeff Wyatt, Thunderbird USA, and to Jill Adams Hale for her valuable research.

And finally: to my editor, Steve Kirk, thank you for your valuable insight and your unerring attention to detail.

Author's Notes

Although this is a work of fiction, I have borrowed some names from people I know or have known.

For those of you who are curious:

Jim Murphy is a UPS man in Gatlinburg who is gracious and good humored and willing to go the extra mile. He has never been a police officer.

Dr. Sam Chang is a very fine doctor at Vanderbilt Medical Center who has kept me on the straight and narrow these last few years. When I told him about his part in my second book, he simply said, "Viva Las Vegas."

Allyson Mecham does work at the Tamarisk Restaurant in Green River and the food I had there was very good.

Laura Crowder is a very caring nurse, and even a better person, in Sevierville, Tennessee.

Stanley Johns was a high-school classmate named John Stanley, who took it upon himself to know where all of us were and to encourage us to come to our reunions. Regrettably, John is no longer with us, our loss.

I have never known anyone like Victor Vargas. Hopefully, I never will.